# THE PLACE
## OF
# HER NAME

THE PLACE OF HER NAME

Copyright © 2024 by S.C. Makepeace.

For information contact : scmakepeaceauthor@gmail.com

http://www.scmakepeace.com

Cover design by Marta Susic

ISBN: 978-1-0683145-1-3

First Edition : December 2024

# The Place of Her Name

## Fires of Irkalla

### Book One

S.C. Makepeace

This book contains strong language; graphic depictions of violence, torture, and death; and scenes of a sexual nature, which some readers may find upsetting.

To my mum,

For listening to the garbled beginnings

of this story on that beach in Hikkaduwa

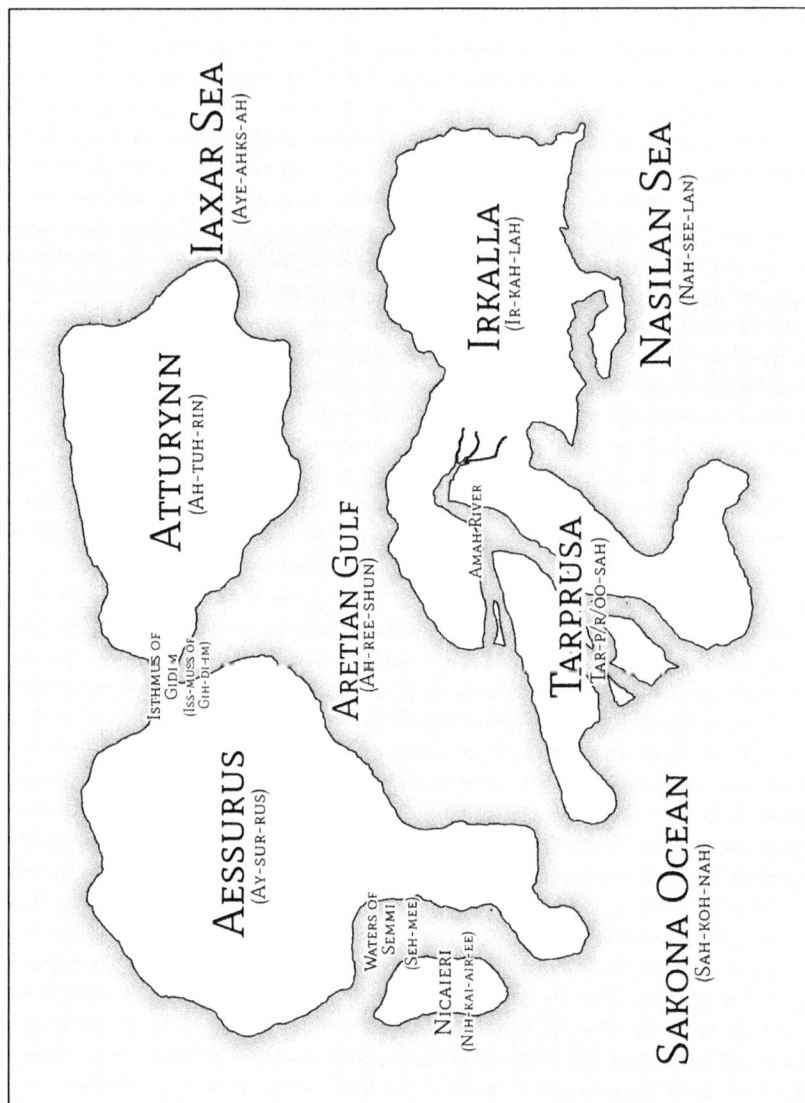

IAXAR SEA
(AYE-AHKS-AH)

NASILAN SEA
(NAH-SEE-LAN)

IRKALLA
(IR-KAH-LAH)

ATTURYNN
(AH-TUH-RIN)

ARETIAN GULF
(AH-REE-SHUN)

AMAH RIVER

TARPRUSA
(TAR-P,R,OO-SAH)

ISTHMUS OF
GIDIM
(ISS-MUSS OF
GIH-DIM)

AESSURUS
(AY-SUR-RUS)

WATERS OF
SEMMI
(SEH-MEE)

NICAIERI
(NIH-KAI-AIR-EE)

SAKONA OCEAN
(SAH-KOH-NAH)

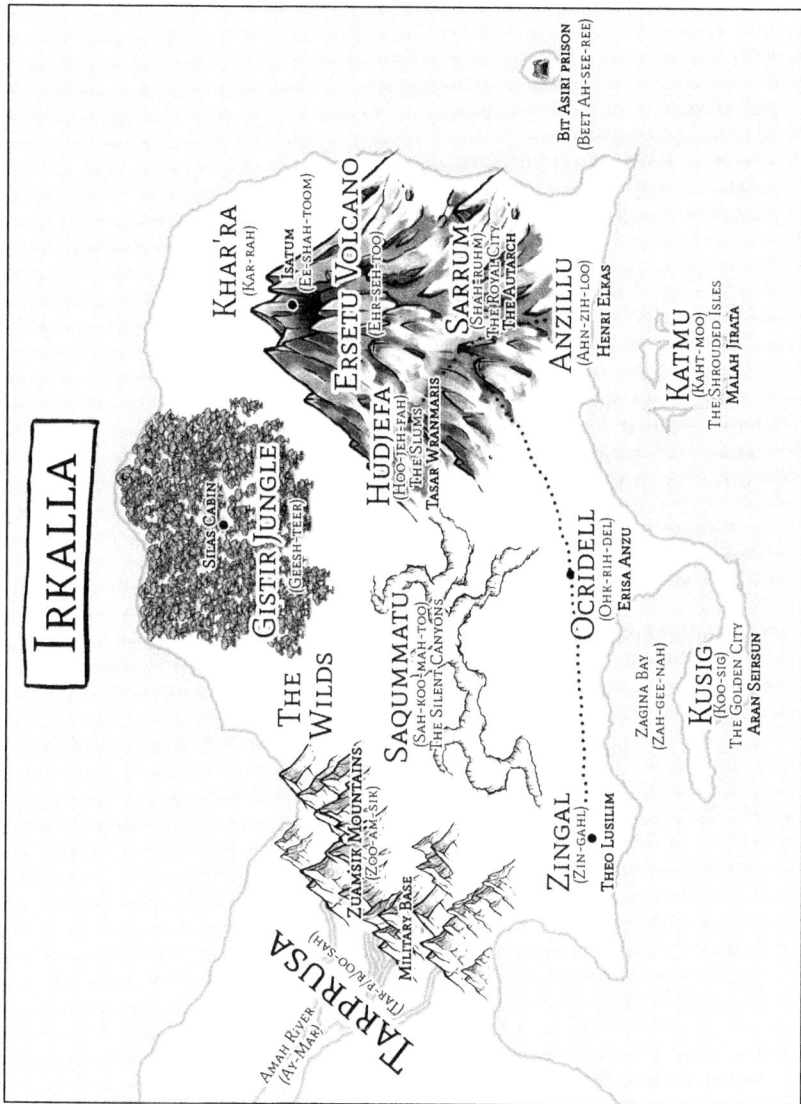

# Pronunciation Guide

## Districts

Anzillu *(Ahn-zih-loo)*
- **Lord**: Henri Elkas *(Hen-ree El-kas)*
- Asila *(Ah-see-lah)*
- ~~Cameron Sangare *(Cam-er-on San-gar)*~~

Hudjefa *(Hoo-jeh-fah)*
- **Lord**: Tasar Wranmaris *(Tay-zar Ran-mah-ris)*
- Cyfrin Wranmaris *(Kih-frin Ran-mah-ris)*

Katmu *(Kaht-moo)*
- **Lord**: Malah Jirata *(Mah-lah Jih-rah-tah)*
- ~~Asor Jirata *(Ay-sor Jir-ah-tah)*~~
- ~~Bail Jirata *(Bayl Jih-rah-tah)*~~

Kusig *(Koo-sig)*
- **Lord**: Aran Seirsun *(Ah-ran See-er-sun)*

Ocridell *(Ohk-rih-del)*
- **Lady**: Erisa Anzû *(Eh-ris-ah Ahn-zoo)*
- ~~Amelyne Fedelis *(Ah-meh-lynn Feh-deh-lis)*~~
- ~~Ava Anzû *(Ay-vah Ahn-zoo)*~~
- ~~Evander Anzû *(Eh-van-dah Ahn-zoo)*~~
- ~~Hue Fedelis *(Hyoo Feh-deh-lis)*~~
- ~~Natara Anzû *(Nah-tar-rah Ahn-zoo)*~~
- Verrill Fedelis *(Veh-rill Feh-deh-lis)*
- ~~Zeti Anzû *(Zeh-tee Ahn-zoo)*~~

Šarrum *(Shah-ruhm)*
- **Lord**: The Autarch *(Aw-tark)*
- Csintalan *(Chin-tah-lan)*
- Tohnain *(Toh-nayn)*

Zingal *(Zin-gahl)*
- **Lord**: Theo Lusilim *(Thee-oh Loo-sih-lim)*
- Corbin *(Kor-bihn)*
- Dana Lusilim *(Dah-nah Loo-sih-lim)*

- Diandra Lusilim *(Dee-ahn-drah Loo-sih-lim)*
- Ezra *(Ehz-rah)*
- Josefine *(Joh-seh-feen)*
- ~~Karasi Lusilim~~ *~~(Kah-rah-see Loo-sih-lim)~~*
- ~~Kyron Lusilim~~ *~~(Kai-ron Loo-sih-lim)~~*
- Nook *(Nuk)*
- Suenna *(Soo-eh-nah)*

## Gods and Deities
- Dumuzid *(Doo-moo-zeed)*
- Ereshkigal *(Eh-resh-kee-gahl)*
- Geshtinanna *(Gesh-tee-nah-nah)*
- Inanna *(Ee-nah-nah)*
- Lamaštu *(Lah-mash-too)*
- Namtar *(Nahm-tar)*
- Nanaya *(Nah-nai-yah)*
- Nergal *(Ner-gahl)*
- Neti *(Neh-tee)*
- Pazuzu *(Pah-zoo-zoo)*

## Places
- Aessurus *(Ay-suh-rus)*
- Amah River *(Ay-mar)*
- Aretian (*Ah-ree-shun)*
- Atturynn *(Ah-tuh-rin)*
- Bīt Asiri *(Beet Ah-see-ree)*
- Ersetu *(Ehr-seh-too)*
- Ganzir *(Gahn-zeer)*
- Gištir *(Geesh-teer)*
- Iaxar *(Aye-ahks-ah)*
- Irkalla *(Ir-kah-lah)*
- Išātum *(Ee-shah-toom)*
- Isthmus of Gidim *(Iss-muss of Gih-dihm)*
- Khar'ra *(Kar-rah)*
- Nasilan *(Nah-see-lan)*
- Nicaieri *(Nih-kai-air-ee)*
- Sakona *(Sah-koh-nah)*
- Saqummatu *(Sah-koo-mah-too)*
- Semmi *(Seh-mee)*
- Tarprusa *(Tar-p/r/oo-sah)*
- Zagina *(Zah-gee-nah)*
- Zuamsik *(Zoo-am-sik)*

And so I unleash the fires of Irkalla to cleanse the plague of mortal sin from this land. Let it scorch the very earth you stand upon, until I bestow the gift of redemption that will restore it to glory.

*Ereshkigal, Goddess of Death and Queen of Irkalla*

# Prologue

I t wasn't a fair fight between the two figures grappling on the side of the chasm. The obvious victor had struck blow after blow, despite having no weapons and their opponent having three. With an audible crunch, the nose of the imminent loser was broken. Their head was thrown back and hood dislodged to reveal a tangle of matted, blood-soaked curls around a pretty face twisted into an angry, exhausted snarl.

"Please, just listen to me! You don't know the truth!" the woman hissed out, throwing a desperate punch. Her opponent grabbed her arm. They used her momentum to swing her around and over the edge of the chasm. The two-hundred-foot drop yawned beneath her, beckoning her down. She cried out as her shoulder dislocated, leaving her body hanging uselessly. She kicked hard, scrambling to find a foothold in the cliff face. Securing the toe of her boot into a crack, she brought her left arm up to clutch desperately at where her assailant had her by the right.

Her teeth clenched as she bit back another scream.

"He's lying to you, I had nothing to do with it! Please stop!" A cold sweat glistened over her forehead, and her expression was etched with pure dread.

The opponent lowered a free hand to grab a jewel-encrusted dagger from the woman's belt and brought it quickly back up through her wrist, slicing hand from forearm. The woman's shrieks of pain and terror echoed through the silent canyons, following her free fall through the swirling mist below and out of sight.

The victor looked down at the severed hand. It was adorned with a ring on the middle finger, which was connected to a bracelet by a thin, delicate chain. The bracelet was now swinging limply, its polished golden shine and inset attachments half-hidden beneath a coating of blood. The hand itself was decorated with a swirling black design, snaking from the fingertips to the knuckles, evolving into several angular symbols and woven patterns across the back of the hand. It would have extended from the wrist up to the forearm, had it still been attached.

Flipping the hand over and noting the six short, golden horizontal lines tattooed onto the palm, the victor carefully returned the bracelet onto the cooling severed limb and placed it gently into a wax wrapping, secured with an intricate purple knot. A symbol of the Palace.

"With regards, from the Autarch," they remarked coldly and slipped the blood-soaked dagger beneath the purple ribbon. Almost hidden within the darkness of their hood curved a small, satisfied smile of a job well done.

Because it *was* a job well done. The woman was definitely dead.

# Chapter 1

## Erisa

Cameron was still inside me, nearing his own release, when I slit his throat. He'd performed so well tonight that I *almost* felt bad for not returning the favor. The blood sprayed over our naked bodies, and I smiled at him as I watched an array of emotions pass over his face. Confusion, betrayal, anger. And finally—sweetest of all—fear.

I continued to straddle him where he sat in his chair until his final, gurgled breaths fell silent. I hadn't meant to kill him just yet, but the letter opener he'd left on his desk had just been too *enticing*. It wasn't surprising he'd kept it sharp. He always was a paranoid little weed, and after his betrayal of the Autarch, he must have been expecting punishment.

Though, perhaps not quite like this.

Using his discarded shirt, I wiped as much of the blood off my skin as I could before it started to crust, and began redressing. Rifling through the paperwork in Cameron's desk, I found what I needed, and after relieving him of his coin pouch, I stepped onto the window ledge, ready to leave. Silently slipping out into the night, I spared a final glance at the office. A half grin rose on my face as I took in the grisly scene his wife would find upon returning home.

I swiftly made my way through the dimly lit tunnels connecting Anzillu to Šarrum, navigating cautiously through the throngs of hooded individuals and underhand dealings. With such a large portion of the realm being underground—concealed in caverns and hideaways throughout the southern and western side of the Ersetu volcano—shadows and illegal activities were constant companions.

Irkalla was a realm encompassing eight districts—nine counting the Bīt Asiri Prison off the east coast—governed by seven houses, all ruled by the Autarch. I made a quick stop at Anzillu's bazaar, trading a few of Cameron's coppers for a bag of sweet spiced pastries and some candied oranges, before leaping onto a tram heading for Šarrum.

The trams under Ersetu were operated on pulleys powered by the volcano's heat and residual magic, creating a direct line from Anzillu to the Hudjefa Slums, passing through Šarrum on the way. Another line traveled west from Šarrum to Ocridell, resurfacing above ground to continue on to Zingal.

It was said that Irkalla was once a beautiful, fertile land, home to the people and gods alike, living in peace with one another. Until the gods became wrathful and tore open the land itself, raising Ersetu to the surface and unleashing the hellish underworld upon the humans to punish them for their greed and selfishness.

Whether there was any truth to it, I had no idea. But I was

grateful nonetheless; I loved Irkalla. I thrived in the dark chaos ensnaring this realm. No one was expected to be anything but themselves and to act in their own best interests. There were no false optimisms and forced niceties here, only brutal means to egotistical ends.

❖ ❖ ❖

I spent the remainder of the hour-long journey to Šarrum cleaning Cameron's blood out from under my fingernails with a small dagger. I silently chastised myself for being so careless when I noticed that some had splattered onto the sleeve of my new silk undershirt. Thank the gods it was already carmine. Grimacing at the offending mark, I rolled the sleeves up to my elbows and pulled my cloak down to cover my arms. I secured the dagger into its sheath at my hip before leaping from the tram onto the platform. The pulleys never stopped, only slowed enough to allow people to jump to and from the carriages.

Šarrum was stifling, situated close to the belly of the volcano, and the smell of sulfur was thick in the air. My clothes stuck to my skin, sweat beading around my hairline under my hood as I skulked toward the Palace at the heart of the city. This district was a sharp contrast to the one I had just left; the bustling, hectic energy of Anzillu was replaced with a more relaxed and refined atmosphere. Šarrum was home to the wealthiest of Irkallian citizens, housed in mansions and dressed in the finest silks. It was still deadly of course. The scheming and plotting of the royal city was unrivaled, and the residents were almost as cutthroat as those residing in Katmu. However, words were the most popular weapon here. Beauty was celebrated in Šarrum, and it masked the ugliest of intentions.

"Good evening, you two," I said sweetly to the guards standing at the main gate of the Palace. Sacha and Joe. I knew every member of staff here and made it my business to know who had access to each area, and their permitted times. The Palace was built into one of the huge caverns beneath the volcano, surrounded on all sides by rock; it was nearly impenetrable. The only access points were two gated tunnels to the southern and western sides of the cavern, as well as a few cracks which could be accessed from neighboring tunnels, if one knew where to look.

"Evening, Kitty Cat!" Sacha winked at me, opening the gate to let me pass. Joe grabbed my forearm, stopping me before he snatched the hood from my head.

"We need to see your whole face before we can let you in," he snarled, "not just your nose and chin."

Looking him slowly up and down, I dug my nails into the hand that held me. I was impressed he didn't wince, I always kept my claws sharp. I was the Feline, and I enjoyed living up to the title.

"But Joe, how could you *possibly* mistake me for anyone else? When you're *so* well acquainted with my mouth," I taunted, a cruel smile appearing as I noticed him fixating on my lips. Hurt flashed across his face before he pushed me through the gate, unable to find a retort. Sacha snorted and I returned her wink as I passed them both, making my way up the short tunnel and into the palace grounds.

The cavern gaped before me, so high I had to crane my neck to see the trickles of moonlight that filtered through thin slivers in Ersetu's surface to kiss the top towers of the Palace. The entire building was crafted from lavastone, looming ominously inside the desolate cave. Torches illuminated the walls, throwing menacing shadows from the razor-sharp spires that reached through the empty space, groping like skeletal fingers. Stone dragons skulked down the tall battlements, teeth bared and tails thrashing. Even frozen, the malevolent guardians watched with glistening moonstone eyes, tracking every movement. The main keep was punctured with narrow windows, lit from within, casting an eerie glow across sentinels patrolling the surrounding turrets.

I walked down the dusty path lined with stalagmites, until the front doors towered before me. Dark wood and elaborately twisted iron depicted the fearsome form of the god Neti, guardian of the gates of Irkalla. His lion head roared down at me, spears held poised in each hand and the long, sharp talons on his eagle's feet shone dangerously from the polished wood. The doors opened and I was greeted by Tohnain, the Palace butler, who as always was dressed impeccably in a fitted maroon tunic embroidered with golden thread.

"He's been waiting almost two hours for you, Erisa," he warned, taking my cloak and leading me through the dark towering archways of the entrance hall toward the Autarch's wing. Tohnain was one of the few people who still used my name, having been head of the household staff when I was first brought to the Palace in my fourteenth year. Ten years had passed since then, but he had remained gentle and kind toward me, as though I was still that frightened child.

Now, I was known by a different name. The Feline: a title that instilled fear into the citizens of Irkalla, causing them to shudder in discomfort at the mere mention.

"I got a little sidetracked while in Anzillu," I admitted, pulling the oranges from my cloak and handing them to him. "I appreciate you keeping him occupied."

He thanked me with a warm smile and popped a candied slice into his mouth before I opened the door to the Autarch's office and stepped inside.

It was a huge room, brightly lit with flaming sconces that illuminated the floor-to-ceiling bookshelves and the enormous table in the center. It was carved from the same ancient dark wood as the front doors, and chiseled into the surface was a detailed map of the four realms. Aessurus and Atturynn to the north and Tarprusa and Irkalla to the south, the two major land masses separated by the Aretian Gulf. Nicaieri was situated off the west coast of Aessurus, but letters and reports covered that end of the table, obscuring the small forgotten territory. The room smelled of old paper and ash; it was comforting and familiar.

"You're late. I expected you back for dinner tonight." The Autarch sat at the head of the ornate table in an equally elaborate high-backed chair and gestured for me to take a seat. He was the embodiment of power and could command a room without speaking a single word. Approaching his fiftieth year he showed no sign of weakness, his tall, strong body still remaining as solid as it had been ten years prior. He was graying slightly around the temples, a shock against the jet-black hair covering the rest of his head.

Had I not known him so well, his icy blue eyes would have pierced right through me; they were so bright and cold they seemed to blaze in the torchlight.

Before I could answer, the door swung open and Verrill strode in, his dark blond hair slightly disheveled and the sleeves of his navy shirt pushed up. His hazel eyes landed on me and widened as he took in the dried blood crusted to my exposed skin. He quickly scanned over me, as if looking for injuries, and let out a small breath when he realized it wasn't mine.

"Tohnain said you were in here," he said to me by way of greeting, and nodded to the Autarch as he sat down opposite me. "Evening, Csintalan. I've received news from the slums; Tasar wants to meet."

Had anyone other than Verrill or myself called the Autarch by his real name, they would have found they no longer had a tongue. Verrill and I had arrived at the Palace on the same day, so many years ago, both orphaned and trembling in fear. I'd been clutching his arm so hard I'd left bruises.

Csintalan nodded slightly.

"Good, it's about time we get that deal finalized." He looked back to me. "Now, why are you late, Kitten?"

He had given me the sickening nickname after he'd found me trying to hide with Verrill in the still-smoldering remains of my family's estate in Ocridell. I'd clawed and hissed at him as he'd tried to get us out. He said that with my face smudged with soot and my amber eyes glowing, I'd reminded him of a feral shadowcat cub.

"Cameron distracted me," I replied, fishing out the letters I'd taken from his desk and handing them over. "And corsets take an *age* to lace back up."

Verrill's jaw clenched as he looked at the floor, away from me. I threw the bag of pastries at him. His face lit up as he caught the scent of his favorite treat and immediately scarfed one down, instantly placated.

Csintalan's lip curled in disdain at both my words and the crumbs now scattered across the table.

"Well, he's certainly been busy. Either Henri doesn't know what his own lackeys are up to, or he's been lying to me. What do you think?" he asked, after flipping through the papers and passing them over for Verrill to read.

"If Henri was in on the deal, he's a better actor than I thought. Cameron made him look like a fool. His pride would never allow him to fake that," I offered. "And there's no mention of Henri in any of the related correspondence. It seems they kept it very quiet."

"Well, it appears Cameron has outlived his usefulness then. We'll have to deal with him at some point," Csintalan sighed.

"I'll see to it," Verrill said, refolding the letters.

"No need, I've disposed of him already." I gave them both a devious smile. "Well, actually, his wife will dispose of him when she gets home and finds his body."

Verrill had to choke down his laugh as Csintalan shot a glare at me.

"You're telling me that not only did you kill a member of Henri Elkas' court after receiving direct orders not to, but you killed him in his own house, which was no doubt full of witnesses? All while knowing that doing so would give Henri the grounds he needs for retaliation. You know very well how difficult he's been this past year."

I rolled my eyes. "Calm down old man, I did him a favor. If he comes crying to you, just show him the letters and he'll be grateful Cam has already been dealt with."

Verrill and I shared a smirk as Csintalan sighed once more, deeper this time.

"You children lack respect and discipline," he groaned, rubbing his temples. "If Elkas does come knocking, he'll have to wait. I'm leaving tomorrow morning. I've got business in the districts to attend to. I'll only be gone a week, if the gods are good. Verrill, you'll need to keep on top of things until I return. Make sure the meeting with Tasar yields fruit. Use this to seal any official correspondence, you already know how to forge my handwriting."

He took off his gold signet ring engraved with the royal crest and handed it over before standing up and looking at me.

"Behave," was all he said before striding out of the room.

"I'm about to leave for Hudjefa, fancy a night out?" Verrill offered, knowing all too well that I could never say no.

"Let's go, drinks are on Cameron tonight!" I chirped, already on my feet.

"You're going like that?" His eyes roamed lazily down my body. I adjusted the lacings of the black corset I wore over my stained chemise and tucked them into the waistband of my trousers, ensuring all of my daggers were where they ought to be. If you ignored the dried blood, I was decent enough for the slums.

"I'll still show *you* up," I countered, taking his arm as we began to make our way through the Palace. He had a handsome, chiseled face, and always looked good in a rakish, careless sort of way. He was a head taller than I was, and had a lean, athletic build. We had both been trained in combat, but Verrill practiced religiously every day, the commitment evident in the lethal grace of his every movement.

"Oh, I don't doubt it." He grinned down at me, his warm eyes sliding to the exposed skin of my left forearm linked with his. He traced the thin silver bands marking my skin with a finger before raising a brow at me.

"Three more this week?"

"Four," I replied, "I cashed one in yesterday to get access to Cameron's house."

"You're incorrigible." He laughed softly, shaking his head.

I rolled my sleeves down, covering the shimmering marks. I had more than the average person and they always caught the attention of a few curious eyes. Once again I scowled at the blood staining the soft fabric, but I knew no one else would notice, especially in the slums.

We continued out toward the main gate, where Joe glowered at me. Verrill was unable to hide the amusement from his voice as he whispered into my ear.

"I heard that you set his bed on fire when he told you he didn't want to hide your ... *courtship* any longer."

"I didn't mean to," I promised. "I was shocked he thought we even *had* anything to hide. When he told me, I got up so fast that I knocked a candle over and the whole bedspread went up like it had been soaked in oil."

He barked out a laugh in response, turning to me, his eyes full of mischief.

"Let's go have some fun!"

# Chapter 2

## Theo

I was trying to run through a dark forest, but my legs were so heavy, like they were made of stone. There was a bright light in front of me and I knew it was safe, I had to get to it, because something was chasing me. It leapt onto my back and I fell, knocking the wind from my lungs. Hundreds of eyes glowed in trees, watching me. I tried to get up to crawl toward that light but claws raked down my back, pinning me down. It was agony. I wanted to get back up, to shift the weight on top of me but as soon as I lifted my head, jaws clamped around my neck, twisting until it snapped. I woke up choking.

12 April

❊❊❊

G ods, I despised gambling dens.

They were bad enough in the more refined districts of Irkalla, but here in the cesspit of the Hudjefa Slums, they were almost more than I could tolerate. I always forgot about the unbearable warmth that plagued the subterranean cities. It was a sickly, sticky heat that harnessed the sour odor of sweat and sulfur to choke you. Especially in Hudjefa, where so many people came to forget everything or be forgotten themselves; it was a writhing crush of bodies, marinated in disease and despair.

This particular den was supposed to be one of the nicer establishments in the city, and I couldn't even comprehend what the worst would be like. The crowded, dimly lit hovel invited a congregation of individuals from every district, packing them in on ten tables scattered about the room. A small group of musicians played in the corner, all of them so inebriated that they didn't seem to notice they were all playing different tunes. Ale mugs littered every surface that wasn't occupied with cards or dice, and topless escorts covered most of the laps.

Had it not been for my tenuous alliance with Tasar Wranmaris, I would never have come. But I was desperate, and he had risked a lot to inform me of his meeting with the Fox. It was only polite that I made the journey into his shithole of a city.

I waited on a small balcony, watching the drunken fools throwing away more money than they possessed on the thrill of chance, when I caught movement from above.

A woman entered the tavern through the ceiling rafters, silently observing the players. She was glorious; dark, silken hair spilled like black ink around a beautiful face, framing golden-yellow eyes so bright they seemed to illuminate the darkness. There was dried blood peeking out from under her chemise, smeared up her throat and speckled under her chin, as though she hadn't thought to clean there. Her hands were stained too, and something told me that it was so frequently the case, she barely bothered to wash it off at all. She watched the bets like a wraith in the shadows, maneuvering from beam to beam, every prowling movement graceful and precise.

She eventually dropped down to join the game, after learning everyone's tells, and placed a few coppers into the pot. She was tall; flaunting a lithe and athletic body clad in fitted garments to show the swell of her breasts and hips, which she used to her advantage. I watched her brush slender fingers over areas of exposed skin, drawing the eyes of players as she reached into their pockets and cloaks, retrieving coin purses and valuables. Three rounds of cards later, and she'd fleeced them all.

She was everything I hated about this realm: the thievery, brutality, and deception, all wrapped in a blood-soaked package, so pretty you didn't even seem to notice it dripping through your fingers. I'd seen many beautiful women in my twenty-seven years, but I was transfixed, my gaze so wholly focused on the lovely demon that I hadn't noticed Nook appearing at my side.

"Any sign of him yet?" he asked, tying his shoulder-length red hair into a knot at the nape of his neck.

"No, he's still in the back room. His men said he'd come and get me when he's ready. The bastard clearly likes making me sweat," I replied, looking at the sandglass by the entrance. I'd been here for more than two hours.

"I know it's easy for me to say, but try not to show him you're stressed. He'll only use it to his advantage." He nodded toward one of the card tables. "Go and have a round to distract your mind, let him see you relaxed and enjoying yourself, so he won't think he's got the upper hand."

He clapped me on the shoulder before leaving the balcony to shamelessly flirt with a group of women gathered around a dice game. I took his advice, heading toward one of the busier card tables, where the woman I'd spotted earlier watched with eager fascination.

I sidled up behind her. Soft strands of jasmine scented hair tickled my nose as I leaned over to whisper into her ear.

"You're still wearing your last victim."

She stilled at my abrupt presence, only for a second. But I noticed.

She gasped, turning to me, a hand over her mouth in mock embarrassment. "Oh goodness, how careless of me!" Her light, silken voice dripped with sarcasm.

Up close, I allowed myself a second to truly admire her. Her flawless olive skin was paler than it ought to be, hinting to years spent beneath the volcano. Those glowing upturned eyes were framed with long, black lashes that nearly brushed her dark eyebrows as she looked up at me. Her lips were tinted a dark pink, the bottom slightly too full for the top. An inverted cupid's bow created a soft, upturned point beneath her straight nose, continuing to tilt down at the corners of her mouth, giving the effect of a permanent petulant expression.

"Whose is it?" I asked, gesturing to the gore adorning her

throat. "Should I be concerned for their wellbeing?"

She snorted.

"Someone beyond your help, hero. Save your concerns for the living, there's plenty that need it here," she remarked, patting my chest as she moved past me to melt back into the crowd.

That was true enough.

As if her words were a reminder of my purpose here tonight, Tasar caught my gaze from the opposite end of the tavern and gestured for me to join him. I wove through the bodies to enter the room he'd disappeared into, almost sighing in relief at the cool whisper of breeze through the open window.

Tasar Wranmaris, like the majority of his malnourished people, was slim. He had a wiry build and a boyish face, despite being a year older than I was. His copper hair lacked the brilliance of Nook's red, but the cunning shine of his dark eyes held my attention.

"Theodoraxion Lusilim." Tasar beamed and I inwardly cringed at the ridiculous name. "Last time we were together, I woke up outside a barn in Kusig, knee deep in horse shit, wearing Karasi's dress and that ridiculous pink bonnet. I've missed you, my friend!"

My jaw clenched at the mention of my twin sister, but I returned his embrace as he said softly, "I was heartbroken when I heard what happened, you know how fond I was of her."

I nodded, sinking into a threadbare armchair by the window.

"Thanks for meeting with me, Tasar. I know things have been tense recently."

He waved a willowy hand, dismissing the thought.

"Nonsense, I understand how these district politics have to play out. We're not the carefree delinquents we once were, Theo. The fact that *you're* the one sitting here is enough of a reminder. Now talk to me, what role do you see me playing in these plans of yours?"

He was getting straight to the point then. Good.

I made an effort to relax into my seat, keeping my voice steady as I replied. "That is yet to be determined, are you saying that you're open to the idea of joining us?"

"Open to the idea of treason, you mean?" he said, closing the window. "I have no doubt of your good intentions, Theo. But do you appreciate what you're asking of me? I told you I had a meeting with the Fox tonight, to give you a chance to make your offer. He had some *interesting* things to say about Cameron Sangare."

"Like what exactly? What does Cameron have to do with anything?" I said, feigning disinterest.

Tasar raised an eyebrow. "Nothing anymore. He was killed a few hours ago. Found slaughtered with his trousers down. A grisly affair, apparently."

"Shit," I breathed. The room was becoming unbearably hot. I couldn't even try to hide the panic flooding my body.

"Fortunately for you, I included *these* in my list of terms for my deal with the Fox."

He handed me a small pile of letters, and I immediately recognized it as my correspondence with Cameron.

"He said no other copies have been made," Tasar continued, "saying it would be pointless, as the damage has already been done. But, Henri Elkas didn't see them."

"That's one small mercy, I suppose."

I felt sick. Tonight was not going at all to plan. A bead of sweat ran down the back of my neck and soaked into the collar of my shirt. I tugged at the fabric, but it only seemed to tighten further.

"Even so, I wouldn't approach him for a while. I imagine he's put enough of the pieces together to be insulted by the fact that you didn't go to him directly," Tasar warned.

I didn't doubt it. It had been a risk using Cameron to go behind his Lord's back. I'd hoped he'd have more time to introduce the idea gently. Henri Elkas was a tricky man, only acting if he believed he was the architect behind every plan. Cameron was to plant small seeds carefully over the next few months, encouraging Henri to approach me himself.

This was a major setback, a failure at the worst possible moment.

"I owe you for this, Tasar," I muttered, the bitter taste of disappointment heavy on my tongue. "What reason did you give for wanting the letters?"

"My district is the poorest, I don't have the same monetary luxuries as the rest of you district Lords. So, I must make my trades in leverage and secrets."

Blackmail; Irkalla's most stable currency.

"Though, he didn't seem to care enough to push the matter," he continued, "you're playing a very dangerous game, Theo. If you think the Autarch doesn't know what you're up to, you're a fool."

"Of course he knows," I retorted. "I'm guessing he doesn't consider me enough of a threat right now to waste time getting rid of me."

"I hope for all our sakes that he continues to be ignorant. But, you still haven't answered my question. What do you want me to do? And why would I risk it?" he pressed. His tone was quiet as his brown eyes assessed me.

"Hudjefa's the poorest district because none of the goods ever make it north of Šarrum. In the last decade, trade has remained central to Ersetu. We've been struggling in Zingal and I know that Kusig has too, though they have their gold mines keeping them comfortable. And I've been engaging in unsanctioned trade with Tarprusa. You don't have that luxury here. Give me anyone who can fight. Out of everyone, you and your people have the most to gain from this reformation." I gave him a grim look. "It won't be an easy war to win, or a quick one. But there's so much that's wrong with this realm. I need to at least try to do *something* about it."

Tasar gave me a sad smile. "It's a pretty dream, Theo. I want to help you, but I will not risk my people, or force them into something that will get them killed. We may be overrun and have too many mouths to feed, but you're forgetting that we house the dregs of society. We *are* the scrapings at the bottom of the barrel. Anyone who *could* fight is needed here to keep the place running. Not to mention we lack the facilities to house and train an army."

He huffed out a small laugh at the idea.

"I'm not talking about forcing them, but asking them," I countered. "I'll have them in Zingal. If you have anyone to spare, let them come to my district. We'll house them and feed them. They can bring their families too."

I didn't mention the barracks we had hidden in the southern region of the Zuamsik Mountains, *that* information was too sensitive to risk.

He considered my words for a few long moments, and I was sure he could smell the desperation seeping from my pores.

"I will give them the choice. I'm sure there will be many willing to take you up on your offer," he said finally, and my heart began to race. "But I do have a few conditions."

"Please, go on," I invited, readying myself for another disappointment.

"I ask that you don't turn any of them away. Don't expect hordes of trained soldiers to come out of my slums. You'll likely find half-mad women and starved children arriving at your doorstep, but let them fight for their chance at a better life here in Irkalla. Where my people lack discipline and fighting skills, they make up for it with sheer determination and a savage will to survive. I also insist that, if they have a change of heart and desire to return home, they're able to do so without repercussions."

Any lingering hint of humor that still clung to his features had vanished while he spoke.

I cleared my throat quietly. "I'll not put swords into the hands of children or the ailing. However, should they wish to help, I'll find them other roles to fill. Anyone who chooses to leave will be able to. Any other requests?"

"My involvement is to remain hidden," he said as he met my gaze. "I support your movement, but I do so from the shadows. The Autarch cannot know of this meeting tonight. I've already burned the letters from you. I ask that you do the same. Finally, if this all goes well, I'd like a formal alliance between us; for you to reconsider the proposal you shot down two winters ago."

My stomach soured at the memory of receiving that particular letter. I had foolishly hoped he had let that go, but of course he hadn't. It was an effort to unclench my jaw to speak.

"My decision hasn't changed, I will not force her hand."

"All I ask is that you take time to think it over," he replied coolly.

I nodded and stood, holding out my right hand to him. "Very well. So are we agreed on the terms? You will take my offer to your people and in return I'll take all that come, allow any to leave and destroy the evidence of this meeting. Then, if we're successful, I'll consider your previous offer."

"Agreed," he answered, taking my outstretched hand and shaking it once.

I watched the thin silver mark etch into his skin, encircling his wrist above two others that were already situated there. Then, I felt the burn on my own hand. I let go of him and looked down to where a single, short horizontal line of gold now shone in the center of my palm.

"Now," he said, clapping me on the back with an easy smile, "get out of here before someone recognizes you."

❖ ❖ ❖

Thanks to his shock of red hair, I quickly found Nook pressing a woman up against the shaded back wall. His mouth was so engaged with hers, he gasped for breath when I pried them apart. He gave me a wolfish grin as we set off for the exit, blowing a farewell kiss in her direction.

Despite the late hour, the tavern was still busy. My hood was already covering most of my face, but I pulled it down further. Nook mirrored the action.

We were almost at the door when I was shoved out of the way from behind. I looked up to see the pretty demon from earlier slip past and into the crowd, winking one yellow eye at me over her shoulder. Her silky black hair was still braided down her back, swaying slightly as she approached a man standing at the bar from behind.

I watched as she pounced onto his back, fisting one hand into his dark blonde hair, the other holding a dagger to his throat. The action was so fast, I had to blink several times to believe what I was seeing. The man didn't so much as flinch, he simply chuckled affectionately, turning his head to look at her, as if this was a common occurrence.

"Come on," Nook insisted, pushing me forward, "let's get out of this madhouse."

He'd clearly witnessed the encounter too.

We were at the Šarrum platform, changing to the western tram line, when I realized she'd emptied my pockets. Nook graciously paid my fare after laughing himself hoarse when I told him. What I didn't have the dignity to disclose was that not only had she had the opportunity to strip me of my last copper, but she'd also managed to slip a note into my cloak pocket.

*If you're going to stand there and watch me from the shadows all night, you can at least buy me a drink first.*

I mentally chastised myself for being so careless. Even with my hood up, she'd somehow managed to recognize me enough to give me the note. I only prayed to any of the gods that might be listening that she didn't know who I was, that she was too preoccupied with the man at the bar.

*Good luck to him,* I thought, shuddering.

❖ ❖ ❖

As tired as I was, I couldn't help but be grateful for the tramline running directly to my district. Compared to Aran Seirsun, it took no time at all to get back home from the Palace.

Kusig, Katmu and Khar'ra could not be accessed by tramlines. Kusig sat across the Zagina Bay from Ocridell, and the strip of land joining the two was unsuitable for the pulley tracks. Katmu was a collection of small islands off the southeastern coast of Irkalla, a haven for pirates and smugglers engaging in black market trade with Anzillu's bazaar. Khar'ra was located in the Wilds, the large expanse of land encompassing everything north of Ersetu—unruly and feral, teeming with monsters and unimaginable horrors. Though it would be perfectly achievable to integrate Khar'ra into the tram network, no one had ever had the desire to do so.

By the time we arrived back at the estate in Zingal, pale pink whispers of dawn were beginning to spill over the jagged crater of Ersetu, feathering into the dark night sky. I savored the coolness of the spring air and faint scent of the ocean as we made our way through the gardens toward the house. It was an impressive manor, standing firm and steady against the storms that occasionally funneled in from the Nasilan Sea, but entirely too big and empty.

My mother was waiting in the kitchen, sitting at the table with a steaming pot of tea ready for us. She filled two mugs, and Nook snatched one gratefully, wincing as he scalded his tongue on the first gulp.

"How did it go?" she asked tentatively, as though scared of the answer.

I fell into a chair beside her, sighing. I didn't even know where to begin. I rested my elbows on the table and let my head fall into my hands.

"Worse than expected."

She said nothing, only waited for me to continue.

"Cameron Sangare is dead, the Autarch had him killed last night."

I heard her gasp softly, but didn't look up.

"By now, Henri Elkas will know why. That Cameron was plotting with me to undermine him. He didn't see any of the letters, but I'm sure his imagination will conjure up schemes far worse than reality. Any hope of us securing a foothold in Anzillu is gone."

"I suppose there is nothing to be done about it now, we knew it was a gamble. One that unfortunately hasn't paid off. And what of Tasar? Did he see you?" she asked, not managing to hide the hopeful tone from her voice.

"He was the one who told me about Cameron. He agreed to give his people the choice to fight, as long as we keep them here."

I finally looked up, reaching for my tea. I knew what she was going to ask next. But my heart still sank when she did.

"And what have you promised him in return?"

"I told him that if we succeed, I'll reconsider his proposal regarding Didi."

My cheeks burned with shame. The room was silent, even Nook held his breath, his azure eyes focused on the table.

"You will do no such thing," my mother hissed, her brown eyes fierce as they bore into mine. "There is something wrong with that brother of his, he's not … right. I'll not have Diandra anywhere near him. And I'll not have her sold off as though she were some broodmare."

I didn't need her to tell me that handing my little sister over like livestock to Cyfrin Wranmaris was abhorrent. She was right, there *was* something unsettling about him. But I didn't have the energy to argue about it now, I needed to sleep.

I drained my cup and rose to my feet.

"Corbin is due to arrive later, I'm hoping he'll agree to help this time," I said as I left the room.

Nook's voice followed me up the dark hallway. "Don't worry, Dana, you know he won't agree to it. And we've still got a long way to go before it's even an option."

Thankfully, I didn't hear her response as I closed the door to my chambers and fell into bed.

❖ ❖ ❖

The sun glared through my open curtains and woke me

midmorning. I was still dressed in my clothes from the night before and grimaced at the smell of ash and sulfur lingering on the fabric. I took the small, crumpled note out of my cloak pocket, and examined it again.

Trying not to think about what it could have cost me, I smoothed it out and stashed it into a drawer, before bathing and changing into fresh clothes.

Corbin arrived shortly after I'd had breakfast. He had been an extended part of the family since before Karasi and I had been born, and after our father died, he stayed close to help our mother raise us. Didi had only just turned one.

I had only seen Corbin a handful of times in recent years. Before Karasi was killed, I'd spent my time drinking and fucking my way through all four realms, Nook, Ezra, and Suenna in tow. Since then, I'd been too busy plotting my revenge and picking up the pieces of my broken family. Guilt lanced through me at the thought. Corbin *was* part of the family too, but it hurt to look at him. He'd spent so much time teaching my twin how to be Lady of Zingal, that I couldn't see him without imagining how much of a failure I must be in comparison to her.

"Hello, my boy." He grinned, holding me at arm's length to look me over. He was half a head shorter than I was, his body leaner with age, but still well maintained. He had dedicated as many years to my combat training as he had to Karasi's political lessons, and I had no doubt that he could still beat me in a fight. His light eyes sparkled at me as he added, "you're looking well."

I returned his smile. "It's good to see you, Corbin. How have you been?"

"Fine for the most part. Though I have to admit, I'm glad this last winter is behind us. It was almost enough for me to move below ground. I felt the cold in my bones."

Despite being offered a permanent residence in Zingal, Corbin had never wanted to move from his little house in Ocridell. It was situated south of the tram line, in the larger part of the city that remained above ground. The rest networked below the surface, through the outer slope of the volcano.

"You know you always have a place here, should you want it." I repeated the offer he'd declined so many times before. He gave me a warm smile and followed me into the main sitting room.

"Are you still having the dreams?" he asked, watching me stifle a yawn. He stood by the hearth, warming his hands.

"Almost every night." I cringed at the thought of the nightmares that had haunted me since Karasi's death. "Mother suggested writing them down each morning to get them out of my head."

"And is it helping?"

*No, not at all.*

"Possibly, it's hard to tell," I replied.

"And I assume your request for my visit wasn't just for a catch up."

"No," I conceded, "there have been developments in my … situation. I was hoping that you would finally change your mind about helping me."

"I'm getting old, Theo. I am not a Lord, I have no lands or people to offer you but myself. And I wish to die in my meadow in Ocridell, the sun on my skin and birdsong in my ears, not on some gruesome battleground with a sword through my gut." He looked at me sympathetically. "I wish you every success in your plan, but I have nothing that I can give you."

"You have sway with the other Lords, your connections are more than enough. I would never ask you to fight, despite the fact that you could likely take down ten of my best men at once," I said, only half joking.

He crowed out a laugh in response, but his gaze went to the mantle. Karasi's bracelet sat on a little pillow beside a portrait of her face etched with boredom. I had forced her to sit for an hour while I sketched her likeness as a gift for our mother's birthday one year. I'd had to bribe her with her favorite sweet bread from Anzillu's bazaar. The memory made my chest hurt.

Corbin quietly inspected the delicate golden chain and connecting charms that would always chime together as she moved. She never took that bracelet off. She'd linked it to a gold ring on her middle finger when the clasp had come loose, fearing it would come off without her noticing.

"Mother put it out last year," I explained. "She said Karasi wouldn't have wanted it hidden away and left to tarnish."

He picked it up gently, his fingers trembling ever so slightly, and brushed one of the lockets with a knuckle.

"Corbin!"

A delighted squeal came from the door as Didi ran to throw her arms around the older man. He'd been caught so off guard, the bracelet fell from his hand and landed heavily on the stone floor. We all watched in horror as the small casing he had been inspecting split from the impact, sending a small red stone rolling across the ground.

Had I not been so shocked, I would have scolded my little sister for her outburst. But I couldn't take my eyes off the bracelet. From where the red stone had been held, a small piece of paper lay folded, nestled in among the pieces of the broken charm. I was over to them before they could react, snatching up the bracelet, stone, and paper to inspect the damage.

"Mother will kill you if she sees this is broken," I warned Didi, without looking at her. My focus was consumed by the tiny, folded note. I opened it, unable to stop my hands from shaking.

*T, you already know who he is.*
*Find the other piece and fix the stone.*

I reread the words four times, begging them to make sense. The stone was a rough half sphere, about an inch in diameter, with a jagged edge which gave the impression it had been cleaved from its counterpart.

"What does it mean?" Corbin's voice was clipped as he stared at the scene, his gaze darting between the stone and the note, his pale skin a deathly white.

Didi was silent, guilt heavy on her delicate features.

"I have no idea," I replied honestly. I put the bracelet back into place on its cushion, angling the broken piece toward the back, out of sight, and slipped the other two items into my pocket.

Tears welled in Didi's eyes. "I'm sorry. I didn't mean to."

Corbin collected his features into a kind smile and took her arm. "It was my fault, Diandra, I've grown clumsy with age. Come on, take me to your garden, I think I saw some new crocuses on my way in."

❖ ❖ ❖

Between visits to the city and preparing for the incoming numbers from Hudjefa, I didn't manage to see Corbin again until two days later. He was sitting with my mother, sipping tea, when I entered the parlor.

"Theo, I've been thinking about what you said," he began, as I took a seat across from him, "*and* Dana has been plying me with those baked apples she knows I can't resist." He threw my mother an amused look. "I will not play an active role, but I will give you some advice that I hope you'll heed."

"I've always taken your suggestions seriously, Corbin. I'd be glad to hear them now."

He hesitated, pulling at a loose thread on his sleeve. "The Autarch has very few friends, and even fewer that he trusts. Whether you like it or not, he knows that you're planning to overthrow him to reform this realm. I'm not sure why he hasn't chosen to interfere yet, maybe he's waiting to see how the other Lords react to your ideas. But, whatever the reason, you need to choose your allies carefully. Your best bet would be to infiltrate his inner circle. If you can convince even *one* of them to sympathize with the cause, they could direct his attention elsewhere."

I blew out a breath.

"You're trying to get me killed, Corbin. Let's say I agreed to this madness, who would be the easiest target?" I asked, in disbelief that I was even entertaining the idea.

"You asked to hear what I thought, and I'm giving you my honest opinion. Now, while they wouldn't be easy targets, they would be the most effective. The Autarch has his pets; the Feline and the Fox, I'm sure you've heard of them."

I had to repress a shudder as he continued.

"No one knows where they came from, but he's incredibly fond of them. They attend every meeting and event, carry out his justice, and have free rein within the realm. From what I know of them, they're nearly inseparable. Where one goes, the other will likely follow. *They* should be your targets."

"Gods help me," I begged, sagging into my chair. "And which of the two is more likely to hear me out before ripping my head off?"

"As to that, I cannot help you. I have, luckily, never been in close proximity to the duo. But, as rumor has it, the Feline likes to play with her victims. Perhaps you could keep her occupied long enough to get your point across."

I'd rather he'd suggested I drown myself in Zagina Bay.

"The Feline." I chuckled. "You really *are* trying to kill me."

He only smiled apologetically.

# Chapter 3

## Erisa

The man's screams ricocheted off the walls of the chamber, his voice hoarse from the effort. I lounged sideways on a bench, resting my boots on the top rail of the backrest as I watched Verrill work. I pushed back my cuticles with a sharp red nail, growing impatient.

"All you need to do is tell me where the shipment landed, Erik, and you can leave."

Verrill's low voice was steady. I could tell he was bored too. We'd been in here for over an hour.

His hazel eyes rested on mine as he pushed the blade deeper through Erik's foot. The bloody creature whimpered, trying once more to break free from the ropes securing him to the chair in the center of the room.

"Please, I t-told you I d-don't know!" Tears ran pale tracks through the blood and grime coating his face.

"It's interesting you keep saying that," Verrill replied, resting the tip of another knife above Erik's thigh, "because one of my Rats happened to find a letter sent *by you,* regarding a shipment of eight children and two dragon eggs to be smuggled in from Aessurus. The vessel was supposed to dock this morning in Katmu, but no one has seen it. So, tell me, where did it go?"

He pushed the blade in two inches, creating thin ropes of blood that snaked around his exposed leg before falling to the floor.

Erik looked ready to faint. Again.

*"Or,* I can ask her"—he jutted his chin toward me—"to come and use those pretty claws to slice into your more …" he glanced down to the urine stain soaking Erik's torn trousers, *"sensitive* parts. I've never had the stomach for it myself."

Any remaining blood in Erik's face leached away and his throat bobbed as he turned his terror-stricken eyes to me. I raised a brow at him.

"If … If I tell you, you'll l-let me leave?" His voice broke half way through the question.

Verrill's voice was silky in comparison. "I promise."

"The b-boat unloaded in Katmu. On t-the most southeastern island. The mists keep it hidden, b-but there's a dock on the western side, half way down. It arrived there last n-night, I s—" His voice cut off as Verrill's knife went through his left eye and into his skull.

I sat up on the bench, watching my friend retrieve his blades and wipe them on Erik's shirt, his expression tired. I knew how much he hated doing these interrogations. Every one of them chipped away at him, piece by tiny piece.

"Was it the truth?" I asked.

"Yes," he responded, his tone empty.

Occasionally, children in Irkalla were born with certain traits, whether these were passed through family lines or gifted from Ersetu, no one knew, but they were like a sixth sense. Verrill, for example, always had an uncanny ability to sense lies. It was one of the reasons why he had such a successful spy network around the realm. It also made him the best candidate for conducting questioning.

I observed him silently as he untied the ropes and dragged the body through the door of an adjoining chamber, where one of his men would deal with it. He returned with a bowl of water and a cloth, which he set down on the bench beside me and began wiping away the blood from his hands.

Verrill had been my best friend my entire life. His father, Hue, had been my father's right hand, and they were as close as brothers. So close that when mine had moved to Irkalla to marry my mother, Hue and his wife, Amelyne, had packed up their life in Tarprusa to move with him. Amelyne had died giving birth to Verrill less than a year later. By the time I was born, Hue and Verrill were a permanent part of our household.

Verrill sighed, wringing out the cloth and placing it next to the bowl of now pink water. He ran a damp hand through his hair, and the dark blonde strands were pushed from his forehead to reveal more of his drawn expression.

"Come on," I urged, taking his hand, "I fancy a swim."

❖ ❖ ❖

There were dozens of hot springs located around Ersetu. Our

favorite one, however, was almost at the very top of the volcano. It was always empty, and I was convinced we were the only ones who knew of its existence. We scrambled through the cracks and hollows in the rock, eventually reaching the surface. We were so close to the crater, that Išātum—the dragon's protected hatching ground—was almost visible. After descending down the face of the volcano for another ten minutes, we arrived. Unlike the near-scalding springs below ground, this pool was a collection of rainwater heated gently from the rock below.

I stripped out of my clothes and leapt in, savoring the refreshing press of the water against my skin. Verrill had said little on our trek up here, and I knew he was still mentally back in that interrogation room.

"You don't have to keep doing it, you know," I said gently, as he slid into the water beside me, "one of your Rats can do it, or we can ask Csintalan to have one of the others take over. He never asked you to in the first place, he wouldn't force you to continue."

He sat on the stone ledge beneath the water, tilting his head back to rest it against the edge of the pool and closing his eyes.

"I'll not ask one of the Rats to do something I wouldn't do myself." He sighed. "Besides, Csintalan wouldn't bother to question them at all, as long as he got his cut from the deal. The trafficking situation is getting out of hand, and we both know he just considers it 'bad business,' yet lines his pockets with it anyway."

I couldn't argue with that. The Autarch was the ruler of a depraved realm, a place which thrived off the innate corruption of human nature. People would come here seeking the freedom

Irkalla's debauchery promised. There were laws, of course—and Bīt Asiri Prison housed some of the foulest monsters in the realm—but for the everyday person, petty theft and the occasional murder were a way of life. To us, the Autarch was different from Csintalan, the man who had saved us all those years ago, brought us into his home and taught us how to survive. We owed him everything, and it wasn't for us to question how he ruled his realm.

"He knows we're trying to cut out the trade from the market, and he's given us free reign to do so," I suggested. "Surely he would have forbidden us to do anything if he wanted it to keep growing."

Verrill shook his head, his eyes still shut. "He's humoring us, Eris. He lets us work on it like it's some little project to occupy our time. He could've given us resources and imposed sanctions at the ports like I suggested, but he hasn't. He even has his own magic, yet he doesn't bother using it. He doesn't care."

"What are you saying?" I whispered, despite knowing there was no one else here.

Verrill and I had discussed Csintalan's rule countless times. But Verrill was almost as loyal to him as we were to each other, and I had never heard him come so close to outright defiance before. Of course, I would do anything for the man who had become a father figure in lieu of my own, but Verrill was different. I always had my mother's name and district to fall back on, but Csintalan had given Verrill the position and respect of the Autarch's second in command. Even I couldn't give him such an impressive title.

"Nothing," he promised, turning to me with a grin. His somber mood vanished and he kicked my legs from beneath me, pushing my shoulders down to plunge my head beneath the water.

I spluttered to the surface to find him swimming away, laughter peeling through the air. I went under again, cutting through the water toward him. Reaching out to wrap a hand around his ankle, I pulled his body down toward me.

I had always been the stronger swimmer, and by the time I finally let him catch me again, we were both spent and panting with laughter. I pushed myself out of the pool and lay on the smooth rock to catch my breath. He followed, lowering onto his stomach beside me, twirling strands of my long, wet hair around his fingers. The afternoon sun caressed his tanned skin and glittered off the water droplets clinging to his long, brown lashes.

"Do you ever wonder what our lives would've been like if we'd have stayed?" I asked quietly, reaching for his hand.

"Sometimes," he admitted.

He stroked a finger softly over the scar marring my left palm. The action threw me back to the day we never discussed.

❖ ❖ ❖

"Wait, Erisa, you're going to pull my arm off."

"Come on, Ver, if we sneak back in through the window in time, Mama will never know we were gone."

I tugged on his hand again, urging him to walk faster.

"She probably already knows. I hope she isn't mad at me," Verrill replied, and his brow furrowed with worry at the thought. He hated disappointing my mother.

I shot him an annoyed look. "Don't worry about that, she's never mad at you, I *always* get the blame."

"Because *you're* always the one dragging us into trouble," he teased, squeezing my hand.

He wasn't wrong. I'd convinced him to sneak out today. Once a month the local Priestess came to the estate to prattle on for hours about the blessings of the gods. It was almost as fun as watching the grainfalls of a sandglass.

"Would you rather have stayed?" I challenged.

He laughed. "Gods no! Priestess Lea hits me with her cane when I slouch."

My lip curled in anger as I tucked that piece of information away for later. The Priestess was going to regret that.

"Then I think you owe me a kiss for getting you away," I insisted playfully, knowing he'd refuse.

A cunning grin lit up his face. "Eris, with the amount of poison that spews from your mouth, I'll die the moment I kiss your lips," he declared.

He cupped his hands to boost me up into the pear tree that stood at our estate's outer wall. Once secured on the branch, I reached down to help him scramble up.

"And besides, I'll be the one t—" His words broke off in a sudden intake of breath.

I followed his gaze to the cloud of smoke billowing out from the house. Even from this distance, the flames licking the walls were visible and terrifying.

Neither of us said anything as we flew across the wall and jumped down, my knees screaming from the impact. Then we were sprinting through the gardens, trampling through the flowerbeds my mother and little brother, Zeti, had spent hours tending to.

"Mama! Papa!" I yelled, racing toward the main door.

Fire tore through the building, the heat of it scorching the air. I slammed my hands against the door, crying out in pain as the small metal design of our family crest burned through my left palm and melted the skin. I tried pushing it again but something was jamming it from behind. I looked over in time to see Verrill smash a stone through a window and climb through. I went after him, the jagged glass slicing deep into my right shoulder.

Almost blind with panic, I followed Verrill as he ran through the house littered with bodies, aiming for the lecture hall. The walls were almost glowing and I couldn't tell if I was struggling to breathe from the heat or from the fear lancing through my body.

I made it through the archway a few seconds after him, but was yanked roughly to the left. A hand covered my eyes and an arm wrapped around my torso, pinning mine to my sides.

Verrill's broken voice was frantic in my ear.

"Don't look, Eris," he sobbed, trying to pull me backward. "Don't look. Let me lead you out. We need to go. Please, don't look. Don't look."

I bit and clawed at his hands as he clung to me. Breaking free from his hold, I turned and looked. And wished I hadn't.

A scream tore from my throat. My family lay at the foot of the dias at the end of the room, crimson soaking the floorboards beneath them and flames beginning to lap at their clothing. What looked like the rest of the household and staff lay scattered across the floor and burning pews, every pair of eyes vacant and unseeing.

"Mama!" I screeched, throwing myself onto her blood-drenched body, shaking her shoulders to wake her up.

Her necklace was gone and a dagger lay embedded in her chest. She was laying far enough away from the rest of my family that I had to crawl to them, vomiting as I saw my father's head was detached from his body. I wailed and shook my sister Natara and then Hue. Neither of them woke up. I moved to Zeti, his small, childish frame crumpled and broken. He was still holding his beloved little wooden horse, its hind legs and tail charred from the fire. I pried it from his hand and clutched it to my chest.

Blood curdling shrieks continued to lash at my ears, and I didn't realize they were coming from me until I stopped to cry out to Verrill.

He was on his knees by our family, tears streaming down his face, anguish haunting his every feature. He pulled the dagger from my mother's chest, and smoothed the hair from around her face, not seeming to realize that his right trouser leg was burning.

Wood groaned above us, the ceiling threatening to collapse. I leapt toward Verrill, nearly pulling his arm out of the socket as I hauled him up. We ran to the door, the heat scorching the soles of my boots, and made it through just in time for the roof to fall behind us. We didn't stop to look, only continued to flee until we reached the open air of the courtyard. Verrill pulled us into the shallow fountain, extinguishing his trouser leg and the smoldering hem of my skirt.

I couldn't breathe. My racing heart pounded in my ears, growing louder and louder. I knew my body was trembling, but I couldn't stop it, couldn't feel my hands. Everything was spinning and I felt my knees buckle. Verrill caught me in his arms and led me to the edge of the courtyard, where we sat under a stone table with our legs tangled together.

He held me tight as I sobbed into his chest, kissing my head and stroking my hair while our entire world crumbled around us.

❖ ❖ ❖

"It's probably for the best though." Verrill's voice pulled me back to the poolside. "We'd have turned feral. Well, *more* feral in your case."

He was still tracing my palm, the crest imperfect, but still recognizable; a songbird soaring, its wings stretched in flight.

I scoffed. "Me? Feral? I'm angelic."

His booming laugh caused a smile to tug at my lips and his eyes followed the movement, remaining on my mouth for a few seconds.

"I need to go," he said quickly, rising to his feet. "I was supposed to meet with Tasar an hour ago."

"What? Why didn't you say anything?" I asked, picking up my clothes and pulling them on.

He only shrugged and gave me a wry smile, clearly unconcerned by the delay.

❖ ❖ ❖

Tohnain greeted me with a small tray of food when I arrived back at the palace.

"The Autarch has sent word that he'll be returning in two days. He's arranged a meeting with the Lords and requires you to be present. Verrill too." He looked over my shoulder, as if expecting Verrill to appear there.

"It's about time, he's been gone almost a fortnight. I'll tell Verrill when I see him. Is Asila here?" I asked hopefully, taking the tray from him.

"She's waiting for you in your room."

I thanked him before climbing the winding staircase.

Asila was rifling through my wardrobe when I entered, throwing various pieces onto the bed and scowling at the others. Being Tohnain's daughter, she had spent a lot of her time at the Palace growing up, alongside Verrill and I, despite being a few years younger. Like her father, she always looked immaculate. Her tight, dark curls kissed the neckline of her lavender gown, which contrasted beautifully with her umber skin. The pale silk plunged low before falling in soft waves to the floor, complemented with matching slippers.

"You need to sort this mess out, we've got less than two days before the meeting with the Lords, and *this*"—she gestured to the pile of clothes on the bed—"is unacceptable."

"It's fine, I think I'll just wear an old outfit," I goaded, waiting for her retort.

"I think not," she snapped, whipping around to scowl at me. "I'll not have you parading around in these dilapidated old rags, it would reflect badly on me."

I sat picking at my food, listening to her mutter under her

breath about how the Autarch *never* thinks of the preparation needed for events before springing them on us with only a moment's notice. Asila was an extremely talented seamstress, and, even though she was only twenty-two, she owned the most successful dressmaker's shop in Irkalla. I didn't bother mentioning that most of those "old rags" were items she'd either made or chosen for me herself.

Two hours later I was in the bustling bazaar of Anzillu, arms laden with bolts of fabric, following Asila as she wove in and out of the stalls on the way to her shop. Her mother was sitting at the till, going through the accounts when we entered, and I only had the time to greet her with a kiss on the cheek before I was ushered into the back.

"Strip," she ordered, armed with a measuring tape and pin cushion. I knew better than to disobey her in here, I'd been "accidently" stuck with those pins too many times.

"I think we'll go with the red. I'm assuming you'll need your face covered?" she asked as she began to measure.

"Yes, though please not a mask."

She snorted as if the idea was ridiculous. I'd always been extremely grateful that Asila had never once dressed me in anything remotely cat-like. Though I enjoyed being the Feline, the "kitten" references that came with it became tiring over the years, and she thought they were downright disgusting.

"Have you seen Malah recently?" I asked, smirking at her as she adjusted the fabric at my shoulder.

Malah Jirata was the Lord of Katmu, recently having taken over the role when his older brother drowned while high on silkleaf.

Malah had been aiding Verrill and I in our effort to rid his district of trafficking vessels.

She fought a small smile. "He dropped by this morning with some Tarprusan silks. He told me about the meeting."

"Hand delivered? I didn't realize he provided such *dedicated* customer service," I said, raising an eyebrow.

That earned me a jab of a pin.

"Be grateful that he does, otherwise I wouldn't have had time to put anything together and you would've been parading naked before the entire retinue."

"What? Everyone's attending?"

I couldn't remember the last time that had happened. Every Lord and his court would be invited.

Her brows furrowed slightly as she met my gaze. "Apparently. He must be planning something big."

We were both silent, considering the possibilities, as she continued her work.

❖ ❖ ❖

I stood in front of my mirror, securing a glittering earring when Asila walked in, gently carrying an elaborate tangle of silver chain.

She looked at me and let out a small, contented sigh. "I really am talented."

There was no denying it. Even though she'd had barely more than a day, I looked splendid. My outfit consisted of two pieces; a tight-fitting bodice and a sweeping skirt that sat seductively at my hips. Both were made from dark red silk and overlaid with chiffon, stitched together with intricate silver embroidery. The chiffon created sheer sleeves that began just beneath my shoulders and ended cinched at my wrists. A slit rose high up my thigh, showing off my silver sandals as I walked.

Asila was almost done fastening the chains, which were the exact width and shade as the tattooed bands adorning my arms. She wrapped two around my waist and attached one on each sleeve at my shoulder, linking them to the thick silver cuff around my throat, so they draped across my chest.

Glancing at her in the mirror, I admired how beautiful she looked. She was wearing an emerald velvet dress that touched the floor. The neckline of the bodice was high, and fastened at the back of her neck. Her back was completely exposed and she'd twisted her hair into a sleek knot high on her head.

The veil she was pinning into my hair was made of the same chiffon as my outfit, the multiple layers stamped together with crystals to hide my face beneath. The same silver chain was used as a net over the crown of my head to keep the material in place where it lay across my forehead and ended above my lips.

As usual, Verrill strode into my room without bothering to knock. He held a mask in his right hand. His suit was made of black velvet that went up to his throat, the material clinging to his muscled form like a lover. Despite the volcano's heat, he looked at ease in the rich fabric.

"Nice embroidery," I complimented Asila, when I noted the small patterns and swirls decorating the dark fabric were the same as mine, in burgundy. She'd made us match, as always.

She shrugged. "I had some thread left over from yours and I wanted you to be cohesive."

Verrill's eyes swept over me slowly, his gaze caressing the expanse of bare skin at my abdomen and chest with such intensity that my face almost heated. I would have been grateful that my expression was hidden from him had he not looked directly into my eyes, as if there were no barrier there at all.

He walked over to us and placed a kiss on Asila's cheek.

"You look wonderful, Asila. Thank you for saving us at such short notice, you really are a treasure." He grinned. "Your father's downstairs, we'll be starting shortly."

"I'll see you afterwards," she said to us both, before leaving the room.

Verrill turned to me and brushed a knuckle softly across my jaw and under my chin, tilting my face up.

"You are exquisite," he breathed, before dropping his hand and pulling his own mask on. It was a black fox face that covered his entire head, blending in seamlessly to his suit, the same dark red patterns swirling up the snout and over the crown of his head between the ears. His brown eyes shone out at me. He looked formidable and enchanting.

The masks were a necessary precaution for Verrill and me. Though our identities were not a complete secret like the Autarch's, we still preferred to remain as hidden as possible. It was much easier to roam the districts freely when people weren't watching your every move.

"Do you know what this meeting is about yet?" I asked quietly.

"I've heard many chirps and whispers, but they're so conflicting, it's hard to tell which ones are worth listening to," he said, cloaking his anxiety with a small laugh. "Whatever it is, it's caused quite a stir."

I took his offered arm and we went to take our place at the Autarch's side.

# Chapter 4

## Theo

I was in a meadow. The sun was bright and I watched bees and butterflies filter through the wildflowers that swayed in the soft breeze. A beautiful voice filled the air around me. I desperately wanted to turn, to see the source of that haunting melody, but I had no body, only consciousness that was floating in that scene of idyllic serenity. I had never heard anything like it before. The song was melancholic and I felt as though my soul was being ripped apart, yet it was the most peaceful violence I had ever experienced, and I never wanted it to end.

28 April

❋ ❋ ❋

Had it not been for both Tasar Wranmaris and Aran Seirsun confirming that this call to the Palace was, indeed, for all of the Lords, I would have been entirely convinced that I was walking to my own execution. I hadn't discounted the idea, it was still a very real possibility that I was about to be killed in front of all the others for my underhand treason. I had, however, no choice *but* to go. If I disobeyed, and this summons wasn't for me, I would be killed anyway.

I glanced over to Nook, Ezra, and Suenna, their faces displaying the same anxious expression as I'm sure my own did. They were my closest friends and despite our occasional arguments over the years, we had always remained close.

We were gathered with the other district courts in the main throne room of the Palace, in the royal city of Šarrum. Nobody looked relaxed. I had left my mother at home with Didi, despite them being members of my own court. I hadn't wanted my sister anywhere near Tasar, or his brother, Cyfrin. The former moved to my side.

"I'm assuming you are also ignorant of the reason for this summoning?" Tasar muttered quietly. His expression was easy and playful, but I knew it was feigned.

"I have my theories, each more horrifying than the last," I responded, unable to hide my own apprehension as easily.

"Then I truly hope you're wrong." He smirked, but moved in closer. "I trust that any new residents of Zingal are provided for."

"Of course," I assured.

More than five hundred of his people had already made the journey from the slums of Hudjefa to fight. I had been pleasantly surprised with the turnout. It had been less than three weeks since my meeting with Tasar, and not only had more of his people arrived than I'd expected, but they had promised more were planning on joining once they figured out how to make the journey with their families without drawing too much attention.

I scanned the room, noting the other district Lords that were now here; along with Tasar from Hudjefa there were Aran from Kusig, Henri from Anzillu, and Malah from Katmu, who was openly flirting with a pretty woman I didn't recognize. The only districts not yet represented were Šarrum, as the Autarch had not yet made an appearance, and Ocridell.

The latter was not surprising; it had not had a residing court for at least a decade, since the passing of its Lady, Ava. I couldn't remember much of the Anzû family; I had been an overindulged adolescent, too uninterested in anything other than my own pursuits to take notice of politics during that time. The Autarch had taken over control of the district, something that had raised more than a few eyebrows. Districts were passed down through family lines, the eldest child becoming Lord or Lady once their ruling parent died or abdicated. If there were no children, the eldest sibling would take over.

No one knew what had occurred in Ocridell all those years ago to wipe out an entire family line, but the effects of it had been felt across the realm. There had never been a gap in succession in Irkalla's entire written history. The districts had been kept within the same six families—the seventh always being the domain of the Autarch—since the end of the God's War. It was the reason why marriages between Lords and Ladies of different districts were discouraged.

The atmosphere crackled with tension. The last district had

arrived nearly an hour ago and the waiting had everyone on edge. The room was tall, the ceiling decorated with a multitude of snarling beasts made from dark wood and iron; the small flames from the hanging chandeliers cast menacing shadows from their sharp teeth and claws. Towering archways loomed up to meet the creatures, many of which were frozen climbing down the stone, looking so real they were unnerving to stare at for too long. The throne itself sat at the top of the dais stairs, made from the same ancient materials as the monsters above and inset with bone and obsidian. The seat was upright, transforming into the enormous, outstretched wings of an eagle, every feather sculpted in minute detail. The arms of the throne each depicted the fierce face of a roaring lion, the manes traveling down to the clawed talons which made the base of the chair.

It was said that the goddess Ereshkigal had sat on that very throne to rule over Irkalla, before the God's War had compelled her to rip the land apart and bring her underworld to the surface. At least, that's what Silas had once told me.

Silence fell the instant the far doors opened and the Autarch strode in and across the dais to his throne. He wore his usual attire; a sleek, black velvet suit, buttoned high to the base of his throat and a black crow mask. The mask was delicate and terrifying; instead of feathers, shiny black scales reached from the top of the sharp beak to the crown of the head, where it transitioned seamlessly into glossy ebony feathers, which lay over short hair of the exact same shade. His entire face was covered, the lethal point of the beak jutting out away from his face and curving up and under his chin. The eye sockets were covered in a fine dark mesh, revealing nothing of the eyes that lay behind. He held his long staff in his left hand, which was made from a peculiar metal that seemed to glow with its own light. It was made of snakes twisting upwards, tangled around one another in a race to the top, where a moonstone sphere lay, about the size of an apple. The shape of the staff was strange, as though it had been slightly warped or melted. At the top there was a small golden setting which looked like it should hold a small orb, but was empty.

The Fox and the Feline entered a few seconds later, and more than a few people shifted with unease. Their reputation for brutality was far reaching and well deserved. Though it had been years since I had seen them in the flesh, there was no denying who they were.

I could see the tall, lean form of coiled muscle under the dark suit worn by the Fox as he walked to his ruler, his fox mask turned to survey the crowd. I didn't manage to notice anything else about him, because my gaze instantly fixed on the Feline. Most of her face was covered, only showing a softly pointed chin and lips painted in the same blood-red as her outfit, which clung to her skin in a divine fashion. The silver chains linked across her body complimented the golden hue of her skin, matching beautifully with the numerous bangles around her arms, shimmering beneath her sheer sleeves.

No, not bangles. *Bargains.*

She had the silver tattoos stretching not only from her right wrist to shoulder, but also mid way up her left forearm. I stared in disbelief. I had never seen anyone with enough bargains to reach beyond their right elbow, let alone to their left arm.

Before I could examine her further, the Autarch sat on his

throne and I heard Tasar's voice in my ear once more.

"The Autarch has his whole menagerie here tonight, even the Rats are present," he whispered, looking around at the Fox's spies that were threading themselves through the crowd, all dressed in the same simple brown masks. "What is it with his creepy animal obsession anyway?"

Before I could answer him, our ruler cleared his throat. Every eye in the room turned to him, where he lounged with his hands resting atop the twin lion heads.

"I'd like to begin by thanking everyone for their attendance tonight," he began, his booming voice echoing, and I almost snorted. As if anyone would dare refuse.

"I am sure you are all wondering why I called you here at such short notice," he continued. "I have very recently been made aware that negotiations of peace have been made between the kingdoms of Atturynn and Aessurus. Any open conflicts between them have been halted with immediate effect, as of two days ago."

Quiet murmurs immediately filled the room. The two northern kingdoms had been at war for hundreds of years. Their small, shared border—the Isthmus of Gidim—had claimed so many lives it was said that those who die on that land never leave and continue the fight in spirit.

The powerful voice once again silenced the room.

"It is not yet known how this will affect us, or Tarprusa. However, we must be prepared. A united front is more important than ever at times of uncertainty, so we must set aside any squabbles and differences to unify our districts. Irkalla must remain *strong,* which will only be achieved if we work together. Spies have been sent out to the other kingdoms to gather information, and I will, of course, relay what I learn as the situation develops. We will commence meetings tomorrow. For the time being, I invite each of you to stay at the Palace, should you wish to."

Everyone watched as he stood and walked down the stairs, flanked by his two pets, to talk to a smartly dressed man. His Palace manager, I realized after a second. I kept the group in my line of sight as I moved closer to my friends.

"Eat and drink your fill from here," I muttered, gesturing to the tables of food provided along the left side of the large room. "We won't be able to trust anything that is sent to our rooms."

"You mean to stay?" Suenna asked, incredulous. Her light brown eyes were wide and she twisted a strand of pale blonde hair around her finger nervously.

"The invitation was a test for the Lords, we all have to stay at least for tonight. I imagine we will all be watched very closely. His speech about keeping a united front was no doubt aimed at me, and those considering siding with me," I clarified, my voice barely above a whisper. "You three can leave in the morning, I'll likely remain the rest of the week."

"We'll be staying as long as you are." Ezra's deep voice was firm. He looked more relaxed than Nook and Suenna, as he ran a hand through his short, dark hair.

"Besides," Nook said, glancing at a pair of lovely women from Aran's court, "what a perfect opportunity to make new friends."

"You're absolutely right," Suenna agreed, eyeing the shorter of the pair with delight, "it would be *rude* not to fraternize for a night or two."

Rather than bear witness to their brazen flirting attempts, Ezra and I made our way over to the food table, overhearing scraps of conversations from the other Lords. It was clear that the news had shaken the majority of the attendants. It was, in theory, a good thing that the war had ceased between the two northern kingdoms, only no one knew what that now meant for us.

Change was coming whether we liked it or not, and we could only hope it was for the best.

"You don't mind him flirting?" I asked Ezra, whose eyes were fixed on the back of Nook's red head.

"Not at all," he replied with a smile, before turning his attention back to the food table, "he enjoys other people, and those girls are very pretty."

Nook and Ezra had a very fluid friendship. It was obvious to everyone around them that they were in love, but they had never openly admitted it or entered into an actual relationship with each other. But I remained silent; as long as my friends were happy, it was none of my business.

"Don't look, but the Fox has his eyes on you," he said quietly, raising a piece of honeyed bread to his mouth.

I whirled around to meet the crafty eyes of the spymaster from across the room. His masked head was tilted to the side as the Feline whispered something into his ear and he nodded.

"I said *don't* look," I heard Ezra mutter behind me, but I ignored him, totally focused on the pair who were now walking toward me.

*Shit.*

I made a desperate attempt to hide the panic in my face with a bored expression. I had hoped to talk to one of them, preferably her, over the next few days. But not yet, not before I'd had the chance to observe them, to look for any information that could help me.

"Lord Lusilim," the Fox greeted me in a smooth, low voice, "what a *pleasure* to officially meet you at last."

"Fox. Feline. The pleasure is all mine," I responded, nodding to each of them.

"I'm *so* glad our reputation precedes us." The Feline's voice was sultry. "It would be *truly* unfortunate if we became irrelevant. I wonder how you cope with it."

Her chin tilted, indicating that she was looking me up and down.

"Play nice, my dear," the Fox warned, his eyes flashing with mischief. "He'll think you are in earnest."

They were toying with me.

"Better to be irrelevant, than play the obedient lap dog ... or cat," I replied, assessing her slowly from head to toe. "Tell me, does he leash you in private too, or just at public events?" I asked, my gaze fixing on the metal collar around her throat.

She gave a small, mocking gasp. "Shocking!"

Her mouth and voice were familiar, and though I wasn't certain, I suspected that a large pair of yellow eyes were hidden beneath that sparkling veil.

She took a step closer. The smell of jasmine, orange, and vanilla invaded my nose and she stood within inches of me, the top of her head brushing my chin as she looked up. One of her clawed hands came to my throat, her sharp nails digging into the skin above my shirt. She was testing me, pushing me to flinch or back down.

I would rather set myself on fire than give her the satisfaction.

"Why don't you come to my room and find out," she purred. "You know, I can—"

"Feline."

The Autarch's voice cut her off and she dug her nails in deeper for a split second before retracting them and returning to the Fox's side. His eyes were wild with mirth.

"Leave us, you two," the Autarch ordered, and they slunk back into the crowd. "I am pleasantly surprised to see you here, Lord Lusilim."

"Is there a reason I would not attend, Your Grace?" I tested, my patience fraying rapidly as my mind spun, thinking of all the different conversational traps he could be laying.

"I should hope not," he said simply. "We'll begin discussions after breakfast tomorrow. I am so glad to have the districts together at a time like this. Tohnain will show you and your friends to your rooms."

He gestured to where his butler stood at the far door.

"I do hope you enjoy your stay here, but be careful with those two," he warned, motioning to his two pets who were now hounding Malah Jirata and the pretty woman I saw him with earlier. I watched her aim a smirking comment at him, causing a slight blush to creep over his cheeks, barely noticeable beneath his russet skin, and he ran a hand through his shoulder-length black hair.

They all seemed familiar with one another, laughing and joking. I would have to be careful when approaching Malah.

Before I could respond, the Autarch walked away, leaving me more confused than ever. He had to know that I'd made plans to undermine him, to encourage change in our stagnating land, and yet he had made no move against me. Not even a whisper of acknowledgment.

I would have to figure out his game, and fast.

# Chapter 5

## Erisa

"You know, a little bit of warning would've been appreciated!" I snapped at Csintalan, as Verrill and I followed him into his office.

He smiled, placing his crow mask on the desk beside Verrill's. "Don't fret, my Kitten, you both played your roles well."

I almost snarled at him, and ripped at my veil, desperate to have it off. The pins securing it tore at my hair and I pulled harder in frustration.

"Yes, and what exactly were those roles?" Verrill asked him coldly, coming behind me and moving my hands away before gently removing the pins from my hair one by one. "You were lucky that everyone was too shocked to notice our own unease," he continued, "and what of Lusilim? Almost everyone knows he's been rebelling against you, and yet, when we go to entice answers out of him, you send us away."

"You schooled your expressions perfectly, as you always do. I was not concerned," Csintalan said. "And in regards to

Theodoraxion Lusilim, I need him pliable."

Verrill fished the last pin from my hair and eased the veil from my head, placing it carefully on the desk. I smiled at him in thanks before turning to Csintalan.

"So you have a plan for him?" I asked, suspicion crawling up the back of my neck.

The sight of Lusilim here had put me on edge. I felt ridiculous for not realizing who he was back in that tavern in Hudjefa and even more foolish that I'd behaved so recklessly that night. Not only had he seen my face uncovered, but he could have easily seen me with Verrill.

"I do," he confirmed, sitting down in his chair, "and I will need you both to be … *welcoming* toward him."

"You want us to spy on him," Verrill assumed in a clipped tone.

"In short, yes," he said, turning to me. "Erisa, I need you to get close to him. We know he has been in contact with the other Lords, looking for allies. What I don't know is who is considering joining him or who has already done so. I'll need you to uncover this information for us to modify our plans accordingly."

"And you think he's just going to tell me if I ask nicely?" I quipped, already skeptical.

He raised a dark eyebrow. "I think that if you utilize all of your talents, you can be very persuasive. He is unmarried, use any means necessary."

*Of course.* I had to fight to not roll my eyes at his insinuation.

"She'll not be whoring herself out to that traitorous bastard!" Verrill snapped at him. "We should just kill him now before he makes another move, I'll do it myself. Tonight."

"You're putting words in my mouth, Verrill, though I truly don't care how she does it. And you will do no such thing. If he dies now, he becomes a martyr to his cause. And, as we don't know who is behind him, we cannot predict if his death will … fan the flame, so to speak."

Verrill's expression was furious, and I could tell that he was considering doing it anyway. Csintalan must have thought the same, as he turned to him, his own temper rising.

"Lord Lusilim is not to be killed until I give a direct order to do so. Do I make myself clear?" His voice was firmer than I'd heard it in a long time. Verrill only sneered at him in response and looked away.

"And what if I don't want to? I have no interest in this Lord or who he talks to. Why would I spend my time in his company? He seems so *dreary*," I complained.

"Is helping this old man out not enough of an incentive?" he asked, humor brightening his features. My unamused expression must have been plain to see, because he continued, "I think I might have something that could encourage you."

He opened a drawer in the desk and retrieved a dagger.

My heart stopped. The dagger had a long, thin blade and an ornate hilt depicting green palm leaves and a single purple date fruit. Verrill didn't even breathe as he stared at the dagger. It was the same one he had pulled out of my mother's blood-soaked chest.

"What is this, Csintalan? How do you have that?" he finally asked, voicing only two of the many questions I now had.

Csintalan's blue eyes glossed over for a brief moment as he

looked at the dagger. "I recovered it when my men cleared the estate."

"And why have you not given it to us before? Why wouldn't you show us? And why now?" I demanded.

"What would have changed if I had? Would it have brought you peace to have your mother's murder weapon in your possession?" he countered. "I want you both to look at it, at the design, and tell me why it is relevant now."

The symbol on the Lusilim family crest was a date palm, sprouting with fruit. I knew Verrill had realized it too when I saw his fists clench.

"And why didn't you tell us this before? That *they* were responsible? And don't you *dare* answer me with another question!" he hissed, angrier than I had ever seen him.

I could see Csintalan make a conscious effort to subdue his swelling temper. He did not tolerate insolence affably and had we not been so close to him, he would have cut this conversation short a long time ago. He let out a long breath and pinched the bridge of his nose.

"It would not have changed the past," he argued, his voice low and steady. "When I brought you into this Palace, you were both heartbroken and vicious. I hadn't realized that I would come to care for you as if you were my own children, and I avoided any mention of the topic that brought you both so much pain. I know it was wrong of me, but as time went on and you both began to heal, I couldn't bear to bring it back up again."

"And what about four years ago?" I asked him, feeling the dull thrum of a headache developing at my temples.

"You were still so focused on revenge, I thought that by killing one of the people responsible, you could finally find some peace. The dagger belonged to her; the one you killed."

Verrill gripped the back of a chair hard enough to turn his knuckles white. "Who even was she? And why are you showing it to us now if Erisa has already killed her? You're making no sense," he challenged.

"I do not need to make sense to *you*, Verrill!" Csintalan shouted. "I am the Autarch! Despite my love for you both, I do not answer to you, or to Erisa. Four years ago, that woman was a threat to me and to this realm. She was also the owner of the blade that killed Ava Anzû. *That* should be more than enough for you!"

I couldn't even remember the last time we'd heard Csintalan use the voice of the Autarch with us. It was cold and terrible. Verrill's head bowed as he scowled at the floor, a flush of color rising to his face. We often challenged Csintalan, but never to this extent.

"I'm sorry, my boy," Csintalan sighed, rubbing a hand over his face, "that was uncalled for. The Lusilim family was often quarreling with yours, an old rivalry that went back generations. I thought that by showing you this blade, it might spark one last desire to exact retribution on their family. They threaten to end us all now."

"I'll do it," I said, rage and exhaustion warring inside me. "I'll destroy them."

❖❖❖

65

I woke the next morning to the sound of Verrill's lyre floating through the open door of my balcony. I pulled on a thin robe and walked out, my bare feet silent on the stone. He was sitting on the divider between our two balconies, his back against the wall and his left foot propped up in front of him. A breakfast tray was balanced on the ledge beside him. He had his eyes closed, head resting behind him as he played a lovely, gentle melody. The few rays of sunlight that filtered in through the top of the cavern illuminated his serene face as he quietly hummed the vocal accompaniment I usually provided. Not wanting him to notice me, I noiselessly sat across the balcony from him on a little stone bench.

We hadn't spoken since last night, too wrapped up in our own thoughts and emotions. I still didn't completely understand Csintalan's reasoning for keeping the dagger from us. But he was right, the Lusilims were the reason Verrill and I were orphans, and whether Theodoraxion was guilty or not, he would still pay. Like our parents, Natara, and Zeti had paid.

I watched as Verrill's fingers caressed the strings in expert ease. I always loved watching him play. His lyre was one of his most beloved possessions and we had spent so many hours of our childhood singing and dancing to the tunes he'd lured from it.

As if sensing me, he opened his eyes and looked at me, giving me a lazy smile.

"Sing for me?" he requested.

"You know I can't, Csintalan wouldn't like it."

His face fell slightly, but he continued on for a few minutes more. He finished the song and placed his lyre down, before grabbing the breakfast tray and swinging his legs down off the wall to join me on the bench.

"Good morning, my music." He grinned at me, popping a grape into his mouth.

I started tucking into the bread and jam. "To what do I owe the pleasure of this melodic awakening?" I asked.

"I was … awake early, and thought we could come up with a plan on how to entice a certain Lord to spill all of his dirty little secrets," he said, another grin flashing across his face, full of mischief. "I do hope you were planning on brushing your hair before the meeting."

I snorted and pushed his shoulder playfully.

"You're never awake early." I noticed for the first time that he was still wearing his clothes from last night, and his own disheveled hair. "You didn't even go to bed last night, did you?"

"Whatever do you mean? Of course I went to bed." He smirked. "Fara and Rena were just keeping me company."

"Oh *please*," I whined, trying not to laugh, "not while I'm eating."

He rolled his eyes dramatically and took a sip of water before handing the glass to me. I quietly studied my friend as we ate. Despite his nighttime escapades, he seemed troubled. He never asked me many questions about the men and women I took to bed, and I tried to extend that same courtesy to him. I wanted him to tell me what was bothering him, but equally didn't want to pry.

"So what exactly *is* the plan?" he asked, pushing the thought from my mind.

I smiled sweetly at him. "Play the affable, docile little woman. He seems the type to lap up any simpering drivel like that."

Verrill almost choked on his pear.

An hour later, I was bathed and dressed in my garments from the previous night and on my way to the Autarch's office. The Lords had not yet begun discussions, only engaging in idle polite chatter between themselves. I spotted Theodoraxion speaking quietly to Tasar, casting furtive glances my way. He must have thought he was being sly, thinking I wasn't watching him through my veil, but I saw.

He was intrigued. *Perfect.*

"Please be seated all," Csintalan said as he entered, his crow mask secured over his face. He could never be seen without it, only the Palace residents knew his true identity, and their tongues had been magically tied with the information. Even if I wanted to, I wouldn't physically be able to speak his name to anyone who didn't already know it.

The Lords sat around the long, ornate desk. There were seven seats, though one remained empty. My seat. I was the Lady of Ocridell, only none of them knew it. Verrill and I sat at the refreshment table that ran alongside the desk, situating myself so that Lord Lusilim was opposite me and I could observe him freely.

Malah seated himself next to him and extended his hand. "Theodoraxion. Malah Jirata, nice to officially meet you!"

"Theo, please," he insisted.

"Thank the gods, we would've been here all day otherwise," I muttered to Verrill.

Theo must have heard my comment because he barely contained a smirk as he shook Malah's hand.

"Great to meet you too, Malah. Please accept my condolences

for the loss of your brother," he said kindly.

Malah grinned, but shrugged away the commiserations. "Thank you, my friend, but my brother was a fool, like my other two before him."

Theo chuckled. "Well, then I hope you don't suffer from the same affliction. We need more than just a pretty face commanding the Isles," he jested and Malah gave a hearty laugh.

"Then it's fortunate that I received the bulk of both brains and beauty from my siblings."

Malah's grin was infectious and I felt a small smile pull at my mouth.

The Lords talked about defensive positions and trade route updates over the next hour. I was only half listening, sharing a few whispered comments with Verrill. All of which seemed to be caught by Theo. I observed him freely, hidden beneath my veil. There was no denying that he was handsome. His dark brown hair was cropped shorter at the back and sides, the longer waves on the top of his head fell almost to the thick, dark lashes framing his alert emerald eyes. A neat, dark shadow of stubble washed across his sharp jawline, and I could see a slight dent in his otherwise straight nose that indicated a previous break. He was taller than Verrill, if only by a few inches, and his bronzed skin and substantial muscle marked many years of hard work under the Irkallian sun.

For the most part, Theo was engaged in the discussion, not so much as glancing my way. There was a lull in conversation and Henri Elkas, Lord of Anzillu, who had been shifting uncomfortably for a while, suggested that we have a short break. He hadn't even waited for everyone to agree before hurrying from the room, his face shining with sweat. How unfortunate.

Theo smiled, rose from his seat, and came to the refreshments table behind me. I kept my face forward, but listened intently as he sampled some of the food and drink.

I almost jumped when I heard his rich, deep voice in my ear.

"Hopefully this will satisfy until I can buy you a real drink," he whispered, his words caressing my skin. "But at least for now, I can watch you freely."

He placed a cup of wine down on the bench beside me.

Well, *shit.* He did recognize me.

*I should never have given him that stupid note*, I thought, silently chastising myself.

"As long as I don't claw your eyes out first," I replied sweetly, remembering too late that I was supposed to be winning him over.

He walked back to his seat laughing, obviously assuming that I was joking.

"A valiant effort." Verrill chortled next to me. I didn't even bother responding.

Theo's gaze rested on me for the remainder of the meeting, when he wasn't answering a question or having a quiet discussion with Malah. The pair had obviously hit it off, but they were talking so low I had no chance of overhearing. It grated on my nerves. And I think Theo must have known because after a particularly long chat, they quickly shook hands and he turned and winked at me.

*Arrogant asshole.*

My fingers inched toward the dagger strapped at my thigh, ready to launch it into his throat.

Csintalan's voice distracted me enough to still my hand. "And

I will need a recent report from you, Lord Lusilim, regarding the reopening of the trade route through the Zuamsik Mountains."

I saw a muscle in Theo's jaw tense. Twice.

"I would recommend a new route through the northern section of the mountains, Your Grace," he replied. "The southern pass has collapsed in recent years, it is unsuitable for use. I think we would be better situated to enter Tarprusa in the north, gaining easy access to transportation via the Amah River."

Now *that* was interesting. Why would we bother creating a new trade route, instead of repairing an existing one? Verrill cleared his throat quietly, sensing a lie. I looked at Csintalan, who gave the slightest nod of his head. He wanted this information.

"Very well," Csintalan said, nodding to Theo, "we will start discussions on a new route. Though I would still like to assess the damage to the southern pass, perhaps I can send someone back with you to take a look."

"By all means," Theo answered, his tone clipped. "But I am more than happy to carry out a full investigation and send you a report with predicted time and monetary costs for the repairs."

"Nonsense, you're far too busy for all that. My dear Feline," he looked at me, "would you mind terribly if I were to send you on this errand?"

"As long as Lord Lusilim is there to escort me, I would love nothing more," I purred.

"It would be an honor, Feline," Theo assured me, suddenly looking very pleased with the outcome of this conversation.

*Perfect,* I thought, *let the games begin.*

# Chapter 6

## Theo

I was drowning. Violent waves crashed over my head and pulled me beneath the surface. I was tossed so violently by the swells of the water that I couldn't tell which way was up. I sank into the shadows of the seabed. The silhouette of a siren rose above me, her long ebony hair swirling around her as she sang to me. So beautiful. I cried out to her, begging her never to stop, not caring as water flooded my mouth and lungs.

"You cannot trust a sailor, they'll entice you in with pretty words and false promises. Then they'll trap you and leave you to suffer. All alone," she crooned sadly, swimming closer. I could just see two rows of small, pointed mother-of-pearl teeth snapping at my face, as death came to claim me.

30th April

⁂

As much as I hated to admit it, I was intrigued. It was my second morning at the Palace, and much like the first, I had to fight to keep my gaze from straying to the Feline. By some miracle, I'd managed to secure at least a week's worth of time in her company. I would most likely regret it, but this was not an opportunity I could afford to waste.

I was not naive enough to think that the Autarch was sending her with me for any other reason than to spy. I knew that he'd likely caught my comment about the southern pass that went through the Zuamsik Mountains, so I would just have to work carefully to keep up the ruse. The southern pass technically *had* collapsed, or at least the entrance to it had after we'd blown it up.

Suenna and I were seated in a large parlor along with the rest of the Lords and their courts. The room was a low hum of strategic discussions. I had sent Nook and Ezra back to Zingal, instructing them to prepare for our "inspection" of the neglected trade route.

"She *is* rather lovely," Suenna mused, following my gaze to where it had landed, yet again, on the soft curves of the Feline. She prowled between the guests, being especially generous with her scathing remarks today.

"So is wild eytelia. It looks and smells wonderful but one petal will have you catatonic and foaming at the mouth within minutes," I retorted, though I still couldn't stop looking.

She took a sip of her tea. "So you're saying she smells nice too?"

*Yes. Like jasmine and oranges and ... and I'm an idiot.*

"I'm saying she tortures and murders for fun, Suenna. She is anything *but* lovely."

As if she felt our scrutiny, the Feline's head snapped to us. She began to saunter over, her hips swaying seductively and I heard the small bells braided into her hair chime softly.

"Feeling musical today?" I smirked at her as she passed by our table.

She stopped in front of me, almost touching my knees, and looked down.

"Be grateful that I am, and that they announce my presence," she sneered at me before looking at Suenna, "otherwise, you might find that I snap up more than one pretty little bird. Wouldn't want them to be caught unawares, would you?"

Her tone was derisive and mocking.

"Careful, you wouldn't want to be caught catching *this* little bird," I warned, jutting my chin toward Suenna, "I'm very fond of her."

The Feline reached out to tilt my chin up with one sharp nail. From this angle, I could almost see her eyes from beneath the navy blue veil she wore today. Without realizing, I leaned forward, anxious to see them again. She flashed me a devious grin and was gone.

"I think I'm in love," Suenna gasped. Her face was flushed.

"She practically threatened to kill you." I chuckled, raising a brow.

"Oh, I know!" she sighed, fanning herself with a hand. I only rolled my eyes at her.

❖ ❖ ❖

That afternoon, I was summoned to the Autarch's office. I was due to leave shortly after, and I could only assume he wanted to take the opportunity to deliver a few final threats to ensure my good behavior.

All in all, this trip to the Palace had gone surprisingly well. I was—to my surprise—still alive. And not only had I been granted unfettered access to the Feline, to try and entice her to join our cause, but she also seemed somewhat interested in interacting with me. I knew it was probably a ruse, but investigating the mouths of gifthorses was low on my priority list today.

I knocked on the office door and was greeted with the masked faces of the Autarch and the Fox.

"Lord Lusilim, please come in." The Autarch's harsh voice welcomed me.

"Thank you, Your Grace," I murmured, moving to put the desk between us.

The pair in front of me seemed a little tense, and I deduced that I'd just interrupted an argument. Despite not being able to see his face, I could practically feel the rage rippling off the Fox. The Autarch seemed relatively unbothered, but the room had an awkward atmosphere.

"I won't beat around the bush," the Autarch began, "the Feline is a difficult creature, she does as she pleases and listens to no one, not even me. I'm giving you this warning as a courtesy, because if I find out that my Kitten has been mistreated in any way, the consequences will be dire."

*His Kitten? What the actual fu—*

"I have asked her to remain masked or veiled at all times," he continued, "and I expect you to grant her every privacy and discretion to ensure that her identity remains hidden."

So she hadn't told them I'd already seen her face. Interesting.

"Is that understood?" he demanded.

My mind was reeling. I knew the Autarch was fond of his pets, but to threaten me directly in regards to the wellbeing of one seemed excessive. Could they be his children? It would definitely complicate matters if that was the case. But no one had heard anything about them until they were at least adolescents. It was harder to tell with the Fox, but I'd gauged the Feline's age to be close to my own. Despite the obvious gap in age, it was possible she was some type of consort to the Autarch, which made his nicknames even more nauseating. Tasar was right, the man really did have a weird obsession with animals.

"Of course," I responded smoothly, "though I expect that if I were to do anything she didn't like, there wouldn't be enough pieces of me left for your own retribution."

He laughed deeply, and clapped his hands together.

"So very true. And I'd be grateful if you didn't mention our little chat with her, I fear I too would be in pieces if she found out I had spoken for her." He chuckled, still amused.

Was he *proud* of her ferocity?

I nodded at him with a smile and headed for the door. As I passed the Fox, his hand gripped my elbow tightly, halting me. My lip curled in a sneer at his touch, before I remembered that, he too, could be useful to have as an ally.

His brown eyes bore into mine as he moved to my ear.

"If you lay a hand on her, I will skin you alive. And I will *enjoy* it," he hissed, moving back to glower at me.

I was sick of this place, sick of the threats and sick of this gods damned *heat.* I didn't bother responding to his threat, just snatched my arm away and strode out of the room.

❖ ❖ ❖

True to form, as soon as we left the Palace grounds and started making our way through Šarrum toward the tramline, the dark veil the Feline wore was torn off and shoved into a pocket of her black trousers. Despite the questionable associations that came with her title, there was no doubt that she embodied it perfectly. Shadows clung to her as she slunk through the dark tunnels with a prowling, calculated grace that I had only ever seen in the shadowcats of the Wilds.

We traveled alone; Suenna had returned with the rest of my entourage in the morning to transport our baggage and relay news of our upcoming arrival.

"You didn't tell them that I'd already seen you without a mask before," I ventured, trying to pry my eyes away from the unusual glowing shade of her own. I had forgotten how truly striking her face was.

"You flatter yourself if you think you're worth the breath I would waste in relaying that useless information," she scoffed, throwing her thick, dark braid back over her shoulder.

I couldn't understand her mood swings. Over the last few days, she had occasionally been almost pleasant, yet positively venomous

THE PLACE OF HER NAME

the rest of the time. Despite her deceptive outward beauty, she was a foul-tempered nightmare.

"Are you going to tell me what your name is?" I asked, which earned me a bored scowl. "Seeing as you've decided to disobey your Autarch's orders and remove your veil, if I call you Feline in front of everyone, your cover is blown. And, as he and the Fox threatened to skin me alive if I put you in danger, I'd rather keep your secret safe."

If I was going to try and put a rift between the trio, I might as well start now. The look she gave me told me I'd hit a nerve.

"They're fools," she hissed, "and it seems you struggle with the same condition if you listened to them."

We'd been waiting on the platform for less than a minute when the tram came into sight. Just before it reached us, I started a quick jog, matching its pace before grabbing a handrail and swinging myself into the carriage. I briefly considered holding out a hand to help the vicious creature behind me, but decided I didn't care enough. She didn't need it anyway, leaping silently into the tram a second later.

"I actually told them I was more frightened of you," I teased. "So, what should I call you? I don't care if you give me a fake name."

She simply looked me up and down, disdain etched on her expression.

"All right then, Sunflower," I goaded, giving her a mocking smile.

Had it not been so amusing, the look she gave me would have made my balls shrivel up in fear. She clenched her left fist and moved her right hand to a dagger at her belt.

"My name is Erisa," she snapped coldly.

It sounded familiar, but I couldn't place it. I only shrugged at her, knowing I wouldn't use it after that reaction. Even if her eyes weren't miniature replicas of the flower, her *glowing* personality was so warm and cheerful that Sunflower just suited her *so* much better.

❖ ❖ ❖

As the tram pulled us above ground and through the outer half of Ocridell, Erisa's expression turned somber. The tram had no windows or doors, just large, empty gaps in the carriage walls to jump inside, and the cool wind whipped stray pieces of hair across her face. The sun was setting, casting a warm glow over the buildings and small markets that sped past.

"Have you been to the outer districts before?" I asked as we eventually reached the Zingali border.

"Not for a long time," she replied quietly, her voice almost sad. I tried to identify the emotion on her features, but I could see little in the twilight of approaching nightfall. She scowled at me when she noticed my scrutiny.

The tram eventually slowed as it approached the platform, ready to loop around the station and begin its journey back into Ersetu. I leapt off first, conscious of her close on my heels, and began making my way through the city toward my estate. Zingal was more spread out than the other districts. Though our population was similar, we had more land to expand into. Erisa inspected everything eagerly, her eyes sparkling at the decorative light sculptures and inhaling deeply whenever we passed by restaurants. She was too proud to ask questions, so I supplied what information I thought might be of interest. She merely nodded to each comment, feigning disinterest.

By the time we reached the long, tree-lined track that led to the manor, she looked almost excited at everything she'd seen, her face open and bright, taking it all in. It was obvious that she hadn't been to Zingal before, and I planned on using that to my advantage. She was shivering, clearly unused to the colder climate outside of the volcano, especially at night. I was grateful that I didn't have a cloak with me, because I would have given it to her, completely fooled by that sweet expression. I was almost relieved to see the scowl creep its way back onto her face when the lit-up house came into sight.

I let out a sigh when I opened the door to the parlor. My family sat waiting with obvious interest and I almost laughed when they caught sight of Erisa's uncovered face.

"If you don't retrieve your jaws from the floor, rats will crawl down your throats," she snapped at them.

Suddenly everyone found something else to look at.

"Everyone, this *charming* creature is Erisa," I said. "Erisa, this is my mother Dana, my sister Diandra and my friends Nook, Ezra, and Suenna, who you've met already."

I gestured to them all one by one as I spoke. She surveyed them slowly.

"How lovely to meet you all," she said sweetly, shocking us all. They each responded in kind and I gestured for her to follow me upstairs.

I wondered if her volatile mood swings were a tactic to derail those around her, making them easier to manipulate.

"This will be your room while you're here. There is a bathing chamber through that door and your luggage should already be inside. Supper will be ready in a half hour downstairs," I stated, and closed the door behind her.

When I returned downstairs, they were all talking in hushed tones. Ezra looked at me as I entered.

"I've got a bad feeling about this, Theo," he murmured.

"There's nothing to be done," I responded quietly, looking at each of them. "I want everyone to watch their words carefully. Despite any display she makes, she's not to be trusted. We'll be leaving for the southern pass after tomorrow's celebrations."

The meal that evening went surprisingly well. Erisa didn't speak much, only responded politely to the few questions put to her. Afterwards, she seated herself by the fire in the sitting room, trying to chase away the chill she was clearly feeling.

"Before we leave for the mountains, we'll go to the city and find a proper cloak for you to wear," I suggested, "otherwise you'll freeze to death."

As if she'd be able to freeze with that burning hot temper.

"Tomorrow?"

"The day after," I clarified, "tomorrow is Tammuz, the beginning of May. We celebrate it here in Zingal at the start and end of the first week … and it's also my birthday."

She said nothing, only nodded slightly.

"I hope you'll join in the festivities," I prompted. "No one outside of this household knows that you're here, so you'll be able to explore freely."

She almost smiled. "I'd like that."

She stretched her hands out closer to the fire, and her gaze lifted to the mantle. She gasped softly, and every part of her stilled.

"Whose bracelet is that?" she asked, quickly pulling her hands back into her lap and clasping them together.

I followed her line of sight to Karasi's bracelet, where it lay on its cushion next to her portrait. My heart began to race at her question.

"That belonged to my twin sister, Karasi," I answered, watching her reaction like a hawk. "She was born three minutes before I was, so was the Lady of Zingal before her murder four years ago. All we received was a severed hand and her dagger. We were never able to find the rest of her body."

I didn't mention the royal ribbon that had secured the package, afraid I would blow my cover. I had never seen the Feline so motionless. She didn't even take a breath for what felt like hours.

"She never took that bracelet off, it was how we knew it was her," I whispered, not bothering to hide the pain from my voice. I reached under my shirt for the little pouch I now kept around my neck, fishing out the bright red stone, hoping that she'd recognize it. If my suspicions were correct, and she'd killed Karasi, then there was a chance she might know something about the stone.

"This was hidden inside the bracelet." My voice was quiet as I held it out for her to see. It glowed faintly in my palm.

She was transfixed, her attention solely on the small ruby object in front of her. After a few moments she turned to me, her expression schooled and completely blank.

"I'm sorry for your loss," she said stiffly, rising to her feet. "I think I'll retire now, I'm weary from the journey."

I nodded and watched her leave the room. My palms were sweating and I was sure she could hear my heart thundering in my chest. I had long believed that the Autarch and his pets had been responsible for the death of my sister, and she had just confirmed it.

Despite what she'd said, she wasn't sorry. But she was going to be.

# Chapter 7

## Erisa

I was panicking. And *furious*.

What was Csintalan thinking by sending me here? Sending me into the house of the woman I'd murdered. Obviously I'd known that the woman, Karasi, had been involved with the Lusilim family, but their *Lady*?

I scolded myself for not realizing it. I never cared to listen to the politics of the districts, was never interested in the reported deaths of Lords and Ladies and court members unless they affected me. With the cutthroat nature of succession, brothers and sisters killed each other all the time to take control of the districts. There were simply too many murders to keep track of.

But the Lusilims knew that Karasi had been killed by the Autarch. I'd wrapped the package myself with that damned purple ribbon.

I had to sit on the bed and take multiple deep breaths to try and soothe the fury and anxiety raging through my body.

He had that stone. My mother's stone. It had been torn from

her necklace but there was absolutely no doubt that it was the same one. I couldn't have counted the number of hours I'd spent gazing longingly into its shimmering glow as it hung from the silver chain at her throat. She always said it was powerful, that it would sometimes whisper things to her about what was to come.

And Karasi had stolen it. The *Lusilims* had stolen it after they'd slaughtered my entire family.

How many of them knew?

Dana, the mother, must have been part of the plan. Diandra looked a little young, but that meant nothing, she still could have played a part. Theodoraxion—what an *absurd* name—he would have known. He would have been plotting the whole scheme with his twin and had shown me that stone to taunt me.

But then why hadn't Csintalan told us? He knew the dagger was Karasi's, and as the Lady of Zingal, she would have been the one to order the slaughter. Yet, he'd refused to tell me who she was, only that she was "one of the people responsible." Maybe he knew that Verrill and I would destroy the entire district, and the only reason he was letting me do it now was because they were on the cusp of open rebellion.

My mind continued to race as I bathed. I missed Verrill already, and desperately wanted to tell him what I'd seen. I could imagine him telling me to stay calm and stick to the plan, make them bleed. I would do just that.

I had tried to be on my best behavior so far. I'd had a few slip-ups when my temper got the better of me, but I could do this. I could be pleasant and polite, maybe not toward Theo, but at least to the others, to gain their trust.

I just had to pray to any of those wretched, long-forgotten gods that Theo wouldn't realize that it was me who had killed his sister.

※ ※ ※

After a fitful night, I woke as soon as the sun began to brighten the sky. I was so used to the subterranean darkness of Ersetu that my eyes opened at the faintest rays of light that crept beneath the curtains.

I worked through drills quietly until Suenna knocked on my door. She looked a little shocked at my sweat-coated body as she brought a breakfast tray into the room.

"Couldn't sleep?" she asked, clearly noticing the dark circles under my eyes.

"I'm not used to the dawn light," I admitted, eyeing the tray. "Thanks for breakfast."

"It's the start of the Tammuz celebrations today. It's hosted here at the manor, but if you want to venture further, there'll be smaller parties throughout the city." She spoke softly, smoothing the silk of her pale gown. She was beautiful, with long, gleaming gold hair, soft brown eyes and a pale, flawless face. She gave me a bright smile before leaving me to eat.

I bathed quickly before changing into a navy blue dress. The bodice was tight with loose sleeves that covered my shoulders. I sheathed two daggers beneath the long skirts and set off outside. Even though it was still relatively early, the grounds of the estate were alive with people.

I hadn't seen much when we'd arrived in the dark last night, but now my breath was stolen by the beauty of it. The gardens stretched out on either side of the main path, full of color and buzzing insects enjoying the height of spring. The smells were truly wonderful, the scents of flowers and trees combined with the aroma of baked goods from food stalls being erected on the lawns. Musicians were tuning instruments and warming up their voices, every one of them practically beaming with excitement.

I decided to take a tour of the gardens. It was obvious that someone cherished each and every flowerbed, and it wasn't long before I saw a small figure hunched over, pruning a young hibiscus plant.

"Shouldn't you be celebrating?" I called out to Diandra as I got closer. Her head swung to me, slightly startled.

"I will soon, I just have to inspect a few areas first," she replied, and a smile lit up her pretty face. "You can join me if you like, I'm almost done and I can show you around the gardens."

I agreed and we spent the next two hours wandering through the color-drenched land and fruiting orchards. Diandra was a true delight, and as much as I tried to prevent any warm feelings developing for the charming girl, it was difficult. She was so bright and engaging. She allowed me to listen as she told me about her happy childhood and her love of plants.

It was obvious that the Lusilim family loved each other; she gushed about Theo and how he and some uncle named Corbin had indulged her passions and interests. Theo had let her have complete control over the grounds to manage as she pleased, and had set aside an allowance for her and Dana to spend as they wished on improving the estate.

By the time we returned to the front of the manor, the celebration was in full swing. The music was louder and food stalls were catering to the many guests who had arrived.

Diandra led me through the craze of people, demanding I try some of her favorite foods. Despite being a Lusilim, she received the same kind smiles as anyone else. The citizens of Zingal seemed very happy with their ruling family, and she appeared to be familiar with most of them, being called Didi by almost everyone she greeted.

After a while, she bid me farewell and hurried off to join a group of friends splashing in a nearby pond. I moved around, listening in to conversations and joining in with a few, before seating myself on the grass beneath one of the huge, ancient trees dotted across the grounds.

The food Diandra had recommended was delicious, a spiced meat and potato pie and some baked pears, the flavors rich and perfectly balanced. The warm afternoon sun was high in the sky as I continued to sit in solitude, watching the revelers drink and dance and play.

It was like stepping into a different realm, everyone was happy and smiling. Maybe it was only due to the celebrations, but there was none of the sullen melancholy or snide malice that afflicted the citizens of Šarrum, Hudjefa and Anzillu.

I had not yet seen him today, but everyone who I'd spoken to or overheard seemed to genuinely like Theo and the way he ran his district. It was difficult to accept that the family responsible for the murder of mine were so loved and respected here.

I finally spotted Theo, enthusiastically engaging in conversations with many of his people, and only occasionally looking longingly over at where his three friends were dancing riotously among the others.

I rose to my feet and slipped into the crowd, moving toward Theo's back, remaining unseen to catch snippets of conversation. It was mostly boring and unimportant, until a bald man approached, his face flushed from the heat and the wine.

"Lord Lusilim, we'd hoped to see you today," he began, gesturing to a slender woman following a few steps behind, with a small child in her arms. "My wife and I wanted to thank you personally for all that you've done for us—for so many of us—in recent weeks."

"Please call me Theo," he replied warmly, shaking the man's hand and then the woman's, "and there is no need to thank me. I trust you're comfortable in your new lodgings? Do you have everything that you need?"

I half hid myself behind a tent flap and observed silently.

"Comfortable? They're fit for nobility, compared to what we're accustomed to! You've been so generous to us all," the man beamed at him, and then leaned closer, his voice quiet. "We're eager to join this fight with you, tell us when you're ready to move."

*Very interesting.*

Theo quickly looked around him and I ducked further behind the tent, remaining unseen. I could only see part of his face when he smiled at the man.

"I just need all of you settling in with your families and getting comfortable, building your strength. It means more than you know that you'd risk so much. I won't make a move until we are better situated with more allies," Theo answered in a hushed tone. "But for now, enjoy the celebrations!"

The man was all smiles and thanks as he clapped Theo on the back and ushered his wife away. I followed them to the outskirts of the revelry, where they joined a group of approximately fifty people. They were enjoying themselves, dancing and singing but for some reason they still seemed to be separate from the rest of the people here.

The pair joined into a conversation with a handful of others, and I tried to move closer to them. Unluckily for me, it seemed as though everyone in this group knew each other, as they eyed me suspiciously, knowing I wasn't one of them. I only caught a few snippets of the conversation before I retreated, not wanting to draw too much attention to myself.

"—requires nothing yet, only to remain committed to the cause."

"—what we've been waiting for, we need this change. To build a better life for the whole of Irkalla."

"But to risk the children? Tasar was clear about the punishments—"

"It's a gamble, but if it pays off, our children will have more freedom than we ever did."

The serious, hushed conversations gradually merged back into the lively music and joyous laughter of playing children. I poured myself a glass of chilled wine and walked across the lawn, the grass soft beneath my bare feet. I had long since discarded my sandals and savored the feeling of the sun and outside air on my skin. It had been so long since I'd felt it like this.

The mention of Tasar had thrown me. I had heard the Rats whisper that he had once been close with Theo and his family, but why had he been mentioned in a conversation on Tammuz? I considered that they may be citizens from Hudjefa, as they looked scruffier and didn't seem to fit in with the rest of the people here. But if that was the case, Tasar must have known. If he had warned them of punishments, did that mean he was promising punishment for those that came here, and was therefore standing against Theo's rebellion?

I watched Theo swing Suenna around the makeshift dance floor in front of the musicians, their faces wild with merriment and wine. Ezra and Nook were whirling around them with partners of their own, their combined laughter filling the air. It was easy to see Theo as the carefree and shameless man that he had been known for before the death of his sister. Before he'd been forced to take this position at the head of the family. I was responsible for that change. Sure, my orders had come from the Autarch, but I had been more than willing to deliver the killing blow. I brushed the thought away before I could dwell on it.

I had wandered back to the refreshment table to put down my glass when Ezra approached me, his light green shirt contrasting beautifully against his dark skin and short black curls. He held a hand out to me, his bright chestnut eyes twinkling in delight.

"Will you dance with me, Erisa?" He dared me with a wink.

I raised an eyebrow at him before giving him a quick smile and placing my hand in his. His returning grin was dazzling, and he instantly had me spinning and swirling through the other pairs and groups. I couldn't stop the laughter that pealed from my mouth as I was turned and thrown by Ezra. This wasn't the calculated, seductive dancing I was accustomed to in Šarrum, this was wild and riotous. It reminded me of how Verrill and I would dance together. A flash of red was the only warning I had before I found myself whirling into Nook's waiting arms. He had me reeling even faster around the clearing, his eyes alive and glowing with delight. I was passed between the pair, twirling so quickly between them that everyone else was a blur. By the time the musicians slowed to close the song, I was panting and flushed. I wiped the sweat from my brow as the pair bowed to me with ridiculous flourish, prying another chuckle from me.

I glanced up to see Theo's gaze fixed on me, the expression on his face unfamiliar, almost angry. Before I could decipher it, he turned to Ezra and Nook, who had been walking over to join him, and began laughing and joking with them once more.

By the time the sun had surrendered to the expanding shadows of night, I was exhausted. I collapsed into my bed in the manor and experienced one brief moment of guilt. I'd promised Csintalan that I would spy and collect as much information about the Lusilims as possible, and instead, I'd spent almost the entire afternoon dancing and delighting in the festivities.

But the moment was fleeting, fading away as soon as I shut my eyes. And I drifted into a deep, dreamless sleep.

# Chapter 8

## Erisa

Theo was silent as he led the way through the main bulk of the city. He was pale today, even with the spring sun warming away the remnants of dew still clinging to the ground. He'd grumbled a "good morning" to me before we'd left, the slight greenish hue of his complexion hinting at a long night of drinking and revelry.

"So, did you enjoy your birthday?" I asked him casually. "With the way you were throwing yourself around all day and night, I'm surprised you're able to walk today. I've seen better dancing on the hangman's gallows."

The look of utter contempt I received almost made me shiver in delight.

"This way," he said gruffly, gesturing toward a bright storefront filled with colorful fabrics and haberdashery. It wasn't as grand as Asila's shop, but it had the same cozy feel inside.

A short, gray-haired woman lifted her head from her needlework and beamed when she saw Theo. She scrambled over the half-finished clothing that had been draped into piles and stopped in front of him. He towered over her as she inspected him at arm's length.

"My darling Theo, you look truly terrible," she scolded. "A night of wine and spirits no doubt. Come through to the back, I've prepared a broth for when Nook finally shows his face. I predicted you all would have overindulged in the celebrations."

He began shaking his head when she turned and finally noticed me hovering by the doorway.

"And who's this pretty thing?" she asked, glancing from me to Theo.

"No one of consequence," he replied curtly, rubbing his eyes. "She needs a warm cloak, do you have one that'll fit?"

I rolled my eyes at his blatant rudeness, but the lady seemed taken aback.

"Of course I do, now go back there and fix your sour mood," she huffed, ushering him through the curtain at the far end of the store.

"Now my dear," she began, pointing to a raised platform, "stand up here and I'll get some options down for you."

I obeyed, watching her totter up a swaying stepladder to reach onto the shelves of stacked fabrics and garments. She descended back to the ground laden with items, somehow managing not to crumple under the weight of them. I stepped down to help her, but she shooed me away.

"I don't know what's gotten his knickers in a twist," she mused. "I've never seen him in such a bad temper."

"He doesn't like me very much," I said.

She looked at me with suspicion, as if deciding that if Theo didn't think that I was respectable and good, then I definitely wasn't.

She didn't ask for my name, and I didn't offer it. I didn't care about people knowing, Erisa wasn't uncommon enough that they would automatically realize that I was the presumed-dead heir to Ocridell. But I didn't trust this woman, she looked old enough to have seen my mother at my age and could possibly see the similarities between us.

I remained still as she threw different fabrics over me, testing for fit and length, before deciding on a navy blue cloak made from soft wool and lined with padded silk. The simple design was enhanced by the silver stitching that matched the delicate clasp at the front.

"It's not fancy like the velvet cloaks or the ones lined with fur, but it's the only one I've got that's long enough to cover your feet without swamping the rest of you. It'll keep you warmer," she explained.

"It's perfect, thank you," I answered, before she disappeared into the back.

Hushed whispers drifted from the doorway but before I could move close enough to eavesdrop, she returned with a large piece of brown paper and began wrapping the cloak into a neat parcel, securing it with twine. Theo returned too, with slightly more color in his cheeks, followed by Nook.

Nook didn't even look tired, his carefree demeanor and happy smile as charming as ever. As if he'd heard my internal musings, he turned and winked at me.

"Thanks for the broth, Nana. You're a lifesaver!" he called

around Theo's bulky form, before disappearing back into whatever lay behind the shop.

"Yes, thank you, Nana." Theo smiled at the woman, before giving her a kiss on the cheek. She huffed something under her breath about silly children, before holding the package out to me.

"I suppose I'll be adding this to your bill, Theo?" she asked him as I took the cloak.

He snorted in amusement. "No, she can pay for it herself."

"I'll be paying for it," I protested at the same time. I didn't want to owe him anything.

I handed over what I hoped would be a sufficient amount of coin, and she raised a gray eyebrow at me before trying to put three silvers and a gold coin back into my hand.

"Keep it, it's a lovely cloak. Thank you," I said, pushing her hands away. The older lady merely nodded and said her goodbyes and we turned for the door.

"Keep that coin close, Nana," Theo called over his shoulder, "otherwise she'll steal it right back."

He closed the door on whatever her response was and continued up the cobbled street. We made a few more stops for Theo to make various purchases and have warm conversations with almost every business owner. He somehow seemed to know everyone and was at least liked—if not loved—by them all.

"Did you pay everyone to be nice to you while I'm here?" I scoffed, watching him shake the hand of a baker who had come running out to give him a box of pastries and two loaves of bread, after seeing him through the window. He'd refused to take a single copper from his Lord, only insisting he save a couple for his "lovely mother and charming Miss Didi."

"It may be a foreign concept to you, but some people are actually likable." He smirked at me. "Although, if it'll make you feel better about yourself, *sure* I paid everyone in the city to pretend to like me until you've finished spying. They'll be so relieved when you leave."

"Funny," I snapped, narrowing my eyes at him. "I'll have you know I'm very likable. I just refuse to make an effort for pompous morons. Like yourself, for example."

"You wound me, Sunflower," he mocked, holding a free hand to his heart.

We walked the rest of the way back to the manor in silence, as I refused to entertain any name other than my own. When we entered the kitchen, Dana and Diandra were chatting away with a few of the workers, sleeves rolled up, helping with the baking and the laundry.

"Oh Theo, you forgot to take Didi's corset to Lola's to mend," Dana scolded, quickly drying her hands to take some of the items we were carrying.

"Sorry," he said quietly, opening the box of baked goods and taking out a small pistachio pastry. "I'll have Ezra take it to her."

"No need," she replied, "Corbin is on his way there now, he just left here. He said to thank you for a wonderful celebration yesterday and that he's sorry he missed you this morning."

Theo's brow furrowed slightly, but he nodded. I hadn't met Corbin, only heard about him from Theo's family. I wondered how we could have missed him on the path to the house if he had only just left. There must be another exit point to get into the city. I'd have to discover it before returning to Šarrum.

"I have some things to attend to," Theo informed me. "Get your belongings ready, we'll leave in an hour. Pack light."

He'd left the room before I could offer a retort.

I had already packed a small bag that morning, so I rolled up the loose sleeves of my undershirt and began kneading some dough with Diandra. We joked about her brother's bad mood and she told me that he almost never lets himself relax and enjoy celebrations like he used to do years ago. She didn't say that the change in her brother was due to Karasi's death, but I knew that already. I laughed when she told me that she had found him asleep on the stairs early this morning, and that he had almost tripped over Ezra—who was lying on the parlor floor—on his way to empty his stomach.

"Call me Didi, all of my friends do," she'd insisted at one point in our conversation. I felt a pang of guilt at the knowledge that I was deceiving her. I wasn't pretending to be nice to her, I genuinely liked Didi. It was just unfortunate that I happened to be plotting my revenge against her conniving family.

Theo came back to find Didi and I giggling over some ridiculous letter she had received from Tasar's brother Cyfrin, of all people. I quickly stored that information away for later.

"Clean yourself up, it's time to leave," he snapped, scowling at me as I walked past him.

"I told you to be careful around her, Didi, what do you—" His voice trailed off as I continued up the stairs and into my room. It seems I wasn't the only one he had a problem with today. I quickly washed my hands and picked up my bag, swinging it over my shoulder.

Didi smiled slyly at me from behind Theo's back and I had to stifle a grin as she and Dana gave us their goodbyes. If I hadn't known that Dana disliked me already, it would have been obvious in the warning glare she gave me as we left.

❖ ❖ ❖

Two horses were already saddled and ready to go when we walked into the stables. Theo approached a large piebald beast that had one blue eye and one brown. He patted it affectionately as he attached his leather bag, bow and quiver of arrows to the side of the saddle.

"I can't ride," I lied, feigning an anxious look toward the bay gelding I guessed was meant for me.

I needed more time to discover something useful. I'd learned next to nothing. If my suspicions were correct, and there was something hidden in the southern pass of the mountains, I needed to discover it and get back to Šarrum quickly, preferably without Theo hot on my tail. Without horses, I could outmaneuver him easily.

"You're joking," he said blandly, looking less enthusiastic than ever.

"Have you seen many horses under the volcano?" I hissed.

He sighed heavily, as though I'd just ruined his entire week—which I probably had—and started unbuckling his bags. He snatched my own bag from my shoulder and strode to the bay horse.

"You'll ride with me, Moth can handle the extra weight as long as we put the luggage on Fergus," he grumbled, displeasure evident in his tone.

*Oh, hell no.*

"Absolutely not! I'd rather walk there."

"That will extend our trip by days, and I need to be back before the end of the week," he shot back at me. He must have sensed that I was going to insist on riding by myself after all, because he hastily added, "and I'm not stopping every five minutes for you to get back on when you fall."

What a mess I'd gotten myself into. If I admitted to lying now, he'd trust me even less and wouldn't let me out of his sight.

Well, *great.* I'd just turned the barely tolerable journey into an insufferable one.

He quickly removed the saddle from Moth, only leaving the blanket beneath, allowing us the space to both be seated comfortably. I was suddenly grateful for the years Verrill and I had spent galloping our ponies through the fields, all the way to the Silent Canyons of Saqummatu, bareback and wild. I felt the ache of nostalgia deep in my chest at the memories.

"Are you able to get on yourself, or do I have to lift you?" he taunted me, knowing I would have to ask for his help without having stirrups to lift myself up. I considered vaulting up to spite him, but that would only expose my imbecilic lie.

Instead, I pulled gently on Moth's reins, guiding him to a low wall. His brown eye watched me suspiciously as I clambered up onto the wall before throwing a leg over his back, and seating myself just behind his withers. I thanked my earlier self for choosing to wear trousers instead of a dress.

I gave Theo a sarcastic smile as he handed me Fergus' reins, which strained as he tried to reach his head down to eat the grass underfoot. Theo leapt onto the wall next to me, and it took all of my willpower not to ride off as he began clambering onto Moth's back, settling himself behind me. He snatched both sets of reins from me, bringing his elbows close to my waist, likely to hold me upright if I began sliding off.

This was going to be a very long few days.

※ ※ ※

Two hours later and we were cantering through the lush meadows on the outer northern perimeters of Zingal. Neither of us had spoken and my thighs were beginning to ache from the years I'd spent out of the saddle.

I started in shock as Theo's rumbling voice broke the long silence.

"Just *relax,* you've been rigid since we left," he grumbled close to my ear. "It's making *my* back ache just looking at you, yours must be agony."

He wasn't wrong, my back *was* hurting. I'd made every effort to ensure that we didn't touch each other. He huffed out an exasperated breath, and circled an arm around my waist, pulling me flush against his chest. I started to protest, but the change in position had me almost sighing in relief. My back muscles practically wept with the reprieve as I sagged against him.

We slowed to a walk as we passed through a stream, Fergus hesitating for a few seconds before reluctantly stepping into the cold water. The late afternoon air was beginning to cool and I shivered slightly, reluctantly grateful for Theo's warmth behind me. He pulled me closer, draping the sides of his cloak over my shoulders as well as his. Mine was currently still tied to Fergus' saddle.

"Thank you," I said quietly, and I felt his chest shake with laughter.

"Never thought I'd get any gratitude from you." He chortled. "The others will never believe me."

"Say anything and I'll set the Fox on you," I snapped, which only increased his aggravating humor.

"Please don't, I'm quite fond of my head being attached to my body," he replied, the levity still evident in his voice. He was quiet for a few minutes before I heard him speak again, this time genuine curiosity infused his tone.

"So what is the deal with you and the Fox? You've always been a pair at the Palace, what's the history? Are you siblings?"

I considered telling him to mind his own business, but after a moment said, "We grew up together. We're the only family we have left. The Autarch found us after we were both orphaned and took us in. He's cared for us ever since and gave us our own roles to fulfill."

"I'm sorry for your loss," he said softly. "I suppose it's fortunate that the Autarch was there to guide you both."

I nodded, thinking about what I'd revealed and what he'd said in return. Csintalan *had* been caring and loving toward Verrill and I, and we had been excited to be part of his Palace court as the Feline and the Fox. But as the years went on, our tasks became more gruesome and morally taxing. We had never complained, never felt as though anything was wrong because we had always followed Csintalan blindly. We owed him our lives, owed him everything, because he had given us everything he could.

But I wondered at what point, over the recent years, had we become just the Feline and the Fox to him. When had he stopped seeing us as Erisa and Verrill, as opposed to tools he could use to do his dirty work? He'd been fine with whoring me out to Theo, and I hadn't even been surprised.

Not that it would have worked anyway. Even if Theo hadn't started off with hating me, he certainly did after I came back with him to Zingal. I wondered what had changed.

"Why *do* you hate me?" The question was out before I could stop it.

I heard him take in a shocked breath, but he remained silent and tense. I foolishly hoped for a moment that he hadn't heard me, but I felt his arm around my waist tighten. His fingers dug painfully into the skin at waist and hip, pinning me to him. His face lowered and I felt his lips brush against my ear, sending warm air across my cheek and neck as he spoke.

"Because I know you murdered my sister."

# Chapter 9

## Theo

I can't even remember much of the dream last night, I had to write this down after I finished throwing up. I was trying to reach the top of a hill. It was so steep and I kept on tripping and stumbling back down. But I was desperate to reach the item at the top. The sun was so bright that I could only see a silhouette of what looked like an upside down shield, embedded into the ground. I was almost there, fingers reaching out and brushing the metal, when my foot slipped. I tumbled back down the hill, rolling over and over. I woke up with my stomach still turning.

2 May

❖ ❖ ❖

Erisa went completely still. I was so close that I could see the rapid pulsing of the vein in her neck, and I could almost hear her mind whirring and calculating.

She hadn't denied it.

Her right hand twitched toward her thigh where she kept one of her daggers. I tutted in her ear, and loosened my grip on her waist to catch both of her wrists in my left hand.

"There's a clearing not far from here," I informed her. "We'll camp there tonight."

She was leaning as far away from me as possible, resuming her impossible rigidity from earlier. Her proud chin jutted up in defiance, to make it clear that she didn't care that I knew, that she regretted nothing.

I almost rode past the clearing, to force her to remain uncomfortable for longer, but I was too tired. I was only a little ashamed to admit that I was still feeling the effects of last night. And I was hungry; we'd only snacked on pieces of bread and cheese as we rode, and I was anxious to have a more substantial meal.

As soon as we stopped in the small, grassy clearing, she tore her hands free and swung her leg over Moth's neck, dismounting swiftly. She tried to hide the slight wince she made as she hit the ground, her thighs must have been aching from the ride. Although, for someone who couldn't ride, she had kept her seat surprisingly well.

"Are you going to kill me?" she asked when she was a few paces away, her eyes darting from me to Fergus' back, where my bow and arrows hung out of reach.

"What would that achieve? Other than ensuring my own death.

And besides," I said, looking over her arms where I knew dozens of silver bands were hiding beneath her sleeves, "I'm not sure I *could* kill you. You terrify me."

I was only half joking; if it was a battle of strength, I would definitely be victorious over her. But she was a true creature of Irkalla, with a speed and cunning that would likely make my defeat swift and brutal.

I dismounted and tended to the horses, feeling sorry for poor Fergus, who had been demoted to pack mule. I relieved him of the bags and saddle packs and started making up a small camp. Erisa watched me intently as I built a fire, staying shrouded in the shadows of the trees. The way her amber eyes almost glowed in the dim light had the hairs on the back of my neck standing on end. They were such an unusual shade, somehow both yellow *and* orange.

"Are you not going to have anything to eat, Sunflower?" I called out, as I finished unpacking the food bag and began warming some of the dried meat by the fire. She stalked over to a bedroll I'd laid out and snatched up her cloak from where I'd placed it on top. She was fully shivering now that the sun had set.

"I could kill *you* at any moment," she snapped at me, leaning over to take some of the food into her lap.

"Always so violent," I taunted, smirking at the perpetual frown of her mouth. "Even if that *were* true, I've given you ample opportunity to do so, and as far as I'm aware, I'm still breathing. Which means your *master* must have forbidden you to kill me. He must need me for something, or I wouldn't be here."

She bristled at the mention of the Autarch, and I saw fresh fury wash over her, confirming my theory.

"What do you want from me then?" she asked, her voice steady. "You seemed pleased when he ordered you to bring me to the mountains."

"Maybe it's because you're so pleasant to be around," I quipped, heavy on the sarcasm.

She just continued to scowl. I wondered if no one had ever warned her that it would be permanent if the wind were to change.

I sighed. "I saw it as an opportunity. You're close to the Autarch. I thought that if I could learn more about you, I could perhaps persuade you to become an ally of the ... *transformation* of Irkalla."

She let out a harsh, bitter laugh. "I told you that the Autarch had raised me as his own and you think I'm going to join in with your rebellion against him?"

"You may not look past Ersetu, but the rest of the realm is falling apart," I began. "The Autarch has kept all of the trade for Šarrum. Katmu and Anzillu are only surviving because they take what they can as the supplies pass through, but everyone else is left to fend for themselves. And since he began importing from the northern kingdoms when he came into power, my farmers have been struggling to sell their produce. Kusig would be in the same predicament as Zingal if it weren't for their goldmines."

"So you're saying that because *your* district is failing, you decided to start an uprising that would disrupt everyone else?" she countered.

"That's not my only reason. I won't even go into the dire state of Hudjefa, you've seen that for yourself. The other issue is the control the Autarch has over the districts. I'm not questioning the role of one ruling over the other six, but he's abusing his power, gradually seizing more control than he's entitled to."

I wasn't sure why I was telling her all of this now. I'd hoped to gain a little trust from her first, but I'd ruined that plan as soon as I mentioned Karasi's death. We couldn't stand each other, and I was sure no amount of logic would convince her to side with me.

"Explain," she prompted, studying me. I knew she was evaluating my every word.

"No one knows how an Autarch comes into power, the method of succession is a mystery," I said, watching her nod in agreement, "but everyone recognizes the change-over by the disguise they wear. I hadn't turned twenty when our current Autarch took over, but I do remember the changes in the realm that started then. I remember only a few days had passed since I'd returned from Tarprusa. I heard the news that Ocridell was in ruins, their Lady's family gone, and the Autarch was staking a claim over the district."

She was motionless, the only movement was the fury flaring in her expression. She said nothing, so I continued.

"That control was supposed to be temporary, but a decade later he's still in possession of Ocridell, as well as Šarrum, earning taxes from both. Then only a few years later, my sister began to question the Autarch. Never directly of course, only in private, but the Rats are everywhere and must have reported whispers to him. That's when Karasi was murdered," I raged quietly, shooting her a hateful glare, "the *Lady* of Zingal. It seemed too coincidental that not one, but two district Ladies had been slaughtered under his reign. I'm sure he's working to slowly annihilate each of the district families, to expand his control over the realm. What better place to start than the outer districts, led by powerful women who dared to question his decisions? Is that not why he ordered you to murder her?"

She stood up abruptly, glaring down at me.

"I didn't even *bother* to ask for his reason. I killed your sister because she was responsible for my family's murder!" she fumed dangerously, her fists already closed around the hilts of her gleaming blades.

"What do you mean?" I asked, completely thrown off guard.

She sneered at me before turning and stalking away.

"Wait!" I called after her, rising to my feet. "You can't just say something like that and walk away! You owe me an explanation!"

"I owe you nothing!" she hissed back over her shoulder, and disappeared into the darkness of the trees.

I slumped back down onto my bedroll and turned to face the fire. It wasn't even late, but I felt the exhaustion leeching away any energy left in my body. Disappointment and anger spread through me like poison. That conversation had gone wrong so quickly, and yet I had no idea where I'd failed so spectacularly. She was either lying or confusing Karasi for another poor innocent she'd slaughtered. My twin wasn't a killer. I knew her better than anyone, knew that she would never leave a child orphaned.

Erisa must have been mistaken.

❖ ❖ ❖

I woke the next morning to find Erisa's bedroll empty and unused. I started packing up when I saw her leap down from a tree branch at the edge of the clearing. Judging by the dark circles beneath her eyes, she hadn't slept, likely watching me the entire night, waiting for me to attack.

I thought about apologizing for offending her last night, but stopped myself. She had *killed* my sister. I wasn't apologizing for shit.

By the time I had returned from the small stream to refill our water skins, Erisa had packed the bags onto Fergus and held both horses ready to leave. I could see her looking around the clearing for a place to get up onto Moth and her frustration at finding none.

"Need a hand?" I sneered.

"Obviously." She could barely get the word out through her gritted teeth as she turned her back to me and bent her left knee. I grasped her shin and boosted her up onto Moth's back, narrowly avoiding her right foot as she swung it toward my groin on the way.

I sighed, handing her Fergus' reins and began leading Moth out of the clearing.

"What are you doing?" she asked.

"I can't jump on with you already up there," I replied, eventually finding a low hanging branch that looked sturdy enough to support my weight.

She refused to even acknowledge me for at least an hour into the ride, likely annoyed she hadn't used the branch too.

"The Autarch informed me that a woman posed a threat to him and instructed me to kill her," she began, startling me with the abrupt change in attitude. "When I showed reluctance to travel to all the way to the Canyons to dispose of her, he told me that she was one of the people responsible for murdering my family. Suddenly, the distance was nothing. I didn't know or care who she was, only that I had to get my revenge. I was obsessed with it. The Autarch had given me strict instructions to keep her left hand intact to send on, he didn't care what happened to the rest of her."

Pain lanced through my chest at her words when I realized what she meant. Hearing her talk about Karasi's death so callously had my fists clenched so hard around the reins that my fingers cramped. Saliva filled my mouth and last night's dinner threatened to resurface at the imaginings of what Erisa had done to "the rest of her." I had spent months searching everywhere for her body, the Silent Canyons included, but there wasn't a trace of her left anywhere. For a while, I'd foolishly hoped that she was still alive, that the hand wasn't hers. But there was no mistaking the birthmark on her little finger, or the tattoos inked into her skin.

Erisa carried on speaking as though in a trance. Like she had kept this confession to herself for years, never uttering a word of it until now.

"She was exactly where he said she'd be, just waiting," she continued. "She was surprised to see me, I think she must have been expecting him. I remember being woefully disappointed in her fighting skills, she was so clumsy and unpracticed that I could've killed her in seconds. I was angry that this bumbling wretch had somehow managed to destroy my entire life. I wanted to feel like I'd had to fight to avenge my family, not for it to just be handed to me. I toyed with her for a few moments, until she started begging, then I just had to get rid of her."

As she spoke, I felt my heart plummet to the pit of my stomach, which clenched painfully, the cramps intensifying with every word. I didn't know whether hearing about Karasi's final moments was a blessing or a curse. Ever since her death, I'd been plagued with the need to know how it had happened, but now that I was actually hearing it, I somehow felt even worse.

"It wasn't her," I croaked out adamantly, and my throat felt thick with emotion. "She wouldn't have done that to anyone. She was *good*. You made a mistake, killed her for nothing."

"I've seen proof!" Erisa retorted, her voice venomous enough to spook Fergus. "She had a dagger with a dark purple date on the hilt, didn't she? On top of some green palm leaves?"

My racing heart sped up. "She did," I confirmed.

"*That* was the dagger Ve— the Fox pulled out of my mother's chest. We still have it at the Palace," she replied, her voice breaking. "And that red stone you found in her bracelet, that was inset in a silver pendant that never left my mother's neck. Your sister stole it when she killed her."

"You're wrong," I fumed.

My head was swimming and my pulse thundered so loudly in my ears I didn't even hear if she responded. Lies. It was all lies. She'd had all night to come up with this rancid story, to make my twin look so guilty that I wouldn't try and seek my own revenge on her.

It wouldn't work, I would take everything from her. I would take the Fox, the Autarch, and the Palace away.

But the dagger. How had she known about Karasi's dagger? It had been passed down from each Lord and Lady Lusilim for as long as anyone could remember. Our father had given it to her after we were born, and she had never been without it. I remembered the day it went missing, she had been distraught, refusing to tell me what had happened. I'd offered to help her look for it, but she had said it was gone forever. She'd found another one a few years later, the one we'd received with her hand; she'd hated it, but refused to get rid of it, saying that she needed to keep it safe.

We had been riding in silence for another hour when Erisa's austere posture slowly relaxed and she began to slide sideways. I considered letting her fall for a second before capturing her with my right arm. She slumped back against my chest, her sleepless night finally catching up with her. I let her stay, enjoying the prospect of her humiliation when she woke.

The terrain became harsher and rockier as we continued on. I had to make a conscious effort not to give in to the impulse to wrap my hand around Erisa's throat and squeeze. The witch was right there in front of me, completely defenseless. Whatever spell of doubt and confusion she had woven into my mind had me seething. I *hated* it. Hated that it was even possible for me to consider believing her. To consider doubting my own twin. But I forced my hands to remain still, knowing I had to make the most of her unconsciousness; the less she saw of the route into the mountains, the better.

Despite the sun rising high in the sky, the climbing altitude introduced a chill to the air, making me glad I had kept my cloak on. Moth tripped on a loose rock, jolting Erisa awake. She spun around to glare at me, as if I were the one at fault.

"Why didn't you wake me?" she huffed, embarrassment

reddening her cheeks.

"You're more agreeable when you're unconscious," I replied coldly.

She turned to face forward again, color flushing deeper across her neck and face. This was the most emotion I'd seen from her and I had to admit, it was satisfying.

Another tense, awkward silence followed in which I allowed myself to fantasize about brutal ways to destroy her, imagining that she might be doing the same.

❖❖❖

As we drew closer to our destination, I made a show of looking at the map often. I knew this route well, but I couldn't let her find out why. I had to be careful to avoid worn paths, which meant taking a slight detour. If she noticed, she didn't make a comment.

We were about an hour's ride from the entrance to the southern pass when I guided Moth into a small clearing, the glint of a stream visible at the far end.

"Why are we stopping?" she asked after climbing down from Moth's back and stretching her arms above her head.

"I only brought enough food for last night. So, unless you want to survive off the remaining bread and cheese, we need to hunt," I said, unsaddling Fergus.

"I'll do it," she said, picking up her bag and stalking off before I could argue. Not that I *would* argue, if she wanted to volunteer, I was more than happy to set up camp and relax.

Though it was the height of spring, vegetation was sparse this close to the Zuamsik Mountains, so there was little point in searching for any fruit or berries. I sat by the fire and took out my notepad to begin sketching. I had always loved to draw, it relaxed my mind in a way nothing else could. I didn't have to think about anything, just allow the pencil to find its own path across the page.

The crackling fire threw flickers of light across the rudimentary version of Erisa's flushed face that was forming on the paper in front of me. Not flushed from embarrassment, but from the exertion of dancing. The bowing figures of Nook and Ezra were in front of her, as if they were two vassals paying homage to their queen. She'd certainly looked regal enough in her flowing gown and wild hair. Anger flared in me once again and the pencil snapped in my hand, slashing a dark line through the sketched outline of her skirts.

It wasn't the first drawing I'd done of her, and likely wouldn't be the last. Sketching the images down helped to remove them from my head, and I wanted to erase them all. I threw the pencil in the fire, irritation fraying my every nerve.

Erisa's footsteps were completely silent as she returned to the camp, the only thing that gave her presence away was the light of the setting sun glinting off a dagger strapped to her hip. Her long hair was wet and dripping and she had changed into fresh clothes. She carried two decent sized fish in a damp shirt and handed them to me.

"Thank you," I said, not bothering to ask where she'd learned to catch fish with her bare hands. She said nothing, only watched me prepare and cook the meal.

We ate, once again, in that cold, stony silence.

***

I spent a few minutes watching Erisa's sleeping face the next morning. It was so bizarre to think that so many in this realm feared the Feline, and yet so few of them had actually seen her. She was fierce, yes, but what truly scared me was how vulnerable she could look in moments like this. No one would suspect the formidable creature that lay beneath.

I had never been a violent man, but something about the Feline angered me more than I could even comprehend. I wanted to *hurt* her, to plunge Karasi's blade into her chest and finally get the revenge I had been seeking for the past four years.

Wrenching my gaze away, I followed the sound of the deep, rapid stream. I stripped off my clothes when I reached the bank and sank under the water, hoping the freezing temperature would be enough to banish the swirling images of Erisa from my mind.

It wasn't.

I returned to the camp with a renewed sense of shame and self-loathing. I was unable to even look at her as I prepared the horses and led Moth to a large boulder. We mounted without saying a word, and continued our journey into the mountains, the icy winds echoing the empty coldness between us.

# Chapter 10

## Erisa

It was safe to say that I was *not* having fun on this trip. And judging by the fact that his mood was somehow even worse than yesterday, neither was Theo.

These past few days had made me truly realize how overindulged and pampered I'd become at the Palace. I was cold, hungry, and aching. But instead of missing the heat of the underworld, I mourned the loss of that part of me that thrived in the wilderness.

As children, Verrill and I had belonged to the outdoors, we had disappeared for days at a time with no more than the clothes on our backs, a few daggers, and his lyre. We would hunt monsters in the Gištir Jungle, daring each other to venture into dark dens and nests, one time being caught and chased by a hooded demon.

Theo allowed his horse, Moth, to choose his own route up the neglected and crumbling path. It looked as though it hadn't been used in the years since before Tarprusa's last invasion of Irkalla, when the trading route closed. It was stark and harsh in these mountains, and I hoped I wouldn't need to stay here for very long. But Theo was hiding something about the pass, and I needed to find out what that was.

We halted in a flat clearing in the valley between two towering, snow-capped peaks that threw the empty space into a chilling shade. This was obviously the beginning of the pass, as I could see remnants of trading facilities and a route carved into the stone leading west toward the Tarprusan border.

Theo tried to tie the horses to an old, broken hitching rail, but it buckled into rotten splinters as soon he put any pressure onto it. I didn't even bother trying to hide my smile when he exhaled a heavy sigh of frustration. He decided just to let the beasts wander, trusting them not to stray too far.

"This was the main trading port, where everyone would rest before or after the journey through the pass," he said, walking toward me. "Everything that remained has just been left to rot."

He gestured around us at the empty crates and discarded wagons, all moved to the edge of the clearing and piled against the far mountainside. "Anything of value is long gone, before you get any ideas," he added bitterly, and began walking down the carved path. "The entrance is down this way."

Small pieces of rock and various abandoned items littered the ground as we walked a few hundred feet toward the entrance. We turned the last bend and I saw, for the first time, what had once been the gated tunnel mouth of the southern pass. It was more than ten feet in diameter, so could have comfortably fit multiple people, as well as horses and carts. Enormous chunks of smashed rock had filled the inside of the tunnel and one of the wrought iron gates had been completely struck off, the other barely hanging on to its hinges.

The tunnel had collapsed from the inside, so he *hadn't* been lying about that. I moved toward the opening, trying to see how far inside the damage went.

"There used to be guards at these gates, to monitor who came in or or out," Theo told me, shifting some of the smaller boulders from the gate that lay on the ground. The bars were bent out of shape but I could still see the design in the middle, a circle made from all seven district crests, with the Autarch's in the center. In the middle of each crest was an object which identified the district; an eye for Šarrum, a two headed lion staff for Anzillu, a key for Katmu, the head of a snake for Hudjefa, a stylus and tablet for Kusig, a date palm for Zingal and a songbird for Ocridell.

"How did it collapse?" I asked.

Theo shrugged his shoulders and looked around, a muscle in his jaw tensing. "Who knows? It was discovered on a biannual inspection a few years back, but by that time, it had been out of commission for a while. As far as we know, it was just a freak rockslide from the mountain, possibly caused by an earthquake."

I spent the next several hours looking around the site, trying to get further into the tunnel, but it was completely blocked off. Theo made no attempt to help, but stayed close anyway, never letting me out of his sight. I noted down a few things I thought might be of interest to Csintalan and decided to go back to the main clearing.

"Done already? I thought you'd want to count *all* the stones in the tunnel, noting down the qualities of each one," Theo drawled, but his feigned bored expression didn't quite mask the anxiety I saw simmering beneath. He positioned himself in front of me on the path, nearly blocking my exit.

"Like *you* would know anything about stones," I gibed, throwing a lazy, pointed look down to below his waistline.

He gave me a wicked, malicious grin and stepped closer, only inches from me. He leant down and began to whisper in my ear. "Oh, you'd lo—"

Whatever he was saying was cut off with a whoosh of air as I ducked under his arm, elbowing him in the ribs as I passed and continued down toward the clearing. I could feel his glare igniting me as I walked away, but I kept my pace slow and apathetic, *daring* him to retaliate.

I felt a twinge of disappointment when he only followed in silence back into the old trading port. *Coward.*

It quickly became obvious that he wanted me nowhere near the stacks of discarded rubble by the way he avoided looking at the eastern side of the clearing, where it lay piled against the mountainside. He tensed whenever I moved in that direction and would make some lame, unassuming comment to try and guide my attention away from the area.

I obliged after a while, knowing I would have to return again tonight to explore further. The heaped rubble seemed to form a crudely assembled set of stairs that led up to a ledge on the mountain. I didn't focus on it for more than a few seconds, to not draw suspicion, but I was willing to bet that whatever had Theo so on edge would be up there.

My stomach was growling loudly by midafternoon, earning a scornfully amused smirk from Theo. He was sitting on some old sacks with his back propped against a rock, sketching something in a small leather-bound book. We had finished the rest of the food this morning, so I knew he had to be hungry too.

"I caught the fish yesterday, it's your turn to get dinner," I remarked, hoping his honor would force him to oblige and leave me alone to investigate for a while.

I enjoyed watching the conflict warring inside his head. He was desperately trying to find an excuse not to leave me here unguarded.

"I'm not hungry," he said finally. "You want something to eat, go get it yourself."

"Fine," I snapped, "but don't expect me to bring you anything."

He simply shrugged one shoulder, not even bothering to look at me as he continued to draw.

I wanted to snap his fingers.

I started back down the winding path that we traveled up earlier and pulled my cloak tight, as the wind attempted to whip it away from me when I left the shelter of the towering mountains. I tried to find a way to double back on myself to see what he was hiding past the clearing, but found nothing except sheer, inaccessible rock. Cursing, I quickly formulated a new plan.

I walked for over an hour without seeing so much as a rabbit, because the landscape was so desolate and barren. What little vegetation I *could* find was too sparse and willowy to even house small birds or rodents. I needed to find *something* for my plan to work. I crept over the gravelly terrain as quietly as possible, scanning the ground and sky for any sign of movement. The sun was setting by the time I gave up. At least the heat of my growing frustration was enough to keep the chill of the air from seeping into my skin, and the bitter taste of failure had kept the hunger at bay. I drained the little water I had left to try and fill my belly and trudged back up the mountain to the camp.

The scene I was greeted with had my blood boiling. Theo was sat by a roaring fire made from some broken planks of wood, plucking a pigeon.

"No luck?" he taunted, glancing at my empty hands.

"Where did you get that?" I demanded, my face so hot from my flaring temper I was surprised it wasn't glowing.

"The sky, *obviously*."

He reached down to retrieve a second bird laying next to his bow and held it out to me, a smug, egotistical smirk crawling across his face. At that moment, I would have done *anything* to eliminate the vexing expression, but I decided that I was too hungry to be proud tonight. And besides, he had just given me the perfect opportunity to put my plan back into action.

While the birds cooked over the dancing flames, I walked over to where I had left my bag by the horses. Making sure Theo had his back to me, I retrieved a small sachet of coarse, pale powder from a hidden inner pocket; ground wild eytelia root. The petals were lethal, but a small pinch of the root powder could knock someone unconscious for half a day. My mother had schooled me in the art of poison making. She had taught me how to utilize common herbs and flowers to treat ailments, avoid pregnancy, bewilder someone into becoming more pliable, or to simply snatch their consciousness. The folded paper had become slightly crumpled during the journey, but it had kept the contents contained. I emptied a large pinch into my palm and closed my hand around it.

Luck seemed to be on my side, as Theo was fletching an arrow when I returned to the fire, completely absorbed in his work. I leaned over the fire to turn the birds a final time, letting my palm open over his, so that the powder would fall and stick to the fatty juices seeping over the skin. Most fell into the fire but I had overcompensated on the dosage. He was about to sleep *very* well tonight. He would also wake up with severe stomach cramps and nausea, but I didn't see how that would be my problem.

As much as I hated to admit it, the pigeon was good. Theo scarfed his down in record time, not seeming to notice the slight bitter taste of the wild eytelia root now dissolving on his tongue. I was about to thank him for the meal when he took a long swig from his very full water skin. I had seen him drain it earlier in the day.

"Is there a spring nearby?" I asked.

He gave me a scathing look. "No."

"Then where did you fill that up?" I nodded to the waterskin in his hand.

"At the stream this morning," he said, smirking again as he held it out to me. "Why? You want some of this too? Need me to feed *and* water you?"

"Go fuck yourself," I replied tartily, to which he winked in response, further increasing my ire.

I knew he was lying to me, but I couldn't see the point of it. Would he really be petty enough to lie about a stream to make me thirsty? He likely wanted me to be eager to leave in the morning and forget about whatever he was hiding up here. Whatever it was, I would soon be on my way to discovering it.

As if on cue, Theo yawned. He stretched his muscled arms above his head before smoothing out his bedroll and blankets next to the fire. I laid down on my own, facing away from him to warm my back by the flames. I was already cold; the sky was completely clear, offering no cover of cloud to abate the briskness of the air.

After a few minutes of silence, I heard Theo shuffling back onto his feet. I rolled onto my back to see him standing over my head as he threw one of his blankets onto me.

"If I have to spend another night being kept awake by your teeth chattering I'll end up setting you on fire," he grumbled and lay back down without another word.

*Well, you won't have to worry about a lack of sleep tonight,* I thought cheerfully.

Less than ten minutes later, he was completely still and breathing deeply. Sound asleep. I counted to five thousand in my head, to be safe, then silently extracted myself from my blankets. I regretted the loss of heat immediately, but was placated by the bright, full moon that shone unhindered through the dark, knowing the light would be invaluable.

I chose my footing carefully as I made my way to the other side of the clearing, looking back every few seconds to ensure Theo was still unconscious. Though, with the dose I had given him, he'd struggle to wake up before midday. A wash of giddiness came over me as I imagined him waking up alone and confused after realizing I had left, taking the horses with me.

The ascent up the stacks of rubble was a little challenging, the low groans of the wood seemed thunderous in the surrounding silence. But I was correct, the piles had created a makeshift stairway that led up onto a stoney ledge that wound around the mountain.

I followed the path, glancing back a final time to see Theo still motionless by the fire, before rounding the corner. There was a sheer drop to my left, but the path was wide enough for me to comfortably jog along it without fearing the fall. The moon illuminated the gentle downward slope that wound back into a small valley between two mountainsides. The trail continued for another five minutes or so before ending abruptly over another sheer drop. Had I been running any faster I may have gone straight over the edge in the dim light.

I considered going back to the camp. I hadn't seen anything out of the ordinary, but this path had been *made*, it had to lead to something. I had turned a full circle before I saw it; another rickety wooden staircase that descended to a second ledge below. It had been tucked away behind the shelf of rock I was currently standing on, hidden in the shadows.

With careful steps, I made my way down onto a thinner ledge this time, holding onto a coarse rope that had been hammered into the stone at waist height. My heart was thundering in my chest by the time I made it around the mountain and into a wide clearing overlooking a large flat expanse nestled into the mountain range.

I had to blink a few times before I believed what my eyes were showing me. Below me, burrowed in a modest copse of tall trees, was what looked to be a small village. There were multiple large buildings and so many huts and shacks, it was difficult to count them all. I sunk to a low crouch, to move closer to the edge of my elevated viewpoint.

There were no people and no fires, though some of the

buildings had thin wisps of smoke rising from chimneys. From my vantage point I could just about make out a large courtyard split into sections, with a row along each edge of something glittering in the moonlight.

Weapon racks.

Now, I saw the other clues more clearly: the circular boards for target practice and the straw bundles used for combat training.

This was a military base.

I was completely stunned. I tried to calculate my location, knowing that I couldn't be anywhere near the Tarprusan border, because there were still mountains surrounding me. I squinted my eyes at a dark shape at the far end of the base below. It just looked like a dark hole, indicating that it must be another tunnel of the pass. Which meant that in the rock below me to my right, there must be a tunnel opening out into the clearing.

My musings were cut short as I was tackled and pinned to the ground, my hands and knees scraping on the rough stone. Instinct took over, and I spun at the waist, my elbow bent outwards. It made contact with something hard and I flipped my legs over, following the momentum and kicking out. A large hand grabbed my legs, holding them down, and I looked up to find Theo rubbing his jaw with his right hand.

*What the actual fuck?*

He used my moment of confusion to shift his weight over me, pinning my legs down with his shins and capturing my wrists with his hands. He was breathless, yet somehow he had still managed to catch me unawares. I had been absorbed in my observations but he had approached me silently.

"What—" I began.

He cut me off. "You foolish, thoughtless girl! You should've just stayed at the camp, instead of sticking your nose where it *certainly* doesn't belong."

I shot up, smashing my head into his nose and he reared back, shifting his weight just enough for me to free my left leg and bring it straight up between both of his. He yelped in pain, retracting in on himself. I wrenched my hands away and began scrambling backward but he grabbed my ankle, pulling me back to him, toward the cliff edge. I lunged out with punches and kicks and slashed my nails, but he dodged most of them and just seemed to absorb the blows I landed.

His large hands wrapped around my neck and he squeezed. The pressure instantly made my face hot and blood pound in my ears. I was at a disadvantage. He was almost lying on top of me, his hips pinning down my own as he held my head over the sheer drop of the cliff.

"Squeeze a bit harder, Theo," I gasped. "I'm starting to feel something."

His eyes were wild, and I knew he was going to kill me, he *wanted* to kill me.

I clawed at his eyes and his cheeks until he had to shift his arms to trap mine beneath them. The brief change in angle allowed me space to bring my right hip up where I reached down and retrieved a dagger. Black spots were appearing in my vision and the dizziness was almost overwhelming. I attempted to plunge the dagger under his rib cage but he shifted his knee forward, trying to knock the blade free from my hand. I sliced into his calf instead. I brought my now free right leg up to kick his chest back, throwing him off balance. He released my throat, flinging his hands out behind him on instinct, to catch himself.

I gasped in one glorious breath after another, clambering quickly to my feet. My head swam as I stood and I quickly backed away from the edge. His eyes were glued to me as I circled him slowly, assessing my every move.

It was clear that I'd seen too much. I knew he didn't intend on letting me live long enough to spread the knowledge. I had to kill him. What a *terrible* shame.

Before I could decide how to strike, he lunged for me, quicker than I ever expected he could be. I ducked under the huge arm he tried to grab me with and went to attack his back. He'd been expecting that and swung his left elbow behind him, striking me in the chest and knocking me backward. He came at me again, and I feinted to the left before trying to dodge right, but he blocked me again. I thrust my dagger toward his neck, but his right forearm halted the attempt. He pushed sharply, trying to force my own hand into my face, but I shifted to my left foot, expecting the move. The tip of the dagger caught the fabric of his shirt and tore it as I spun away, leaving the upper half of his chest bare except for the small leather pouch hanging from his neck.

*Damn, he's attractive,* I thought, chastising myself as soon as it formed. We were moving again, each of our moves blocked by the other. I didn't have time to dwell on the similarities of our fighting styles, I could only learn and adapt.

"Come on, Sunflower," he taunted breathlessly, "is that all you've got?"

Anger flared hot inside me and I knew that was his goal. I went in for another strike and he caught my wrist on an upward arc of his arm, causing the blade to slip from my grasp. He'd taken the bait. As he reached for the fallen dagger, I grasped his right shoulder and swung myself around to his back, kicking my feet into the backs of his knees. We flew forward and he landed hard on the stone. I snatched the dagger from the dirt and brought it up to his throat.

The small pouch dropped to the floor in front of him as I cut through the cord, dragging the blade across the soft skin of his neck. He seized my hand and pushed it away from his jugular. Pain lanced through my wrist as he twisted it, causing the weapon to fall back to the ground.

His grip was vice-like on my arm as he dragged me in front of him once more. Small, dark trails of blood were seeping out of the small cut I'd made at his throat. The look in his eyes told me he had tired of our little game; he was ready to end me now. Which was a shame, this was the most riveting fight I'd had in a while, I was enjoying myself.

I bit down hard into the hand he had wrapped around my wrist, and he released it, hissing as I drew blood. I made a lunge for the knife, but dipped my body at the last second and snatched the fallen pouch from between his knees and turned quickly to scramble away from him.

I managed to take two steps before he captured a fistful of my hair, pulling me back. I glanced down at the blood coating his left calf and kicked out, striking at my previous cut.

He crumpled to the ground and I fled, sprinting across the clearing and down the narrow path, not daring to look down.

I was almost at the top of the rickety stairs when I heard him thundering after me. I kicked out hard against a supporting beam and the top four stairs dismantled and fell into the empty space beneath. It wasn't much of a head start, but it would have to be enough.

A brief glance back told me he was limping across the narrow ledge, holding tight to the rope. I refused to waste another second before I began my sprint back to the camp.

The upwards incline made my thighs burn almost as much as my lungs. My whole body felt like it was on fire, but I didn't dare stop. Somehow, over my rasping lungs and deafening heartbeats, I could still hear him behind me. I pushed my body beyond its limits but he was still gaining on me.

The main clearing came into view and I hurled myself down the steps, the battered planks of wood bowing beneath the impact. Small flames still burned brightly in the center where we had made our camp and I raced to it, snatching my bag up and over my head, where it smacked against my back with every stride.

Moth and Fergus were eyeing me warily from the edge of the clearing, shifting uneasily as I sprinted toward them. I slowed to a jog to try and avoid spooking them, and was grateful when Moth stood his ground. I grasped his bridle and began running again, his loping trot easily keeping pace. The clearing narrowed to the exit path and I used the low, collapsing wall of stone to spring onto Moth's back. He was bigger than any other horse I had ridden before and I wasn't sure if I could have executed a running vault without the additional height. I urged him into a canter and looked behind me to find Theo at the top of the stairs, watching me escape.

The descent down the mountains was treacherous, and I slowed as much as I dared when the loose, rocky terrain threatened to trip Moth. The last thing I needed was for him to break a leg.

We reached the flat plains at the foot of the mountains, and I tried to urge him on, but the beast was in a temper, his ears pinned back and tossing his head in agitation. Every few strides he would try and turn back toward his companion and his master. I regretted my decision to not take Fergus instead, but I didn't have time to dwell on it, Theo was bound to be in pursuit.

Luckily, the moon was still bright in the sky by the time trees and thickets began repopulating the landscape. I headed southeast, hoping to skirt around the canyons in Saqummatu without venturing too close to the borders of Zingal.

As soon as I could hide myself effectively in the wilderness, I dismounted. Though I expected it, it still stung slightly when Moth immediately spun around and galloped away, back the way we had come.

I hauled myself into a nearby tree, climbing up into the thick canopy. My body was aching and exhausted, the lack of proper sleep and food catching up with me. I gently touched the tenderness at my throat, a souvenir from Theo's brutal caress. I wouldn't be surprised if I had bruises in the morning. I should have killed him, should have gone for the dagger instead of the pouch he always carried with him, but I was foolish. All I could think of was getting my mother's stone back.

I would make time to finish him off later.

A faint red glow illuminated the darkness as I opened the drawstring pouch. I tipped the contents into my palm and gasped.

The moment the ruby stone touched my skin, my vision went black.

❖ ❖ ❖

Fire burned my retinas, the heat of the flames caressed my skin, and the booming explosions had my ears ringing so loudly that I almost couldn't hear the shrill screams rending the air. Hundreds of scenes and images flashed before my eyes, immersing me in each with devastating detail.

Irkalla was burning.

My mind raced through the visions of buildings reduced to ash, families being torn apart, and endless, meaningless slaughter.

Then I saw Csintalan as the Autarch, sitting on his throne in the middle of a burning battlefield, laughing maniacally at the carnage. There was something white poking out from his clenched left fist. In his right hand he held his staff, the warped snakes writhing as though alive. He stood and began to walk in my direction, only stopping a few paces from me.

"Look at what we've achieved, Kitten," he said, gesturing to the bloodbath continuing around us. "Think of what more we could do once you bring my stone back to me."

The voice did not belong to Csintalan. It was the cold, unfamiliar sound of many combined into one. His gaze fell to my hands, and I looked down. I was holding my mother's stone in one hand and an identical copy in the other, the jagged edges seeming to match perfectly.

"Don't let him have it!" A cry sounded from my right, and I

saw Verrill sprinting toward me, covered in blood. I didn't know if it was his own or if it had come from another.

A clap of thunder shook the air, reverberating through the ground so hard the fighting halted momentarily. I whirled back to Csintalan, to see that he'd struck the field with his staff, impaling the soil.

Then, the shrieking began anew, but not from fighting. The earth had started splitting, seizing people from where they stood and snatching at their feet as they tried to run. Verrill was at my side within seconds and tried to get me to move, to flee with him, but my feet were rooted to the ground, snakes coiling around them to anchor me down. He pulled at my arms and tried to lift me by the waist but I was immovable.

"Go! Run, Ver! Now!" I urged, trying to push him off me. But he was stubborn and refused to leave my side, even as the ground crumbled away from beneath his feet.

I cried out as his body started to descend down into the gaping depths below. I clung to him with every ounce of strength in my body, holding him close to me as I fell to my knees.

"Fix the stone, my music. Fix it and use it," he insisted, his hazel eyes boring into mine, pleading with me to understand. A second later he was ripped from my arms and pulled into the ground.

I screamed his name again and again, but I couldn't see him through the darkness that had swallowed him up.

"Do something!" I shouted to Csintalan, who was still standing before me.

He cackled another harsh, peculiar laugh that sounded like a dozen voices in a single note. He opened his left fist and threw something in my direction.

A little white songbird lay crushed and broken on the ground before me, its feathers bent and ruffled.

"Fix the stone, Erisa."

My mother's voice was the last thing I heard before the earth parted beneath me, and consumed me whole.

❖ ❖ ❖

When I opened my eyes, I discovered that I was back in the tree I had sought refuge in. I felt nauseous, unable to comprehend what I had just experienced. I knew it had only been a vision, but it had felt so real.

I looked down at my trembling hand, where the red stone still lay in my palm, the surface warm to the touch. The rest of the contents of the pouch had been emptied too; a small, folded note, some matches and two small pencils.

I unfolded the note.

*T, you already know who he is.*
*Find the other piece and fix the stone.*

Fix the stone. What did that even mean? My mother had worn it around her neck for as long as I could remember, and it had always looked like this. She had often told me that she heard whispers of the future from being close to it. I had no idea what I had just experienced, but it certainly didn't feel like a whisper. It had forced me into a vision that I prayed would never come true.

Hanging my head, I choked out a ragged sigh as I decided on my course of action. Carefully, I made my way back down the trunk of the tree and started walking. Though it had felt as though I had been trapped in that horrifying vision for hours, the moon was still full and bright in the sky, allowing me to detect the hoofprints Moth had made in the loose, dry dirt.

I followed them. I needed answers.

# Chapter 11

## Theo

Once again, I was in that damned forest, running for the light. But this time, I wasn't being pursued, I was the pursuer. I was holding Karasi's replacement dagger, the gaudy jewels set into the hilt uncomfortable in my hand.

A flash of russet fur caught my attention. A small fox was hiding in the brush, its beady eyes cautious and assessing. Only when it began to back away slowly did I realize that *that* was what I'd been chasing. The creature bared its teeth at me, a low snarl escaping its muzzle, and anger flared inside me.

I had no logical reason to hate this animal, but I did. Before I could stop myself, I hurled the dagger in the fox's direction. It vanished into the undergrowth, barking out a mocking laugh. But I knew I'd hit it, that it would die, and regret filled my mouth with bile.

4 May

❖ ❖ ❖

Damn it all.

I knew I had lost Erisa the second I saw her leap onto Moth and canter away. Of course the lying bitch could ride, I didn't know why her deceit even surprised me anymore. But when I saw Moth coming back toward Fergus and I some time later, I knew I would never see her again. Any hope I had of tracking her was gone.

I swore loudly and dismounted, leading both horses to a small gap in the trees. Exhaustion drove me to lay a bedroll out, and I examined the slash on my leg that pulsed angrily. I washed the wound quickly with a splash of water.

I scowled at the waterskin. It had been so incredibly foolish to risk getting supplies from the barracks while she hunted, no doubt fueling her suspicions. My head began to swim as I thought about the repercussions of my inability to keep my people hidden. Erisa would be on her way to the Autarch right now. She had been heading southeast, likely aiming for the tram station in Ocridell. But if I was wrong and she bypassed the city entirely, I would waste time waiting for her to arrive, instead of preparing Zingal for the inevitable sacking and my own torturous execution.

Hindered by exhaustion, I decided to rest until dawn, when I would have to race back to Zingal to try and get as many out as I could. I wasn't naive enough to believe that we had any chance of standing our ground right now. We were still too few, and lacked skills and weapons. I hadn't had the chance to make the crucial alliances this operation needed.

I had failed everyone.

***

For once, I awoke after a dreamless sleep. The absence of my nightly visions would have alarmed me, had I not found myself bound at the wrists and ankles. I pulled on the rope, but it only tightened further. How I had managed to sleep through that, I had no idea. When I saw Erisa perched on the ground beside me, I assumed I was still unconscious.

"Good, you're awake," she said, the early morning light glistening off a small vial of dark liquid in her hand. "I had you inhale some to ensure you wouldn't wake when I tied you, hope you don't mind."

She gave the bottle a little shake. If not for the pain in my leg, I would have been convinced I was dreaming. I had no explanation as to why she would come back and tie me up, if not to kill me.

"Why?" I asked, not even sure which question it referred to.

"Why did I bind you? Or why did I come back?" she said, but didn't wait for a response before continuing. "I bound you so you wouldn't try to kill me again, and I came back to get some answers."

She shifted so that she sat closer to me, and I could see the new smattering of freckles across her nose and cheeks. The deeper tones of her olive skin had flourished from spending the last few days in the sun, after being so long underground.

"Number one, what d—" She hesitated, before demanding, "How did you wake up? You should have been asleep for hours last night."

So, I had been right. I could have kissed Corbin for teaching me all he knew of herbal remedies and poisons.

"I went through your bag," I said, enjoying the look of indignation it produced on her face. "Nook's grandmother, Lola, uses wild eytelia root powder to sleep, I know its smell. I replaced yours with salt. I almost thanked you for seasoning my dinner last night."

"You just happened to be carrying ground salt with you?" she questioned, obviously irritated.

I shrugged, avoiding answering. After looking through her bag I had gone down to the barracks and retrieved the salt when I refilled my waterskin. I didn't know if she was planning on poisoning me, but my distrust had paid off.

"Is it a military base?" she said, testing me.

"Of sorts." She had already seen it, I saw no point in lying now. I pulled on the ropes again, but even when I tried twisting my hands free, they remained tightly knotted.

She held out a small, crumpled piece of paper that I instantly recognized as Karasi's note. "What does this mean?"

"You came back to ask me about *that*?" I asked, completely confused.

"If you don't cooperate, I'll leave you here and return to Šarrum. I'm sure the Autarch will be *fascinated* to learn about what's going on in the mountains," she snapped.

I didn't dare begin to hope that I still had a chance to keep that information hidden. But for whatever reason, she *had* come back.

"I don't know what it means," I answered honestly. "I found

it in Karasi's bracelet along with the red stone."

"But it's obviously addressed to you."

"Well then she clearly overestimated my investigative abilities," I retorted. "What are you even doing here?"

She was silent for a moment, weighing her words carefully.

"I told you that my mother always wore this stone in a necklace, she said that it would... inform her of events that were yet to happen. She said that she'd hear whispers of the future, but I never heard anything from it. I just assumed she was teasing me. Then last night, I had a vision as soon as it touched my hand. I was ordered to fix the stone. Afterwards, I saw this note and assumed you would know what it meant."

"And now you know that I don't?" I pressed.

"It doesn't matter, you're still going to help me find out. Do you have *any* ideas?"

"One," I replied, making an effort not to curl my lip at her impertinence. "I was hoping an acquaintance of mine would know something, though figuring that note out isn't exactly on my list of priorities."

"It is now," she said. "If I untie you, will you try to kill me again?"

Every word just increased my confusion and annoyance. But she was worried; whatever she had seen in her "vision" had clearly shaken her.

"What did you see?"

"A future I'd like to avoid," she finally admitted. "So, can I trust you to cooperate if we work together?"

I snorted. "Work together? Are you joking? You're probably

just lost and need me to show you the way back to Zingal. You'll sell me and my people out the second you return to the Palace."

"I will not," she said steadily. "I'm not going home until I find out what this stone is and how to fix it. You said you wanted to use me to get to the Autarch. I'll allow you to do it. He demanded I do the same to you, so he'll expect me to stay with you anyway."

"So whose side *will* you be on then?" I questioned, completely unsurprised that the Autarch had sent her for more than a trade route inspection.

"I am on nobody's side but my own," she clarified, "but your secret is safe with me, unless you make a move against me."

For some reason beyond my comprehension, I actually believed her. That likely made me the biggest fool in Irkalla, but the fact remained.

I decided to play along, hoping that I could come up with a plan to silence her permanently without giving the Autarch reason to suspect me.

"All right then, Sunflower," I smirked, "as much as I enjoy being tied up, are you planning on leaving me bound all day or shall we get moving?"

Her temporary civility evaporated and she tugged the ropes tight enough to pinch before releasing them. She looked at my calf as she loosened the ones around my ankles.

"It'll fester if you don't treat it," she said sharply, as though I was the one who had caused the injury, and not her.

"I'll see to it back in Zingal," I muttered, rubbing the raw skin at my wrists.

"Don't be ridiculous, there's plenty of useful herbs around

here, now that we're away from those cursed mountains."

She was gone before I could protest. In the daylight, I confirmed that she was right. The wound was long and deep enough that infection could easily take hold. I got up and limped toward the bags. It smarted keenly when I put weight on it, and I guessed the muscles were likely torn from running on it the previous night. I retrieved a needle, thread, and some bandages from a small emergency bag and sat back down, mentally preparing myself.

I had sewn plenty of other people's wounds in the last war, but Nook, Ezra, and Suenna had always been there to patch me back up when needed.

"You'll need to boil that first."

I jumped as Erisa's voice rang through the clearing. I had never known anyone to move so silently. I had been listening for her to get out of bed the night before, and somehow, hadn't heard a thing. I had even given her my cloak, so that the extra fabric would rustle when she moved. But, after a few hours of hearing only the fire crackling, I had turned to see if she was even breathing, only to discover that she was missing entirely.

"We don't have time to build a fire now," I replied. "We need to be back in Zingal by tomorrow night."

"Is that where your *acquaintance* is?" she asked, placing some herbs down on a flat piece of stone.

"No, I need to return for the last day of Tammuz. I told the others that if I'm not back by then, it means you've either killed or kidnapped me."

She sneered at that but said nothing. She snatched my waterskin and poured some water over the herbs and began grinding them with another stone. I wanted to point out that this was hardly more sanitary than the needle and thread but decided it was better to pick my battles.

"Give them to me," she ordered, holding her hand out. "You look greener than a virgin on her wedding night."

"I thought you said they needed boiling," I challenged.

"If you'd rather risk a rotten leg than wait for a fire, I won't stop you. The wound needs closing regardless."

I started to place the needle and thread into her outstretched hand but halted the action. I took her hand into my own, inspecting the palm. She tried to snatch it away but I held on, crushing it so I could take a closer look at the scar marking her skin. The image was distorted and blurred, but there was no doubt as to what it was; the soaring songbird of the Anzû family crest. Slowly but surely, the pieces fell into place.

"Erisa Anzû," I stated. It wasn't a question. I knew I had recognized her name from somewhere.

She gave no answer, only wrenched her hand from mine and snatched up the needle and thread. Without being gentle, she ripped my trouser leg away and doused my leg with more water before starting to close the wound.

I hissed through the pain and allowed my mind to wander as a distraction. I knew there had been something that I was missing, but I hadn't expected this. She was the Lady of Ocridell, and yet no one even believed her to be alive. Lola had muttered something to me about her resemblance to "young Ava" but in my fragile state, I'd taken no notice, only assigning the comments to the mad ramblings of old women. Now I realized she was talking about

Lady Ava Anzû. If I had ever seen her, I couldn't remember doing so, but Lola would have watched her take over the position from her father.

I thought about what Erisa had said about Karasi, that it had been her blade that killed Ava. I couldn't make sense of it. I knew that Karasi would never commit such an atrocity as to wipe out almost an entire family, but I could remember her being so inconsolable after she returned without that dagger. She never explained how she lost it, or where she had been. I couldn't believe that I was even doubting her, but something about it didn't sit right with me. The longing to speak to her one last time surged through me again, as it had so many times since her death.

Erisa was tying off the last knot of stitches, making quick work of the task. She had removed her cloak and tied her hair back, revealing a slight shadow around her throat. I was shocked to find that the sight of the bruises caused a small lashing of guilt to twist through my gut. I shut it down immediately. Had it not been for this extremely unexpected and tenuous agreement, she would be on her way to damn my entire district. Whatever atrocity she had seen from that stone, I was grateful for it.

The green salve Erisa had concocted stung as she smeared it over the neat row of stitches, before binding bandages tight around my leg. I tried to do it myself, but she insisted on completing the task. If I had thought that she was able to feel guilt, I would have assumed that was the reason for her cordiality.

Despite her equestrian abilities being no longer secret, the fact remained that we only had one saddle to tie the bags to. So, much to the annoyance of us both, she had to join me on Moth once more.

Retying the saddle bags took longer than before, as she had stripped the rope from them to tie me down, but we were on our way back to Zingal by midmorning.

Erisa rode behind me this time, to lessen the chance of her leg *accidentally* swinging back and into my damaged one. She was more comfortable this way, holding on only to the back of my cloak, and I could relax knowing she was unlikely to fall.

Conversation was strained and as the day wore on, we barely exchanged a dozen words between us before making camp in the early evening. We were both exhausted and starving, but the springtime heat had returned now that we were lower in altitude. Erisa left to hunt immediately, claiming that my leg was too much of a hindrance to be useful, so I may as well set up the camp. I didn't argue, my leg wasn't exactly painful, but I didn't see the sense in delaying its healing.

I had refilled the waterskins and stoked the fire to a delightful roar by the time she returned with a large hare. We ate and prepared to sleep in silence, and I was surprised when she broke it.

"Who is your acquaintance?" she asked, not needing to elaborate for me to know who she was talking about.

"His name is Silas. He's the one who introduced me to Ezra and then thrust Nook and Suenna on us too," I reminisced fondly.

"When was this?"

I had to pause for a moment to work it out. "Almost eight years ago, during Tarprusa's last invasion. We were in the cavalry division of the army."

"And you think he can help us fix the stone?"

"I don't know," I said. "He's a very peculiar man, and

incredibly old. If anyone knows anything about it, then it'll be him."

"Oh great, so the whole realm could be riding on the potential knowledge of a wrinkled, old kook. Fantastic," she snapped and rolled over to turn her back to me, huffing out an angry breath.

I was desperate to know what she had seen. I knew it had to have been terrible for her to come back and ask for my help, but I doubted that she would give me any answers, especially when in such a bad temper.

✤ ✤ ✤

The next day, our conversation was light in comparison to the heavy press of storm clouds that loomed overhead. Erisa agreed to keep silent about the mountains but was resolute on not aiding my efforts until she could determine the meaning of her vision.

I knew she was second guessing her loyalties to the Autarch. I could only hope that she had seen his true colors in that vision. In return, I would take us to Silas and try to solve the riddle of the stone. I didn't really have a choice in the matter if I wanted to keep my people safe, but I had to admit, I was curious too. She proposed striking a bargain, but a single glance to her decorated arms would reveal to anyone that she collected deals like trophies, and I had no desire to earn a strike on my palm for this. I didn't want to be indebted to someone like her.

The rain began as a soft shower in the late afternoon, but quickly matured into a downpour. Moth spooked as a thunderclap rumbled overhead, and Erisa had to throw her arms around my waist to keep her seat behind me. I hated the way my pulse began to race at the contact. I was about to shove her arms away from me, but she removed them before I had the chance. Disappointment and relief warred against each other inside me at the loss of contact.

With the skies truly opened, I suggested we find somewhere to wait out the downpour and Erisa agreed. Though the air was hot and sticky, I could feel her occasional shiver behind me whenever the breeze picked up. We had made good time today, and were approaching the upper reaches of Zingal. There was a small barn set into the trees a few dozen paces from the path, and I turned the horses toward it.

With Moth and Fergus joining us, it was cramped inside the building. The air was thick with the smell of moldering hay, but it was dry enough. Erisa wasted no time in stripping off her tunic and wringing out the sodden fabric. She wore only a thin white chemise underneath—the cloth slightly transparent from the rain—and it clung to her like a lover's caress.

"Keep your eyes to yourself, or I'll pry them from your skull."

I glanced up into her scowling eyes before letting my gaze fall momentarily back down to her breasts. It took an obscene amount of effort to peel my eyes away. I gave her a lazy smirk, hoping to irk her into lashing another spiteful comment at me, but she only rolled her eyes and turned away.

I couldn't recall ever hating someone so much. Not only was she vicious and ill-spirited, she had openly admitted to killing my sister. And yet, here I was, unable to stop imagining tearing that chemise away and pinning her up against the barn wall.

Maybe I didn't hate her, maybe I only hated myself for this

obscene lapse in judgment. It had been too long since I had been with someone, and I made a mental note to find Josefine at tomorrow's celebrations. I sat on the floor, leaning my back against the wall, and shut my eyes to prevent my gaze from returning to Erisa. The stale barn air stirred as she sat down beside me, and my entire being became solely focused on the heat of her arm less than a half inch from my own.

Before I was able to stop myself, I looked at her. She was examining my face openly, her eyes lingering on my mouth. The atmosphere in the barn became almost too close and charged as I fixated on her parted lips, stained pink from the acid that dripped from her every word. I commanded my eyes to close and turned my face away, but my arm remained next to hers, the closeness scorching my skin.

Almost an hour later, the rain slowed to a light drizzle. With daylight already fading, it would have made sense to spend the night in the barn. But I was keen to return home, to bathe and eat a proper meal. And with the loaded energy coiling between us, I couldn't trust myself not to do something foolish.

"Let's go," I ordered, practically leaping for the doorway, desperate to escape into the open air.

Erisa donned her cloak and we departed.

# Chapter 12

## Erisa

Night had long since fallen by the time we reached Theo's estate in Zingal, and I was extremely grateful to discover a hot meal waiting for us in the parlor.

"I'd like to send a letter, who shall I give it to?" I asked Theo after we both finished inhaling our bowls of stew.

He narrowed his eyes in suspicion. "You can give it to me. I'll see that it's sent."

Despite the fact that he obviously—for good reason—didn't trust me, it was still vexing to know that he would read whatever correspondence I sent. I walked over to a little desk in the corner of the room and retrieved a pencil and a small piece of paper. I quickly scribbled a note addressed to the Palace and handed it to him for inspection.

*Come find me V.*

He looked over the note, turning it over before raising a single dark eyebrow at me. "Is this it? You haven't even signed it."

"He'll know it's me," I assured him simply.

He didn't look convinced, and reanalyzed every word in the hopes of finding some illicit, hidden meaning.

I hadn't told Theo that I was intending on having Verrill accompany us to visit Silas. I didn't think there would be an issue, as he planned on asking Nook, Ezra, and Suenna to make the journey as well. I missed Verrill desperately. I couldn't remember the last time we had been separated for so long and I needed to talk to him about everything that had happened in the past week.

I spent so long soaking in the hot bath that I came out with pale, wrinkled skin. I had only enough energy left to pull on a nightgown and sink into the plush bed. The second my head hit the pillow, I was asleep.

❖ ❖ ❖

The following afternoon, Didi and I were watching a heated game of Conquest between Theo, his three friends, Dana, and Lola. Music and dancing crowded the celebrations around us, and the air was thick with delicious smells from the food stalls next to the game table.

Lola was in the lead and only two points away from winning when Ezra played a devious hand, causing a cry of outrage from everyone at the table as he moved to take the leading seat. The more the players drank, the more competitive they became—and from the expression on Didi's face, I could tell that she was glad to be watching, rather than participating.

The final round was brutal; Theo, Ezra, and Dana were tied in the lead, and each of them pulled out all the stops to snatch that final winning point. Theo passed on all four goes, then annihilated everyone else in the fifth pass of cards. Not even the barrage of abuse hurled at him from his friends and family could wipe the satisfied smirk of victory off his face, and he gave a flourishing bow to them all.

"That was disgraceful." I grinned at him. "I didn't think you had it in you."

"Well, I've spent the last week in your *beguiling* company. Some of your traits were bound to rub off on me sooner or later."

I narrowed my eyes at him, not wanting to play into his taunts. He waited for me to respond and seemed dissatisfied with my silence.

"No biting remark? No cutting retort?" he goaded. "Consider me disappointed, Sunflower."

"Yes well, I prefer not to have a battle of wits when my opponent is unarmed," I replied sweetly.

Theo's face split into a resplendent grin and he threw his head back and laughed so heartily that the sight of it made my breath catch. The others chuckled, hearing the exchange, the passions from the card game already forgotten.

After numerous attempts from Nook to have me dancing, I finally relented, allowing him to lead me to the dizzying clearing once more. I was spun and twirled with even more ferocity than I had been seven days ago, and I surprised myself by loving every second.

The people of Zingal were easy and enjoyable companions. Everyone was open and accommodating, even the ones who knew what my role was at the Palace. Any grudges were fleeting and dissolved into cordial bantering.

Nook passed me into the arms of a new partner, and I looked up expecting to see Ezra once again but was greeted by Theo's jubilant expression that he had been wearing all day. He wrapped a strong arm around my waist and clasped my hand in his and we set off into the other couples. He matched our pace to the speeding music, twisting and turning us both until we were breathless and sweating. Even then, he continued on—stepping so long and fast that my feet barely made contact with the ground—and never once passed me on to another partner.

The music slowed and he brought me close to his chest, my already hammering heart redoubling its efforts for an entirely different reason, as his scent of cedar and ginger enveloped me.

He skated a large hand up over my back, skimming the pale-yellow fabric of my dress that clung to my heated skin. He brushed my curls off my shoulder and gently traced a thumb over the bruises at my neck. He chuckled humorlessly to himself before dropping his hand and walking away, leaving me feeling ever so slightly dejected. I got over it quickly as I threw myself back into Ezra's waiting arms.

Despite the recent vision, I found myself having the most fun I'd had in years. The unfettered delight of the Zingali people was contagious, and I was able to store all of my new and existing worries into a little hidden section at the back of my mind.

No other district celebrated Tammuz. Zingal was said to have once been the domain of Dumuzid, God of Agriculture, and the Festival of Tammuz celebrated his marriage to the Goddess Inanna. Even if that weren't the case, the district provided the majority of the realm's produce. The celebration of spring seemed the most important holiday here.

"Ugh, he is shameless."

Didi's voice came from my left. We stood at the refreshment table, where I had been draining my third goblet of water, both of us flushed from dancing. I followed her gaze to where Theo stood lounging lazily against a tent post, talking to a pretty woman with light brown curls that bounced to her shoulders. I watched him brush a strand from her face and tuck it behind an ear before leaning in close and whispering something that made her giggle.

When he turned his face to kiss her, I felt as though I had swallowed something unpleasant. The sharp sting of my closed throat sunk heavily into my stomach as I watched him deepen the kiss. I looked down at the water in my hand, and then at the empty flagons of wine on the table that I'd helped deplete.

"I think there's something wrong with the wine," I said to Didi, grimacing.

"Maybe you've just drunk too much of it." She chuckled and pulled me back into the dancing. She must have been right, because my stomach settled almost instantly as we started to move.

The festivities continued through the night, rivaling even the most riotous of parties I attended in Anzillu. By the time the eastern sky began to pale, I was so exhausted that I had to practically drag myself back to the house. Dana was bustling about the kitchen when I entered, looking slightly tipsy as she fussed over a kettle.

Lola slumped in a corner chair, snoring loudly, clearly having little struggle with sleeping tonight.

"Here you go, dear," Dana said kindly, "take this up with you."

She placed a mug of tea and a small plate of sandwiches in my hands before giving me a kiss on the cheek and ushering me upstairs. Dana's hostile behavior toward me had eased with each drink she'd had today. I was still suspicious of her. Theo, I was sure, was ignorant of the plot against my family, and for my own peace of mind, I had to believe that Didi was too. I had become quite fond of the young woman in such a short space of time. But Dana *had* to have been involved in some capacity. Despite her recent kindness toward me, I didn't know how to look at her without suppressing a shudder, thinking about the role she could have played.

❖ ❖ ❖

I rose late the next morning feeling a lot better than I deserved, though my feet still ached from the dancing. Most of the others seemed to be faring much better than they had after the celebrations at the start of the week. Nook appeared paler than usual, and Ezra couldn't stop yawning, but they both greeted me with a smile when we all breakfasted together.

I hadn't seen Theo since watching him kiss that woman by the tent, but he arrived in the dining room only minutes after me, Suenna at his side. She had surprised me by not ranting and raving at Theo for his obvious show of affections toward another woman last night. Theo had said he was fond of Suenna in the Palace, and

I had assumed they were involved with each other. But then again, they wouldn't be the first couple to enjoy additional parties and I certainly wasn't one to judge.

Theo sat at the table and began informing us of the journey we were to make over the coming week. We would travel east to Ocridell before heading north, skirting around the Silent Canyons of Saqummatu and on to the Gištir Jungle. We had to travel by horseback, as the tramlines ended in Hudjefa and there was no easy route out of the volcano.

"You still haven't told us why we're trekking halfway across the realm to see that grumpy old bore," Nook said, looking at Theo expectantly. Despite their jibes, they all seemed to have a deep respect and tone of reverence whenever they talked about Silas. Whoever this man was, he had clearly made an impression on the group, and I could tell they were fond of him.

Theo laughed. "Is catching up with an old friend not reason enough?"

"He could at least meet us halfway," Nook argued. "That jungle gives me the creeps."

"He can't, he doesn't know we're coming."

The whole table became silent and very still. They all looked at Theo as though he were about to deliver the punchline to the joke. When he didn't, Ezra spoke up.

"Very funny, Theo," he said. "Last time we tried to sneak up on Silas, Nook almost lost the top half of his head."

"Shame he managed to stop himself." Suenna grinned at Nook. "Would've been an improvement."

"You know you're just jealous," Nook replied, ruffling

Suenna's pale blonde hair. "Not everyone can pull off such vibrancy."

Whatever hesitancy the group had to give Silas a surprise visit, it was forgotten as soon as some coffee and pastries were brought in. I noted that Theo favored the pistachio flavor, as he had three off the main platter and swiped another from Suenna's plate.

❖ ❖ ❖

We set off just after midday, leaving Didi in a fit of rage after Theo refused to let her join us. Despite her pleas and complaints that she was hardly ever allowed to leave Zingal, he was adamant.

"I don't understand why you didn't let her come with us," I said to him as we rode out of the estate.

"I don't need to explain to you how I run my district," he snapped, "and considering the state of *yours,* you can hardly question me about anything."

He said it quietly enough that the others behind us wouldn't hear. It was the first time he had spoken directly to me all day, and had avoided looking at me since yesterday afternoon.

"Touchy," I ridiculed, drawing out the two syllables. He had clearly developed yet another issue with me after we danced yesterday, and I didn't know—or care to know—what it was. Maybe I'd accidentally kicked his bad leg.

I hoped so, and I hoped it hurt.

Theo sighed. "She's the heir to Zingal, I can't risk her."

"Are you expecting this to be such a perilous journey?" I asked.

"*You're* coming aren't you?" he said, raising an eyebrow at me. "There's bound to be at least one unexplained death along the way."

I shrugged in response and looked back to where the others had fallen behind. Nook's gelding, Grazer, was certainly living up to his name, stopping every few paces to snatch any available vegetation in the surrounding area. Nook must have been familiar with him because he held the reins loosely, barely seeming to notice when they were wrenched from his hands.

To my intense relief, we each had our own horse. I had been assigned to Fergus, and was pleased to find that he was alert and responsive. Theo towered above me on Moth; the beast clearly held a grudge against me, as he would snap at me whenever I passed too close and watched me carefully with his mismatched eyes.

Yesterday's warm weather had given way to a cooler, cloud-covered sky that prematurely darkened the end of the day. When we reached the Ocridell border, we stopped to make camp for the night. Theo had decided against staying at an inn, as the road had been uncharacteristically busy with trade wagons and he wanted as few people as possible to know of our trip to the jungle.

The tents were erected quickly and efficiently by the four friends, who had the process practiced to perfection. I watched them all laugh and banter with one another as we ate around the fire, wondering how many nights they had spent exactly like this. If I was prone to feeling lonely, the sight might have invoked the emotion. I missed Verrill. And though I didn't see her everyday like I used to, I missed Asila as well. It was a comfort knowing that in Anzillu she was only ever a tram ride away from the Palace.

We had brought multiple tents for us all to sleep comfortably, but I insisted that they needn't bother putting one up for me. I didn't trust them enough to allow them easy access to me while I was unconscious, so preferred to stay outdoors.

"You sure we can't tempt you inside?" Nook teased, waggling his eyebrows. "We can keep each other warm."

I opened my mouth to reply, but Theo beat me to it.

"Leave her, Nook," he snapped, "she'd keep you warm by setting fire to your bedroll."

Nook winked at me. "Too bad. I like it hot. Goodnight, Erisa."

I bid both him and Ezra goodnight as they climbed into their tent. I didn't bother wishing Theo the same as he retreated into the other tent where Suenna was already settled. My irritation deepened as I heard her giggling at something he said. The pair laughed and chattered for what felt like hours and the same sharp, twisting feeling in my stomach returned.

Was I sick? For a fleeting moment, I panicked at the thought of pregnancy, but I religiously ate three boiled shadow cap mushrooms at the beginning of every week, so ruled that out. Luckily, the feeling abated as quickly as it had come, and I relaxed into an easy slumber.

❖ ❖ ❖

The city of Ocridell came into view midmorning. Our group rode through the sparse villages of the northern outskirts, and I noticed the paucity of inhabitants. These hamlets had once teemed with thriving communities, but were now almost deserted. I knew the population of my former district had been waning since my family's death, but seeing it up close for the first time felt like hot coals had been lodged in my chest.

We made a brief stop to refill our waterskins and to inquire about any food available for trade. No one was particularly hopeful of the latter, but we still had to try.

"Why didn't you take up your role as Lady?" Theo asked, as he and I walked to the well in the center of the settlement.

"Not only was my family murdered, but the entire staff and household of my estate. The Fox and I were supposed to be in that fire," I began, not even sure why I was telling him. "When the Autarch found us, he took us to the Palace, telling us that whoever was responsible would likely come for us if they knew we still lived. I was in my fourteenth year, so my options were somewhat limited."

"But that was what, ten years ago? Did you not consider returning in all that time?" he pressed.

"Occasionally," I replied, "but I have nothing to offer these people. I doubt they would want the Autarch's assassin and torturer to step back into command, even if my training for the role *hadn't* been cut short."

He pondered over my words while hoisting the water bucket up from the belly of the well. A prickle of awareness washed over the back of my neck, causing the hairs to stand on end. I shifted closer to Theo, bending down to where he leant over the well wall. He cringed away from my closeness, shooting me a scathing glare, but was held in place by the weight of the water bucket.

"We're being watched," I whispered into his ear, noticing the slight shiver that ran through him. He nodded once and continued his work.

I straightened and casually observed our surroundings. A few villagers were going about their everyday tasks, no one paying particular attention to us. I inspected the shadowed spaces between the dwellings, the feeling of someone's eyes on me never lessening, but found no one.

We started walking back to the others in silence, Theo casting furtive glances in every direction. I was about to snap at him for being so obvious when a hand closed over my mouth and an arm encircled my waist, hauling me backward into a dim alley between two houses. I bent my head forward before snapping it back into my attacker's face, but they were expecting it and used my movement to hold my head back, exposing my throat. I relaxed into the solid chest behind me as I recognized the tangy, familiar scent of sage and juniper.

His velvety voice caressed my ear. "Hello, my music."

Theo appeared in time to see Verrill peppering light kisses down the side of my neck, holding me flush against his body. He paused, releasing me and I tried to spin to greet him but he was focused on the yellowing bruises that circled my throat. He locked his gaze on mine, fury flaming bright in his hazel eyes as he turned to where Theo stood—looking equally as angry—shifting his eyes between Verrill and me.

I opened my mouth to stop Verrill, but he flew at Theo before I could get a single syllable out. The two men moved so fast I could hardly see what was happening, until Theo landed a blow to Verrill's chest, pushing him backward. Verrill corrected himself by pivoting, kicking out swiftly into Theo's gut, doubling him over and pouncing on the temporary weakness.

I watched for a moment, thoroughly enjoying myself. I knew from personal experience that Theo was a talented opponent, but to see him hold his own against Verrill was impressive, especially as he was still recovering from his injured leg.

"Leave it, Verrill," I said, and he dropped Theo from where he held him in a headlock.

"What the fuck?" Theo rasped.

"I warned you not to lay a hand on her," Verrill said in a low, dangerous voice, "and it looks as though at least *one* has touched her throat."

Theo straightened, his look of confusion turning into a mocking sneer as understanding flooded through him. Verrill wasn't wearing his disguise, and Theo had figured out who he was.

"Oh but she *loved* it," Theo taunted. "She was practically begging me to squeeze harder."

Verrill's gaze shot to me, silently demanding a confirmation. I rolled my eyes, pushing past the pair of clowns. I didn't need Verrill fighting my battles for me, and besides, it was old news. They followed behind me and I could feel the tension rippling through the air between them.

"I see you brought a horse for me," Verrill said as we reached the others, his belongings already sitting on the ground by the group. They looked at him with interest and then questioningly at Theo, who shook his head and strode over to Moth. We had brought a spare horse to carry the luggage, meaning that with a quick redistribution of saddlebags, Verrill was seated and we were on our way once more.

"You might have mentioned that he was coming too," Theo huffed, riding at my side.

"I didn't realize I needed to," I said, "you saw the note I sent."

He looked at me in disbelief before riding forward to join Ezra at the front of the group. Verrill took his place beside me.

"So, where are we going?" he asked, excitement brightening his face. My mood had improved dramatically since his arrival and I gave him a wide smile.

"The jungle," I answered, enjoying his look of mischief as he remembered our previous adventures there. I lowered my voice to continue, "I have so much to tell you, Ver. So much has happened since I left."

We fell back further behind the group, and I told him almost everything in hushed tones. The only thing I left out was my discovery of the barracks in the mountains, not because I didn't trust Verrill, but because I knew he was loyal to Csintalan. And even though I knew he wouldn't say a word if I asked him not to, I didn't want to put him in that position. I needed to find out exactly what that vision meant before making a judgment on the Autarch.

"Do you have the stone with you now, maybe I could see if it shows me anything?" he asked.

I shook my head. "No, I gave it back to Theo, I didn't want to see that again."

When we stopped that evening, we tested the theory. Verrill's cheerful expression dripped away, leaving an agonized look of terror. He practically threw the stone back to Theo before looking at me with wide, haunted eyes. He trailed his gaze over every inch of me, searching for something that wasn't there.

Not yet, anyway.

We set up an additional tent that night, and I slept in Verrill's arms, as I had done so many times growing up. He had been quiet that evening, refusing to tell me what he had seen. Even though I was desperate to know, and compare his vision to my own, I didn't push him on the matter, allowing him his privacy.

❖ ❖ ❖

The path thinned as we continued north, navigating between Ersetu and the Silent Canyons. I glanced behind me as the incessant scratch of Theo's pencil grated on my final nerve. When he wasn't frantically scribbling away each morning, he was sketching secretive little drawings into his notebook.

"Do you have to do that now?" I snapped, turning my head to glare at him. "It's driving me crazy."

"I consider your mere presence to be a lesson in tolerance, so we're even," he drawled, looking at me as though it bored him to do so.

I gestured to the canyon on our left. "That beast of yours will run us all off the edge if you're not paying attention."

"Moth will be fine," Theo replied without looking up again, the corner of his mouth twitching, "he happens to have an *excellent* rider. The way I see it, I'm perfectly capable of controlling him and occupying my time. And if you're worried, you clearly don't share the ability."

"Yeah, I probably *would* see it your way," I muttered, "but I just can't seem to get my head far enough up my own ass."

"Nice to know you're thinking about my ass," he said, winking at me as I turned back to scowl at him. He huffed out a smug laugh and the noise of it made me want to peel my skin off.

We set up a small camp in a cave along the edge of the cliff face. There wasn't enough room for the tents and the horses, so we lay the bedrolls directly around the fire. Theo had shot a small goat we had seen on the path with his bow, the arrow landing cleanly through one eye. We sat chattering while the meat roasted. Verrill plucked a cheerful tune from the strings of his lyre, much to the delight of Nook, who began prancing around almost instantly. Verrill tried to coax me into singing, but I refused, feeling the press of Theo's gaze on me.

Shadowcats ruled Saqummatu and prowled the shadows of the canyons with deadly ferocity. Though they were not often seen, their attacks always betrayed their presence. We decided to take turns in keeping watch over the entrance of the cave, allowing each other to rest peacefully.

Theo offered to take the first watch, agreeing to wake me at the second turn of a sandglass. I lay there, watching his silhouette against the moonlight, appreciating the way the muscles in his bicep bunched as he dragged a hand through his dark, tousled hair. I turned away from him, annoyed at myself for letting his looks distract from his vexing personality. After what felt like an eternity of failing to sleep, I sat up and noticed Theo staring at me.

"Can't sleep?" he murmured when I sat down beside him at the cave's entrance.

"No, you can go," I replied quietly, "I'll cover the rest of your watch."

He shifted closer, reaching around me to trap my body against the wall with his chest. I stopped breathing as his mouth swept across my neck, his lips only a hair's breadth from my racing pulse. He lingered, pressing his body against mine, pinning me in place. After a moment, he pulled back, waterskin in hand from where he had retrieved it from behind me. His smug look of satisfaction fractured slightly when he took in my flustered expression. From the moonlight, I could see the black of his pupils dilate into his green irises as they fell on my mouth. He'd become caught up in his own game; he *wanted* me. The knowledge sent a shiver down my spine as I decided to turn the tables.

I let my mouth part, sighing softly, looking at him through my lowered lashes. His attention was solely focused on me, on my tongue that ran over my bottom lip and on my fingers that I trailed across my collar bone and down to the fastenings of my chemise, toying with them. He watched me hungrily, his expression so intense that my cheeks flushed with heat.

I leaned forward, bringing my face so close to his that his lips parted to kiss me. Triumph made me giddy as I bypassed his mouth and trailed my tongue up the side of his neck up to his ear, coaxing a low groan from him.

"Do you want me now, Theo?" I whispered, attempting to sound mocking, but my voice was so breathless the effect was almost ruined. "Do you want to have me so close to where I killed your sister?"

I leaned back, smirking as he brought a hand up to grip my

jaw. A low, derisive chuckle escaped my throat when he *still* couldn't stop himself from looking at my mouth, despite the hatred etched onto his face. A cool gust of air blew into the cave, making me shiver. Theo let go of my face and stood, before removing his cloak and throwing it over my shoulders. He said nothing as he walked back toward the fire, stealthily adjusting his trousers as he went.

Warmth seeped into me, though it had little to do with the cloak. No matter how cruel I was or how hard I pushed him, Theo's interest just seemed to swell. He was like a sickness I couldn't shake. I smiled to myself, wondering how I could use this information and what I could gain from softening to him. By showing him more of myself, I could use it to manipulate him further.

At least, that was what I kept telling myself.

# Chapter 13

## Theo

I dreamt of Erisa. She was on her knees in front of me, her mouth so wonderfully engaged, I couldn't find it in me to miss the usual poison that seeped from it.

11th May

❖ ❖ ❖

"What are you even writing? I can't imagine you have such insightful thoughts during the night that you have to note them down every morning."

Erisa's voice punctuated the silence of the cave. Nook and Ezra had gone to see how far the nearest stream was and Suenna was still asleep on her bedroll, deaf to any noise before the sun had fully risen. Erisa sat with Verrill's head in her lap, his eyes closed as she stroked his hair.

I tried to suppress the wave of jealousy that washed over me at the sight. That was not expected or welcome.

"Yes well, if I was as inexperienced in the concept as you, I would doubt the possibility of an insightful thought too," I gibed, taunting for a response.

"Oh please, I've *forgotten* more than you've ever *known*," she snapped, huffing out a breath when she noted my triumphant smile. Verrill chuckled and my humor vaporized instantly.

"I write down my dreams from the night before," I said, in answer to her original question. "I find it helps to see recurring patterns in them. And, it gets them out of my head so I don't think about them again." Though last night's dream would definitely be hard to remove.

"Now that *is* sad," she scoffed, earning another smile from me. I tried not to dwell on the fact that enticing scathing remarks from her brought me immense joy. That was a lake I really *didn't* want to be fishing in.

I quickly stowed my notebook into the inside pocket of my jacket, praying to the gods that she wasn't interested enough to steal it and read last night's contents. The reminder had my blood heating, and I looked at the culprit again, where she still sat with the Fox. Her hair was braided down her back, and I longed to untie it, to run my fingers through the curls and wrap it around my fist. I shook my head, banishing the thought and seriously contemplating my evident insanity.

"I forgot," Verrill chirped from her lap, "I brought you something."

He reached over to his bag and pulled out what looked like a small wooden horse. Though it was hard to see clearly in the cave, the back end appeared to be burnt. The way Erisa beamed at Verrill had my gut twisting with envy; I had never earnt a smile from her that wasn't mocking. And I hated myself for caring.

❖ ❖ ❖

Disaster struck later that day. We were quickly washing in the stream Ezra and Nook had found when Verrill's mount broke free and bolted into the nearby trees. The cause of the panic shot straight after it, in the form of a black, lethal feline. I lunged for my bow and arrow, but the shadowcat had already disappeared.

"Fuck," I muttered, the sentiment echoing that of the others in the group.

"It fled north, maybe we can catch up with it," Ezra said hopefully.

I nodded, though we all knew that it was unlikely. Moth's eyes were wild, the whites showing as he tossed his head and I stroked his neck, trying to calm him. Guilt lanced through me as I thought about the poor creature. I should have been more careful, more alert of our surroundings.

"None of us saw it, you're not to blame."

Erisa had snuck up beside me and placed a hand on my forearm. Her eyes were wide as she looked at me and I waited for the snide comment that was sure to follow. Only, it never came.

"We'll have to double up," Nook said, coming to stand beside us. "Erisa, you can join me on Grazer and give your horse to Verrill." He looked down to where Erisa's hand still lay on my arm and smirked at me. "*Or*, seeing as Moth is already used to you …"

"Come on," I muttered to her, tilting my head toward Moth. "I'll boost you up."

To my profound surprise, she cooperated without complaint, waiting patiently while I tied our bags to the other horses. After finding an outcropping of rock to use as a mounting block, I sat astride Moth with Erisa in front of me.

"I didn't expect you to be the sentimental type," I said, watching her twirl the wooden horse in her hands, "does it mean something to you?"

"It belonged to my brother, Zeti," she said softly, "he loved horses, and my father whittled this for his third birthday. He never put it down. This is all I have left of any of them." Her voice was so sad that my arm moved instinctively to wrap around her, but I stopped myself, instead brushing my thumb over the back of her hand.

I had expected to be shot down, for her to hiss at me to mind my own business. My surprise was eclipsed only by my desire to know more, to learn everything I possibly could about this woman.

"I'm sorry about your family, Sunflower, truly. Having my father and Karasi die was difficult enough for me. I can't imagine losing the rest of them too."

"I didn't lose them all, I still have Verrill." She sighed happily, glancing at where he rode ahead of us, talking animatedly with Suenna and Ezra.

"Are you two lovers?" I asked, attempting to keep my voice casual. She laughed quietly and shook her head. I waited for her to explain, but she remained silent so I pressed, "He's clearly in love with you."

She remained silent for so long that I was relieved when she finally spoke again.

"Verrill and I are all that we have left. We fear how much we could hurt one another by saying the wrong thing, and certain topics can never be closed again once they're breached. He'll never ask because he knows I can't lie to him, and whether I give a favorable answer or not, everything would change between us. I think the thought of that is worse than the outcome." She let out a small chuckle before continuing. "Our parents used to tease us about how we would be married one day, and I was in love with him as a child and in love with the idea of us always being together. But after the fire, we were both so desperate to never be parted that we knew we wouldn't jeopardize that with a change of relationship."

Once my flare of jealousy subsided, my perspective on the Fox shifted as her words sunk in; I pitied him and pitied their situation. How many times must he have repressed his words and feelings in fear of losing her, and I wondered if she had ever done the same.

Eventually, I decided that she probably hadn't, imagining that if she wanted something, she would just take it, regardless of the consequences.

"Poor Foxy," I murmured, only half joking.

"He does well enough for himself," she said, "and he knows I'm too selfish to decide anything. I let him get away with far too much already."

I thought back to where I'd found him grazing kisses up her exposed neck, and agreed with her wholeheartedly. At least she could recognize her selfishness, acknowledging that she would keep him there—knowing he wouldn't say anything—to ensure that he never left. I quickly abandoned my musings, knowing that he would probably make good on his promise to skin me alive if he ever found out that I pitied him. I knew nothing of their situation and had no right to make assumptions.

Looking down, I found myself tracing the silver marks around her arm, astonished at her tolerance of the gesture. Something had shifted between us, and I couldn't stop myself from taking advantage of her newfound cordiality.

"So many deals," I whispered into her ear, "you must drive a hard bargain."

It struck me again how lethal this woman was, and how much influence she had in our realm. It made me wonder how many of the district Lords had promised her payment for nefarious deeds.

"I'd offer you firsthand experience," she mused, "but I don't think you could afford me."

"Of that, I'm sure." I chuckled, imagining the anxiety induced by waiting for her to come and collect payment, dreading the cost. I tried to banish the small part of my brain that told me to make a deal with her anyway, to ensure she'd have a reason to find me again once this was over.

❖ ❖ ❖

The next morning we awoke to a jolting screech that sounded like claws scraping through metal. I sat up in the tent I was sharing with Ezra and Nook, straining to hear any further movement, but the air was silent once more. I had suggested that we spend the night in the jungle to avoid showing up at Silas' door after dark, but after the restless night we'd all had, I think I would have rather risked our friend's wrath. The second the camp had been set up, the cacophony of shrieks, growls, and snapping teeth had begun.

I crawled outside, making as little noise or movement as possible, and nocked an arrow. The whole world was green; moss covered every inch of ground and tree trunk that wasn't sprouting plants or vines. The dense canopy clouded our view of the sky overhead, punctuated only by the emergent giants that towered at least a hundred feet above us. The damp, humid air clung to the back of my neck as I scanned the area.

A sliver of movement caught my eye and I slowly turned my head to the left. A reptilian creature roughly the size of a chicken was slinking up a thick vine, its beady blue eyes trained on a golden butterfly on the branch above. It was a bizarre creature; a long, snakelike body of dark green stripes on lighter green scales carried on four clawed bird feet. At its throat it had a flap of bright blue skin that morphed into red as it reached its scaled belly. The blue skin expanded like a toad, and I lifted my bow to take aim.

"That's not what made the noise."

I jolted, snapping my head to the right, where Erisa stood, tense and observant.

"How do you know?" I asked, my voice so low I almost couldn't hear it over the thundering of my heart.

"It's a gourqut; it doesn't make a sound," she answered, peering into the vines of the understory before glancing back at me, "and I wouldn't recommend eating it, you'd break out in hives and that pretty face would be ruined."

When she was happy that the unknown creature was gone, we packed up and hastily departed, everyone feeling eager to move on. During the next hour's ride, Erisa schooled me on the creatures we passed. The least threatening was the ground nesting yeuaww bird, which was named after the sound of its call. It had an orange turkey body with the feathers giving way to black scales half way up its long neck, where a snake's head weaved threateningly. Erisa pointed out that it was unusual to see one alone as they usually ran in flocks, using their large numbers as a defense to make up for their lack of wings.

"Verrill and I used to spend a lot of time here as children," she explained, when I had asked her how she knew all of this information, "we even drew a bestiary. It was terrible." She spoke too fondly for me to mention that I couldn't think of a place less suitable for children to play in.

The dense forest cleared as we reached the edge of Silas' land, and I saw Verrill whip his head around to look at Erisa, who nodded subtly. I couldn't ask her what that was about without betraying my own growing anxiety. Though I was once close with Silas, almost every interaction had always been on his terms, and he *hated* surprises.

Nobody spoke as his cabin came into view. It was large, but made entirely out of the same wood as the surrounding trees and covered in moss and creeping plants, so that it was completely camouflaged into the sprawling jungle. The same jarring shriek I'd heard that morning now echoed around us, and I shuddered as I saw the source of the noise.

About the height of an average man, the monster vaguely resembled an elongated, emaciated monkey. Its elbows and knees were joined with a wing of skin so thin that daylight revealed the blood vessels throughout. Sparse brown hair covered the thin body and crept up over the skeletal head, stopping above the wide red eyes that appeared too big for their sockets.

"That's a gexling," Erisa whispered, her eyes fixed on the creature as it let out another wail, "they're female and usually harmless. It's their male counterparts, the skuvlas, that you need to worry about."

Her words did little to console me. Nothing about the long bony fingers tipped with curved talons looked remotely harmless. As we came closer, I saw the double row of tiny sharp teeth inside its mouth before an incredibly long, thin gray tongue lashed out toward us, making everyone flinch. It watched us approach the cabin, its haunting red eyes never blinking.

The front door opened and Silas strode out, his face adorned with a wide, almost feral smile that displayed most of his white teeth. He had changed slightly since the last time I'd seen him; his usually shorn black hair had grown to his ears and stubble shadowed his jaw. His chestnut skin had deepened, indicating limited time under the volcano, but his black eyes were as alert as ever.

"Theodoraxion," he exclaimed brightly, looking from me to my friends, "and the rabble!" I heard the others laugh as I dismounted, lifting my hands to Erisa's waist without thinking, helping her down. Silas caught the action and stared at Erisa, before darting his gaze to Verrill. He looked back and forth at them with narrowed eyes, before huffing out a brief laugh.

"And who do we have here?" he asked, gesturing to them.

I introduced them quickly, and once the horses were untacked and secured in a paddock at the rear of the house, we went inside.

"I'm sorry for not sending word we were coming," I began, taking in the cozy interior of the cabin, "it was a spur of the moment decision. I know you dislike surprises."

"Fortunately, I was forewarned of your arrival," Silas replied, gesturing out of the window to where the gexling remained perched in the tree, watching us. "As nice as it is to see you all, I can't begin to imagine the reason why you came all this way to visit me."

He was a gracious host, supplying us with food and drink as pleasantries were exchanged between our old cavalry unit. Though he seemed genuinely pleased to see us, there was something skittish about his behavior, constantly casting quick glances to the ceiling whenever the floorboards would creak above us.

"Do you have guests?" I asked. "We can leave as soon as we've spoken." Though the thought of spending another night in the jungle was particularly unpleasant.

"Of course not." Silas chuckled. "No one is crazy enough to visit me here." As if sensing my need to speak to him alone, he ushered Erisa and I into a small adjoining room and we sat at a low wooden table. He gave me a pointed look before leaning forward and asking. "So, out with it, my friend, what can I do for you?"

I reached into my pocket to retrieve the leather pouch and handed it to him. Upon seeing the stone, he flashed me a look I couldn't decipher before staring back down at it. He tried to hand the pouch back to me, refusing to touch the stone, and I put it down on the table in front of us.

"Where in Ereshkigal's deep hell did you find that? And why would you split it?" he gasped, eyes wide. I'd never seen him so ruffled, and the sight made me almost nauseous with anxiety.

"Erisa's mother had it, then Karasi … found it," I explained, looking at the floor to avoid Erisa's hateful glare. But, rather than argue, she waited with bated breath while I gave Silas Karasi's note to look at.

"And where did Lady Ava get this stone?" he asked quietly, staring directly at Erisa, who had turned pale with the shock of the recognition. I didn't question how Silas knew who she was. Despite his youthful appearance, he was old and had hoards of knowledge beyond my comprehension. But I was glad that his tone was low enough for none of the others to overhear.

"She had it set in a pendant since I was a child. She never said where she found it, only that it was a gift from an old friend," Erisa explained, watching Silas warily. When he made no reply, she asked, "What do you mean it's been split?"

"Anyone with a functioning pair of eyes can see that it's half of a sphere," he huffed, but mused to himself, "I didn't think the bastard was crazy enough to lose it, but maybe that's *why* he's crazy …"

"But what is it," I asked, "and who lost it?"

He looked at me for what felt like an eternity. Long enough for me to shift uncomfortably in my seat and glance at Erisa, who looked equally baffled. Silas laughed quietly and nodded to himself, as though making a decision.

"Would you believe me if I said that it was the eye of my

daughter?" He chuckled, flashing me a mischievous grin.

I had to repress a sigh of frustration. "Silas, please, we don't have time for your games."

"All right my friend," he said, looking at the pouch, "when the gods … departed, each of the seven guardians of Irkalla bestowed a … *gift* upon their human successor. What you have there is one of these seven relics—or half of one at least—that was given to the heart of the realm; to the Autarch."

"What nonsense," Erisa hissed and turned to me. "I can't believe I let you drag me all the way out here to listen to the ramblings of some jungle freak."

"Be careful, girl," Silas warned before I could do the same. "I am older than your worst nightmare. And *far* more terrifying."

"I don't care how wrinkled your balls—"

Her snapping words were cut short as Silas shot out a hand and grabbed her arm. Her pupils flooded the orange irises in fear and her breath faltered.

She let out one keening, whining note.

I lunged for his arm, suddenly desperate to get it off her, but his other hand pushed against my chest, locking me in place. My whole body was frozen and I could do nothing but watch the color drain from Erisa's face while her too-full bottom lip began to tremble. Several seconds crawled by before he released us both and I could move again.

"What did you do to her?" I growled, the front of Silas' shirt clenched in my fists as I held him up to my height. I didn't even remember moving.

"Sit down you fool," Erisa snapped, and I swung my gaze to

look at her. She would have looked shaken if anger hadn't dominated her features. When I obeyed, she turned back to Silas, who was grinning like an imbecile. "You mean this belonged to the Autarch?"

"Not necessarily to the current Autarch, but to the original position, yes," Silas answered before turning back to me. "And I imagine Karasi wanted you to find the other half and put them back together."

"For what reason?" I questioned. No one I knew had ever spoken about these gifts from the gods, because no one—apart from Silas—really spoke of the gods at all; they were just half-forgotten stories, withering away over time.

He took a moment to choose his words. "Well, you want to destroy him, don't you? There's your answer." He nodded to the pouch. "The stone is the Autarch's power, a way to channel their magic. Without it, it becomes unstable. I can't even begin to imagine why it would be cleaved in two."

"When I touched it, I had a vision," Erisa said, not quite voicing the question I knew troubled her.

"It was the future," Silas confirmed, "or at least a version of it. The stone is known for presenting images of past and upcoming events. Do you have these visions too, Theo?"

He looked puzzled when I confessed I had never seen anything from touching the stone but nodded and said, "I'm afraid that's all I can tell you about it."

"Do you know of any way to track the other half?" Erisa pressed, her eyes calculating.

Silas sighed heavily and scratched the stubble on his neck.

"No, but I know who might. The Beldams in Khar'ra will be able to answer your questions. But you have to be careful, the old hags are sly and tricky. Though they won't necessarily lie, they'll give you riddles and double meanings. I wouldn't trust anything they say."

His expression was bitter, as if he were remembering something particularly unpleasant.

I clapped him on the shoulder. "Thank you, Silas. You're a true friend."

"Don't thank me for this, Theo. I only ask that we speak no more about it, this is old magic that I refuse to take part in. I know that I won't be able to convince you to leave it alone and I fear that my meddling will just cause more interference. But be careful, both of you."

# Chapter 14

## Theo

Thunder rippled through the air around me as the pressure of the storm pressed against my skin. I was blind, the blackness of night dominating my vision so completely that I could barely see my hands in front of my face. Lighting struck, blinding me again. The flash of light burned onto my retinas so I could still see it long after it disappeared. Thunder rolled, rattling my bones. Lightning flashed again, and this time, I saw a huge figure bearing down on me, silhouetted against the violent illumination. It stalked closer with every burst of light, and terror clawed at my senses as I made out the vast, outstretched wings and large, feral eyes of a dragon.

A warm glow traveled up its long throat and I had just enough time to see its enormous, razor-sharp teeth before fire consumed me.

15 May

❖ ❖ ❖

We stayed at Silas' cabin for three nights as we planned our trip to Khar'ra, enjoying the luxuries we had been missing while camping. Somehow, the cabin seemed to extend indefinitely, able to house each of us in our own room, no doubt due to Silas weaving some of his own enchantments into the foundations. He had never been forthcoming with his abilities or any personal details about himself, but everyone was entitled to their own secrets, and I had never found a reason to pry beyond my own curiosity.

Though our host catered for our every need, he was surprisingly elusive in his own home. He would often sit with us, reminiscing on our shared experiences in the last war, cracking jokes, and supplying us with wild tales that had us clutching the edges of our seats in anticipation. But, when he wasn't with us, he was nowhere to be found, something that Erisa picked up on before I had. I tried to tell her not to search for him, to not pry into his private life, but after being snapped at one too many times, I let her get on with it. She would have to learn the hard way.

Rising from the plush armchair in the sitting room, I went to the small window overlooking the paddock, checking for the third time this morning that the horses were alive and unharmed. Silas chuckled at my fear of them being eaten or whisked away by the jungle demons when I first broached the topic.

"Nothing comes onto my land uninvited," was all the cryptic bastard had to say on the matter. Somehow, that hadn't reassured me.

Despite writing it down, last night's nightmare still plagued me. Even though dragons lived almost exclusively in the northern kingdoms—only coming to Irkalla to nest—I still found myself searching the skies. I had never seen one up close, but the dream last night had felt so real. Like a bad omen.

Movement snagged my attention back to the room. Verrill had leapt from his own seat and was crossing the room to where Erisa had just entered, her expression victorious. It was so smug and triumphant that unease twisted in my gut, knowing that only something truly terrible must have happened to have made her *this* happy.

"What is this, Eris?" Verrill asked, inspecting her arm closely. I stalked toward them, having to angle my head around him to see what was wrong, barely resisting the urge to shove him out of the way. A new silver band encircled her left bicep. It was thicker than usual, and shimmered brightly, as if made from smoldering moonlight. In addition to the strange appearance, it lay too far above the others on her forearm to be a normal bargain mark.

Before I could speak, Silas strode into the room, his nostrils flaring in rage as he glared at Erisa. He moved to press something into her hand, which she slipped into her trouser pocket without so much as glancing at it. Then, with one last sneering look at her, he left.

"What have you done, Sunflower?"

❖❖❖

The wild noises of the jungle sounded worse now that we had left the somehow silent safety of Silas' cabin. We rode throughout the rest of the morning and into the afternoon, everyone shifting their eyes to every new sound or rustle of leaves.

Erisa refused to tell me what had happened with Silas, but I wasn't a fool. I knew she had somehow made a bargain with him. I had seen the proof on his right palm as he'd shaken my hand in farewell; a solitary gold line, glowing like embers cauterizing his skin. I couldn't decide whether it was her pure idiocy or flaming boldness to flirt with death that astounded me more.

"I hope you know what you're doing," I murmured into her ear, "he's a very precarious man to be bound to."

"What is he?" she asked, sounding entirely unconcerned.

Silas had always radiated pure power. I had never asked *what* he was or where he came from, knowing that he would tell me if he deigned me worthy of the information. All I knew was that he definitely wasn't human, or at least, not anymore.

"Dangerous," I replied in a low tone, enjoying the tremor that ran through her as my lips brushed her ear. She shifted, pressing her back flush against me.

She turned her head to the left, skating her cheek along my mouth until it reached her own, stopping when our lips were almost touching. My heart faltered, and my breathing would have too, had I not been so suddenly desperate to suck in the whispers of breath that she exhaled. My eyes were glued to her mouth, so entirely focused on how I wanted to taste it, to experience the tang of her spite across my tongue. My left hand dropped from the reins to her hip, digging my fingers into her skin to pull her even closer, barely managing to bite back a groan at the friction.

"I'm not surprised you think so," she breathed, trying not to appear as affected as I was, "deep down, lesser men always know their place beneath their superiors."

Her tongue darted out to swipe up once along my parted lips, before snapping her head forward again with a low, vindictive laugh.

"I'd happily let you show me my place beneath *you*, Sunflower," I rasped, nipping at her ear. Her titillating breath trembled as she leaned her head back, allowing me greater access to her neck and jaw. I indulged, caressing the soft surface with my mouth, not caring that any of our travel companions could easily see us by simply turning around. My hand was gripping her hip so hard as she moved against me that I was sure I was leaving bruises. The thought of it sent another thrill of pleasure through me, before I loosened them, skating my fingers up and along the inside waistband of her trousers, tracing her silky skin.

The deep flush that spread up her neck to her cheeks was so pleasing that I almost had to continue. But, the flash of her anger when I withdrew my contact was worth it, enacting my own revenge on her endless teasing.

❖ ❖ ❖

Dusk was approaching. Though the sky was not yet visible through the jungle canopy, the light shades of jade and emerald turned dark and menacing, shielding the terrors that were beginning to lurk around us.

"Stop!" Verrill's voice rang out through the eerie silence that had stalked us for the past five minutes. I followed his gaze, straining my eyes into the dim underbrush. My stomach rolled at the sight; what was once a child—no more than four feet tall—hung from a low branch by one desiccated, pale hand. A little girl, I guessed, by the long braids matted with blood from a gaping hole above her left ear. But that wasn't the cause of my nausea; it was the rest of her body that I could see through the tatters of her clothing that made vomit burn my throat.

She had been completely drained, becoming a depleted shell of empty, shriveled skin that swung limply from where she was fixed to the tree with a waxy gray substance. Every ounce of fluid, muscle and soft tissue was gone, leaving a gaunt, flesh-encased skeleton behind. Nook vomited, causing Suenna to follow suit.

"What are you doing?" Erisa hissed, when I dismounted.

"We need to take her body down to burn," I replied, looking at where her hand gripped my shoulder, "she deserves to find peace."

"Don't touch her," she snapped, her nails digging into my skin, "it's a trap. She's covered in mucus and once it sticks to you, it won't come off. You'd have to rip your skin off to get free."

My own horror was mirrored by everyone else, except Verrill, who looked at Erisa intently, questions burning behind his eyes.

"What did this?" Suenna asked, tears pooling in her brown eyes.

"A skuvla," Verrill answered. "We should find somewhere to sleep soon, before night falls; it's likely still close by, and they're nocturnal."

We ate in silence, chewing half heartedly and jumping at every noise that sounded in the darkness, which consumed the outer border of our campfire's light. Erisa and Verrill were convinced that the skuvla was following us, based on the foul odor of death and decay trailing in the humid air. But they were confident that as long as the fire remained bright, we'd be safe. Apparently, skuvlas hated the light.

I sat at the entrance to the tent, my friends behind me as I watched Erisa and Verrill adding more wood to the three fires burning around the camp. They were speaking in hushed tones, too low for me to hear. It was only when they added to the fire protecting the horses that I could pick up a few words.

" … don't understand why you wouldn't just let … could've left him there … don't need him anymore, we could carry on by ourselves to … " Verrill's disjointed voice quipped.

"I don't have to explain myself to you, Ver," Erisa snapped, irritation amplifying her voice. He seemed undaunted by her temper, pushing her further and I strained to hear more.

"I don't like him. He's not trustworthy and yet you're becoming so … familiar with him," he said, brushing a loose strand of hair behind her ear. "Please, just be careful, my music. Don't forget what their family did to us."

Indignation boiled beneath my skin. I didn't care what he said about me, but for him to blame my entire family for something that they had no part in angered me. Despite my qualms about Karasi's role in their misfortunes, my remaining family were completely innocent. How could *she* be angry when she had murdered my twin?

"I haven't forgotten," Erisa hissed, ire crawling back onto her features, as though she *had* forgotten and was furious with herself for it. She handed Verrill the collection of small, leftover bones from dinner, wrapped in paper. "Put these in the dark over there to draw it out, I'm going to find some more wood, everything is so damp around here."

Without thinking, I grabbed my bow and went after her, slipping out of the tent while their backs were turned. I followed her into the dark jungle, only stopping for mere seconds to allow my eyes to adjust, so as not to lose her. Though I made every attempt to keep my steps quiet, they seemed deafening in comparison to her silent footfalls. She stopped at a fallen tree, and began snapping away thin twigs.

Raising my bow, I nocked an arrow, aiming at her temple. I needed this to be over, this repulsive, sick fascination I was beginning to have with her. But my arm lowered of its own accord, my anger and self-loathing resurfacing with a vengeance at my own weakness.

I watched her for a few moments before pouncing, snaking an arm around her waist and a hand around her throat. Her body froze in shock before she reached for a dagger.

"You should be more careful, Sunflower," I purred, my anger still simmering beneath my skin. "Who knows what sort of untrustworthy creatures you'll find sneaking up on you. Even those you're so *familiar* with."

She struggled in my hold, and I loosened it enough for her to spin and face me. Her eyes glittered in the dim light, hatred brightening them from within. Crowding her with my body, I walked us backward, pressing her against the wide trunk of the fallen tree.

"I should've known you'd be eavesdropping like a common rat, always scurrying around and sticking your flea-ridden nose into everyone else's business. Scamper back to the sewers like the rodent you are, Theo." She practically spat my name, though her lips parted as I squeezed my hand around her throat, dropping her gaze to my mouth that was only inches from hers.

My last thread of self-control snapped, and I crashed my lips to hers, desperate to silence her hateful mouth, to tame it into soft pliancy and soothe the caustic burn of her corrosive words. Her head tilted, deepening the kiss and her hands gripped my hair tightly, forcing me closer. She wrenched at the strands, the pain causing pricks of pleasure to dance down my spine.

I released her throat, dropping both hands to cup behind her thighs to lift them around my waist. Our moans blended as I ground into her, absolutely wild with desire. I wanted her, *needed* her.

Just once. Just this once to get her out of my system, so I could return to hating her in peace and finally be able to kill her. She fumbled with the fastening of my trousers as I practically ripped her bodice open, before trailing devouring kisses and bites down her neck and chest.

A high-pitched, keening wail sounded above us, and I looked up in time to see a dark body drop from the tree over our heads. I flung Erisa to the side, stepping to shield her with my body.

There was just enough light for me to make out the stretched, prowling limbs of what could only be a skuvla. Like the gexling, its gangling form was thin and wiry, but instead of a round skull, its head was elongated into a long, narrow snout that ended in a lethally sharp point. My mind swirled with grisly images of it burying that snout into a person's skull, liquifying their insides and sucking them back out.

I looked to where I'd dropped my bow; it lay a few feet in front of the creature that was watching us with enormous black eyes.

"Give me your dagger," I breathed to Erisa, who began moving as I slowly backed us away. "As soon as I say, run back to the camp, as fast as you can."

"Don't be ridiculous," she hissed, but pressed a blade into my palm anyway.

"Now!" I let the dagger fly, hitting the skuvla in the side and charging toward it, dropping at the last moment to slide in front of it and sweep its spindly legs from under it. It fell with a quiet thud as I gripped my bow, but instead of being disoriented from the fall, its clawed hind legs flipped and rotated its sender body right way up as it prowled toward me, snapping. Another small blade flew past my ear and sunk into the creature's neck, halting it for half a second, giving me enough time to reach for my fallen quiver and extract an arrow.

It was almost on top of me before I shot it clean though its head and Erisa's boot flew out to kick it away before it fell onto me.

"Let's go back, we won't need the extra firewood anymore," she said, cringing as she extracted her daggers from the skuvla's glossy skin.

❖❖❖

It was a relief when the dense jungle morphed into an open, sunlit forest the next afternoon. We stopped to refill our waterskins in a little stream that meandered through small clearings dotted throughout the trees, deciding to stop in one for the night. Everyone dispersed to different areas of the brook to wash and relax. I was finishing up a letter to Corbin when I heard faint echoes of music from a nearby meadow hidden by the trees.

I walked toward it, observing the beams of sunlight that filtered through the gaps in the glowing leaves, reflecting off pollen that was floating on the soft breeze. Erisa was sitting on a mossy tree stump next to the stream, face tilted up toward the warmth of the sun. Her eyes were closed in blissful enjoyment as Verrill lounged on the ground beneath her, his hands dancing easily across the strings of his lyre.

Standing in the shadow of an oak, I watched the pretty scene. The music slowed to a mournful melody, Verrill's eyes never leaving Erisa's face. As if she could feel his attention on her, she looked down at him with a small smile, before opening her mouth and starting to sing.

The wordless notes pierced the air and cascaded across the wildflowers, the melancholy sound contrasting with their vibrant color. I felt as though the air had been sucked from my body. I had never heard anything so beautiful. And I realized, it was the same voice that I'd dreamt about all those weeks ago, yet somehow it was different.

I listened, not knowing whether the emotion coursing through me was the highest elation or the deepest sorrow, only that I could almost hear my own soul. My spirit was called to that indelible tune.

Every note that passed her lips was caressed by one of Verrill's. He was so enraptured that I doubted he had even noticed that he'd risen to one knee at her feet, wavering his own melody to harmonize effortlessly with hers, matching every contour and crescendo. His entire being was playing only to her, the rawest proclamation of love I had ever beheld and not a single word was spoken. No matter how much I wanted her, I would never have that, could never compare to that.

My throat was painfully full as Erisa's final note scorched my entire being before it faded, breaking me free from her siren's call. I finally turned away from the idyllic, dreamy scene that would, no doubt, haunt my nightmares.

# Chapter 15

## Erisa

The rain began at dawn, creating a loud, persistent pattering against the tent that roused me from my sleep. Verrill snored softly beside me, his features relaxed and boyish, reminding me of when we were little. I watched him as I let my mind wander over everything that had happened in the last few days.

Theo had saved my life, and it was as though he hadn't even given it a second thought. He could have jumped back when the skuvla had leapt from the tree, leaving me to my fate. But he hadn't; he had actively pulled me out of danger, not even realizing that if that creature had so much as touched my bare skin, it would have been over for me. And when he'd told me to run, I didn't know why I hadn't, why I had stayed behind and helped him when he had just given me the perfect opportunity to be rid of him.

I was under no illusion that I had a single selfless bone in my body. I rarely did anything for anyone unless it benefited me in some way. So, what the hell would I gain from saving Theo? I didn't have an answer, only that the thought of him dying and it not being at my hand made me so uncomfortable that I had to push the thought aside. I hid it away with the memory of Theo's mouth on mine and how the heat of his kiss had ignited me from within.

The silver band around my left bicep shone as I traced a finger across the surface, slightly thicker than the others. It still had the same burning appearance as it had when the bargain had first been struck, as though it was scoring into my flesh over and over again. An image of Silas flashed in my mind, making me shudder; I had never met anyone whose aura would visibly pulse with power. He terrified me, but it appeared that I wasn't *quite* sane enough to turn down an opportunity of trapping him in a deal.

I definitely had a problem.

He had been acting cagey since we'd arrived at his cabin, trying too hard to appear relaxed. I knew from that first day that he was hiding something, so every time he disappeared, I skulked after him until I found it. No matter how formidable someone might be, there were always secrets to be found and weaknesses to extort.

"I worry about you, Eris," Verrill muttered sleepily, and I looked down to see him watching me inspect the mark on my arm. He reached out a hand to brush a finger lightly across the other bands encircling my forearm. "One day, you'll back the wrong person into a corner and they'll decide that killing you is far easier than owing you a favor."

"You can't kill the person you owe, Ver."

His brows pinched in concern. "No, but that doesn't mean someone else can't kill you for them, and there's a lot of people who would do anything to be free of you. You're too conniving for your own good."

A deviant smile spread across my face. "But I have such a talent for blackmail, it would be a shame not to use it."

He shook his head and stretched back out on his bedroll. I copied the action, getting comfortable before musing quietly, "Do you think there's a limit—like how you can only owe six bargains at a time? What happens when I run out of space on my arms?"

"Please don't make enough to find out," he said. "There's only so much a body can take, and I've never heard of anyone having made as many deals as you."

I smiled again. "You worry too much. Besides, one of these marks belongs to you."

"The only bargain I'll ever make," he replied, placing his hand in mine, palm up, presenting the single golden line to me. "I dread the day you decide to call it in."

"I won't," I promised. "I like having you tied to me. That way you can never leave me."

"That suits me just fine. I'll happily belong to you forever."

"I know," I teased, nudging him playfully with my shoulder. "Come on, we should get up, I can hear the others moving around."

Breakfast was a miserable affair; the ceaseless rainfall soaked into everyone's clothes and shoes, causing a chill despite the warm spring air. We packed up and left without delay, hoping to make it to Khar'ra by late afternoon. The promise of somewhere warm and dry to stay in the city spurred us on.

Theo hadn't spoken to me since the skuvla attack, when he'd pulled me to the side before we reached the camp and thanked me for saving him. He hadn't even let me respond before returning to his tent. I had been about to thank him in return, but decided that if he couldn't be bothered to wait for my reply, he didn't deserve it anyway, and considered the case closed.

The deluge continued as we rode, and my mood soured with every cold drop that ran down the back of my neck. Theo's silence persisted well into the morning, speaking only to offer me food or water from his bag.

"Have you been to Khar'ra before?" I asked, not knowing why I suddenly cared about making conversation with him.

"Once, after the last war finished," he said. "Nook, Ezra, Suenna, and I traveled around the realms, wanting to see as much as possible. It's a strange place, everyone watches everyone else, but not always in a bad way. It felt like both the safest and most dangerous place in Irkalla."

"What do you mean?" I pressed, trying to temper my excitement at hearing him say more than one word at a time. It was unusual for me; I couldn't remember the last time I'd actually been interested in hearing someone speak, aside from Verrill, Csintalan, and Asila.

"It's as though you're never alone there. Someone is around every corner, but you never know if they're there for innocent or nefarious reasons. One night, Suenna went missing; a cloaked man grabbed her from us in the street and just disappeared. We searched frantically for hours before he returned her. Turns out, he'd taken her to pull out one of her back molars that had been bothering her for days. We were all completely baffled, especially when he refused any payment offered, only asking that we leave the rotten tooth on his neighbor's doorstep."

"And she was awake the entire time?" I said, not knowing

what to think of this ridiculous story.

"Yeah, she said he barely touched her, only enough to remove the tooth. A wise decision by him, because I would've broken each of his fingers if he had."

I felt that hot, twisting feeling in my stomach flare up again at his words. Was that … jealousy? Fascinated, I inspected the strange emotion, not remembering a time when I'd felt it before and not sure how to get rid of it now. The realization had me almost laughing out loud. I was *jealous* of Suenna and her relationship with Theo.

"Are you two … together?" I asked, preparing to sink my blade into his thigh if he confirmed my previous suspicions. He let out a booming laugh, his chest shaking against my back and I snapped, "Are you going to answer or not?"

"Why," he purred, "are you jealous, Sunflower?" He chuckled as I sunk my elbow into his gut behind me, and I could hear that stupid smirk on his face as he said, "We've only ever been good friends. *You* are more Suenna's type than I am, and she'd likely be disgusted that you thought otherwise."

"Then she clearly has excellent taste," I retorted, facing forward to hide the smile trying to stretch itself across my face.

"Undoubtedly," he agreed, pressing a soft kiss to the top of my head. The action was so tender that it warmed my chest, and I allowed myself to forget—just for a moment—why I should hate it and to relish the feeling of his arms around me.

❖❖❖

Khar'ra *was* strange. The entire district appeared to be surrounded by a wall, but it was too low and narrow to keep anything out and was made entirely out of what looked like bones. As soon as we passed through the seemingly pointless iron gates, the air changed, becoming thick with magic that pressed against my skin like tendrils of smoke. If Theo noticed it too, the only acknowledgement he gave was a slight tightening of his hands around the reins. We led our group toward the heart of the city, the swirling wind moaning through the towering buildings like unsettled spirits, whipping at my damp clothes, and making my teeth chatter.

It was only late afternoon, but the city was gray, as though it had never progressed past dawn on a cloudy morning. In fact, I struggled to find a single flash of color and looked back to our group, discovering that any vibrancy had been leached away. Even Nook's hair had lost its fiery hue, appearing dull and lackluster instead. Pale eyes watched us from windows and dark corners as we moved past, and I could feel their stares as though they were physical touches scraping across my skin. I now understood what Theo had meant by them always watching.

A child, about twelve years of age, appeared in front of Moth, causing him to spook and toss his head in agitation. Theo slid a warm arm around my waist, holding me steady. Had I not been so cold, I would have pushed it away, repelled by his casual touch.

"Follow me. They've been waiting for you to arrive," the child said, but remained standing in front of us, their black eyes observing. I couldn't guess their gender, owing to their shaved head and androgynous features. They wore gray baggy clothes, the only color on them being a blue circle tattooed around the crown of their head.

"Lead the way then," Theo urged, his voice strong enough to calm the nerves that were creeping up the nape of my neck. He must have known something I didn't, because if it were up to me, there would be no way in hell I'd be following that creepy kid anywhere.

"She's taking us to the Beldams," Theo murmured to me, as though sensing my confusion.

"How do you know she's a girl?" I asked him.

"Males are not permitted to enter the inner temple," he explained, "all of the acolytes must be female, to honor Ereshkigal."

"How do you know all of this?"

"Silas," he said simply, and I repressed a shudder at the mention of his friend. Apart from the Priestesses who would come and lecture us as children, I didn't know a single person who still believed in the gods, and even then, I was sure they only chose that vocation to avoid paying their taxes.

Khar'ra was barely mentioned in the other districts, and honestly, I could see why. It was dreary, and even by Irkallian standards, felt sinister and macabre. Everything seemed slightly odd or distorted here, the buildings were crooked and the rats had six legs instead of four.

For the next ten minutes, we followed the child, and I could barely keep my eyes from darting between the strange, mutated animals and the direct but vacant stares of the citizens. She led us alongside the bank of a trench filled with stagnant water, thick mist grazing the surface and obscuring whatever lay on the other side.

Finally, we arrived at a narrow stone bridge, its access barred only by a small wooden gate, which the girl unlocked and ushered us through. The mist enveloped us halfway across, the gray veil snatching at our vision until we were blind. It reminded me of the swirling mists that encased the islands of Katmu; they were nicknamed the Shrouded Isles for this very reason.

Theo tightened the arm he still had around me when the mist cleared and the temple came into view. It was smaller than I expected, with a cylindrical body of dark lava stone surrounded by tall, coiling pillars that curved around the roof to create a spiral dome. It would have been elegant, had the coils been uniform instead of varied and disjointed twists, giving it a haunting atmosphere.

A dozen acolytes came forward to take the horses, all dressed in the same uniform, though their scalp tattoos were slightly different. Most of the older looking girls had thicker blue bands encircling their heads, two of whom having additional black runes inked over the top. Their long gray robes swirled the mist lingering at our feet and I wrinkled my nose in disgust when I noticed the ground writhing with shiny brown cockroaches.

"Only three," one of the girls said sharply, halting Nook, Ezra, and Suenna where they trailed behind Theo, Verrill, and I. Theo looked back at Ezra, who nodded and held back with the other two.

I snorted out a laugh as Theo tried to smooth out the wrinkles in his jacket.

"What?" he said, grinning at me as we moved toward the temple. "First impressions matter, especially as we're asking them for help."

"Oh yeah? What impression did I make on you?"

He huffed out an amused breath. "You don't make

impressions, Sunflower. You make cavernous holes."

We were ushered up the stairs to a tall, arched door that led into the temple. Even though darkness had fallen, I still had to allow my eyes to adjust to the dimness inside. The circular room appeared empty, with a single candle in the center, the area of illumination not even reaching the walls. The door slammed shut behind us and I whirled around to find that it had disappeared into the stone. My hand went immediately to a dagger at my hip when a low cackle echoed around the circular room.

"That will not help you here, girl," the voice said. It was raspy and dry, as though the owner had spent one too many nights smoking silkleaf and laying into the liquor. We turned around the room, trying to find the source, but we were the only ones standing within the candlelight.

It smelled dank and musty, and I could hear the whispers of robes trailing across the black wooden floorboards in the shadows around the dark outer perimeter.

"Over here, my sweets," the voice cooed, and I spun to see three robed figures emerging from the shadows, their hoods covering their faces.

They clearly had a flair for the dramatic.

The candle in the middle of the room shone brighter, in tandem with six other torches that ignited on the walls. I stared in bewilderment at the warped proportions of the room; it was at least three times the size it had appeared from the outside. Seven stone columns climbed the walls to the ceilings, each of them depicting one of the guardians of Irkalla. I couldn't remember them all, but I recognized the menacing forms of Ereshkigal, Neti, and Nergal.

I turned my attention back to the three figures who were now sitting on the floor in front of the candle, gesturing for us to do the same. Obeying, I sank to the ground along with Theo and Verrill, already uncomfortable and cursing the way the floorboards dug into my ankles.

It was only then I realized I was sitting in front of the Beldams, the ladies who ruled this district, and I had no idea how to address them or what manners I should adopt. I decided to just stay still and be quiet, finding it hard to care about proper etiquette when my socks were still wet and their temple reeked of mildew.

"We know why you are here," the rasping voice announced when we were all seated on the opposite side of the candle. It sounded as though it was the middle woman speaking, though I couldn't be sure as her hood was still covering her face. Before we could offer a response, she continued, "Show us the stone, boy."

Theo said nothing as he retrieved the stone from his pocket and held it out to her. None of us managed to contain our gasps as the middle woman lowered her hood. If I had thought she'd indulged in too many consecutive nights of putrefaction based on her voice, her appearance more than confirmed it.

Her face was gaunt, her skin the palest shade of gray and stretched over her skull like translucent paper, showing every blue vein and blood vessel beneath it. Her cheeks were sunken and hollow, pinching at the narrow mouth of brown teeth concealed by thin blue lips. But it was her eyes that had caught everyone's attention; or the lack of them. Where her eyes should have been, lay only dark, empty sockets of shriveled skin. She had one wide, blue eye tattooed onto her forehead, sitting just beneath the inked band encircling her bald head. It was so detailed and precise that it looked almost real.

A white, bony hand emerged from her dark gray robes and she gripped Theo's wrist where he held the stone out in his open palm. It was so bright and vibrant compared to the muted grays that it almost hurt to look at.

"Look, sisters," the woman said, bending over Theo's hand, "the Orb of Nanaya. It is finally before us. And how it *calls* to me."

"It's power was stronger before the break," the woman on the left said.

"And will be again, when it is whole once more," said the one on the right. All of their voices had the same hoarse tone, which—despite being low—seemed to echo around the room.

"How was it split," I asked them, "and how do we join them back together?"

"It was pecked in half by a naughty crow who kept one piece and offered the other to his songbird," the left replied. "Greedy, ungrateful little bird."

"The two halves will sing to each other," stated the right, "there will be nothing you can do to stop their unification."

"Where's the other piece?" Theo asked, his voice deep and smooth compared to their whispered croaks.

"It resides in Ganzir," the middle woman offered. Unease began to creep up my spine from hearing the ancient name of the Palace. I felt Verrill stiffen beside me.

"It never left," continued the woman on the left.

"And will never leave incomplete," said the right.

What were these women? Some kind of deranged act for a past, present, and future freak show?

"I received a vision from the stone," I began, looking at where the middle woman still had Theo by the wrist. "Was it the future? Will the Autarch destroy Irkalla?"

"What will you do when I say yes?" the one on the right mused. My stomach sank at her words as she practically confirmed what I had seen. I had to find a way to stop Csintalan.

"But why would he do it?" I asked, silently begging them to just give a straight answer.

"Why does the starving boy forgo a meal when presented with an outstretched hand and a kind word?" said the middle, only fueling my irritation. Though I hadn't been expecting much, their answers were completely useless.

"If you're not going to give us any helpful information, we'll just leave," Theo growled, finally managing to release his hand and shoving the stone back into his pocket.

"But we have not yet taken you below," the right said to me without looking at Theo or Verrill. "There are so many horrors awaiting you inside our temple, Erisa Anzû. Wouldn't you like to see them?"

Wow, *tempting*.

The men on either side of me bristled, and Verrill gripped my arm as Theo's voice rang out loudly in the quiet room. "She's not going anywhere with you alone."

"Look, sisters," said the middle cheerfully, "see how they swarm her."

"How sweetly their hearts will break for her," chirped the right. "Can you hear how she'll tear them out, dear sisters?"

Theo began shifting to his feet. "This is madness," he hissed.

"You'd know, wouldn't you, Theodoraxion Lusilim," said the left. "How many times has she driven you *mad* with longing? When lust clouds your vision and you find yourself alone in a cold stream, stroking your cock to the thought of her wrapped around you. Her siren song could lure you down into the deepest depths of depravity."

I almost laughed out loud at the woman's unexpected vulgarity. Theo, to my surprise, turned to wink at me without any hint of embarrassment on his face. But Verrill's hand tightened on my arm and she turned to him.

"And you, Verrill Fedelis," the woman continued, her tone mocking, "how many lovers have you taken with closed eyes, seeing only *your music* behind your lids? You've let so many into your bed, but none into your heart. Tell me, pretty Fox, when you touched the stone, which vision frightened you more; the one where you saw the flesh bubble away from her bones, or the one where she was round with your child?"

"That's enough!" I snapped, unable to hold back the rage surging through my veins at the sight of Verrill's pale, haunted face. The women quieted.

"Is there a way to defeat the Autarch?" Theo asked, sounding tired.

"Of course there is," the one in the middle said. She smiled, showing every jagged, stained tooth. "But to master one, you must master them all. Only the combined relics of the gods have the power to change the realm."

"What are these items? Where are they?" I pressed, though the terrifying images Silas had planted into my head made me fear their response. They flashed in my mind in quick succession; a dagger cleaving through scaled flesh, a shield bowing beneath a crushing weight, and tears of blood streaming down a face wild with fury.

"Come below with us, my dear," the middle woman urged, "and we'll give you the answers you seek and more."

She held out one of her skeletal hands to me and I reached out one of my own, my heart pounding in my chest.

"Erisa," Theo whispered, his dark green eyes wide with concern.

Before either of us could say anything more, the woman's hand clasped around mine, and she hauled me to my feet with surprising strength. Too fast for my eyes to process, I was being shoved down through a trap door, the stone steps damp and slippery. I heard the yells of Verrill and Theo from behind me, but when I tried to turn back, I was pushed forward and down into a dark tunnel.

A few seconds later, gravity seemed to tilt, and the tunnel opened into a wide, towering chamber. There were no sculptures or decorations apart from a huge mosaic that covered the entire floor. The image depicted a fur-covered woman, only she had the head of a lioness with long, gray pointed ears that stood upright. Her long, clawed fingers matched the sharp talons of her hawklike feet, which rested on either side of a donkey's back. Snakes hung from her shoulders and wrapped around her waist and legs. Two dogs and a pig flanked the braying mule.

"Who is that?" I asked, unable to hide my bewilderment.

"Lamaštu," all three women said together, their voices merging into an awful, ubiquitous timbre, no longer the separate voices of the past, present, and future trio they'd presented upstairs.

I had heard little of Lamaštu, and from that image, decided I wanted to keep it that way.

I stepped back as the women walked slowly toward me, their hoods concealing their faces. They began circling me and I struggled to push down the wave of nausea that had my heart pounding in my throat. I opened my mouth to tell them to let me go when they all reached out and joined hands.

An ache formed at my temples as the dark room vanished and I found myself flitting through visions and images faster than I could comprehend them, until one of them settled; an old, worn key, the metal nicked and dull from use.

"The key of Neti; the great gatekeeper of Irkalla." The voice of the Beldams rang out around me, the eerie resonance making my skin crawl.

The visions continued, as did the voice, providing me with knowledge of each of the seven gifts. The shield of Nergal, the god of war. The snake's head of Namtar, the god of fate. The songbird of Pazuzu, ruler of the wind. The dagger of Dumuzid, the god of agriculture, and his sister Geshtinanna, goddess of scribes, and her stylus. And finally, Ereshkigal, the goddess of death, holding the Orb of Nanaya in her palm.

My head continued to swirl with images, and with each passing second the pain in my temples grew. Another image, and for a second, I thought I was seeing myself before realizing it was my mother. She stood above me, no more than ten years of age, clutching a fistful of dawn waxcap mushrooms.

"Hello, I'm Ava," she chirped with a bright smile as she held out her empty hand to me.

Pain exploded in my head as the next image formed. A dark-haired woman lying on an altar, covered in blood. A figure towered above me but my gaze was downcast, daring only to look at the enormous clawed feet of an eagle before me. I threw my arms out to lay them on the ground at the figure's feet, and realized that the blood covering the woman was from the deep lacerations in my own wrists.

"I will do anything!" I said, but the pained male voice was not my own, nor was the language I spoke.

My head swam in agony as the vision changed. All I could make out was a body falling toward me, and I reached out, desperate to catch whoever it was. I didn't see whether my hand closed successfully around the woman's ankle before darkness swallowed me completely.

# Chapter 16

## Erisa

The sound of raised, angry voices filtered through my unconsciousness, beckoning me away from the dark oblivion of sleep. My head was pounding, and I felt as though it was detached from my body, floating above the ground.

"—not our fault her mind was unable to handle so many truths. Her susceptibility to the stone should have warned her away from seeking more."

"Then you should've used me, it doesn't show me anything!"

"Where did you think your dreams come from, stupid boy?"

Warm hands crept beneath my shoulders and knees, and then my body was weightless, the warm smell of cedar and ginger enveloping me. I pried my lids open and the dark spots clouding my vision ebbed away to reveal Theo's face, his eyes wild with unrestrained rage. Tremors wracked through my freezing body, and he tightened his arms, cradling me to his chest.

His mouth opened, but before he could form his retort I heard Verrill's voice to my left. "If she's hurt, I'll burn this place to the ground."

My head swam as I dragged my eyes over to him. He was standing between us and the three Beldams, a knife outstretched in his hand. We were still in the inner temple and the menacing face of Lamaštu leered up at me from the floor. The woman on the right cackled, the sound so sharp and harsh, it ricocheted around the room.

"Then be quick with it, Fox, you never know when your last grain of sand is due to fall," she said.

I groaned at the violent pulsing in my skull and the two men whipped their gazes toward me, and I met the deep green of Theo's eyes, which were almost black in the dim light. He looked up to Verrill who nodded sharply and stayed rooted in place, knife still poised, while Theo carried me behind him and out of the room.

"We'll be seeing you soon, Feline," a voice trailed after us.

Once we emerged into the main temple, I tried to turn and look for Verrill.

"He's coming, I can hear him," Theo murmured into my hair. It was only when I heard his approaching footsteps for myself that I allowed myself to succumb to the ensnaring lure of unconsciousness once more.

✤ ✤ ✤

Something cold and wet nudged my hand. Groaning, I opened my eyes and peered at my surroundings. I was lying on a thin bed in a gloomy, sparse room that smelled of stale air, but it was dry and I finally felt warm again. Apart from the bed, the only furniture was a small chest of drawers and a single wooden chair, which sagged under Theo's sleeping form.

My hand was jostled again and I looked down to find a dog pressing its damp nose into my palm, its pale blue eyes stark against its dark brown fur.

The door creaked open and an elderly man walked in, carrying a tray laden with two bowls and a hunk of bread. My stomach growled at the meaty scent of the stew. Theo jolted awake and his eyes instantly flew to me, softening when he realized I was awake.

"Will you be needing anything else?" the man asked, placing the tray at the end of my bed and looking at Theo.

"No, thank you. We'll be leaving within the hour," Theo responded, still not shifting his gaze from me.

"Very well. To me, Shula," he called to the pretty bitch leaning her head into my touch. Obediently, she leapt up and followed him, her tail wagging as he muttered, "Good girl."

"How are you feeling?" Theo asked, shifting his chair to the side of the bed. He looked tired, and the pale gray light filtering in through the small window gave me no indication on what time it could be.

"What happened?" I questioned as I sat up against the headboard.

"A few minutes after you disappeared into the inner temple, you started screaming," he said, running a hand through his already tousled dark hair. "It sounded as though you were being ripped apart. The second we heard you, we were at the door. They'd locked it somehow and I had to practically rip it off its hinges to get through. Then we found you in that room, writhing on the floor, unconscious. I thought Verrill was going to kill them. I considered stopping him, only because I wanted to kill the old hags myself, but getting you out was more important."

"But you said men aren't allowed inside the inner temple," I jested, trying to lighten his dark mood. "Ereshkigal might punish you for eternity for disrespecting her."

"I've been in hell ever since I first set eyes on you, Sunflower," he muttered. "The Beldams were right, you've driven me mad. Ereshkigal's torture would pale in comparison to every second of purgatory I've endured since I tasted heaven on your lips."

My breath caught, and I stifled a shocked laugh. I looked away, picking at a loose thread on the blanket. Underneath the poetic, flowery nonsense, his words seeped like liquid fire into my veins. They ignited something deep within my soul that yearned to reach out and show him just how sweet the afterlife could really taste.

Despite that thought, I was no longer sure that I *wanted* to kill him. And that terrified me more than anything the Beldams could have shown me. So I remained silent and avoided his gaze, while my heart thundered in my chest and I grappled with myself to resist the urge to either stab him or kiss him. Or both.

He cleared his throat softly and pulled the tray toward us, picking up a bowl for himself and beginning to eat. Neither of us spoke again until after we had finished the food.

"Where are we? And what happened to my old clothes?" I asked, not able to see my bag. Somehow, I had changed into a fresh set of clothing, though I could tell by the sticky feel of my skin that I hadn't bathed.

"We're still in Khar'ra, just outside the temple moat," he replied. "I had to find the closest place to warm you up, your lips were blue from the cold. Suenna and Verrill dressed you and went with the others to find an inn where we could keep the horses. We'll go to them as soon as you're ready."

"How long have I been asleep?"

"About half a day. You were thrashing about so much for the first few hours that when you finally stilled I had to wake you briefly to ensure you hadn't died."

I nodded, though I had no recollection of anything after leaving the temple.

❖ ❖ ❖

Theo led me through the somber streets of Khar'ra, glancing back every few seconds to make sure I was still there. He had wanted to wait longer to leave after seeing me sway on my feet when I got out of bed, but I refused, anxious to get back to the others.

The further we walked from the temple, the busier it became. But instead of everyone shoving each other out of the way as they would in the other districts, the people here seemed to maneuver and slip into every available space to avoid touching one another. Theo's arm twitched toward me for the third time and I sighed before closing the short distance between us and taking it in mine. He visibly relaxed, and held me firm beside him. I'd known he wanted to take my hand as soon as we left, but I'd enjoyed watching him squirm, torn between wanting to ensure I wasn't snatched like

Suenna and not wishing to incite my temper.

By the time we reached the inn, my feet were sore and my head had begun to ache again. The building itself appeared disordered and top heavy, with too many sharp, angled stories balancing atop a narrow foundation. Theo had to enter sideways in order to fit his broad shoulders through the doorway, but his annoyance disappeared when he saw me laughing at him. The atmosphere inside was as bright and sunny as the outside was gray and dull, and the smell of food and ale was thick in the air.

I immediately spotted Verrill sitting with the others at a table in the far corner, and Theo and I wove through the patrons toward them. They all looked relieved to see us, and I was surprised at how much Theo's friends appeared to care about my wellbeing. I had grown fond of the trio and while I wasn't sure if we would be considered friends, it was nice to know they were concerned for me.

"Thank you for getting me changed," I said to Suenna, as I slipped into the seat next to her. She smiled and squeezed my hand in response, before I told them about what the Beldams had shown me.

"I know there was something else," I murmured, my brows pinched in frustration. "After they showed me the items, there were other images. I just can't remember anything else apart from the blood. There was so much blood."

"You got the information about the relics, that's all that matters," Ezra reassured me.

Commotion at the entrance had everyone turning to see a fist fight breaking out between two inebriated men, the alcohol making them careless and off target with their punches. But it was the nearby prostitute that captured my attention; she was using the upheaval to distract from the careful conversation she was having with a middle-aged man. He was muttering something into her ear, not so much as glancing down to where she had her assets on display. They each pressed a single finger to the shell of their right ear before he slipped away and out of the building.

Rats. They identified each other by gesturing to an ear; to show they always had one to the ground.

She confirmed my suspicion when she sauntered over to our table, hips swaying and lashes fluttering until she seated herself in Verrill's lap. To everyone else, it would appear as a regular proposition, but I didn't miss the finger she gently tapped to his ear before leaning down and whispering into it. He nodded and she melted away into the other patrons.

"He needs me back in Šarrum," he said, meeting my gaze. I knew he was talking about Csintalan, and though I hated the thought of him leaving, I also knew that he wouldn't be able to disobey. The others must have made their own assumptions, because no one questioned him.

"You're leaving now?" I protested when he started to stand.

"I have to, Eris, you know what he's like."

"Take the horse, Verrill," Theo insisted. "Leave it in Ocridell and we'll pick it up on our way back."

I stood as Verrill thanked him and followed him out to the stables at the back of the inn. He was quiet as he saddled Fergus and secured his bag. I couldn't help but feel as though there was something he was leaving unsaid between us and the silence felt heavy, in a way it never did with him.

"Verrill …" I began, but didn't get another word out before he turned to face me and gripped the tops of my arms. His eyes held such sadness and profound longing that it shattered my heart.

"I'm sorry, Eris," he choked, and pulled me tight to his chest. "You shouldn't have had to listen to what they said and I should've stopped you from going into that temple with them, should've stopped them from hurting you."

"Ver, do you want to talk about what they said?" I whispered, my heart thundering at the prospect of broaching our most forbidden topic.

"No, it doesn't matter," he replied, stroking my hair down my back. I opened my mouth to argue, but he cut me off, "Please, my music. Please don't."

I nodded, acquiescing to his request and breathing in the familiar scent of sage and juniper that clung to his clothes as I buried my face into his chest.

"I don't want you to leave," I whined.

"I don't want to leave *you*," he said, planting a kiss on my temple, "and I promise I'll never do it again. Just come and find me when you return."

We said our goodbyes and I watched him ride away before reentering the inn and heading back to Theo and his friends. They were all leaning forward across the table and talking in hushed voices.

"… redistribute them and send a division to the Isles. I'm sure we can convince—" Ezra's voice broke off as he saw me approach and they all straightened in their chairs, the silence thick in the air. Theo ran his gaze over me, his brow furrowed with indecision, before snapping it to Ezra.

"Please continue," he prompted.

"Theo," Ezra hesitated, looking between us, "I think this is a conversation we should have in private. No offense, Eris, you know I adore you."

"It's not a problem," I said, smiling at him and rising back to my feet, but Theo caught my arm and pulled me back down.

"She can stay and hear it too. I trust her."

My eyes bulged as I looked at him in disbelief, and I knew the others had expressions that mirrored my own. He gave me a tight-lipped smile, and even though his expression was firm in his decision, I could practically see his eyes begging me to not make him regret it.

*What a foolish man*, I thought. I'd given him no reason to trust me and had made no promise of continuing my silence.

"Be reasonable, Theo," Nook said, "as lovely as she is, she's not yours and owes you no loyalty."

And there it was; the first rift in their relationship. Though I technically hadn't chosen a side, it would be short sighted to not catalog how I could manipulate this further, if I *did* decide to offer Theo up to Csintalan in the future. If I could destabilize the close circle of his court, their plans would crumble from the inside out.

"This isn't about that," Theo argued. "Erisa's input could offer advantages we would never even consider. And I'd like to think she cares enough about the people of this realm to realize how many are suffering under the Autarch's rule."

He looked at me hopefully, but I kept my face blank. If I was being honest with myself—and I usually was—I didn't care about the people of Irkalla. I only cared about *my* people in Irkalla, and I'd suffered too much loss to broaden that scope beyond a small handful of individuals. Unfortunately, that handful contained Csintalan and, as much as I hated to admit it, Theo had also crept his way in.

Logically, I knew Theo was right, citizens in every district—especially my own—had been suffocating under Csintalan's leadership for years. Illicit activities had proliferated in his neglect, but I'd thrived within it. If there was a way to overthrow the Autarch without betraying Csintalan, I'd back Theo all the way, if only to enjoy the chaos that would undoubtedly follow. But it was a fool's dream; an impossibility.

"That's my point!" Nook countered, his pale face flushing from embarrassment. "You'd *like to think* she is, but you don't know. You're letting your fascination with her blind you. Sorry Erisa, but you're not exactly known for your philanthropy."

Nook avoided my gaze, and looked ready to die from shame at reprimanding his Lord. I watched as Ezra clasped one of his hands and squeezed encouragingly.

"No need to apologize," I assured him. "I was hoping to go and clean up anyway. Do we have rooms here yet?"

"I'll show you," Suenna said quickly, rising to her feet and leading me upstairs to a small but comfortable room on the second floor. My bag had already been placed in the adjoining bathing chamber.

"I hope the boys didn't offend you," she began. "They can be completely brainless sometimes."

I grinned at her. "Not at all. They were right, you have no

reason to trust me."

"It's only because Theo has worked so hard to get us this far and we know how much he cares and how much he's risking."

"Of course." I nodded, and watched as she hesitated by the door, playing with a stray strand of hair.

"Theo has been a shell of himself since Karasi died, barely going through the motions," she murmured. "He's come alive again since he met you, Erisa. Keep challenging him; we love having our friend back, and I'm sure we've got you to thank for it."

Mercifully, she slipped away before I had to think of a response. I was surprised to feel a twinge of guilt from her words. She was thanking me for antagonizing Theo enough to make him move on from Karasi, when I was the reason he'd lost her. Not for the first time, I wondered if he planned on telling his friends that I was the one who had murdered her, and how they would treat me once they knew.

Upon entering the bathing chamber, I decided that Khar'ra's lack of hot running water promoted it to the most miserable district in the realm. After calling for the tub to be filled to a near scalding temperature, I stripped off my clothes and lowered myself into the water, hissing at the heat. It was a relief to scrub away the grime and old sweat from my skin and I enjoyed lathering soap into my hair to work out the dried mud and dust clinging to the strands.

My skin was wrinkled by the time I heard Ezra's voice outside the door asking me if I wanted to join them for dinner. I dressed quickly and braided out my wet hair before making my way back downstairs.

My heart lurched when I saw Theo glaring at me as I

approached and sat down in the seat opposite. I'd become accustomed to his jaunty, flirtatious expressions and remarks, and the absence of them stung more than I wanted to admit. I stretched my leg out under the table, skimming my foot lightly up his lower leg. His eyes flared at my teasing touch and his molten gaze met mine for less than a second before he snatched his leg out of reach and looked away.

He remained mostly silent throughout the meal, only replying when his friends directed questions at him, and based on their confused expressions, they knew as much about his ill temper as I did. Deciding to ignore him, I threw myself into conversation with the others, and we laughed and joked our way through the evening. We were on our third game of cards when Suenna addressed him.

"Oh for goodness sake, Theo," she snapped, "you're such a bore when you behave like this. If you won't tell us what's wrong, go and wallow somewhere else."

He leapt to his feet and threw one last glare my way before stalking upstairs, muttering under his breath about murdering temptresses determined to ruin his life. Ezra and Nook smirked at each other when I stood up to follow him and Suenna winked at me.

Theo wasn't in my room when I entered it, and as I had no idea where the others were staying, I couldn't seek him out. Ignoring the traitorous stab of disappointment, I changed quickly into a nightgown and slid into bed, the events of the last day finally catching up with me.

A floorboard creaked outside my room, and I looked over to the door, noticing that the light coming through underneath was blocked. My heart began to pound in my chest, knowing that it was

Theo.

I crossed the room and unlatched the door, swinging it open to reveal Theo's thunderous expression. His hair was damp and I could smell the soap fragrancing his skin.

"What are you doing?" I asked, arching a brow at him.

I watched as he raked his eyes down my body slowly before he pushed past me into the room and began to pace. He halted immediately when he heard the lock click back into place.

"Do you regret it?" he demanded. "Do you regret murdering Karasi?"

"No," I replied honestly.

He blew out a breath and began pacing again, running his hands through his already disheveled hair. I sat on the edge of the bed and watched him, the tension between us building with every step he took.

"You're killing me, Erisa. Whenever I'm with you, I forget all the things you've done and I have to remind myself that you're the reason why my life went to shit. The others were right, I can't think straight when it comes to you. And I think about how I would've killed those women for hurting you, when I would've told you every damn secret I've ever known and smiled like a fucking fool when you'd turn and whisper them back into the Autarch's ear."

I tilted my face down to look at him through my lashes, hoping the weak lighting of the room would conceal my rapid breathing.

"Then what do you want, Theo?"

He was in front of me in two strides, gripping my chin tightly and forcing my head up to face him. Heat engulfed my entire body and my skin became feverish under his touch.

"I want *you*, Erisa. I want to explore every brutal, violent inch of you until I discover each of your knives hidden within your sweet words and caresses. I want to taste every drop of poison that flows from your tongue and the feel of your throat beneath my hand as you douse me in cruel words. And I fucking hate myself for it. I want to feel your heart against my soul so I can rip it out of your chest and destroy you like you've destroyed me."

Desire flooded my veins at his words and I ran my tongue along my bottom lip, relishing in the way he desperately tracked the movement.

"Do it then," I whispered.

He left the words hanging in the air for a heartbeat before his mouth was on mine, devouring me like I was an oasis in the desert. His hands flew to my hair, gently tracing the length of my braid before finding the tie and discarding it. I moaned into his mouth as my hair unraveled and he ran his fingers through it before winding it around his fist and pulling it tight, angling my head up to deepen the kiss.

We were a tangle of fumbling hands and heated limbs as we tore away our clothes, aching to remove any barrier left between us. I couldn't remember ever needing anyone so desperately. Even as our sweat-slicked bodies were flush against one another, I needed him *closer*. I wanted to sink into his skin and never leave.

"Gods, I fucking hate you," he breathed against my throat as my back bowed off the bed and a cry escaped my lips.

"Show me how much," I panted, dragging my nails across his back.

He showed me in the way he explored and worshiped every

inch of my body, in every moan and sigh he captured with his mouth, and every nip and scrape of his teeth. I reveled in the tender brush of his fingers, the ministrations of his mouth against mine. And I had never known anything as sweet as the taste of my name as it rolled from his lips and onto my tongue.

# Chapter 17

## Theo

Pain radiated through my right leg and it buckled beneath me, sending me crashing to my knees. I was at the top of a cliff, and I could hear the sea churning below. A cry rang out in front of me and my heart stopped when I saw Erisa hanging over the edge, her limbs tangled in a net that slowly slipped away from its tether. My head swam in agony as I forced myself to stand. I needed to get to her. I managed three steps before my leg gave out once more, agony lashing through me and causing my vision to ebb. Then I was crawling toward her, dragging my useless leg behind me, ignoring every jolt and stab of pain and watching in horror as the rope frayed strand by strand.

I didn't make it in time.

19 May

❋ ❋ ❋

My eyes snapped open and I had to push down the bile that had crawled up the back of my throat. A heavy sigh of relief left me as I felt the warmth of Erisa's body against mine. My rapid heartbeat slowed as I relaxed, completely entranced by the way sleep had softened her features into a vision of serene beauty.

She was always exquisite, but right now, I felt as though the sun could rise and fall a thousand times over and I would still be captivated by the sight. My mind spun over the events of last night and I tried not to linger on the memories of the way she felt beneath me or the sound of her sighing my name.

*She's not yours.*

Nook's words made my jaw clench, because he was right. I had become so wrapped up in her presence that I had willingly forgotten who she was and what she'd done. She made it so easy to be affectionate and playful, and I had thrown myself into it, ignoring the many reasons not to. And last night …

Nook's words had snapped me back to reality, and I was furious with her for the effect she had over me and even more furious with myself for being susceptible to it. I had let my anger run away with itself all evening, loathing the sick obsession I had with her, agonizing over every smile and laugh she gave to my friends. I had found myself outside her door with no recollection of walking there, not even knowing if I planned to send her away, fuck her, or kill her. But I knew the second she had locked that door and sealed us inside, there was only ever one option.

Guilt and self-loathing suffocated me at the thought of how I had betrayed Karasi, and how I was still betraying her by not smothering Erisa in her sleep. I knew I would never be able to do it now; the blind panic I had experienced in my nightmare had confirmed what I was already beginning to suspect. Erisa had dug her claws deep into my chest and then left the wounds to fester, her poison seeping into my bloodstream.

Careful not to wake her, I gently extracted my arm and reached down to retrieve my jacket from the floor. Withdrawing my notebook from the pocket, I began to write, detailing what I could remember from the dream.

The Beldams had been right; I was a fool. For months I had repeated this bizarre ritual, never once considering that the stone in Karasi's bracelet, which I now knew was the Orb of Nanaya, was responsible for the *visions*. I had always assumed they were a trauma response from learning of my twin sister's death, never realizing that they had started after Karasi's bracelet had been returned to us, and only intensifying since I had actually touched the stone.

My musings were interrupted by a small groan, and I looked over to see Erisa stretching, the blanket falling away from her naked body. My throat dried at the sight. I had thought if I allowed myself to indulge in her once, it would alleviate my fixation with her, but I'd been so incredibly wrong. Now I was entirely consumed by her, no matter how I wished it were otherwise. Her amber eyes caught mine, and my stomach dropped when she swiftly looked away.

"Last night was a mistake," she muttered before slipping out of bed and pulling the discarded nightdress over her head.

I knew I should be relieved at her regret, and disgusted that I felt none, but I wasn't. Despite the nausea turning my stomach, I prepared myself to agree, to tell her that it would never happen again.

But my traitorous mouth disobeyed. "Come on, Sunflower. Don't pretend like you didn't enjoy yourself."

"Oh please," she hissed, "I've had chest infections that have satisfied me more."

I was confident enough in my abilities that her jibe sent a thrill through me, the need to push her ire further overwhelming.

"You wound me," I mocked, placing a hand over my heart.

"Stop it, Theo," she snapped. "Don't pretend like there was ever anything between us."

"Really? Is that why you betrayed your *master* to help me? The man who took you in. Maybe you don't really care about him after all," I sneered, collecting my clothes from the floor.

"He was … *is* like a father to me." Her voice was laced with warning.

I ignored it. "Was he? Or did he just raise you to be another weapon for him to wield?"

She was silent and hurt flickered across her face, telling me that my remark had hit a nerve. I felt as though someone had punched me in the gut.

"Get out," she ordered, her voice a quiet tone of simmering rage.

"You're scared, Erisa," I said, "scared to admit that you care and scared to admit that you're feeling guilty about it."

"I said get out!" she seethed.

Her glare singed through my shirt and into my back as I turned and walked to the door. I was about to step into the hallway when her clipped voice stopped me.

"You're wrong. I *don't* care. Last night was fun, but it meant nothing to me. *You* mean nothing to me."

I didn't look back at her as I exited the room. My chest was tight as I stalked downstairs and a hot ball of fury wedged itself into my throat. Rationally, I knew that she was lashing out like a cornered viper, but her words still fucking hurt. And I was angry at myself for letting them affect me.

This could all have been an act, a way to gain my trust and manipulate me for the Autarch. Sure, she had freely given away all of the information about gathering the relics to destroy him, but all of that could have been a fabricated ruse to lure me to my death.

Suenna was sitting at one of the benches, a steaming mug of tea in her hands. She looked up as I sat down but said nothing when she saw the expression on my face, only reached across the table and squeezed one of my hands in hers.

I had regained control over myself by the time Nook and Ezra joined us. They had a few moments to bombard me with questions and taunts before Erisa appeared and they fell silent. Their trepidation of enraging her brought a reluctant smile to my lips.

She greeted everyone politely and wasted no time in beginning discussions on the possible locations of the relics. Grateful to have something else to think about, I engaged enthusiastically in the conversation. We agreed to return to Ocridell and Zingal first; I knew where Dumuzid's dagger was and Erisa could guess where the songbird of Pazuzu would be. After we secured both items, we would approach the other district Lords.

"And we're supposed to just trust that you're telling us the truth about what the Beldams showed you?" Ezra voiced the question we were all thinking, his eyes focused on Erisa. "After you've made it clear that you're loyal to the Autarch."

She shrugged. "It's your choice whether or not you want to believe me. If I didn't want you to know, I wouldn't have told you. My reasons shouldn't concern you as long as we have the same goal."

"But they do concern me," he replied, "we're risking our lives and our families putting our faith in you. The least you could do is offer your motivations."

"Insurance. Leverage. Blackmail. Whatever you want to call it," she said. "If there is a way to remove the Autarch and destabilize the entire realm, I want to know about it."

I wasn't exactly surprised by her answer, but it made me even more curious to know what she had seen from the Orb of Nanaya.

❊ ❊ ❊

It took three days of riding to make it back to Ocridell. Three long, torturous days of Erisa's warm body against mine and her warm scent of jasmine diffusing into my lungs, as intoxicating as silkleaf vapors.

I regretted giving Verrill the horse and was relieved when we picked it up again to continue on to Zingal. We decided that it would be better to come back to Ocridell via the tram to look for the songbird, to avoid drawing attention to our search.

It took another day to reach Zingal, and everyone felt the relief of a warm bath, proper meals, and plush beds again. I hesitated outside Erisa's room the evening of our return, hand raised to knock for a few long moments before I dropped it back to my side and walked away. We hadn't spoken any more about the night at the inn and I knew she was actively avoiding being alone with me, likely out of fear that I would bring it up.

*** ***

The next morning, I was awoken by the same nightmare of Erisa falling from the cliff. I had experienced it every night since the inn, the only difference being the space I closed between us. Every time I managed to crawl nearer to her, close enough to reach out and grasp the rope, only for it to slip through my fingers. And close enough to see the fear in her eyes as she fell. The growing hope of succeeding made the ache of failure even more unbearable.

Dawn light mellowed the sky into a pale pink as I made my way to the Lusilim urnfield. It was a small, gated space dotted with headstones and plaques to commemorate the former Lords and Ladies of Zingal.

Sighing, I sat on the ground beside Karasi's headstone, regret twisting my stomach as I stared at her empty plot. Even though we hadn't found her body, I hoped that she had still managed to find peace in the afterlife, wherever that was.

It was believed that Irkalla itself had been the home of the dead when the gods still walked the earth. If that was true, no one knew where they had gone when the realm was transformed.

It had been a long time since I had found myself here, but the area had been well maintained by Corbin. He came every fortnight with Didi to remove any weeds around the blossoming flowers she had planted.

I murmured apologies as I dug into the ground. It was sacrilegious to unearth someone's remains, but since Karasi's ashes had never been buried here, I hoped that she wouldn't mind. My shoulders slumped in relief when my fingers touched the cold metal of the dagger, and I pulled it from the ground, seeing a hint of color from the jeweled hilt hidden beneath a layer of dirt.

It was uncommon to bury items belonging to the deceased, but I hadn't had anything else to put beneath her headstone. Unease danced across my skin as I considered how different things might have been if I had decided to bury Karasi's bracelet instead of the dagger all those years ago.

"What am I going to do, Kara?" I murmured to the empty grave, smoothing the upturned earth as best as I could. "I've made such a mess of everything."

Of course I received no answer.

I allowed myself another moment to wallow in self-pity before standing and returning to the house. The waking sun had warmed the air and I basked in the springtime scents of honeysuckle and cut grass as I neared my home.

"Is that it?" Erisa's voice punctuated the silence of the kitchen as I washed the dagger, the encrusted hilt quickly returning to its previous gaudy shine. I flipped the blade, holding it out for her to inspect. Both edges were still impossibly sharp, despite the years it had spent buried in the ground.

"You tell me," I said, watching her examine the weapon. As

soon as she had described the colorful jeweled dagger from her visions, I knew it had to be this one. Karasi had been adamant about keeping it safe, and I wondered if she'd known of its importance.

"It looks different," she muttered after a minute, "the coloring's wrong. It should have a green shine to it, and a date fruit on the back."

My brow furrowed. "The only green dagger with a date I know of is the Lusilim blade, and that hasn't got a single jewel on it." According to Erisa, it was the weapon that had ended her mother's life. "Maybe you're remembering it incorrectly?"

"Maybe," she said doubtfully, flipping the blade over one more time before handing it back to me. "Let's worry about it after we've found the rest of them."

I nodded in agreement. The silence was suddenly charged between us, and I could see the moment she realized that we were alone. Her eyes darted to the door, already preparing her escape for when I decided to ruin her day by talking about *feelings*. Despite my desire to clear the air, I also wanted her to feel comfortable around me again, so I said nothing as I prepared a pot of tea.

"When do you want to leave for Ocridell?" I asked as I joined her at the table and placed a steaming mug in front of her. "We can wait a few days if you're tired from all the travel."

"No, I'd rather get it over with," she replied, a nervous agitation clipping her words.

"I have some business to attend to this morning, will you be ready to go after lunch?"

She confirmed she would be, before clearing our mugs and venturing into the gardens. I watched her out of the window until she disappeared from sight, her black curls shining like wet ink.

My mother was waiting for me in my office, armed with estate reports and district matters needing my attention. It was times like this that I felt a fleeting second of resentment toward Karasi, for having the audacity to die and leaving me to deal with this bullshit. I wasn't a patient man when it came to paperwork; I preferred the stimulation of physical tasks over the idleness of desk labor.

I had just finished reading a dock master's letter detailing an attack on his small unit of fishing boats when Nook entered the room. Ezra and Suenna followed him in.

"We've got an update on the numbers," he said, pulling up a seat.

Last night, I had asked them to discreetly scope out information on the military camps situated around Zingal. After returning from the Zuamsik Mountains with Erisa, I had ordered an evacuation of the site, leaving only enough personnel to avoid suspicion if it was breached. It had been difficult to relocate so many people, but I hadn't wanted to leave anything to chance.

"Our current total from Hudjefa stands just shy of eight thousand, approximately seventy percent of which are fit to fight," Nook informed me. "The remainder have already taken up supporting roles where possible. They have people working the fields, making weapons and armor, maintaining the houses, and running additional drills. They're surprisingly self-sufficient."

"There have been roughly a thousand deserters," Ezra chimed in, "most leaving due to family ties, but we've been surprisingly lucky at keeping this quiet. We've only had two of the Autarch's men come sniffing for information, meaning that when people are leaving, they're not selling us out."

"Fortunately for us, I believe the citizens of Hudjefa are as tired of the Autarch's rule as we are," I surmised. "I hadn't expected so many to come. What of the mountain base?"

"Nothing," Suenna replied. "No one has so much as set foot in that direction. Whatever Erisa saw, the Autarch hasn't caught wind of it."

Warm satisfaction ran through me at her words. I was half expecting to return home and find our cover blown and the military base destroyed. Erisa was connected enough to the Palace by Verrill's Rats that any information she had could easily be passed to the Autarch under my nose.

"Good," I approved. "I'd still like to wait a few more weeks before sending everyone back. Erisa still hasn't given the Autarch a formal report of her southern pass inspection. Though we all knew it was a ruse, I'm sure he'd like to keep up appearances. I'll suggest to her about making a visit before he has time to summon her now Verrill's returned."

"We'll need to make arrangements soon," said Ezra. "We're well over capacity with the mountain base closure. Can't we send more men to Katmu?"

"I'm planning on talking to Malah as soon as possible," I said. "I can't imagine he'd have a problem with it but I'd like to make sure first."

Meeting Malah Jirata had been an unexpected perk of my latest visit to the Palace. I had been pleasantly surprised to find him wholly dissimilar to his elder brothers and eager to improve the lives of his people. I had known too little about him to directly question his loyalty to the Autarch, but he had been forthcoming in his frustration regarding the trafficking issues he'd been facing. I offered to send him a large portion of my fighting men to aid him, and he gladly accepted. It had allowed me to distribute my forces across two districts. Should Zingal fall, I would have a backup in Katmu.

"We'll need to be careful about moving so many people. Across land will be too obvious, but Aran Seirsun will see if we use ships," Ezra continued.

I scratched at the too-long stubble beneath my chin. "I'm planning on visiting Corbin after Erisa and I finish in Ocridell. I believe his house is close to the Anzû Estate. He might know of a more discreet route through Ersetu."

We discussed the logistics of the potential transfer for another hour before moving to the dining room for lunch. Upon entering, I noticed Erisa and Didi already there, gossiping between themselves. I had never heard Erisa giggle before and I became transfixed by the sound. I didn't realize I was staring at her until Suenna barged my shoulder and gave me a wry look, unimpressed but amused by my behavior.

"Will you let me come with you this time?" Didi pleaded with me.

I sighed. "No, you already know I don't want you under the volcano right now. There are too many things that could go wrong."

She whispered something in Erisa's ear, who laughed heartily before returning to her meal. The thought of them becoming friends should have scared me. I wanted to shelter Didi from the harshness of our world as much as possible, and Erisa embodied the worst parts of it. However, I would do anything I could to ensure Didi's happiness and I was enjoying Erisa's smiles too much to separate them.

But it still felt wretched allowing Didi to befriend Erisa, knowing that she was the Feline, the one who had murdered our sister. And if she found out, Didi would never forgive me for concealing it.

Erisa and I left shortly after lunch and as we walked, I tried to rebuild my mental walls against her influence. I knew she would likely abandon me as soon as we found the relics. She could probably find them herself, but she needed me to get access to the Lords. If she approached them as the Feline, the Autarch could get suspicious and discover her plans, assuming he knew of the relics.

I had briefly considered dropping her as soon as we'd gone to the Palace to get the other half of the Orb, but the idea made my stomach sour. I could lie to myself all I wanted, but the truth was that I didn't want us to part ways. I enjoyed her scathing remarks and vicious glares as much as I enjoyed her quick wit and bright smiles. Even though I knew it was foolish, I found myself trying to find ways to lengthen or delay our trip, knowing deep down that when it came to a close, I wouldn't want to say goodbye.

I made an effort to keep our conversation light throughout the journey to Ocridell, noting how she became more on edge the closer we traveled to her former home. Tension radiated off her the second we set foot in the deteriorating district, and she set off without saying a word.

I followed her south through the city, disheartened at the obvious signs of struggle displayed by the crumbling buildings and hungry citizens. My few childhood memories of Ocridell had been full of color and music. The city I saw now was almost unrecognizable.

"It used to be so beautiful," Erisa said quietly as we passed by a row of abandoned storefronts. When we passed through Ocridell on the way to Silas', we skirted through the northern part of the city. I could tell from the horror on her face that she hadn't been to the southern side in years. I wanted to comfort her, but didn't know how.

Eventually, we arrived at a pair of metal gates flanked by a tall stone wall. The gates had been chained shut, so she continued around the wall for another few minutes, stopping at the base of an impressive pear tree. Erisa stared at the tree for several moments, and the sadness in her eyes felt like a knife twisting in my chest.

"Boost me up?" she asked quietly, reaching for one of the lower branches. It was the first time she had ever asked me for help and my foolish, irrational heart leapt at the request. Once she was secured on the branch, she reached a hand down to help me up. I took it gladly and climbed up next to her.

"This is how me and Verrill would sneak back in without being seen," she said, sighing deeply before leaping onto the wall with practiced precision.

I followed her into the overgrown grounds, and through the now-wild gardens to the house. It was a miserable sight. The charred remains stood barren and forgotten, the blown windowpanes crunching underfoot as we neared the heavy front door. Erisa briefly placed her left hand on the metal frame, her palm closing over her family crest, an exact copy of the scar on her—

Realization hit me like a battering ram and I had to turn away, fighting down the sickness threatening to rise up my throat. A loud groan pulled my attention forward again and I saw Erisa pushing the door open, fighting with the rusty hinges. After only a second of hesitation, she continued inside, carefully navigating through the burnt, empty remains of the estate and up a winding staircase to the top of a tower.

"You think the bird is in here?" I asked, looking around the ruined room. My voice sounded deafening in the surrounding silence.

She walked to the empty window frame and pointed out. "No, it's over there."

I followed her finger to where a weathervane was perched on the roof over the main entrance hall. It was such a strange color, it somehow looked black one way and then gray as soon as the wind moved it.

"This was my room. I'd sit here and watch it spin in the breeze. It would taunt me. I always wanted to get to it but I was never tall enough to reach up onto the second roof." Her voice was almost a whisper.

The weathervane was situated on a section of roof that lay roughly eight feet above the rest, and I could almost imagine Erisa as a stubborn, determined child growing red with anger at not being able to jump high enough.

"I'll go get it," I offered carefully. I expected her to refuse; she was tall for a woman and even though I knew she still wouldn't make the jump, I thought she would want to try anyway. Instead, she simply shrugged and stepped aside so I could climb through the window.

"It wouldn't feel right to take it without Verrill," she explained when she saw my bewildered expression. "Besides, I want to see if any of my old things survived the fire."

A large number of the tiles were either cracked or missing, but the roof remained mostly stable as I crept across it. Moss and lichen had taken advantage of every empty space on the dark slate, causing the grip beneath my shoes to occasionally slip. Sweat misted my brow by the time I reached the ledge. It was higher than I had originally thought, and it took three attempts for my fingers to grasp the stone overhang above me. My hands screamed in protest as I hauled myself up, the sharp drip edge cutting into my skin.

After taking a few seconds to catch my breath, I moved carefully to the weathervane. The glass songbird was white, approximately the size of my fist, with a translucent black outer shell. It was held to the weathervane with thin, snaking metal that coiled around its neck and tail. I snapped it off easily and inspected the bird in my palm. The outer layer seemed to catch the light in such a way that the color looked different from every angle. Everything from black to silver to pearlescent.

After securing it in an inside pocket, I turned to make my way back to Erisa. I crouched down at the edge of the platform, preparing to grip the tiles with my hand and gently lower myself down. But before I could position myself, the ledge beneath me crumbled under my weight, causing me to fall down onto the lower roof. I slammed onto my back and barely felt the sharp pain radiate down my spine before the lower roof gave way under me.

Then I began to fall.

# Chapter 18

## Erisa

I was running.

The succession of events was so rapid that I could barely comprehend how I had ended up sprinting through the scorched remains of my old home. One moment, I was frozen in horror watching Theo fall and the next I was moving, blind panic catapulting me forward. Without even registering my surroundings, I raced to an old drawing room on the first floor, praying that Theo had fallen there, instead of all the way down into the entrance hall.

My relief at finding the correct location was short-lived after I threw the door open to see Theo's legs sticking out from beneath a pile of rubble. The old, stale air was thick with disturbed dust and ash as I flew toward him, ripping away broken pieces of wood and roofing.

"Theo!" I shouted, my fingers already bleeding and splintered from the rough edges of the debris.

No answer.

I shouted again, continuing until I uncovered him completely and saw his unconscious face, filthy from the soot. After inspecting the length of his body for impalements and finding none, I decided I needed to move him in case more of the roof collapsed.

I knew he should be kept still until I could determine if he had any neck or spinal injuries, but I didn't want to risk further debris falling on top of him. Fueled by adrenaline and fear, I gripped his upper body beneath the shoulders and dragged him out of the room and down the hallway. He still hadn't stirred when I gently set him down, and I pressed an ear to his chest to listen for a heartbeat but couldn't hear anything over the pounding of my own. Instead, I raised two trembling fingers to his neck and almost choked in relief at finding his pulse strong, if a bit too fast.

I desperately looked around me for anything I could use to help him, but my thoughts were so erratic I was bordering on hysteria. I needed him to wake up so that I could assess the damage. Neither of us had brought any water, the water taps in the house would be useless and the nearest well was on the other side of the estate, if it was even still functioning. So, sitting close to his side, I did the only thing I could think of and gave him a sharp slap across the face.

"Wake up, Theo!"

I had dealt with countless injuries in the past and not once had I lost my composure like this. Logically, I knew I shouldn't be slapping him or splashing his face with water, but I was desperate to see him wake up.

Theo groaned, opening one eye and then the other before coughing loudly. I gently pushed against his chest when he tried to sit up and he furrowed his brows in confusion.

"What the—" he croaked, looking around and settling his gaze on me. He stared at me for a long moment before his eyes widened and he looked down at himself. "Oh shit."

"How do you feel?" I asked as he tried to sit up again.

"Like I've eaten a whole urn of ashes," he said. He tried to wipe the dirt from his eyes, but his hands were so covered in dust that he just smeared more across his face.

"But where are you hurt?" I pressed, anxiety leaching into my voice. "Can you feel everything?"

"Unfortunately," he said, after flexing each hand and foot. "I think I've cracked a few ribs though."

I rose to my feet. "Don't try to move yet, I'm going to see if I can find some water."

Quickly surveying each of the nearby rooms, I found a somewhat livable area in one of the old parlors. The settee was dusty but fortunately not entirely burnt. I ran back outside toward the well, praying it hadn't dried up over the years.

The pump was rusty, and I had to throw my body weight into moving it the first few times before it loosened. When the water spouted, it was brown and lumpy, but eventually turned clear again. I quickly rinsed a nearby pail and filled it, clamping a hand over one of the larger leaks in the wood, before taking it to the old parlor in the house and returning to Theo.

"Can you walk?" I asked when I reached him. He hadn't moved from where I had left him, though his eyes reopened at my question.

He winced as he sat up. "I think so."

It took our combined efforts to get him to his feet, and though he leaned on me the whole way, we made it to the parlor. Once I had him stretched out on the settee, his grunts of pain finally stopped. All of the glass cups had been smashed or cracked but I managed to find a metal goblet in one of the disheveled display cabinets and filled it with water.

"Here, drink this," I said, propping Theo's head up and pressing the goblet to his lips. He drank greedily and coughed once more before slumping back down and closing his eyes. "Stay here, I'm going to go into the city to get a healer."

"No," he wheezed, wincing as he reached a hand out to grab my arm, "don't leave, I'll be fine soon. I'll see a healer when we return to Zingal, I just need a minute to rest."

I nodded, feeling exhaustion slowly replace the adrenaline that had coursed through my body for the past half hour. I scanned the room for any clean-looking cloth but found none. Sighing, I ripped away a strip from the bottom hem of my shirt and soaked it in the water before lightly washing away the dirt from Theo's face and hands. He groaned in contentment at the touch but kept his eyes closed, his breathing even and slow.

It was then that I remembered the bird. If he was still awake, he didn't stop me as I gently reached into the pockets of his jacket. I pulled out a notepad, then went to the other side to retrieve the songbird.

It was nothing short of a miracle that the smooth glass surface was still perfectly intact, though I suspected it would take more than a fallen roof to destroy it. It thrummed with power, making my fingers tingle slightly. Caught in mid-flight, it looked exactly the same as my family crest, soaring on the wind. I had half hoped to be shown something when I touched it, and the disappointment in seeing nothing gnawed away at the relief I should have felt.

Unable to help myself, I turned to the notebook. Knowing that I shouldn't look inside made the prospect far too tempting to refuse. I flicked through the pages, almost bored to tears at the content when I turned to one of the loose papers.

It was a drawing. Of me.

It was from Tammuz, and showed Nook and Ezra bowing toward me after our dance. The sketch was so detailed, I could see the flush of exertion on my cheeks and the heave of my chest mid-breath. There was a deep lead gouge that slashed across my skirt, as though he had used the pencil to try and cut me through the paper.

My heart hammered as I extracted the other loose papers tucked into the pages of the notebook. Apart from a few of Nook, Ezra, and Suenna, they were all of me. Drawings of me sat at a campfire, riding a horse, braiding my hair with a scowl etched across my face. There was one of my naked body stretching, the blanket falling over my hips and my cheeks heated at the attention to detail.

My breath hitched as I saw the final drawing. I was sitting on a tree stump, my smiling mouth open on a song and Verrill knelt on one knee at my feet, his lyre in his hands. It was beautiful. I recognized the scene immediately as the meadow we had stopped at on the way to Khar'ra. I hadn't even realized Theo had been there, but my throat felt heavy as I looked at the depiction of the idyllic scene, the glow around Verrill and I shaded to black, giving the perspective of a lonely observer.

S.C. MAKEPEACE

Over the next half hour or so, I inspected each of the drawings, marveling at Theo's skill and trying to suppress the warmth spreading through my chest.

"Didn't anyone ever warn you about the dangers of curiosity, Feline?"

My hands stilled on the drawings as Theo's voice broke the silence. I met his gaze, looking for traces of anger at my prying, but found none. He was just watching me, as though he had been the whole time. Swallowing, I tilted my chin up defiantly.

"What are these?" I demanded.

"Drawings, obviously."

"I didn't realize you were so obsessed with me." I rolled my eyes, trying to mask whatever emotion had my pulse quickening and my cheeks heating.

"Oh, but I am," he affirmed, sitting up slowly and leaning toward me without a hint of embarrassment marring his features, "you invade my every thought."

"You're pathetic," I sneered, looking him up and down. He reached out to clasp my chin firmly in his hand, and indignation and desire flared within me when he smiled at my harsh words.

"If I'm so pathetic," he murmured, pulling my face toward his own, "why did you bother saving me?"

"I need you to find the other relics," I hissed, wanting to rip my eyes out for straying to his lips without permission.

Theo chuckled to himself and roughly pushed my chin away before rising shakily to his feet. I opened my mouth to demand he lie back down, but his expression turned triumphant, so I snapped it shut again. Besides, I was torn between wanting him to lie back down and rushing back to Zingal to get the healer.

Quickly tucking the drawings back into the pages, I handed him his notebook and the songbird, which he placed into his pockets. Saying nothing, I ducked under his arm, placing it over my shoulders, and encircled my own around his body, keeping it low to avoid putting pressure on his ribs. He murmured his thanks and we began slowly making our way out of the estate.

I maintained my steely silence all the way to the outer wall, which I looked at hesitantly, before extracting myself from under Theo's arm. After collecting a few old pieces of garden furniture, I was able to make a somewhat climbable set of stairs to the top of the wall. He would have to jump down from the pear tree on the other side, but there wasn't a lot I could do about that.

To his credit, Theo made the detour without complaint, even though he was obviously in considerable pain. We continued on toward the city, but by the time we made it to the tram platform, I could no longer keep my anxiety in check. His face had grown paler by the minute and a cold sheen of sweat coated his skin.

I considered searching for a wagon to take us to Zingal, since Theo refused to see a healer in Ocridell, but decided that we couldn't spare the time. When the tram came into sight, I tucked myself tighter under his arm, grabbed the belt at his waist and hauled us both into a running jump, only just clearing the distance to the carriage.

Exiting the tram was just as taxing and it took every ounce of my strength to keep us from stumbling over upon landing. Theo had been quiet for the entire ride, and I could feel the panic clawing its way back up my spine. He sagged against me, his breaths short and shallow, as I heaved him toward the Lusilim estate.

I almost cried out in relief upon seeing the date palms marking the entrance to the track leading to the manor, when a gray haired woman caught my attention.

"Lola!" I yelled, watching her nearly drop her wicker basket in horror as she saw Theo. She started toward us but I called out to her again, "Fetch a healer, I'm taking him up to the house!"

I didn't waste any time to see if Nook's grandmother had obeyed my command. Instead, I carried on, forcing my knees not to buckle under the weight of a near-unconscious Theo. As soon as the house came into view I was shouting again, calling for help until his friends and family swarmed us. Nook and Ezra tried to relieve me of his weight, but I refused, only letting them help me carry him upstairs to his chambers. Only when we had him lying safely on his bed did I let him go.

# Chapter 19

## Erisa

A warm breeze whipped at the hair around my face as the tram sped toward Šarrum. Theo had been mostly unconscious for the past four days, with the healers treating him for several cracked ribs, a bleed around the lungs and a liver contusion. Despite their reassurances that he was improving, I was sick with worry and had spent most of my time sitting by the door outside his room, never quite able to go inside. He didn't need me there, he was unconscious, and between his mother, sister, and friends, there was always someone sitting at his side.

This afternoon, I couldn't take it anymore and practically ran to the tramline, sprinting after one already departing and only just making it into the last carriage. I needed to do something productive, so I'd decided to head to the Palace and try to find the other half of the Orb. Unfortunately, as soon as I caught my breath, I was desperate to return to the Lusilim estate, in case Theo's condition deteriorated. There would be nothing I could do, but the thought of not being there suddenly made me nauseous.

Swallowing hard, I chastised myself for my foolishness and mentally ran through the possible locations of the Orb. Even if Csintalan hadn't known what it was, he would have hidden it carefully. That was assuming he even knew of its existence, it was possible that the stone had been stashed away somewhere in the Palace by a previous Autarch.

Despite the added heat of the approaching summer season, I pulled my cloak on as the tram approached the Šarrum platform and secured the hood over my face, concealing everything but my mouth. I should have felt at home in the heat of the volcano, slinking into dark corners and cutting my way through narrow spaces in the rock. But the familiarity felt confining instead of comforting. I had spent a decade navigating these tunnels and for the first time since arriving at the royal city, I felt the desire to leave again.

"I'm relieved to see you, Feline," one of the guards called out as I approached the western gate of the Palace, "you've been gone for so long, some of us were starting to get worried."

"You know me, Medo, I like being mysterious." I smiled when I reached him, and glanced at his companion. "Who's this?"

"Alekos," the man said, eyeing me suspiciously. Something about him looked familiar and I racked my brain to place him. He was the man I had seen talking to the prostitute in the tavern in Khar'ra. I knew Verrill had his Rats placed almost everywhere across the realm, but in the Autarch's Palace staff seemed bold, even for him.

"What a pleasure to meet you," I said, breezing past the two men and continuing up to the Palace.

Tohnain greeted me at the doors and I couldn't help the grin that spread across my face. I had missed him more than I realized, and hounded him with questions on how he had been and what updates he had on Asila. Eventually, he shooed me away with orders to change out of my dirty boots before traipsing even more mud across the floors.

I made my way upstairs and thankfully heard the moans of pleasure coming from Verrill's room before I barged in, and instead continued onto my own chambers next door. After a swift change of clothes, I went to the Autarch's office, where I found Csintalan sitting at his desk, poring over letters and reports. His expression brightened as soon as he saw me.

"Erisa." He beamed, standing to pull me into an embrace. "How are you, Kitten? I didn't know when you'd be back and I've heard so little from you."

"It's been a busy few weeks," I murmured, relishing in the familiar comfort of his arms. He hadn't embraced me like this for years and the bitterness I felt toward him due to the visions waned slightly.

"Well," he said, sitting back down, "what information do you have for me?"

"Nothing of value," I lied, a small twinge of guilt settling in my stomach. "The southern pass has completely caved in. The damage is irreparable, so we'd be better off starting a new one in a different section of the mountains. Whatever Theo lied about during that meeting, I didn't uncover it."

"That is unfortunate," he said, though he appeared unconcerned. "But what about Theodoraxion? What knowledge have you gained from your time with him?"

"He is a complete fool," I decided truthfully, "but if he's planning on moving against you anytime soon, he's not spoken of it in front of me."

"But is he beginning to trust you? If you can't win him over then there's no point in you being there."

"Yes, but it's been difficult to win him over while he's trying to kill me for murdering his twin sister!" I snapped, hoping to see even a flash of remorse about sending me into a death trap. When he simply raised a brow, I continued, "Why didn't you tell me? You sent me there knowing he would likely figure it out!"

He gave me an indulgent smile. "Kitten, if I thought you would let yourself be killed by Theodoraxion Lusilim, I wouldn't have let you leave. I didn't spend ten years training you for that inconsequential boy to do any major damage."

I bristled in defense for Theo, but kept my expression blank and nodded, accepting that he simply withheld the knowledge as an added challenge. Ignoring his questioning look, I walked round to his side of the desk and opened the drawer to his left. The green dagger shone in the dimness inside and I plucked it out, inspecting the small purple date adorning the hilt, before slipping it into my belt.

"I miss having you at home," he said, "and I know Verrill does too. Try and speed things up."

I made no answer, not trusting my voice to remain steady as the guilt increased. I had loved my father, but Csintalan had stepped in and cared for Verrill and me when any other person would have left us in that crumbling ruin. And though I was still furious he had sent me into a trap, he had also given us everything and trained us to survive.

And I was lying to him.

"Feline," Csintalan's voice rang out as I turned to leave the room, "I expect your next report to be less disappointing."

Without responding, I closed the door and walked away, trying to keep my emotions under control. I spent the next hour rifling through cupboards and drawers throughout the Autarch's wing of the Palace, looking in every hiding place I could think of before huffing out a frustrated sigh and leaving to return to my room. As I was passing by the main hall, I saw Verrill running toward me from the other end of the hallway.

"Why didn't you come and get me?" he scolded into my hair as he wrapped his arms around me.

"I went straight to your room when I arrived, but you were … occupied."

Looking up, I saw a slight blush creep over his cheeks and he turned away, clenching his jaw. He never liked to talk about the people he took to his bed, and after our visit to Khar'ra, I had more of an understanding why.

"I heard Theo is unwell," he said quietly as we walked back toward our rooms.

"Of course you did." I chuckled, though the mention of him made my anxiety demand I forget the stone and return to Zingal immediately.

"You're worried," Verrill observed, his expression dark.

I sighed, unable to hide my emotions from him. "It was bad." We slipped into my room and I closed the door, not wanting anyone to overhear. "Csintalan doesn't know?"

"The Rats are loyal to me," he said, leaning against the wall, "but I'll tell him after you return to Zingal. If he hears it from anyone else he'll start to question my effectiveness."

"Or *your* loyalty," I worried.

"Eris, he knows I'm only loyal to you."

I huffed out a laugh and gave his shoulder a playful push, before sitting on my bed facing him. Despite Csintalan's fondness for us, it still made me uneasy to hear him talk like that. Verrill had control over the Rats, but Csintalan could have his own spies within the Palace. And while I didn't think he would punish Verrill for saying things like that, I knew he could threaten me to force him into doing almost anything.

"Do you want to do something tonight?" he asked, giving me a devious smile. "I heard that there's a party in Anzillu, where our favorite seamstress will be attending with a certain sailor."

"I can't," I muttered, "I'm going back to Zingal."

"To check on Theo?" Verrill asked, hurt flashing across his face for less than a second before he smoothed it into indifference. I barely nodded before he added, "Why did you come back?"

I pulled the dagger from my belt and presented it to him, but he didn't take it. Instead, he looked away, focusing on the floor. Despite my yearning to comfort him, I knew he wouldn't want me to.

"Okay, let's go!" I said, jumping to my feet and banishing my unease. "I need to catch Asila in the act so I can tease her until the end of time."

But Verrill only shook his head.

"No," he said softly, "go back to Zingal, I know that's where you actually want to be. I'll collect the evidence you need for tormenting Asila."

I shook my head. "I can go back tomorrow."

"But you want to go back tonight." He paused for a second before adding, "You care about Theo."

It wasn't a question, but he gave me a searching look, waiting for my confirmation anyway.

I forced out a rough laugh. "Don't be ridiculous."

Verrill gave me a sad half-smile before ushering me out of the Palace.

And I let him, because he was right. I did care.

# Chapter 20

## Theo

I had too many nightmares to write down. I saw Erisa fall from the cliff over and over until I eventually jumped down after her.

30 May (I think)

❖ ❖ ❖

The motion of falling jolted me awake and I snapped my eyes open. Though I remembered briefly regaining consciousness a few times, I felt properly awake for the first time in days. Looking down to the warmth I felt at my side, my heart stopped when I saw Erisa sitting on a chair next to me. She was asleep with her head and torso on the bed, holding my hand firmly in both of hers and resting them against her forehead. She looked incredibly uncomfortable.

I squeezed my hand around hers, until her eyelids fluttered.

She looked up quickly, relaxing when she saw my attempt at a smirk.

"You're awake," she breathed.

"I believe so." My voice was hoarse from misuse.

She let out a long breath and bent down to rest her forehead against my arm, still holding on to my hand. It was dark outside and she looked tired, but the purple smudges beneath her yellow eyes made them appear even brighter.

"Come up," I said, patting the bed next to me. She hesitated for a second before joining me, curling herself against my arm and facing toward me.

"You scared me," she whispered, her words barely audible in the silent room.

"And here I thought I meant nothing to you," I teased and silently chastised myself. I hadn't wanted to make a joke about her being there in case she left, but I couldn't help myself. To my surprise, she huffed out a soft laugh and pressed a light kiss to my shoulder, and I felt my heart swell almost painfully in my chest.

"That's okay, we can't all be as intelligent as me," she remarked with a smile.

I watched as her eyes closed and her breathing deepened, entranced by the serene expression that softened her features. I stared at her until my own eyes drifted shut.

❖ ❖ ❖

Battling through the fog of confusion that met me upon awakening,

I eventually made out shouting in the hallway.

"I want you out of this house! Leave before I make you!" my mother shrieked, and I shook my head to try and clear it because that couldn't be right; I hadn't heard her raise her voice in years.

"And how exactly do you plan on doing that?" Erisa hissed, her voice still carrying despite the low and dangerous tone. There was a scuffle in the hallway and I could hear the yelps of several people as I forced myself to my feet.

"Get off me," Erisa snapped. "I don't want to hurt you."

That was all the encouragement I needed to make it to the door. Swinging it open, I saw the source of the commotion. Nook and Ezra had Erisa pinned to the floor, and even though I knew she could easily escape the hold, anger surged inside me.

"What is this?" I demanded, noting my mother's glare and Suenna holding a sobbing Didi. Everyone's heads turned toward me.

"Oh Theo, my darling, go and lie back down. You should be resting," my mother said, coming over to usher me back into my room.

"No, tell me what's going on." When she didn't respond, I cursed. "Tell me, mother!"

"That *demon*," she shrilled, pointing at Erisa, "murdered your sister. She admitted it to us last night and then I found her asleep next to you. No doubt plotting to kill you next!"

I groaned, pinching the bridge of my nose. "I can't deal with this right now." I was feeling slightly lightheaded from standing up after sleeping for so long. "Ezra, Nook, let her go."

As soon as they did, Erisa stared at me for a long minute

before disappearing downstairs and through the backdoor in the kitchen. I followed slowly, not wanting to have this conversation standing in a hallway, but led the way into the parlor instead, to give Erisa time to get away.

"Theo, did you not hear what I said?" my mother cried, trailing after me. "She killed Karasi. Left her body to rot somewhere instead of returning it to us."

Her voice broke into a sob at the end and I had to work to keep my expression neutral as I sank into a chair. I waited until everyone was in the room before speaking again.

"I know."

"What do you mean you know?" my mother wailed. Didi's sobs doubled in intensity and my heart broke watching her cry.

"It means I know," I said. "I found out before Tammuz and she confirmed it when we were on our way to the mountains."

The silence that followed stretched on for an eternity.

"And you let her live?" my mother sputtered. "You let her come into our home and eat at our table?"

I felt wretched and miserable. "I'm sorry for not telling you, but it wasn't like that."

Suenna's expression was furious. "So what, you fuck her once and suddenly you're cuntstruck? Blind to every wrong she's ever committed? What the hell were you thinking, Theo?"

"Oh Theo, you didn't," my mother cried, "please tell me you didn't."

"Enough!" I shouted, my head swimming. "Do you think I wanted this? Do you think I don't hate myself for it? The Autarch ordered her to kill Karasi, and she did it without knowing who she was. And I'm not saying that excuses her actions because it doesn't, and every time I think about it I feel sick. But I couldn't help fa—" I broke off, putting my face in my hands. "I tried, I really fucking tried to keep on hating her."

"But Theo—" Didi began, her eyes red and puffy.

"Are you all forgetting that Erisa saved my life not once, but twice?" I snapped, cutting her off. "She has had countless opportunities to kill me during the last few weeks and as far as I'm aware, I'm still here. Thanks to her."

"I won't stand here and listen to this. Come on, Didi," my mother said, leaving the room and taking my sister and Suenna with her. Ezra avoided my gaze and Nook followed the others out, his face full of accusation and betrayal. They were fond of Erisa, and despite not being close to Karasi like Suenna was, I knew they were hurt that I'd lied to them.

"Give it time," Ezra said, finally meeting my eye, "they'll come around."

"They'll never forgive her," I murmured, shaking my head.

"Do you?" he asked.

"No," I answered truthfully, hanging my head. When I looked up, he was already gone, and I sat alone, with only my own misery to keep me company.

In my mind, Erisa existed as two versions: the Erisa who I could laugh and joke with, and the Feline who had killed my sister. I had been too confused and wrapped up in my own emotions to reconcile the two, but I knew I needed to. I needed to either forgive her and move on or cut her out of my life completely, for the sake of my family.

The choice made my stomach churn with guilt. Because it shouldn't have been a choice at all.

⁂

I didn't see anyone but the healer for the rest of the day, who informed me that my recovery was going well and that I should continue to rest and regain my strength. It was the last thing I wanted to do, there were so many tasks that needed my attention and I couldn't think about any of them. My mind was spinning with possible future scenarios, each one laced with guilt and self-loathing, because no matter how much I tried, Erisa was at the center of them all.

She still hadn't returned by the time I went to bed that evening, and if I hadn't known how capable she was I would have gone out to search for her. I wondered if she had fled Zingal and returned to the Palace. The thought of her leaving twisted painfully in my gut, even though it would make my decision for me.

The curtains whispered softly against the floor and the light breeze brought the scent of wild jasmine, orange, and vanilla into my bruised lungs, soothing the aches and pains away. I opened my eyes to see Erisa crouched on the windowsill, watching and waiting.

"Now who's obsessed?" I said, the joke falling flat against my dark mood.

She stepped inside the room and silently walked toward me. After removing her cloak and boots, she climbed onto the bed and resumed the same position from the previous night. Then, reaching down, she pulled a dagger from her belt and placed it on my chest.

"I thought you'd want to have it back," she whispered.

I knew what it was without touching it, but lifted it in the air anyway. The decorative palm leaves adorned the hilt, surrounding the purple date that glittered in the moonlight. It had been years since I had seen it, and somehow it hadn't lost any of its shine. My throat felt thick as I held Karasi's treasured blade in my palm, the enormity of her death crashing through me once more.

"Why did you tell them?" I asked, placing the dagger on the side table.

"I didn't want you to lie for me anymore," she murmured. "And I guess I felt guilty about lying to them myself. Especially to Didi."

Taking in a deep breath, I turned to face her fully, resting my forehead against hers.

"I can't take back what happened," she continued, "and I don't believe in regretting past actions. But I do wish that she hadn't been your sister."

And if Karasi had to have died, I wished it would have been anyone else that had killed her. But wishes aren't horses, and beggars don't ride.

Sighing, I gently trailed the backs of my fingers across her cheekbone, savoring the softness of her skin beneath mine.

"Do you want me to leave?" she asked quietly.

This was it; the moment I needed to make my decision.

"No."

My answer was firm and decisive, and though the guilt threatened to drown me, I couldn't bring myself to regret it. I stared

261

at her mouth and was unable to stop myself from brushing my lips against hers.

The gentle kiss quickly turned feverish, developing into a desperate clash of tongues and teeth. Erisa sighed against me and I cradled her neck, tracing the column of her throat with my thumb, feeling her pulse quicken beneath my touch. Ignoring my injuries, I stripped her bare, following each trace of my fingers with my mouth and tongue, until she was writhing beneath me.

"Theo," she panted, "lie back down, you're still healing."

I obeyed, knowing that I would follow any command she gave with that desire-laced purr. She could ask me to commit any unimaginable sin and I wouldn't hesitate for a second.

Looking up, I revered her as one would a divine being as she straddled me, carefully avoiding putting pressure on my chest. My hands roamed over her, tracing every line of perfection before settling at her hips and gripping tightly. Everything about this was wrong, I was betraying everyone I loved and yet nothing had ever felt this right.

Erisa threw her head back and her black hair cascaded down her back to brush against my knuckles.

Her pace quickened, and with every rise and fall of her body, I realized I had never truly been religious until now. Erisa was my Inanna, Goddess of Love and Queen of Heaven, and I would gladly lay down my life to worship at her altar.

❖ ❖ ❖

The next morning, I awoke alone. The intoxicating scent of Erisa still lingered on my bed sheets, but they were cold and empty. Though I hadn't expected her stay, I still found myself despondent in her absence. Reaching over to my side table, I retrieved my notebook to write down my latest nightmare and found a short, scrawling note inside.

*Continuing the search. Try not to miss me too much.*

Beneath the note, she had drawn a simple sketch of a sunflower, and the sight of it brought a grin to my face, which refused to leave until I made my way downstairs to the breakfast room. I suspected Erisa had left to avoid creating even more tension between my family and friends, and I would have to try my best to smooth things out as much as possible before she returned to Zingal.

As expected, my mother and Didi were waiting for me and their hushed voices halted upon my entrance. My mother looked more reserved but just as severe as she had yesterday. I was glad to see Didi's mood had improved, the redness around her eyes had gone and her cheeks were dry. My mother opened her mouth to speak as I joined them at the table, but I held up a hand to stop her.

"Before you say anything, I'd like to apologize," I began. "I should have told you as soon as I returned from the mountains, but I let my own confused emotions get in the way. I convinced myself that I needed to keep Erisa around to stop her from exposing the mountain barracks, and that meant hiding the truth from you all so she could stay here. But deep down I think I was secretly glad of the excuse."

"I can't forget what she did to this family, Theo," my mother said, "nor can I forgive her for it."

"And I would never ask that of you," I assured her. "I know I've put you all in a terrible position, but I never intended on taking it this far. And I suppose I wanted to avoid reopening old wounds, because knowing who killed Karasi doesn't change the fact that she's gone."

My mother's mouth pinched. "Then what *are* you asking of us?"

I shook my head. "I don't know. If I want to take down the Autarch, I need to find the rest of these relics and Erisa has agreed to help me do that."

"And what does she want in return? I don't trust her, Theo. She could ruin us … more than she already has."

"If that was her plan we'd already be dead," I said softly. "She won't hurt any of you, I'm sure of that."

My mother didn't seem convinced, and this time Didi turned her large green eyes to me. She looked so much like my mother, but we both shared our father's eyes; the Lusilim green.

She sniffed, tears threatening to spill once more. "Why did you let me get so close to her? I thought she was my friend."

"I'm so sorry, Didi. I know she was fond of you," I said, hating seeing her so upset. Though I knew I wasn't giving her the whole truth. How could I admit to her that I had liked watching them become friends? That the thought of Erisa building a relationship with my little sister had been too appealing for me to put a stop to it?

My mother glanced toward the door, where Nook, Ezra, and

Suenna were standing. She cleared her throat and smoothed her skirts before speaking again.

"There are plenty of women, Theo. Nice girls from good families that I can introduce you to. Or what about Josefine? You were fond of her not so long ago, and she would suit you much better than some Palace executioner."

"She's Erisa *Anzû*, mother."

Their expressions morphed into genuine shock, and I spent the next half hour explaining almost everything that had happened in the last month, including Karasi's potential involvement in the Anzû slaughter, which my mother vehemently denied. But even she did not have an explanation of how the Lusilim dagger had come to lodge itself in Ava Anzû's chest, nor could she account for Karasi's actions during that time.

It was by no means an easy conversation, but after it was over, I felt a weight lift from my shoulders that I hadn't realized I had been carrying.

My friends remained with me after my mother and sister departed to the gardens, and though I didn't say it, their presence was comforting. We worked through the rest of the morning in a tense atmosphere. It wasn't until we were well into the afternoon, drawing up multiple plans and placement strategies for our growing army, that the tension eased and our easy companionship started to return to normal.

While I had been healing, Verrill had sent a message notifying me about a small conflict on Tarprusa's eastern coast, along with his wishes for my speedy recovery. Though I knew the spymaster had eyes and ears everywhere, I couldn't help feeling slightly disconcerted about his apparent access to my household's private affairs.

❖ ❖ ❖

The next few days passed in a similar, uneventful pattern. I had fallen so behind on my paperwork that most of the reports and correspondence had become obsolete. The strain between my mother and me had lessened, and though I knew Didi was still upset, I tried to make it up to her by spending each morning in the gardens, helping her tend to the flowerbeds and plants.

Truthfully, I was actively occupying my time to avoid fretting over Erisa. I hadn't heard anything from her or about her, even though I knew the Rats ran rampant around my district and she was beginning to have almost as much control over them as the Fox.

Corbin stayed for two days and helped me look over the current state of affairs in Zingal, offering advice on how best to transport my forces from Katmu back to the mainland when the need arose. I told him about Erisa, without mentioning her role in Karasi's death, and he had seemed so genuinely happy for me that I felt a fresh wave of guilt at my concealment.

"I'm pleased for you, my boy," he had said, smiling. "I'd like to meet this young lady, see if she's as fierce as you say."

The morning after he had departed, I was in my office redrafting a letter to Malah Jirata for the third time when I felt the cool press of metal against my throat, and a pair of soft lips at my ear.

"I have a gift for you." Erisa's melodic voice sent a shiver of delight down my spine and I basked in her scent once more.

"You know, it's incredibly rude to enter someone's house unannounced," I said, turning my head to smile at her.

"If you don't want visitors, you should start locking your windows," she replied, perching herself on my desk in front of me and reading my letter to Malah. She let out a snort of amusement. "Why is this so formal? You know we can just go and visit him without arranging a meeting, I happen to have an open invitation to the Katmu citadel."

"That *is* good to know," I said. "You mentioned a gift?"

She gave me a devious smile and hopped down from the desk to walk back to the window, where a shield lay propped against the wall. She handed it to me and I angled my chair toward the light to see it in more detail. It was no longer than the length of my arm and made of a gleaming metal with a large depiction of a lion-headed mace on the front. Surrounding the two heads were multiple divots in the surface, giving the shield an unfinished appearance.

I almost gasped in amazement. "Nergal's shield? Where did you find it?"

"Henri Elkas has quite the collection of old trinkets stashed away in Anzillu," she said. "Who knew he was such a hoarder?"

"Henri gave you the shield?" I asked, astonished.

Her eyes gleamed. "Yeah … sure he did."

"You stole it."

"Stealing is such an *ugly* word." She pouted, twisting the end of her braid around her finger. "I merely borrowed it from his vault … like a surprise loan, with an indefinite return deadline and no interest. Though, I do have to mention, he won't be joining your efforts to take over the realm. He's still a little sore about the Cameron situation … sorry about that."

"I'm not *taking over the realm*," I protested, shaking my head at her thievery. Though I had to admit, her methods were efficient.

She rolled her eyes. "Whatever you say."

I looked down at the shield, focusing on the shape of the divots; they looked like six place holders for smaller items, and I could make an educated guess at what they were. Reaching into my desk drawer, I retrieved the jeweled dagger and placed it into the groove along the top of the shield. It fit reasonably well, but not perfectly; the shape was correct but the depth wasn't.

"It still doesn't look right." Erisa hummed, looking over my shoulder. "Where's the other one?"

"It's still upstairs in my room."

She was out of the room in a flash, and I roamed over the rest of the indents. Beneath the dagger, there was a long, thin space, likely for the stylus. There were two larger spaces, one in the center, between the two roaring lion heads, and one on the bottom right, each of which would probably fit the songbird. Beneath a smaller, intricately shaped space on the lower left was an eye etched into the shield surface, but the iris remained empty, almost the same size as the Orb of Nanaya, if it were whole.

"Try this one," Erisa said, making me jump. I had never known anyone to move as silently as she did. She held out the palm leaf dagger toward me and I tried it in the space.

It still wasn't right.

Taking it back out, I placed them both on the desk in front of me, examining them together for the first time. I had never thought too much about the flat design of the hilts before, but now that I was paying attention I saw that the grooves of the palm leaves on one hilt matched exactly to the jewels on the other.

I put them together, pressing them side by side and almost yelped in surprise as they began to thrum with energy. A shimmering green rippled over the joined blades, making them appear as one.

Erisa gasped. "That's exactly the one I saw."

I placed the joined daggers into the shield, finding the fit to match perfectly, and not quite being able to believe what I had just witnessed.

"Well that's that one done," Erisa chirped, apparently over her shock and at ease with the blatant display of magic. "So, are we going to Katmu?"

I chuckled and shook my head in disbelief, before standing and placing a hand on her lower back.

"Lead the way, Sunflower."

# Chapter 21

## Erisa

This recent truce between Theo and I was, although tentative, not unwelcome. I imagined that, like myself, he was expecting the thin threads of our new civility to snap under the slightest tension, but I found myself enjoying the result of it all the same. Our conversation on the tram ride into Ersetu was lively and diverting and he teased me relentlessly about my flawed sense of morality, which amused me exceedingly.

"Do you know what your problem is, Theo?" I asked, after he made yet another mention of my "sticky fingers."

"I have no doubt you'll tell me," he remarked with a smirk.

"You give too much attention to the methods, when you should be focusing on the results. You're so high and mighty, you forget that down here in the real world, little sacrifices must be made for the greater good."

He raised an amused brow. "And whose greater good is that? I often hear so much about this *greater good*, and the very many sacrifices made in the name of it, that it's hard to keep track of who it actually benefits."

"Human kind in general, if the histories are anything to go by."
I smiled.

"Ah, but histories are only ever written by the victors,
Sunflower," he said with a grin. "The fact that the virtuous always
eventually prevailed over the wicked is a matter of perspective. I'm
sure both sides of every historical conflict believed they were
making a great many little sacrifices in the name of battling against
evil."

I laughed. "Are you doubting your cause?"

"Not at all," he assured me. "I am perfectly susceptible to that
particular flaw that has afflicted so many of our kind before. I truly
believe in making Irkalla a better place. But if you were to ask your
Autarch, or any of the wealthy citizens in Šarrum, they would no
doubt say that I'm in the wrong."

My brows furrowed. "Then why bother? I've seen how happy
the people of Zingal are, why don't you just content yourself with
the improvement of your own people and leave the rest of the
districts to their own Lords? It seems like an elaborate scheme just
to get revenge over the Autarch."

"He needs to pay for his crimes against my family, and for
every other little offense he commits without penance," he said
decisively. "But if I were to kill him, it would have a rippling effect
throughout the realm. I need to have a plan in place to improve the
lives of others, instead of just chasing this goal for selfish reasons."

I pondered his words for a long moment, concluding that he
was much more rational than myself. I was more of a strike-first-
and-avoid-the-consequences kind of person. And while I admired

his good sense, it seemed like a terribly boring way to live.

"So, are you saying I shouldn't have stolen the shield?" I asked him, playful once more.

"Absolutely not," he replied. "I'm taking your advice and focusing on the results. I'm sure poor Henri can lament your methods enough for the both of us."

❖ ❖ ❖

There was a general air of unease at the Šarrum platform, and from beneath my lowered hood I could see more whispered deals and passing of notes than usual. Theo said nothing until we were on the tram line to Anzillu, and even then, it was too crowded for him to remark on anything other than the stifling heat.

Though the likelihood of seeing Henri was slim, I clung to the shadows as much as possible. He was unlikely to know about the missing shield yet, but as soon as he did, I would be his prime suspect. He had been incredibly onerous to arrange an audience with, and I had needed to cash in several favors to make it happen.

"You're almost down to one arm," Theo said when he noticed me tracing the remaining silver bands on my left wrist. His eyes flicked up to the thicker band on my bicep, marking my bargain with Silas and then he looked away again.

"I made my own payments for the shield," I explained, gesturing to my bare forearm. He only nodded and I was grateful he didn't push the subject.

Henri Elkas had always been a difficult man, and it had been a risk for me to show up in his office as the Feline, under fabricated orders from the Autarch. I could gauge enough from his behavior to be confident in his disdain for Theo—and loyalty to Csintalan— all of which was supported with the correspondence I had swiped from his desk. But I had to hope that after Cameron's misgivings, he was still too cautious around the Autarch to mention my visit or my line of questioning.

Theo remained close behind me as I cut through Anzillu's bazaar toward Asila's shop. Though I had been to see her before cornering Henri, I couldn't resist stopping by whenever I was in the area. Unfortunately, the shop was closed but I chatted to Theo about my friend the rest of the way to the seafront.

It was late afternoon, which meant the main harbor was still a bustling commotion of offloading shipments and a frenzy of sailors. The smell of fish and salt was thick in the air and the darkening sky was clouded with billows of steam rising from food vendors.

By exchanging a few silvers, I secured passage to Katmu's main island for Theo and myself, and we climbed the swaying gangway to the deck of the ship. We didn't have to wait long before the sails were raised and the vessel lurched forward. Looking out toward the small specks of land in the distance, I tried to soothe my nerves. I had been to Katmu once before, accompanying the Autarch on a visit to Malah's eldest brother.

❖ ❖ ❖

The ship groaned against the waves and I clung to the railing, another dry heave bursting from my throat. Cold sweat plastered the veil to my face and I fought the urge to rip the whole thing off and cast it overboard into the thrashing waves below.

"We're almost there, Kitten. It'll be over soon. Here, drink this."

Csintalan held his waterskin toward me and I reached for it gratefully.

"But we've still got to come back!" I protested after taking several refreshing swigs of the cool liquid.

"We can wait until the sea is calmer for our return journey," he said. "Even if it takes a few days. I'm sure you'd enjoy exploring the island in any case."

Though his face was obscured behind his crow mask, I knew he was smiling and I allowed his words to comfort me. I almost wept in relief when we eventually made it to port and I took my first shaking steps back onto solid ground.

"Remember your training, Kitten," Csintalan advised as we walked toward the main gates of the stronghold, "and know that whatever the outcome, I'm already proud of you."

My chest warmed at the statement, but I lifted my chin defiantly. "I'm still angry at you for not letting Verrill come with us."

"The *Fox* has his own tasks to be getting on with," Csintalan said, subtly chastising me for forgetting to use Verrill's title. "And I want you two to be able to operate separately. You're much too dependent on each other at present."

Making no response, I walked by his side into the main hall of the castle, where Bail Jirata, Lord of Katmu, sat in an elegant chair on the raised dais. His younger brother, Asor, stood beside him. The pews were filled with citizens, each of them anxious to know the reason for the Autarch's visit.

I had occasionally been out with Csintalan in public, but this was the first time I had been close enough to really see how others reacted to him. Though everyone bowed their heads slightly, some were cringing away from him in fear, rather than as a show of respect.

"Your Grace, you are very welcome," Bail called out, apprehension leaking into his tone. "I hope you will not keep us in suspense much longer as to the reason for your visit. We have been eagerly awaiting your arrival."

"Apologies," Csintalan began, his voice carrying effortlessly to each corner of the room. He settled a large hand on my shoulder before continuing. "My dear little Feline was not feeling so well after the sea crossing. Cats rarely do well in water, you know."

He chuckled softly at his own joke, pausing to allow every eye in the room the chance to settle on me. This was my first public introduction and I felt each gaze heavy on my skin. My already racing heart pounded so loudly in my ears that I could barely hear Csintalan announcing Bail's profit skimming and unsanctioned trade dealings with Tarprusa. He declared Asor—the source of the information—to succeed in being the new Lord of Katmu and sentenced Bail to death.

"Come now, Kitten," Csintalan whispered to me, "let's see those claws."

I swallowed down the nerves and nausea that were closing my throat and took a deep breath to steady myself. Every thrum of my heart fed adrenaline into my frozen limbs, shaking the numbness away as I prowled toward Bail.

"Please, Your Grace! Asor is the snake, he's the one who was—" Bail's voice broke off as he saw me approach, and he looked at his Autarch and then back to me. "A child?"

Without giving him a second to act, I threw my first dagger. It landed through his left foot, pinning it in place. The second went through his right, and I whirled around him as he stumbled, slicing through the backs of his knees. I could barely hear his cries as I severed each arm at the elbow and stood behind him with my hand in his dark hair, exposing his throat.

I looked to Csintalan, whose large crow head nodded once, before I dragged my blade across Bail's throat, marveling at the way the onlookers now cringed away from *me*, instead of their Autarch.

For the first time since my family's slaughter, I had *power*.

❖ ❖ ❖

"—than I thought."

Theo's voice shook me from the memory, and I looked over to see him pointing at the band of mist surrounding the islands. He must have noticed the confusion on my face, because he dropped his hand and moved closer to me.

"I said, I'm surprised the fog has cleared today, it looks like it might rain," he clarified. "Have you ever been here before?"

"Once," I replied, "though it was a long time ago, I wasn't yet sixteen. I imagine there have been a few changes since then."

When we disembarked, I spotted a little girl with a brown ribbon in her braid playing dice with some other children beneath a loading station. She stood when I approached and I crouched down to her height.

"What a pretty ribbon," I said, brushing over it before swiftly tapping a finger to her ear. Her eyes sparkled and I leaned in closer to whisper, "Run along and tell your Lord he has a visitor."

Her smile brightened when I pressed a few coppers into her palm and she sprinted away toward the citadel. Theo and I navigated our way through the bustle of the dockyard and as we approached the thick, towering walls, I found that it looked exactly as it had almost a decade ago. The colorful stonework depicted the snarling faces and hybrid bodies of the ancient, fierce creatures of Irkalla. The hulking form of Neti stretched from the ground to the battlements, his lion head roaring to warn off any unwelcome intruders. The scene was menacing in the approaching dusk.

We were stopped at the gates, and I smiled in recognition at the guard. She was even taller than me and at least twice as wide, and I could see Theo eyeing the axe strapped to her back warily. She was one of Malah's favorites and she would often accompany him to Anzillu when he was transporting high value items. Her face fell when she recognized me.

"What a happy accident," I said brightly, grabbing her right hand noting the single gold line etched across her palm before she snatched it back. Tracing a single silver band on my left wrist. "We need to enter."

"Is that an official exchange?" she snapped, eyeing me with

disdain.

"Let me rephrase," I said. "We need to enter the citadel, complete our business and be able to exit safely, without being followed, obstructed, or detained."

The guard nodded and opened the gate to let us through. I didn't bother looking down at the burning sensation on my wrist to know the bargain had been fulfilled and the silver band would already be gone. That was the great thing about open-ended bargains. Without needing to specify terms, I could cash in my payment anywhere, at any time.

Malah was waiting at the gates of the inner wall, where his face broke out into a beaming smile when he saw us. The little girl skipped away out of sight.

"Shouldn't you be veiled?" Theo muttered into my ear as we approached.

"Malah knows my face," I explained, though it was a bit late for him to be worrying about that now.

"Welcome, my friends." Malah grinned when we reached him. We exchanged greetings, and he led us through a maze of winding hallways and drawbridges until we entered a private office.

"I have to say, I *am* surprised," he began, after closing the door. "I'd expected a visit at some point from you Theo, but never would I have guessed the *Feline* would accompany you. Please tell me what business could possibly bring you both here."

"We're looking for something," I said, wanting to get straight to the point. "An ancient item, believed to have belonged to an original guardian of Irkalla, passed down from one Jirata to the next. Do you know of anything like it?"

"Did you know that Katmu was said to be the entrance to Irkalla?" Malah mused, not answering my question. "Seven islands, one for each of the seven judges. When a person died, their soul would come here to face judgment for their sins."

"Riveting," I said dryly.

"You saw the great Gatekeeper Neti in the stones of the outer wall, Feline. So if you have knowledge of the old gifts, you should be able to ask me about one in particular."

"Do you have the key?" Theo pressed, amusement poorly hidden beneath a serious expression.

"That depends," Malah teased, looking at me. I held out my right hand, raising a brow in challenge, but he only laughed. "Oh no, absolutely not! I've learned my lesson the hard way about making deals with you, Feline. I only need a small favor."

"Go on then," I encouraged, unable to resist the smile that pulled across my face at his easy temperament.

"I'm hosting a bit of a gathering tomorrow, I sent you a message about it to the Palace, but," he looked at Theo, "perhaps you weren't there to receive it. All I ask is that you attend."

"And how could I *possibly* find an outfit at such short notice?" I laughed, guessing his scheme immediately.

He gave me a wink. "Ah, well fortunately I have commissioned a favorite seamstress of yours to sort my own clothes. If she knew you were attending, she would be sure to make an appearance herself." Another glance at Theo. "The Fox has been invited too, though his Rats have made no answer yet."

"We'll be there," I promised, already excited to see Asila again. "Now, the key?"

Malah's hands were already going to a chain around his neck, which he pulled free from beneath his shirt. Hanging from the small links was a large, elaborate key. It was about the length of my hand but every surface of it was covered in delicate designs that swirled from the intricate bow to the pin centered between two symmetrical bits.

"Would you allow us to take it back to Zingal?" Theo asked, admiring the small, twisted piece of metal.

"Unfortunately, I cannot," Malah confessed. "If I were to give it away, I'd be disgracing the entire Jirata line. Though I'm sure my elder brothers would have argued that that ship had sailed long ago."

"Luckily for us, the dead cannot speak," Theo said, before leaning back in his chair. "I'll be frank with you, Malah. I know we've not been acquainted long, but it seems you and Eri—the *Feline*, are friends. We're here together, on the same side. I've no doubt you've heard of my goals to unite the realm by removing the Autarch. You've confirmed my men have been useful in tackling your smuggling issues, and I'm hoping to move more here to aid you. I'm not asking you to supply any soldiers, because I know you have little to spare, but if you want to aid our campaign for the sake of your people, the key is all we need."

"And if I can't give it to you? Will you withdraw your aid from Katmu?" Malah asked.

Though I had suspected some secret dealings between the two men since I saw them shake hands in the Palace, Theo had never confirmed it or disclosed any details to me. The fact that he was letting me listen now meant that he had either forgotten that I didn't already know, or he trusted me enough to keep his secrets.

Each option was undeniably foolish, and yet sadly, equally as probable.

"No, I won't," Theo assured him. "I understand what I'm asking of you and if you decide not to take a side then I'll respect that. Your brothers didn't share your interest in your people; they were selfish and greedy. I want us to be friends, Malah, to build a relationship between our districts."

"We only need one thing from you," I added. "If you can't give us the key, then the chances of success are severely reduced."

"Are you truly a part of this scheme, Feline?" Malah looked at me, every soft feature turning serious. "You and the Fox are betraying the Autarch?"

There are countless times in life when decisions can be thrown away into the meaningless abyss of trivial consequences. This was not one of those times. I had always been adamant about not taking a side, but I knew that I now stood at a very distinct crossroads. I had to choose between Csintalan and Theo, to turn my back on either mine and Verrill's hero or the struggling population of Irkalla. Csintalan had saved us, raised us as his own, but then I thought back to the hungry people in Ocridell, *my* people, who had been forgotten and discarded.

"I cannot speak for the Fox, but yes," I said finally, any lingering uncertainty vanishing beneath the sureness of my decision, "I am with Theo."

My pulse quickened as I looked at Theo, whose answering smile made my heart skip and my stomach fill with bats instead of butterflies. He beamed at me, happiness radiating from his every pore as his dark green eyes regarded me with such deep and open affection. He was beautiful, and I was choosing him.

"In that case," Malah said, holding the key out to us, "here. I expect to have it back when this is all over."

He showed us the way to the guest rooms and entreated us to join him for supper that evening. My stomach growled in acceptance of his request and he left us to settle into our chambers with a smile on his face.

Theo never made it to his own room; as soon as we were alone, he spared no effort in showing me just how much he appreciated my declaration of loyalty to him.

Conversation flowed easily between our small supper party that evening. I had been extremely pleased to find Asila already seated upon entering, and a small, shy smile crept onto her face when she informed me that she had been staying in Malah's home for the past week. He had put her up in one of the finest wings in the citadel and prepared a sewing room for her to work in, furnished with enough items to put a haberdashery to shame. My heart warmed toward Malah at seeing my friend's poorly concealed happiness.

"I have something for you to wear, of course," she said quietly after the meal, "Malah told me you would be attending. Though, now I realize that was merely a ploy to entice me over here."

We laughed through the rest of the evening, poking fun at both Theo and Malah, who seemed to be getting along handsomely, and retired with the promise of continuing the gaiety the following day.

❖❖❖

Theo's arm tightened around my waist, rousing me from sleep and I could feel his heart beating erratically beneath my cheek. Light whispers of dawn crept beneath the thick curtains, illuminating his face as I looked up at him. His long black lashes twitched from the rapid movement of his eyes beneath his closed lids and his full lips were pulled down into a frown.

Reaching a hand to his face, I tried to smooth away the crease settling between his furrowed brows. I knew he received visions from the Orb of Nanaya almost every night and that they often haunted him long after he woke up.

"Theo," I whispered when his breathing turned into short, fitful pants, "you're dreaming. Wake up."

As though he had been waiting for permission, his eyes flew open. They remained wide and wild for half a second before he found me. He breathed a long sigh of relief, before burying his face in my neck. Desire shot through me as he trailed kisses across my throat, shoulder, and collarbone, while holding me so close it was almost painful.

Whatever he had seen had shaken him and I could still feel the thrashing of his pulse against my skin. I relaxed into his touch, allowing him to trace across my body as though assuring himself I was still there. He took his time, memorizing every dip and curve until I was flushed and pliant in his grasp. He kissed away every sound that escaped my lips, replacing each with groans of his own.

"Tell me you're mine, Sunflower," he murmured against my ear, his voice dark and rasping. "Lie to me and tell me that you're mine. Let me pretend that I can have you. Just this once."

"I'm yours," I breathed. "You have me."

# Chapter 22

## Theo

*I saw Erisa die for the first time. I'd seen her fall night after night, but this time I saw her body broken and crumpled on the ground. Her sunflower eyes were cold, empty and unseeing.*

*5 June*

❊❊❊

Katmu was unlike any of the other districts. Though they were separated by choppy waters, the communities on each of the islands were so tightly knit with one another, they rivaled the familial citizens of Hudjefa. Malah had spent the day showing me around his district, proudly pointing out the things he had already improved and the areas he would like to focus on in the coming years.

Despite his young age, he was already one of the better Lords I had known. It was clear that he loved his people and that they loved him. He knew what his weaknesses were and wasn't afraid to ask for advice. He plied me with questions as he pointed out each fault in defense on the islands, indicating where the smugglers were getting in and out. I gave him the best advice I could, and despite stressing to him that I was no sailor, he jotted down everything I said so that he could talk it over with his council at a later date.

"Theo," Malah began during a light supper that evening, "I've been dying to ask about you and the Feline. I know the Autarch sent her with you, but how did you become …" He waved a hand in the air between us. "Whatever you are?"

How could I even begin to answer that? I had no idea what he already knew about Erisa or what information was safe to reveal.

"She killed my sister," I blurted out, unable to stop the words from spilling from my mouth. There was a bitter edge to my voice and I mentally cringed away from the painful memory.

"Ah, right." Malah hesitated. He scratched the back of his neck for a moment, before smiling and meeting my gaze once more. "Did you know she killed my brother?"

"I …" My voice trailed away, because now that I thought about it, I *did* know. The vague memory of hearing about the young Jirata Lord being supplanted by his adolescent brother resurfaced. "Your eldest brother, Bail?"

Malah nodded. "The very one. I had only just turned twelve when she came here and sliced him open in front of everyone. I remember watching from the side of the dais, holding my little sister Calia and being absolutely mesmerized. I think I fancied myself a little in love right then."

He must have seen the shock on my face because he laughed, flashing his pearly white teeth. "Bail was a tyrant, to all of us. I won't bore you with the details but we all feared him. She was like an angel, a savior, and I was too enraptured to even see the gore she left behind. Everyone else did though, they all began to fear her that day, just as they did the Fox."

I thought back to Erisa's vacant expression on our journey to Katmu. If this was the first time she had returned since killing Bail, how had it affected her? As far as I could remember, no one had heard of the Feline before Bail's execution. Her life had changed here, and she'd barely matured beyond childhood.

"The Autarch shouldn't have put her through that," I muttered, voicing my thoughts.

Malah shrugged. "Maybe not, but she wields the title like a weapon now. Looking back, that was obviously his intention; Bail's crimes were minor but the Autarch was relatively new himself. He wanted to make an impression, and wanted his pets to do the same. It worked wonderfully. Asor was so terrified of the Feline, he licked the Autarch's ass like his lips were glued to it."

Before I could answer there was a soft knock at the door and I looked behind me to see who had entered the room. Though half his face was covered with a simple navy fox mask, I knew from the dark blonde waves and lethal poise that it was Verrill. He was dressed in a matching navy suit and carrying a small bag in one arm. One glance at Malah told me that his presence was welcome and not entirely unexpected.

"Fox"—he grinned, gesturing to a seat at the table—"come and join us, we were just discussing your charming Feline."

The way Malah said *your* Feline to Verrill made my teeth clench so hard they almost cracked. Even though I knew it was the truth.

"I would, but I'd prefer to just see her instead of talk about her," he said, before handing the bag to me. Inside was a set of clothes; a neat black suit with emerald thread detail.

"These are mine." It was almost a question.

"I need to speak to the Feline," he said lazily. "I went to Zingal yesterday, only to hear the Rats chirping about seeing you here. She can never resist a party and I assumed she'd rope you into it as well, so I brought these along for you in case you didn't have anything suitable to wear." He looked down at the clothes I was wearing. "Good thing I did."

"Thank you, that's … very helpful."

"I didn't do it for you." His tone wasn't malicious or unkind, simply truthful. "The Autarch will hear reports from tonight, so this needs to look like a planned event for Malah to declare his allegiance to the Feline and myself. And by extension, the Autarch." He looked at Malah, who nodded, before turning to me. "And Theo, he expects the Feline to have beguiled you enough to derail your plans. You'll need to act as though you're completely captivated by her." He sneered down at me, his expression turning cold. "Shouldn't be hard for you; you're already obsessed."

"As if you're not," I replied. But his words did little to affect me. I wasn't obsessed, I was merely *dedicated.*

Verrill snorted out a humorless breath. "He's hoping that the Lords will see you in public with her and therefore won't trust you when you approach them. The Autarch expects everyone to know her loyalty lies with him."

He gave a cordial nod to Malah and strode out of the room.

Before I could stop them, tendrils of unease nipped at my heels. I knew the Autarch had sent Erisa to ensnare me in one of her lethal traps, but hearing it so plainly from Verrill was unnerving. Because she *had* planted her traps, and I had seen her do it and had practically skipped into them. I had let her learn about the locations and movements of my army and about each of my alliances.

*No*, I thought to myself, *she hasn't told him about the barracks in the mountains. They're still safe. She's on my side ... I hope.*

❖ ❖ ❖

The party was an impressive affair. The soft glow of the enormous chandeliers illuminated the high, sweeping arched walls of the grand hall. A group of musicians performed on the raised dais, their music sweeping over the dancing couples and setting the pace for the steps. Even the individuals by the refreshment tables were swaying to the beat and laughing at the cheerful atmosphere.

As splendid as the ambience was, as soon as Erisa walked in, it was impossible to focus on anything else. How could I even comprehend something as mundane as the decor, when the most extraordinary creature was across the room from me? She was veiled, the deep blue material obscuring every part of her face above her mouth, which was painted a dark red. Her dress was made from silk—the same shade as her veil—and the tight bodice swept elegantly up her torso to tie at the nape of her neck, leaving her back completely exposed.

She took Verrill's hand, his outfit the perfect complement to hers. My heart throbbed painfully as I watched them twirl around the other couples, their movements so familiar and natural it seemed entirely effortless.

It wasn't until he leaned down and whispered something into her ear, causing her to throw her head back in laughter, that I had to look away, jealousy flooding my mouth with acid. I had to work for every single grin and laugh, and she gave them to him freely. Not that I minded the toil, I chased the reward of her smiles, but watching them together pained me.

My shift in focus allowed me to observe the way the other guests interacted with them. They would cringe away, their fearful eyes following every movement and ears straining to catch every comment in hopes they didn't hear their own names.

It was such a contrast to how I had seen people act around Erisa in the past few weeks. By simply donning her Feline persona and uniform, she was seen as an entirely different person. The thought unsettled me; she looked so comfortable and at ease being the Feline. Was she really so different as the Erisa I knew?

After what felt like an eternity of watching the Autarch's pets whirl around in each other's arms, I could no longer bear it and made my way over to them.

"Mind if I cut in?" I asked, rudely interrupting their hushed conversation.

"Mind if I cut *you*?" the Fox muttered as he melted away into the crowd, who were subtly glancing as I took Erisa's hand and led her into a dance.

289

Those glances morphed into blatant stares as I allowed my hand to caress the expanse of her exposed back and skimmed her jaw with my lips. They knew who I was, and rumors had been circulating for almost a year about my treasonous plots. This parade could be my greatest show of strength, or the Autarch's most effortless—and successful—way of undermining me.

"That was very rude," Erisa chastised with a smirk. "The Fox was in the middle of telling me a very interesting piece of information."

"I don't give a fuck," I crooned, delighting in the goosebumps that rose on her skin as I nipped at her earlobe.

"But you might when I relay it," she whispered, placing her arm around my neck to shield her mouth from view. "The Autarch is gathering his own forces. The Fox tells me he's conscripted citizens from Šarrum and Anzillu so far and is planning on approaching Aran, Malah, and Tasar. It's already causing quite a stir among the people. So, if you were planning on talking to them, I'd recommend that you do it soon."

This new development was hardly surprising, but I couldn't help the feeling of dread that settled in my gut. Up until now, the Autarch had remained a silent and stagnant opponent, and I couldn't help but wonder what had caused him to finally start taking action against me.

"We'll go and visit Tasar tomorrow," I said, only realizing after the words left my mouth that I had assumed she would come with me.

To my relief, she nodded. "I think we need to find the other half of the Orb as quickly as possible," she murmured. "I had a look for it while you were still unconscious but didn't find anything. We need to try again, and be successful, because we won't have much time left after he talks to the other Lords. He'll be keeping a closer eye on me."

"And the Fox, can we trust him?"

She only snorted and I knew she rolled her eyes before pressing her temple against my shoulder, allowing me to lead her through the dance.

"What's the reason for this party anyway?" I asked when the music slowed.

Her smile lit up the room and I yearned to peel back her veil to see if her eyes were just as bright. She tilted her head to where Malah was dancing with the seamstress, Asila.

"It's her birthday," Erisa explained quietly, "though Malah would never admit to it."

"Are they together?"

She grinned. "No, Asila's only a few years older than him, but she says he's too young for her. She likes him anyway, even if she pretends she doesn't." She was quiet for a moment, then added, "I need Malah to get her and Tohnain out, in case everything falls apart."

"Tohnain …"—I paused, trying to recollect—"the Palace butler?"

"Yes, he's Asila's father, and I'm fond of him."

We danced through two more songs before she tried to pull away from me. My arms instinctively tightened until I felt her nails pierce the skin of my biceps. I couldn't see her eyes, but I could feel their glare penetrating through the veil and a whip of excitement cracked through me at her anger. She walked away toward Malah, taking her warmth and jasmine scent with her.

I had realized soon after this evening had begun that I was considered a sort of pariah by almost everyone in the room. With the Fox and the Feline present, only a few very brave souls risked engaging in a conversation with me, and even then, they were brief. No one wanted to be seen talking to me, in case they were accused of participating in any of my illicit schemes.

It suited me just fine. I was relieved not to have to entertain the meaningless ramblings of court morons or the unwelcome advances of ambitious women. Making the most of the opportunity, I skulked between couples and lingered around the refreshments, picking up pieces of furtive conversations and covert discussions.

"Lord Lusilim." The Fox's quiet voice halted my meanderings and I stopped beside him, following his gaze to where Erisa was dancing with some puffed-up airhead I recognized from Henri Elkas' court. He was prancing about the floor like someone had stuck pins in his sickly velvet shoes.

"At least try to control your facial expressions," Verrill sneered, "you're embarrassing yourself."

"You weren't an asshole on the journey to Khar'ra," I murmured, "what changed?"

"Has she sung for you?" he asked, ignoring my question.

"Not directly," I said, trying to keep the dejected tone out of my voice, "but I've heard her sing."

He smirked, as if he knew exactly when I had heard her sing. *For him.* His expression was one of poorly concealed delight, as though I had just confirmed she preferred him over me.

"She gets it from her mother," he offered. "Ava had the voice of an angel and could persuade you to do just about anything by using it—a gift she passed down to her daughters. I rarely get to hear her now, unless we leave the Palace. The Autarch forbade her to sing when he took us in."

"Why are you telling me this?"

"I hear chirps from all over the realm," he went on, still ignoring me. "Because you never leave Zingal, as soon as you do, it's all anyone can talk about. And unfortunately, I've had to listen to the unending foolish prattle about the *handsome Lord Lusilim* on his adventures to Khar'ra with a mysterious dark-haired beauty."

"I'm assuming you're getting to the point?"

He scratched along his jaw before turning his cold brown eyes to me. "For whatever unfathomable reason, she seems to be … *fond* of you, which isn't something she's known for. I'm not warning you, Theo, I'm *promising* that if your plan is to betray her or trick her in any way, I'll make you wish that you'd died alongside your sister."

"Ah, you're jealous," I drawled. His threat would have annoyed me, had I been paying him any attention at all. But my eyes were fixed on Velvet Shoes across the room, and to where his greasy fingers were creeping inside the silk of Erisa's dress.

I decided that I wanted to rip his hands off.

The muscles in her back tensed in discomfort and she leaned away from his face as he brought it to hers, his hands roaming and groping greedily.

I hadn't realized I was moving until Verrill's hand clamped around my arm, halting me mid-stride.

"Do you think she can't handle herself?" he hissed as I moved to shake him off. "He'll be dealt with by the end of the night."

As if on cue, the man howled loudly enough for the musicians to falter and for everyone to look around. At first, I couldn't see why he had cried out, Erisa had twisted in his arms so that her back was to his front. Then I saw the blood; she had sliced the fingers of his right hand off, the ones I had seen go under her dress. She held his arms under hers, pinning him in place while she chopped his thumb off. After turning and tucking his fingers into the front pocket of his jacket, she lifted his left hand.

"Now, do I need to remove these too, or can you keep them to yourself?" she said sweetly, the silence of the room allowing it to carry effortlessly.

"No … I'm s-sorry," he whimpered, doubling over and clutching at his ruined hand when she let go of him.

Without hesitation, four men came running over to the pair, two of whom shooed the wailing man off into a side room while the other cleaned up the spilled blood off the floor. One of them handed Erisa a cloth and she thanked him and began cleaning her hands and dagger.

Scanning the room, I found that even though there were a few sickly pale faces, no one looked particularly surprised. I caught a glimpse of Malah, who wore a disgruntled expression and waved to the musicians to resume playing.

"Pity about your dress," Verrill said as Erisa approached us.

Though it was hardly noticeable on the dark fabric, she had small splatters of blood down the length of her skirt. I knew I should be horrified with what I had just witnessed, but when I remembered the way that man had touched her without permission, I concluded that losing his fingers wasn't enough of a punishment.

"Oh no, Asila is going to murder me." Erisa sighed, glancing down at her dress before searching the room. "Where did they take him?"

"Will you wait a while, my darling?" Verrill asked her, brushing a loose strand of hair behind her ear. "He's one of Henri's, I want him to give me some answers before you dismantle him."

Erisa huffed out a displeased sigh. "Ugh, you can have him then." She grabbed my hand, pulling me away. "I want to dance again."

Without giving the Fox a second glance, I followed her back into the crowd that had resumed their revelry with renewed vigor, and threw myself into enjoying her undivided attention.

❖ ❖ ❖

"Do you think I'm a fool, Theo?" Tasar asked me the following morning.

Erisa and I had sailed back to the mainland after breakfast. The journey had been uncomfortable; the thick blanket of mist surrounding the islands had been low enough to skim the sea's surface and it had whispered cruel and disturbing promises into my ears.

It was known for its sentience, and renowned for its malicious remarks and distressing visions. It had susurrated confirmations of my fears; telling me that I wasn't strong enough to win this war.

That I was dooming everyone I loved and I would have to watch them all die around me.

Even Erisa had grown pale and quiet until we emerged out of the other side.

"Of course not," I replied carefully.

"I may not have direct access to the Rats, but some of them are still my citizens, I still hear whispers," he began, before looking pointedly toward Erisa, who sat in a small chair in the corner of his office. "I'd like to think that I'm clever enough to deduce that you've brought the Feline into my house, but I'm really hoping that you'll prove me wrong."

"You're not wrong," Erisa answered before I could speak. "Am I not welcome, Tasar?"

He rested an elbow on his desk and pinched the bridge of his nose, letting out a deep sigh of frustration. "Theo, you've just arrived uninvited to my house, asked me to give you one of the only treasures I own, and tried to conceal one of the most influential people in the realm from my notice."

"She's working with us," I said, looking at Erisa, "she can be trusted."

"And do you have any proof?" he protested, looking at me as if I were a mad man. Maybe he wasn't entirely wrong about that.

"I know that you were the first to send your people to Zingal," Erisa began, her golden eyes fixed on him, "and I know where they're hidden, what they're doing, and who they're speaking to."

"What do you mean?" I demanded. I hadn't made it a secret that some of Tasar's people were now comfortably housed in my district, but I had never openly told her.

"Honestly, Theo," she said, rolling her eyes as if it were obvious how she knew. Turning her attention back to Tasar, she continued, "I could've outed you weeks ago, you would've been executed for treason and your brother would be sitting here instead. You should be grateful that I'm on your side."

"And what exactly do you get out of this?" Tasar asked her. "You've been the Autarch's pet for longer than I've been Lord, why would you betray him?"

"I have my reasons."

"Then I have my reasons for not giving you the snakehead," he quipped.

"Tasar, if you give it to us, we have an actual chance at winning," I explained. "The Autarch is already planning his move against me. You allowed your people to come to me in the hopes of a better future. Help them turn those hopes into a reality."

"Have I not given you enough? Risked enough for you?" he argued. "I fulfilled my end of the bargain, Theo. And you've yet to fulfill yours."

"I told you I'd consider your request if we were successful. With your relic, we're more likely to *be* successful."

"Well, I want you to consider it now. Agree to marry Diandra to Cyfrin and I'll give you the damn thing," he snapped.

Erisa stood abruptly, throwing me a scathing look before narrowing in on Tasar. "Didi will not be included in any deals without her permission. I think you're forgetting, Tasar, that Cyfrin owes *me* a debt," she seethed, pointing to a silver band on her arm. "I'd hate to have to call in that favor when the fighting gets *really* nasty."

"You're blackmailing me," he said.

She smiled sweetly. "Yes."

Tasar rubbed his face with his hands, looking more tired than I had ever seen him. With another deep sigh, he produced a key from around his neck and opened a drawer in his desk, withdrawing an ornate metal box. He flipped the lid open, revealing an obsidian snakehead nestled in a bed of red velvet, which looked muted compared to the glistening crimson of its eyes. The jaws of the snake were wide open, brandishing needlelike fangs and a delicate forked tongue.

Erisa wasted no time in snapping the lid shut again and swiping the box from the desk and placing it into her bag.

"Be careful, Tasar," I warned, "the Autarch will likely be approaching you soon about supplying him with men to fight against me."

"Then I'll tell him to go down into the slums and get them himself." He smiled, but it was half-hearted and didn't touch his eyes. "Now get out of my house and take that demon with you."

# Chapter 23

## Erisa

"How did you know about Tasar?" Theo asked as we slipped through the tight tunnels in the upper caves of Šarrum.

"It was a lucky guess," I admitted, pulling myself up into one of the larger cracks in the wall above us. "I overheard some of the people from Hudjefa speaking about Tasar during Tammuz. So between that and the conversations I've heard you have with the other Lords, I assumed he was the first to agree to help you."

I reached down to help him up, guiding him through the near-blackness of the volcanic caves. We had to bypass both of the guarded Palace gates, to avoid being seen. Luckily, I knew these tunnels like the back of my hand.

"I do trust you, Erisa," Theo said, his breath heavy from exertion. "I wasn't just saying that to sway Tasar. I do trust you."

"You shouldn't."

We were silent as I continued to lead the way down the dark passages, our footsteps muffled by the thick layer of dust and small rocks that had settled on the ground over the years. Whispers of light began to trail in through fissures in the stone and I gripped Theo's hand tighter, picking up the pace.

"I thought we were going to the Palace," Theo said as we arrived at the entrance to the cave. The soft orange glow from within lit up the expression of wonder that had blossomed onto his face.

"We will, I just thought we could make a small detour to one of my favorite places."

The cavern was the size of a large mansion, and completely empty apart from a single tree in the center. The deep roots pulled lava from below the rock in thin channels underneath the bark of the trunk, lighting it up from within. It radiated all the way to the tips of the branches and into the veins of the black leaves, which glowed like fire.

"I don't know what it's called," I murmured, my voice sounding too loud in the peaceful silence, "and I haven't found another one like it."

"It's incredible," Theo whispered, following me as I moved to sit on a large rock closer to the illuminated tree. The stone was hot beneath me and the stifling air felt heavy in my lungs, but the familiarity made me feel at ease.

Disturbed by our footsteps, lava beetles took to the air and surrounded us like small floating pieces of smoldering coal. We watched them dance lazily on the non-existent breeze before settling onto the candescent trunk of the tree. I leaned against Theo's shoulder and he pressed a light kiss to the top of my head before resting his cheek against it.

"Will you sing for me?" he rasped after a long while, his words faltering with uncertainty.

The request caught me so off guard that I couldn't control the small gasp that escaped my throat. In the past ten years, no one but Verrill had ever asked me to sing. It was something I had shared with him and no one else; he would play his lyre and I would sing to his tune, sculpting his emotions into elated joy. It was how I expressed my love for my oldest and dearest friend. It felt wrong to give away something that he cherished so ardently. And yet, for some reason, a small part of me wanted to say yes.

"Come on, we need to hurry, I don't know whether the Autarch is at the Palace or not," I said, already on my feet and heading to the exit.

"Erisa," Theo began, catching my arm to stop me, "I'm sorry, forget I asked."

To avoid looking at the hurt that marred his perfect features, I turned and led the way through the darkened tunnels once more. The image of the glowing tree was burned onto my retinas as we sunk into the black abyss of the subterranean maze that networked and spidered beneath the surface of Ersetu.

We emerged out of a narrow crack in the wall of the Palace cavern, and after warning Theo to be cautious of the sheer drop beneath us, I instructed him to follow my every move. I hopped between stoney outcrops and the tips of stalagmites in a series of practiced moves.

"Try not to put too much weight on the stalagmites," I called back to Theo, "they're more fragile than they look." I cringed away from a broken one that had taught me that lesson three years ago.

Fortunately, we made it safely to the ledge opposite my

balcony and I took a second to acknowledge two white ropes tied to Verrill's.

Fueled by muscle memory, my body flung itself over the short distance and onto the warm tiled floor leading to my room. I moved out of the way so that Theo could follow, and failed to stifle a laugh when he fell awkwardly onto his knees upon landing.

"Come on," I said, pulling him up, "the Autarch could come back any minute."

"How do you know he's not here?"

I pointed to the ropes. "One rope means the Autarch is absent, two ropes mean that we've also left the Palace, so he could have come back before we returned. It's useful for when we know we're in trouble and want to avoid him."

Theo scowled at the ropes before following me through my rooms and into the Palace. I moved silently, clinging to the walls. I had expected to wince at Theo's inability to keep quiet, but quickly became impressed with his stealth. I was headed in the direction of Csintalan's private chambers, hoping that he would keep anything of value close to him, since I hadn't found anything in his offices during my last search.

Knowing he had set enchantments at his door to inform him of intrusions, I took us to the floor above his, and dropped down out of the window to his private balcony. As soon as Theo hit the ground beside me he jumped as though something had stung him.

"What the—" he hissed, pulling out his leather pouch from under his shirt and tipping the Orb of Nanaya onto his palm. It was glowing impossibly bright and he swapped it from hand to hand as if it was burning him.

"It's in there," he said quietly, looking at the balcony door, "it's calling to this one."

Slowly edging toward the window, I looked inside, praying that the room was empty. It was. I extracted two pins from my bodice and quickly picked the lock on the door, before swinging it open.

I had only been inside Csintalan's chambers a handful of times, and it looked exactly the same as I remembered. A wide, four-poster bed dominated the room and mahogany furniture decorated the edges, each surface littered with books and half-written correspondence. Black crow feathers lay scattered across the papers.

"Where is it?" I asked Theo, who was inspecting the foot of the bed carefully.

"It's somewhere around here but I just can't see anything."

I knelt down, running my hands gently over the wooden bedframe, looking for a hidden latch or closure but found none. An almost imperceptible groan sounded beneath my left knee when I shuffled forward and I looked down to examine the floorboards. One of them was ever-so-slightly sunken.

It took me three minutes to pry the plank from the floor when I couldn't find the mechanism to open it and inside lay a plain, unremarkable wooden box. I gently lifted it out and opened the lid. As soon as I saw the contents I gasped, unable to move or breathe.

The box hosted a collection of odd trinkets and keepsakes, but my attention was caught on the top item. Nestled among a handful of dried dawn waxcap mushrooms, a lock of dark brown hair tied in a red ribbon, and a small stack of letters, was my mothers necklace.

My hands trembled as I lifted it from the box and brought it closer to my face. The silver of the chain and pendant casing gleamed like it had been freshly polished, and the red stone in the center glowed as if it were lit from within.

"What's wrong?" Theo asked softly. "That's it, isn't it?"

"This is my mother's necklace," I croaked, not knowing if my eyes were burning from the light of the Orb or from the threat of unshed tears. Looking up at Theo, he glanced between the stone in his hand and the one in the necklace.

"So does that mean … Did Karasi not—"

"I don't know," I admitted, unable to come up with a single explanation as to why Csintalan would have this necklace and not give it to me.

I grasped the pendant, the contact with the stone instantly instructing me to pry it from the metal casing. It hummed with power, the vibrations making my fingers tingle uncomfortably and I held my hand out to Theo for him to give me the other half. As soon as he did, my body was compelled to obey the Orb. I smashed the two pieces together, blinding myself as the light emanating from them illuminated the room.

I felt my eyes roll back as the vision seized me.

❖ ❖ ❖

"You can't eat those!"

A little girl, about eight years old, halted in front of me and slapped the mushrooms out of my hand before snatching them up off the floor. She had dark brown hair, with streaks of gold that shimmered under the sun.

"These are called dawn waxcaps, because if you eat one, you'll never see another day break." She smiled, holding out her right hand. "Hello, I'm Ava. What's your name?"

"My name is Csint-" my voice broke off, before I squeaked out, "my name is nothing. I am no one."

She scrunched her brows in confusion as she tried to understand the words through my fumbling, thick accent.

"That's silly," she said, taking my hand in hers. "I'll give you a name if you don't have one. Your hair's black like a crow, they're such pretty birds. I think I'll name you …"

❖ ❖ ❖

"Stop petting me and listen," Ava scolded, "you asked me to sing but I can't concentrate with you stroking my hair."

"But it's so soft," I teased, twirling a shimmering golden strand around my finger. She turned her large, honey-brown eyes to me and I laughed at her petulant expression.

"I'm sorry, my songbird." I smiled, releasing her hair and smoothing it over with my fingers once more. "Please sing for me."

Instantly placated, she indulged me, igniting me from the inside out with every sound that passed through her lips. Knowing how much she'd love it, I silently called to the birds around me.

*Come here,* I commanded. *Come to me and sing with her.*

305

Within seconds, our meadow was alive with a flutter of wings and melodic chirps. I called a crow to land on my shoulder and when she saw it, Ava's smile was brighter than the sun.

❖ ❖ ❖

"But why?" I demanded, my voice almost breaking with agony. "We love each other, Ava. Marry me instead."

Tears streamed down her face, tearing my already broken heart to pieces. She clutched at my hands, sobs shaking her entire body.

"Because I'm to be the Lady of Ocridell," she sniffled, after gaining control of her cries, "it's what's expected of me. I *begged* Papa. I begged and begged but he said no. He said you're n—"

She broke down once more into chest-heaving wails.

"I'm no one," I finished bitterly.

❖ ❖ ❖

"You stole it?" Ava exclaimed, her warm eyes wide with disbelief.

"I promised that one day I would get it for you."

She gasped softly as she looked at the necklace I'd brought her, nestled in a long box, lined with black velvet that made the red stone stand out even more.

"This is really it."

"The Autarch's stone," I confirmed. "His power."

"And you split it?" she asked, looking up at me.

"I told you," I murmured, brushing a strand of hair behind her ear. "I will give you anything, my songbird. Anything you want, I will find a way to give it to you. We're a pair, two halves of a whole. I will share everything I have with you. Feel how the stones call to one another, just like us."

"I can't take this," she said softly, moving to close the lid.

I stopped her hand and gently lifted the necklace from the box. Slowly, I moved behind her to fasten it, taking care not to catch any strands of soft hair.

"You know it's too late," she lamented. "I'm already married, Co—"

"It doesn't matter," I said, pressing a finger to her lips, "we can still be together. I can get rid of Evander, he's nothing. Just say the word, Ava, and I'll do it."

"I'm sorry."

❖ ❖ ❖

"What more do you want from me, Ava?" I yelled, before reeling back. I had never raised my voice at her before, never lost my temper. I took a few seconds to collect myself before continuing, "I did it. For you. I defeated the Autarch, became the most powerful man in the realm. *For you.* And I'm still not good enough?"

"It's not about that," she argued. "I have a family now."

"And what about my family? You're the only one I have!" I hated how desperate my voice sounded, my long-forgotten accent thick in my distress. "It was supposed to be us. We were supposed to be married with children. I would have done, will *still* do anything to have you, my songbird. Come with me to the Palace. Bring your children, I'll raise them as my own. If they're yours I already love them."

"You left!" she accused, tears streaming down her beautiful face. "You disappeared and I didn't see you or hear from you in years! I sent you letter after letter and you never responded to a single one!"

"What letters?" I shouted, losing control of my temper once more. I had become increasingly unstable in recent years. I felt like my psyche was slowly chipping away piece by piece. "I told you to write to me if you wanted to stay in contact and I received nothing from you!"

"I don't understand," she faltered, nervously fingering the necklace I gave her so many years ago. The sight of it soothed my agonized heart.

"Here are your damn letters," Evander said, striding into the room without even trying to conceal that he had been eavesdropping. He threw a wad of letters tied in twine in my direction. The sight of him boiled my blood into a simmering rage and my unbalanced magic struck out like a cornered snake.

I knew it was because I had split the stone, that over the years the Autarch's magic I had gained was unhinging, and I was barely able to leash it in.

I grabbed Evander by the collar, dragging him out of the room and locking the door, almost blind with fear that I had put Ava in harm's way. I heard her pounding against the wood, shouting at me to open it.

"You stole them?" I seethed, hauling him through a door and into a large chamber filled with people. I could barely see them turn to look at us through the haze of red obscuring my vision.

"She needed to forget you! What could you possibly offer her? Other than a life of being constantly on the move, only just scraping by. You could never give her what she deserved. I could!"

"You know nothing!" I bellowed, desperately trying to regain composure. It felt like I was trying to hold onto water as it slipped through my fingers.

"I know who you are," he sneered. "No matter how high you rise you'll still be that filthy little boy traveling with the circus. You're no one, and will always be no one."

My magic lashed out of me like a whip, splitting the air with a deafening crack. I could barely feel my body. It felt like I was floating, watching the series of events that stretched on for hours, yet were flashing by so fast I couldn't stop them.

The room was on fire and I watched in horror as Evander tried to shield two children—Ava's children—from the second wave that shook the air and reverberated up through the ground. I howled in agony as I tried to control the power that was pouring from my skin in a flood of pent-up magic I had spent years suppressing.

Bile scorched my throat and I heaved repeatedly at the realization of what I had just done. I was no stranger to killing, I had ended more than a few lives to get where I was today and had never thought twice about it. But this was Ava's family. I was hurting the only person I had ever loved. And I knew I would never forgive myself.

A blood-curdling scream rang out behind me and I whirled to

see Ava stumbling toward her slaughtered family, her left arm swinging limply from where she had forced the door open.

"NO!" she screamed, clawing and hitting me as I tried to hold her in my arms and shield her from the destruction I had created. She reached down for the stolen dagger in my belt.

"Do it," I begged, exposing my chest and neck for her to sink it into my skin. "I'm so sorry, my love."

A soft gasp escaped her lips and her beautiful honey eyes widened. I felt no pain, and realized too late that it was because the dagger was not in my own chest.

It was in hers.

❖ ❖ ❖

My vision cleared and I was on my feet, running for the balcony. Barely making it to the railing, I vomited over the edge, heaving until my throat was hoarse and my head pounded. Theo stood beside me, holding my hair back and rubbing slow circles onto my back. I leaned into his touch, allowing him to support my weight as the agony of watching my family die came crashing into me.

I was grateful that Theo knew not to ask about what I had seen. I knew I didn't have the strength or mental capacity to relive it. Instead, he returned the box to its space beneath the floorboard and retrieved the empty necklace from the floor.

After closing the balcony door, he silently followed me out of the Palace, through the tunnels, and back to the tram station, keeping my hand grasped firmly in his for the entire journey back to Zingal.

# Chapter 24

## Erisa

It wasn't until Theo and I had arrived back at his house in Zingal that I allowed myself to break down. I couldn't remember the last time I had cried, but as soon as we made it back to his room, he laid me down on his bed and held me in his arms while I wept.

Everything I had known since leaving Ocridell could have been a lie. I could have spent the last decade of my life practically worshiping the man responsible for mine and Verrill's misery. And though I was desperate for answers, for Csintalan to deny everything, I knew deep down that what I had seen had been the truth.

I wanted to kill him, to make him suffer for every wrong he had committed. Not just against my family, but Theo's too. I had killed his sister on Csintalan's orders, let him trick me into believing it was her fault. My mind was a flurry of confusion and hurt. I yearned for Verrill, wanting to unburden my distress onto him.

"Tell me, if you need to," Theo murmured, sensing my

torment.

So I did. I told him about what I had seen, letting him brush away the tears that streamed freely down my cheeks until they dried completely.

"We'll make him pay, Sunflower," he promised. "We'll get our revenge."

I allowed myself another hour in his arms before pulling myself together. Since my family's slaughter, extreme emotions had become foreign to me, and I'd forgotten about the blocked nose and pounding headache that accompanied crying. The discomfort just added insult to injury and despite being too wretched to eat, I forced down the small supper Theo brought up to me out of spite. I wouldn't allow this to weaken me, I would help Theo gather his forces to strike out against the Autarch.

His family and friends avoided me the rest of the evening, with his mother outright refusing to be in the same room as me. The only kindness I received was from Ezra, who gave me a quick smile as I joined them in the parlor on Theo's request. I knew the rift in the household was bothering him. I would have left the house altogether if he hadn't insisted on me staying the night.

Though I had no right, I found myself feeling disappointed in the coldness I received from Didi and Suenna. Apart from Verrill and Asila, I didn't have many friends. Everyone was too scared or too useless for me to build any sort of relationship with. Which usually suited me just fine. I used people for as long as it benefited me, breaking any bonds before they had the chance to. But with Didi and Suenna, I had recklessly allowed myself to take comfort in their kindness and enjoy their company.

I decided that killing Karasi had been more trouble than it was worth. Four years later and she was still causing me problems.

Usually, I couldn't care less about the open hostility I received from people, but tonight, I couldn't stand it for another second. I rose from my chair, ignoring Theo's gaze, and made my way to the guest room upstairs. My small bag of belongings were still where I had left them after returning from Khar'ra and I pulled out Zeti's small wooden horse and cradled it to my chest as I fell asleep.

✢ ✢ ✢

"What exactly is the Autarch's power?" Theo asked the next morning on our journey to Kusig. We were taking the horses to avoid the walk from where the tram line ended in Ocridell. Fergus pulled on the reins, eager to get ahead of Moth.

"He's never told me," I replied, "and if I've ever seen him use it, it's been subtle enough that I haven't noticed. Even if he had, I'm sure I wouldn't be able to talk about it. His magic binds me so I can't even tell you his name."

I thought back to what I saw in the vision, of him being able to annihilate an entire room of people within seconds. He had never displayed power like that in front of me before, but I had seen small aspects of it in the way he effortlessly commanded the respect and attention of everyone around him.

"But if the stone is the source, do you think he felt it when the two halves were joined together again?"

"I think so," I answered. "He felt it become unstable when he split it. I just hope he's not strengthened by it coming together again."

The sun had risen to a warm glow, the promise of summer soft against my skin as I tilted my face up to the cloudless sky. The air was salty from the ocean, and I could see the tempestuous waves of the Nasilan Sea on their journey to thrash against the distant Tarprusan coast behind us.

"Do you think the roads are emptier than usual?" Theo asked when we stopped for some food at midday.

"I'm not sure," I admitted. "Before the spring I hadn't been anywhere near Zingal since I was a little girl."

"Something doesn't feel right."

He didn't elaborate, only swatted at a fly venturing too close to his face. We sat in the shade of a large tree, allowing the horses to rest during the heat of the day. I lay down with my head in his lap, watching him, allowing myself a few precious moments to admire him without his notice. Worry lines creased his brow, and I longed to reach up and smooth them away, but stopped myself. His eyes were the exact shade of the dark green leaves above us, illuminated by the sun.

Closing my eyes, I could almost pretend that this wasn't temporary, that this brief moment of peace could stretch out before us with no end in sight.

"Right now, everything feels right," I whispered, falling prey to my own delusions.

He let out a contented sigh and traced lazy circles and patterns across my face. Each feather-light brush of his fingers left trails of fire in their wake and for the first time in a long time, I permitted myself to imagine a different future.

❖ ❖ ❖

My anxiety increased as we traversed through the southern outskirts of Ocridell in search of an inn for the night. After Theo's accident and my recent visions, I never wanted to return to my former home. I stiffened in the saddle as I saw the tall wall of the estate in the distance. What was once a haven of happy memories was now a prison of waking nightmares, haunted by echoes of the past.

"Will this do?" Theo said reluctantly, pointing toward a run-down boarding house with a sign hanging onto the post by a single nail.

I glanced at the storm clouds rolling in from the sea. "I think a bedroll on the ground would be better than anything they can offer in there. But it looks like it'll be a wet night, so at least we'll be dry."

"Let's hope so," he muttered, handing me Moth's reins while he ventured inside to enquire about a room.

Despite the outward appearance, the interior of the house was surprisingly pleasant. Two hours later, Theo and I were bathed and fed. Though the meat in the stew had been questionable, combined with the fresh bread it had alleviated the hunger brought on by the long day's ride.

"You're cheating!" Theo accused as I won the third game of cards in a row.

"Prove it," I challenged, knowing he wouldn't be able to. I'd bet every coin in my purse that I'd spent more time in gambling dens than the righteous, upstanding citizen that was Lord Lusilim. I knew every trick in *and* out of the book.

"Fine," he said simply, raising a brow at me, "if you're playing dirty …" He placed down a final card that had definitely already been played, completing his flush and winning the round.

"Using my own card against me? What a dirty trick!" I beamed at him, pleased with his nefarious ploy.

My heart skipped when he saw my smile; he looked at me as though I was the gravity that pulled the tides, or the wind beneath a dragon's wings.

The door opened and the owner walked in, her pale hair twisted into a neat knot at the back of her head. She looked anxious, smoothing the brown apron at her waist.

"Lord Lusilim?" she said, wringing her hands.

"Yes?"

"I was told to relay a message to you, and the young lady." She hesitated, quickly glancing at me. "I was told to tell you that 'he knows,' and that 'you shouldn't go back.'"

Theo held my gaze for a moment before smiling at the woman.

"Thank you," he said kindly and waited for her to exit the room. When we were alone once more he murmured, "A message from Verrıll'?"

I nodded. "He must have sent Rats to every inn and boarding house between here and Zingal."

The confirmation of our suspicions weighed heavily on our minds that night. Csintalan knew that someone had stolen and fused the Orb, and I was almost certain that he knew it was me.

❖ ❖ ❖

From the dark circles beneath Theo's eyes, I deduced that he'd slept even worse than I had. He said little during breakfast and his weary expression only deepened when we trudged outside into the muddy remnants of the recent late-spring shower. There was an unseasonal bite to the air and I shivered, pulling my cloak tighter around my shoulders.

"Did you not sleep well?" I asked Theo after his eyelids drooped for the fourth time in the last hour.

"No," he replied gruffly. "I haven't had a single dream these past two nights – ever since you fused the stone. Now I can't seem to sleep at all."

"Maybe it's because we left the Orb in Zingal?"

He shook his head. "I don't think so. They stopped the night we returned from the Palace. Not that I'm complaining. They were terrible."

"Oh?" I pressed.

Theo had never spoken of his night visions, and I'd never felt the need to pry. I could have looked in his notebook, but I wanted him to offer the information freely.

"They're mostly about you," he murmured, without meeting my eye. When he finally looked at me and saw my expectant expression, he sighed. "You haunt me in my nightmares, Erisa. I've seen you die again and again, and I'm always powerless to stop it.

It kills me."

"Really?" I teased, trying to brighten his dark mood. "I would've thought you'd enjoy the opportunity to be rid of me."

His voice was so low that I barely heard it. "Not anymore."

Winding down the paved path, we gently descended to sea level. The thin strip of land connecting Kusig to the mainland was busy with merchant carts and travelers, each person focused solely on the journey to or from the golden city.

The road widened on the approach to the city, the banks lined with food stalls and peddler wagons, trading rich fabrics and glittering jewelry. Owing to its gold mines, Kusig had always been a wealthy district. Though in recent years, it had faced the same struggles as the rest of the realm. The dense population was a reserved community; their isolation from the rest of the realm made them untrusting of outsiders and unwilling to socialize.

It was late afternoon by the time the gates came into view and the sun reflected off their golden surface with blinding ferocity. They were open, allowing unfettered access to the ornate architecture beyond.

One look at the city was all that was needed to confirm Kusig's main export. Each building was adorned with gold detailing, throwing warm light across every other surface, elevating it into luxury. The Seirsun estate looked like a miniature palace, almost every feature gilded and sparkling.

"We seek an audience with Lord Aran Seirsun," Theo informed the two men standing guard at the grand double doors at the main entrance. Their uniforms were a deep red velvet that hugged their figures perfectly.

319

"Welcome, Lord Lusilim. He has been expecting you," one of the guards said, motioning for a stable hand to fetch the horses.

"You'd think they at least use a different color inside the house," I muttered to Theo as we were admitted into the entrance hall. Almost every surface was covered in gold; a motif that continued throughout the whole house. I could feel a headache starting to develop.

"They certainly have a theme," Theo replied under his breath. The butler led us to what I assumed was Aran's office and offered us a seat on a gilded bench outside the door.

"Are we telling him who you are?" Theo asked while we waited, scraping some dried mud off one of his boots. When it fell to the floor he swiftly glanced around before kicking the clump of dirt under a decorative cabinet.

"If we need to," I replied, just in time for Aran to emerge from the room.

"Welcome, both." He smiled, gesturing behind him, "Please come in."

The gaudy office was almost painful to look at. Everything shimmered in the setting sun that shone through the floor-to-ceiling windows and lit every extravagance ablaze. Aran was dressed impeccably as always, his dark purple velvet suit contrasting wonderfully against his paler features. Theo and I seated ourselves in plush chairs in front of a large glass desk. When he opened his mouth to speak, Aran held up a hand.

"I already know why you are here, Theo. I've received several threats from the Rats instructing me to aid you."

"That makes my job a lot easier then." Theo smiled. His

expression was convincing enough, but I noticed a tightness around his eyes, hinting at his underlying unease. He leaned forward, bracing his hands on the desk. "Does this mean you'll help us?"

"That depends. Tell me what you need."

"Besides Katmu, your district commands the largest fleet," Theo began, leaning back in his chair once more. "With your proximity, it would make the most sense to make you the first line of defense against attacks across the Zingali coast. Any people who can fight will be welcomed into my army, with ranks befitting their station."

"So you need fighters?" Aran prompted.

"In short, yes. And one other thing." He paused for a moment, weighing his words. "We need Geshtinanna's stylus."

"I don't know what you're referring to—"

"You cannot lie to *me,* Aran," I hissed.

His handsome, sun-kissed face paled in recognition at my voice. I'd said the exact same words to him during his last interrogation with Verrill and I. He quickly schooled his expression into a lazy smirk and brushed a hand through his golden hair.

"Well, I have to say, Feline, I didn't expect you to be such a beauty," he exclaimed, gaze casually roaming over my face. "But those eyes … I can't decide if you're more menacing with or without the veil."

I glared at Aran, while nudging Theo's leg with my knee. He'd stiffened at Aran's words and I didn't need him getting defensive. Unfortunately, Aran caught the motion through the glass.

"I have to hand it to you, Theo, you're a braver man than I." He chuckled, his pale blue eyes gleaming with an unspoken challenge.

"We're getting off topic," Theo responded smoothly, betraying none of the irritation beneath the cool exterior. "Do you have the stylus?"

Aran smiled. "I do. I don't have an issue with helping you, but I'll not do so for free. Men and ships are one thing, but the stylus is special. It won't come cheap."

"What do you want?"

"Kusig is a lonely place," he began, sighing dramatically. "We're so far away. No one ever seems to want to make the journey down the cliff to get to the city, because they know they have to climb back up afterwards. We're so cut off from the other districts, even Khar'ra gets more action than we do."

"*Fascinating* story, Aran," I drawled, "any chance you might be nearing the end of it?"

He smirked again at my disinterested expression. "I want us to be better connected, to be able to transport goods up the cliff without needing wagons. One of my engineers has designed a pulley system but the cost would be … substantial. I would also require new trade terms with the other kingdoms, with a lower tax on my gold profits."

Of course this wasn't about connecting his people to the other districts. He was so full of shit it was no wonder he perfumed himself so heavily in sandalwood oil.

"If it is in my power, I will do it," Theo vowed and held out his right hand. "Shall we seal it?"

"I believe you." Aran dismissed the proffered hand with a smile. "I'm not in the habit of binding myself to others"—he glanced down at my marked arm—"it can end so nastily."

"Are you afraid, Aran?" I challenged, reaching out my own hand and wiggling my fingers to taunt him.

His striking face split into a grin and he laughed, lighting the room up like sunshine. "Of you? Yes I am!"

He invited Theo and I to stay the night but offered his apologies that he would be absent for supper. I made no effort to appear disappointed and happily followed one of the staff to the guest rooms, grimacing at the shimmering decor that dripped from every surface. Even the bathtub was coated in gold.

Theo and I ate in a small parlor next to our rooms, and I tried to casually steer the topic of conversation away from Aran or the stylus, sensing that we were being watched. It wasn't until I snuck into his chambers that night that I addressed my concern.

"Something doesn't feel right," I admitted, resting my face against his chest and enjoying the sensation of his fingers trailing across my bare back.

"Aran's always been a little … eccentric," Theo murmured.

"He's not though," I argued. "He pretends to be foolish and vain, but it's just a mask for him to hide behind. He's calculating."

"You worry too much, Sunflower," he said, skimming a finger up my waist. "He's already agreed to give us the stylus."

"I don't trust him, Theo. You need to be careful with this, especially if the Autarch knows about the stone."

"I will," he promised, "but let's not make rash decisions. Let's give him the chance to prove himself."

❖ ❖ ❖

My suspicions didn't abate by the next morning, especially when we were greeted by a servant over breakfast, informing us that Aran had rushed out of the estate at dawn on urgent business.

"He is unlikely to return before the end of the day," he added, setting a small gilded box down on the table between us, "but he asked that this be delivered to you."

I lifted the lid and peered inside to find a folded note on top of a long, thin writing utensil, with a sharp point and a flat, flared end. It was—of course—made from a gleaming gold metal. Unfolding the note, I read Aran's neat, slanting words.

*My contribution to Irkalla.*
*May it prove useful to you, my friends.*

Carefully, I extracted the stylus from the box's silk lining and inspected it closely. It was surprisingly light and much less remarkable than I'd expected the final relic to be.

"It's quite dull," I concluded, handing it over to Theo, "if you ignore the gold. I thought it would at least glow or hum with power or something to make up for it. At least the key and the snakehead were interesting."

"Maybe you have to write with it," Theo suggested, before pressing the sharp tip to Aran's note. He made a discontented noise when it did nothing. "Well, at least it seems like the right size for the space in the shield."

"I suppose there's no point in waiting around for him to get back?"

"I guess not," he agreed, "there's no way of knowing when he'll return and we can't wait around here for days. I do find it strange that he didn't want to give it to us himself."

"I told you, there's something not right here," I insisted. "I feel like we're missing something. He didn't even mention if he's sending any men to aid us—" the gleam in his eyes made me pause and rephrase, "to aid *you*."

"Well, there's no point in pushing him for more," he said. "Not yet anyway. We've got the stylus, that's worth more than any number of men."

"Or so the Beldams say …"

He looked up, searching my face. "Do you doubt them? After the power you've seen from the Orb?"

"I just think we— *you* should focus on strengthening your army now we've got the last relic. You need to be ready for the Autarch, he still holds the majority of the realm."

"Then let's go back to Zingal and prepare," he decided, rising to his feet. "I want to be the one to strike first."

# Chapter 25

## Theo

Verrill,

I'm receiving chirps about your movements from within the volcano. While I appreciate your heroic efforts, they've not exactly yielded the results I asked for. The last delivery was still one feline short, and I'm growing impatient.

I look forward to your explanation, which I have no doubt will be full of more prattling excuses. If you're struggling in your role, you only have to say the word.

Theo

20 July

❖ ❖ ❖

I could hear sputtering and choking from the other side of the door before I had even reached it. Throwing it open and striding into the room, I found Erisa standing over a writhing form, pouring water over a cloth-covered face.

The sight of her made my heart lurch and my step falter.

"Help me!" they gurgled, straining toward the sound I'd made upon entering. "She's crazy!"

They were bound to a simple wooden chair, which was tilted back against the low water trough in the corner of the barn.

"Focus on me, Beso," Erisa crooned, lifting the jug of dirty water to splash over his face once more, "he won't help you."

"What did he do?" I asked.

She turned to look at me and I drank her in almost desperately. Blood was splattered up her pale-yellow dress, across her face and into her braided hair, betraying her soft look of innocence. The skirt was torn, revealing an expanse of toned, tanned thigh. Her sleeves were short, and I noticed her arms were almost completely free from bargain marks. Aside from Silas' smoldering band on her left bicep, she only had five remaining on her right forearm. The sight made me uneasy.

"Apparently, he was the last person to have seen Silas in person," she explained, twirling the end of her braid around her fingers. The yellow ribbon was stained with blood. "And it just so happened that when I eventually tracked him down, he was sniffing around the Lusilim family vault. I was happy to ignore the petty theft, until I heard him muttering to his imbecile companion about the shield. They made the mistake of trying to hurt me after I caught them." She leaned over to check the pieces of pale-yellow dress fabric securing him to the chair and smiled in satisfaction. "I'll leave you in here awhile, Beso. Let's see if your memory improves while I'm gone."

She stuffed the sodden cloth into his mouth and turned toward the door. Just as she was about to walk past me I moved to stand in her path, halting her. I crowded her, moving us backward toward the wall and reached my hand up to wrap it around her throat, slamming her into the wooden panels. The side of her mouth tipped up and she raised a brow, challenging me.

"I haven't seen you in almost three weeks, and that's how you greet me?" I growled, pushing my chest flush against hers.

"Stop pouting, Theo," she jeered, "you look like a petulant child."

The bite of her insult was softened by the slightly breathless delivery as I thrust my legs between hers, pinning her in place. I squeezed her throat tighter for a brief second before releasing it, capturing both of her wrists and restraining them above her head. Her eyelids fluttered as my other hand threaded into her hair, pulling her face up to meet mine.

"I've missed you," I murmured, skating my mouth up her neck, feeling her pulse racing beneath my touch and not caring about our captive audience sitting only a few feet away.

"Don't be pathetic," she gasped before crashing her mouth to mine, her lips frantic and demanding. She forced her tongue into my mouth, tilting her head to deepen the kiss. Without breaking it, I released her wrists to fumble wildly at the laces of her bodice.

"Fuck," I hissed, as a jolt of pain lashed through my palm. I looked down to see blood dripping from a slice across my hand and a blade protruding from between Erisa's dress and corset.

"Oops," she breathed, fighting a small smile from forming, "I forgot that was there."

Throwing the dagger to the floor, I grasped her waist and pulled her back to me, finding her mouth once more.

"Get off, you fool," she snapped, pushing me back, "you'll get blood all over my dress and ruin it."

"It's already ruined, Sunflower." I smirked, raking my eyes over her disheveled appearance.

She was even more beautiful than I remembered. Especially with her cheeks flushed and her dark hair escaping the neat braid.

"Yes, well, I can't remember the last time I cleaned this," she huffed, retrieving the weapon from the floor, "and you'll just whinge about your hand until it's sorted."

"It's nothing," I promised, following her out of the barn, "just a scratch."

She scowled before turning her back to me and leading the way up to the house. Under the brilliant light of the summer sun, I cataloged every change that had occurred since I had last seen her.

Her hair was shorter, ending mid-way down her back rather than at her hips. Her skin had deepened beautifully and the fresh smattering of freckles across her face indicated hours spent beneath the summer sun. She had a new gash across her left forearm, the skin raised and freshly healed.

"Where have you been?" I couldn't stop the question that came out once we were seated in the kitchen. Erisa ignored me, busying herself with preparing a bowl of water and finding bandages for my hand.

"Did you find Silas?" I asked, when she sat back down and took my injured hand in both of her own.

"No," she admitted, bitterness seeping into her tone. "I searched everywhere, chased every lead and followed up on every rumor. And still nothing."

"But you said he gave you a way to summon him?"

"He did," she confirmed, "but I'm only to use it when I want him to fulfill his bargain. We only need to talk to him about the shield and I'm not wasting it for something so trivial when we could need him later down the line. He's purposely avoiding me."

Her voice was as sharp as her hands were gentle. The cut on my hand wasn't nearly bad enough to warrant this much attention. Yet she cleaned and sanitized the wound with such a soft tenderness, that I couldn't help but suspect her fuss over her dress was a cover for wanting to tend to my injury.

I let my mind wander as she worked. After returning from Kusig, we had placed the stylus into its place in the shield, but nothing had happened. We tried taking each of the relics out and reinserting them in different spaces and in different orders, but it had remained unchanged. Though no one had known what it was supposed to do, everyone had agreed that it should do *something*. There were no visions or voices, no transformations, and not so much as a whisper of the power we had experienced from fusing the two halves of the Orb of Nanaya.

All of our letters and messages to Silas had remained unanswered and I had reluctantly agreed to remain behind in Zingal to coordinate our forces while she went to find him.

"Maybe we should try the Beldams? They must know more than they told us last time," I offered.

"I did try. I went to Khar'ra after turning Silas' cabin upside down, but they refused to see me." She tied off the bandage and tucked in the remainder, before looking up at me. "So I broke into their temple and tried to set it on fire."

"Tried?" I laughed, failing to keep a straight face.

"They must have seen me coming and had men there ready to chase me off. One of them got a lucky shot," she said, gesturing to the fresh scar on her arm. "I got past the rest and tried to knock one of the torches down but it wouldn't catch so I had to run. They screamed at me to never return and that '*Lamaštu will remember.*' It was all very dramatic, you would've loved it."

"Lamaštu? I thought their temple was for Ereshkigal?"

"So did I, but there's a large mosaic of Lamaštu on the floor of their inner temple. Seeing as I didn't wait around to ask them about it, I just added it to the growing list of questions I have for Silas."

I couldn't help but feel disappointed in my friend. Silas had never let me down before, but he hadn't answered a single letter I had sent asking him for help.

"If I didn't know how difficult he is to kill, I'd be worried that something had happened to him," I admitted.

"How *is* he that difficult to kill?" she questioned. "I know he's not normal, but I don't understand why."

"Neither do I really," I said, allowing myself to drown in the molten amber of her eyes. "All I know is that we'd been surrounded on a raid one night during the Tarprusan war. It had been a trap to lure our squad away from the others. They cornered us outside an old woodmill, outnumbering us four to one. Silas promised that he'd get us out, that we'd all make it. But even though we'd all seen him annihilate every opponent on the battlefield, none of us were foolish enough to believe him.

"Ezra went down first, and then Nook, who dove on top of him. Suenna and I tried to drag them both back but we were getting overrun ourselves. Silas was a machine, cutting through men and women like a wild beast, but we could barely stop to appreciate it because more were coming. He shouted at us to get into the mill, that he would take them down. We obviously refused at first, knowing he would only be sacrificing himself for us to die later. But he was adamant and Ezra was bleeding badly. So me, Suenna, and the three others in our squad grabbed him and Nook and retreated back into the mill."

Her eyes widened in disbelief. "And Silas took them on by himself?"

"He did, and he lived. Ten very tense minutes later, he knocked on the mill door and just about fell in when we opened it. He was covered in slashes and stab wounds, but was somehow still breathing. I couldn't believe it when I looked outside and saw over fifty bodies on the ground."

"You're lying," Erisa insisted.

"I swear on Ersetu that's what I saw," I vowed. "He lost consciousness not long after that and we all thought he'd died because I'm *sure* his pulse stopped, but he woke a few hours later, right as rain. His wounds had closed and his bruises had disappeared. When I questioned him about it he said, 'I've tried to kill myself a thousand different ways and have never managed to stay dead. I'm a powerful creature, Theo; if I couldn't succeed, those men didn't stand a chance.' He didn't elaborate further and

I've never asked him to."

Her eyes were wide and she shook her head slightly, as though she didn't fully understand. Not that I could blame her, even after all these years I still had trouble with it myself.

"I spoke to Verrill last week," Erisa said finally. "He mentioned that Malah has reinforced Aran's fleet around the coast, and that the soldiers from Kusig are holding the external exit points of Anzillu, stopping Henri's men from exiting the Volcano via the harbor."

"You saw Verrill last week?" I demanded. "I sent that bastard a letter three days ago asking if he knew where you were and he didn't even bother responding."

She smirked. "He said you've been trying to keep an eye on me. Were you worried about me?"

"You didn't send any letters," I said, not wanting to admit how anxious I'd been to hear from her.

She shrugged. "I didn't see the point. So what's been happening?"

"You probably got most of it from Verrill," I grumbled, my longstanding jealousy flaring to life once more. "Aran's men have successfully cut off Anzillu's access to the harbor, and along with Malah's support, have surrounded us on the coast … not that the Autarch can get his army to the water now, but they're there in case of a breach. After you left, the Autarch approached Tasar and ordered the slums to be locked down. Tasar evacuated as many of his people to Ocridell as he could but got caught doing it. He officially declared loyalty for me in his defiance and has been locked in the Palace ever since. I was surprised the Autarch didn't just kill him."

"Verrill mentioned that he's working on an escape plan for him," Erisa informed me, her brows creased in concern, "but he needs to be careful. Even with control of the Rats, the Autarch has his own spies now and could find out he's still got access to the Palace."

"The Rats won't betray him?"

She shook her head. "No, they're loyal to him … and to me. We have ways of confirming their loyalty. It's everyone else I'm worried about. The Autarch has put a bounty on both our heads. He knows I've betrayed him and knows that Verrill is loyal to me, rather than to him. He wants us brought to the Palace alive."

I tried to suppress a shudder as I imagined what he would do to her if she was caught.

"I don't want you leaving again," I announced, my voice firm. "It's not worth the risk. We can figure out the shield here."

"I don't care what you want," she snapped, standing up and heading to the door. "You don't command me. I'll take any risk I deem necessary."

She was gone before I was even out of my chair, and I looked out of the window to see her heading back toward the barn. I felt a jolt of sympathy for the man inside, who I suspected was about to pay the price of her vexation.

Before I could go and intervene, the door opened behind me.

"She's back then?" Nook's voice rang out through the quiet of the room, causing me to turn. He was leant against the doorframe, his hands full of papers.

"She is," I replied, gauging his expression. My friends and

family had alleviated some of their animosity toward Erisa in the two weeks we'd spent here after returning from Aran's district. Though Dana and Didi would refuse to be in the same room as her, my friends had put aside their differences and had worked hard to include her in the plans and strategies regarding the armies. At first it was because they realized the power she held with the Rats—who were now the only reliable channel of communication between our troops—but then they started slipping back into their previous joking and bantering, clinging onto the fragile threads of their previous friendship.

Nook nodded. "Good, you can finally stop harassing the Fox for news. I've got the latest reports if you want to see them?"

"Sure." I followed him to my office and threw open the window to entice some fresh air into the stuffy room.

"So, first on the list," Nook began, rifling through the letters and producing one written on heavy, pale green paper, "Khar'ra has officially declared allegiance for you."

"What?" I sputtered, unable to contain my shock and confusion.

"I know, it's a surprise to everyone. No one even thought of asking them to choose a side, but they chose one anyway."

"When was this?"

"Yesterday," he replied, handing me the letter to read. "This is a copy."

I scanned over it quickly, then paused before rereading it again slowly. The Beldams had written directly to the Autarch demanding him to remove his forces from their borders, where they had been excavating an exit from Hudjefa—through Ersetu—leading straight to Khar'ra.

*Autarch,*

The Gods demand that you, son of no one, who came from nowhere, relinquish your power and authority to Theodoraxion Lusilim, son of Kyron Lusilim, acting Lord of Zingal and Ereshkigal's promised gift of redemption. Great Autarch, your future is written and you will perish, cold and alone beneath the falling leaves of your lover's throne.

*The Ladies of Khar'ra*

*21 July*

*Copy made 22 July*

Though I could barely make sense of their riddles, the overall message was clear; they pledged their support to me, and were entreating the Autarch to stand down. I knew he never would. The fighting hadn't even begun and he still held the volcano.

"I can't believe they're still supporting me when Erisa tried to burn their temple down," I said, perplexed.

"She did what?" Nook yelped.

"Maybe it's a trap in retaliation," I mused, more to myself than to a wide-eyed Nook, "but then what would we gain from that, we haven't asked them for anything and they've not offered anything …" I trailed off for a few moments, thinking. "Do you think we need to send forces to the new opening in the volcano to help defend their borders?"

"It sounds like they have it covered, there's a letter here reporting that one hundred of the Autarch's men slit their own throats after passing through." He cringed. "Whatever magic they're using, it seems to be effective to some extent."

"Very well." I nodded, quickly drafting a letter to the commander of the mountain barracks. "Will you send this for me, I want them to be ready in case Khar'ra does call for help."

He left me to sift through the correspondence alone. It was mostly official letters recounting messages I had already received from the Rats. The sun was low in the sky by the time I wrote my final response, just in time for a knock to sound at my office door.

"Come in," I called, clearing my desk.

"Good evening, Theo," Josefine said as she closed the door behind her. She was wearing a pretty blue dress that matched her eyes perfectly. Half of her light brown curls were pinned at the back of her head.

"Josefine." I smiled. "What can I do for you?"

"We've been having some supply issues for weaponry in the lower camps and I have an idea how to alleviate it, I just wanted to double check with you first."

I hadn't been aware of any issues, and I made a mental note to chase up whoever was in charge of that communication channel. I had placed Josefine in charge of hosting the camps of Hudjefan soldiers as her family owned a large portion of the land between the Lusilim estate and the Zuamsik Mountains. She had been doing an excellent job of ensuring each of the soldiers were housed, fed, and clothed appropriately for their training.

"Of course," I said.

"As you know, the mountain barracks have been supplying the camps with weapons from their forge, but they've been experiencing material shortages and can't keep up with demand. This means that by the time the shipments reach the camps closer to the city, the weapons are usually gone. I propose we reopen the steelworks on Tolani Seko's land and start another line of production there. There's plenty of metal left over from the tramline that's just being wasted."

"You would need to ask Tolani for permission, but it sounds like a wonderful solution." I didn't need to feign how impressed I was at her initiative.

She grinned. "I already have, he's agreed to it as long as you approve."

"You're extraordinary, Josefine," I complimented, "I truly wouldn't have been able to manage this without your help."

As I spoke, I heard the sill outside my window groan and saw a few loose strands of dark hair out of the corner of my eye. But I kept my gaze on the woman in front of me, pretending to be ignorant of Erisa's spying.

Josefine smiled sweetly and moved around the desk to stand between my legs, reaching out and running her hands through my hair. It was a move she'd done many times before, but not since I'd met Erisa.

"Can I come and see you tonight?" Josefine cooed, moving her hands down to the collar of my shirt.

"I can't tonight," I said, rising from my chair. She didn't move to put any space between our bodies, only dropped her hands to her sides.

"Have I done something wrong, Theo?" she whispered sadly. "I know you always said it was temporary and I'm fine with that, really I am. But I thought we were good together."

"Josefine, you're a delight. Like the first kiss of spring sunshine, or like the warm taste of sweet apple pie and sugared tea. You're a treasure," I said, brushing a stray curl off her face, "any man would be lucky to have you as his wife."

Her blue eyes were glistening as she looked up at me, and I kept my focus on her face as I heard the telltale groan of wood from the windowsill, indicating Erisa's departure.

"But I'm not the one for you," I said, squeezing her shoulders gently. "I'm sorry if I have done or said anything to make you think otherwise."

She nodded, swiping away the single tear that had escaped down her cheek, and walked from the room, never letting her dignity waver for a second. She *was* lovely, but no matter how hard I had tried in the past, I could never give her everything I knew she wanted.

I waited a few minutes before following her out and heading upstairs to the hidden room at the end of the third floor hallway. Sliding my hand along the mahogany panels of the wall, I pushed the fifth one gently, hearing the snick of a latch. The small door opened and I crouched down to step inside, lighting the small lamp I'd brought from my office. I sighed a soft breath of relief when I saw the shield still safely stored away. It was a routine I had practiced every day for the past few weeks.

I took a moment to inspect its gleaming surface. Each of the relics fitted perfectly into the grooves of the metal. The conjoined daggers were slotted along the top, above the stylus which ran parallel beneath them. The snakehead hissed between the two roaring lions etched into the face of the shield. To the right of the lion staff design was the Anzû songbird, wings outstretched mid-flight. And to the left, nestled beneath the elaborate key, was the Orb of Nanaya, glowing the same vibrant red as the eyes of the snake in the center.

Lightly tracing my fingers over the ancient objects, I willed one of them to finally show me where we were going wrong. Something was missing, but I couldn't understand what it was.

Sighing, I rubbed a hand over my face, feeling the tiredness settle into my limbs. Though my sleeping had improved, I'd missed Erisa's presence and worrying about her made the nights long and restless. A devilish smile stretched across my face when I imagined how enraged she'd be with me right now.

Suddenly, I was desperate to see her. I glanced over the shield one last time before exiting the hideaway, locking the door and making my way down to the second floor.

Pausing to listen outside the door and hearing nothing, I entered my room assuming Erisa was elsewhere, but found her perched on the settee beneath the window. Her lips twisted into a cruel smile when she saw me.

"Hello, Sunflower," I said, glancing around the room. Everything was still where I'd left it and she hadn't set fire to the curtains or the carpet. Her calmness was making me nervous.

"Theo," she chirped, "I just came to congratulate you."

"On what?" I asked, taking stock of her polished appearance. She had bathed and changed since I'd seen her earlier, swapping out her ruined dress for a simple gray one.

"Where is she?" Erisa smiled, making a show of looking around, "I'd so love to be introduced to your *darling* little wife."

"You're jealous," I hummed, stalking toward her.

She lifted a teacup toward me when I reached her, but I batted it away and leaned down to rest my hands on either side of her face, pinning her against the arm of the settee.

"Don't you want a taste, Theo?" she goaded, lifting the cup to my face.

"Not of that." Without breaking her stare, I took the cup and placed it on the table behind her head, wincing as the scalding water sloshed over my knuckles.

"But I made it just to your liking," she sneered as I leaned closer, "I know how you like your sweet pies and sugary tea."

Her words came out like acid, biting and corrosive and I wanted to lap them up.

"You're wrong," I murmured against her ear. "I like my pies sour and my tea bitter. And nothing tastes better than the venom on your tongue."

I captured her mouth with my own and pressed her against the soft cushions with my chest, groaning as her sharp nails scratched across my scalp.

Gripping beneath her thighs, I lowered myself to my knees in front of her and pushed her legs apart. My face was instantly lost beneath her skirts, and I indulged greedily, my trepidation over her quiet, jealous rage completely forgotten.

It wasn't until later that night, when I pulled back the cover of my bed and found Beso's severed head beneath the sheets, that I was reminded of her ill temper once more.

# Chapter 26

## Erisa

Eris,

Tohnain has left the Palace. I tried to track him down at Asila's shop, but she and her mother are gone too. Obviously, I've sent Rats out, but there's no sign of a struggle so I'm hoping their disappearance has something to do with Jirata.

I'll send word when I know more.

Verrill

27 July

My music,

As suspected, Malah was behind it. He's begged me to ask that you don't remove his balls for stealing your friend away without telling anyone. I told him I'd ask nothing of the sort.

I miss you desperately.
Your Verrill

30 July

❖ ❖ ❖

Dearest Feline,

I'm writing to inform you that, as requested, I have established a plan to keep our lovely mutual friend and her family safe. Though she was stubborn, she eventually agreed.

I don't want to include details here in case this note should fall into the wrong hands, but rest assured, she will be taken care of.

Your friend,
Malah

1 August

Eris,

Cyfrin Wranmaris has requested the help of the Rats to retake possession of Hudjefa. As you may well be aware, most of Tasar's citizens have scattered themselves between Ocridell and Zingal but thousands of them have disappeared into the Wilds. You know as well as I that this does not bode well, and I have told Cyfrin as much.

However, if you could coordinate the Rats on your end of the realm to gather as many as you can find, I'd be very grateful. The Hudjefans are angry and want their home back. Though I'm sympathetic to their plight, their anger encourages them to stand with us against the Autarch, and for that, I'm grateful.

I will send further instructions once we have a clearer understanding of numbers.

Yours always,

Verrill

7 August

P.S I saw a dragon today. It was flying over the Iaxar Sea and I watched it from the top of Ersetu. It reminded me of the time we saw one hunting in the Gištir Jungle.

Erisa,

Though it physically pains me to agree with that oaf, Theo is right in wanting you to stay away. I am working with Cyfrin on a plan to free Tasar, but our usual routes into the Palace have been blocked or destroyed.

Please, my music, I am <u>begging</u> you not to attempt to come here. The Autarch is desperate to get to you and is becoming more volatile each day.

Please stay safe in Zingal.

With love,

Verrill

12 August

Feline,

As requested, please find enclosed my official report regarding our success in retaking Hudjefa. With your help and expert direction, we managed to re-enter our home through the new opening in the volcano. My people are alight with passion and called out my brother's name all the way to victory. I wouldn't be surprised if he heard them from his cell in the Palace, and I know his heart will swell with pride when he hears the news.

Once again, I find myself indebted to you. Consider this letter another one of my bands around your wrist, a favor I will gladly return at any time. You need only ask.

Your faithful servant,
Cyfrin Wranmaris

29 August

# Chapter 27

## Theo

Tasar,

In response to your letter last week regarding tensions within the volcano, I have made the decision to bring our plans forward. I have sent word to Malah and Aran to ready the divisions they have in Katmu and Kusig.

Based on the advice given very forcefully by the Feline, I have not informed them of your divisions still hidden in the mountains, and they remain mostly ignorant of the ones camped in the northern parts of Zingal. That information remains solely with you.

Though I do not expect, nor ask, you or the citizens of Hudjefa to fight, I wanted to inform you of our accelerated plans to enable you to prepare yourselves. It is likely that when we enter the volcano, many will try to flee via your district.

We begin our march in three days.

Stay safe, my friend. I hope that the next time we meet, this will all be over.

Theo

14 September

***

A bead of sweat dropped from the tip of my nose and landed with a soft thud on the leather of Moth's saddle. I swiped the back of my hand across my forehead for what felt like the hundredth time in the last hour. Even this late in the afternoon, the sun was unbearable; no one could ever remember a summer as blistering and intense as this one.

Despite the heat, the army marched on; slowly but surely toward the eastern borders of Zingal, our sights set on the towering volcano looming in the distance.

Even though I had left the reserve division in the mountain barracks behind, under Suenna's command, the sheer volume of men and women surrounding me was enough to make me almost hope for a victory.

Our numbers weren't as great as the Autarch's, but our soldiers had chosen to fight. I hadn't bought them or forced them into anything. They were here because they believed in the potential greatness of our realm.

I called out for our company to halt and build camp, not

wanting to wait until dark. Though walking through the heat of the day tired everyone, marching through the night wasn't an option. As soon as the sun dipped below the horizon, the nights became uncharacteristically cold. The Beldams had sent warnings that it was because change was coming and the gods were waking up, disrupting the weather. I paid no attention to their ramblings, I had more important things to focus on.

My council joined me in the large meeting tent a few hours later, everyone peering around the large map on a table in the center.

"The Rats have reported movement across the tramlines here," Erisa informed us, pointing to the section of the map between Šarrum and Ocridell.

"But the trams have been out of operation for weeks, since the Hudjefans sacked the city," Nook replied, gaining murmurs of agreement from the others.

"That's just what was reported," Erisa said, her tone steely.

"Then we've got to consider that the Autarch's got them up and running again," insisted Ezra. "Even though the explosions destroyed the line between Hudjefa and Šarrum, the westerly line was only damaged, he could have had it repaired."

"But we would have seen trams come from Ocridell if that was the case," said Didi, who despite my best efforts had refused to be left behind.

"They could have cut the line short," Ezra offered, rubbing the stubble on his chin.

"Whatever the reason for it, we can't do anything about it at the moment," I decided. "We've just got to keep in mind that when we reach Ersetu, we might face additional challenges."

"I've already sent word of the developments to Malah," Erisa said when I looked at her, answering my question before I could voice it.

"Should we change our route?" Nook asked.

I shook my head. "No, we continue as planned until we know more. Aran will meet us with the rest of his division in Ocridell and send a ship signal to Malah to bring the rest of our army to Anzillu. We'll surround them from all sides. With Tasar blocking Hudjefa and Khar'ra defending that exit point, they'll have nowhere to go."

"And the battle location?" Ezra asked.

"I'm still hoping he'll have the sense to surrender." I sighed, rubbing a hand over my face. "But if he doesn't, we'll still aim for Anzillu. The tunnel network in Šarrum will cause its own difficulties and we'd be on better footing if we can push them out into the open. We've made plans for every possibility, so we'll just have to play it by ear and hope for the best."

We spent the next two hours discussing camp logistics and marching routes for the following day, and by the time I'd eaten and returned to my tent, my body was slow and weary.

I was pulling the blankets around me when Erisa came in, silent as always, and stripped, before joining me on my bedroll and pressing her frozen feet against my legs. She ignored my half-hearted, grumbled complaint and settled herself into my arms.

I was in love with her. I wasn't foolish enough to try and convince myself otherwise. And though I hadn't told her, we both knew it. She maintained the opinion that whatever we were right now, was temporary. That after the war was over, we'd go our separate ways and never have to see each other again. The thought of it was agonizing, and I knew I wouldn't be able to let her leave. She'd have to kill me to get away.

I brushed my thumb lightly over her cheek, mapping every freckle. I opened my mouth to speak but she cut me off, pressing her fingers over my mouth.

"If you're going to beg me to go back to Zingal, you can forget it," she warned.

It wasn't what I was going to say, but she had reason to suspect it. For the past few weeks I'd pleaded with her to stay behind. It wasn't that I thought she couldn't look after herself, I knew first hand that she could. But the Autarch would suspect her to travel with my army and I was worried that he would capture her and try to use her to control me. I was frightened, because I knew it would work, that I would abandon everything to save her.

"I think I learned that lesson four days ago when you promised to rip my tongue out if I asked again," I murmured against her fingers before gently biting the pads.

"I'm glad. It's one of your more talented body parts, it would be a shame to lose it."

"Ah, you mean the constant flow of intellectual words that come from it," I teased.

"Certainly not," she disagreed, patting my cheek, "your head is merely a decorative feature, but it's pretty enough to make up for the lack of function. You're lucky I'm clever enough for the both of us."

"And here I thought it was just your ego inflating your head so outrageously," I said in feigned wonder, "how silly of me to not realize it was just trying to accommodate your brain."

"Theo," she said quietly after a moment, the lingering humor falling from her face, "I want you to be careful. The Autarch is cunning, he will have an escape route planned, even if we can't see it."

"Are you still trying to call me inept?" I joked, trying to take the worry from her eyes.

Her brows furrowed. "I'm being serious. If you let yourself get hurt, I'll be so mad, I'll make you wish they'd killed you."

Her words caught me between the ribs and she scowled at the grin spreading across my face, which only made it wider.

"I will make every effort to stay safe, Sunflower. You have my word," I vowed. "But only if I have yours in return."

"Don't be ridiculous," she sneered.

"Now *I'm* being serious. I won't be able to concentrate if I think you're going to be making foolish decisions and risking yourself unnecessarily. You're my—"

"I'm not *your* anything, Theo," she hissed, glowering at me.

"Yes you are," I growled, pinning her beneath me. "You are *mine*, Erisa Anzû. And if you think for one second that I wouldn't rip the world apart to get to you and annihilate every single person responsible for hurting you, you're very much mistaken."

A delighted shudder ran through her as I said her name, and her lips parted, her gaze darting to my own.

"I'm not," she rasped, her voice betraying her too, "we're nothing."

I huffed out a laugh and kissed her gently, murmuring against her soft lips, "Your lies taste sweeter than any other poison."

Drawing back to look at her, my heart pounded in my chest at the thought of her being captured or killed. In less than three days we would likely be fighting for our lives, and as prime targets, the possibility that both of us would make it out alive was incredibly slim.

My breath caught as I stared into her large, warm eyes, knowing she was realizing the same thing. I could no longer contain the words I'd held back for weeks.

"Erisa, I need to say it. I need to tell you that I lo—"

"Don't!" she snapped, putting a hand to my mouth. "Don't you dare say it."

She kissed me before the pain in my chest could destroy me completely. Even though I never expected her to return the sentiment, having her deny me from saying it felt like the worst kind of rejection. She didn't even want to hear it.

Despite the fissures feathering across my heart, I allowed myself to get lost in her as I had so many times before, refusing to tarnish any of the time we had left together. If we survived the next week, I would lay myself bare before her, and make her listen to every word.

But deep down she knew how I felt, and for now, that would have to be enough.

❖ ❖ ❖

"Whose ships are those?" Erisa called from the edge of the cliff the next morning, the wind whipping the words from her mouth.

I followed her pointed finger to a small fleet of ships on the horizon. Squinting my eyes against the glare of the sun reflecting off the water, I could just about make out the unfamiliar shape of the vessels.

"Are the sails blue?" I had to cup my hand around her ear so she could hear me.

The ships looked like they were sailing from the west, which couldn't be right. I'd ordered Malah and Aran to recall the majority of their fleets to transfer the army from Katmu all at once, so it made no sense that they would be so far away from the coast.

"It looks like it, but it must be a trick of the light! None of the Irkallian fleets are blue!" Erisa shouted, pulling me back from the viewpoint so that we could talk from the shelter of the camp. "Maybe they're just waiting out of sight so the Autarch doesn't get suspicious, we don't know how many spies he has in Katmu. They don't look too far, less than a day away I'd say."

"You're probably right," I agreed, deciding to wait until I saw Aran tomorrow to ask him about it.

The concern was quickly swept from my mind as everyone threw themselves into dismantling the camp. Thanks to the numerous drills carried out over the past few weeks, the process was well practiced and took less than an hour. We were marching before the sun had regained its scorching heat.

Erisa rode by my side, patting Fergus on the neck whenever he shied away from the clanking of metal or the bellows from the horns. She remained quiet as we neared Ocridell, our brief snippets of conversation never venturing toward my almost-confession of the previous night.

"Are you nervous?" I asked her later that afternoon.

"What makes you say that?"

"That's the third time you've oiled those daggers since we left yesterday morning," I replied. "I don't think the Autarch's army will mind if your blades aren't gleaming. You'll cut through them all the same."

"That's where you're wrong." She grinned, holding up the oil bottle and cloth. "I made this from creeping bindweed, if it gets into your bloodstream it congeals the blood, eventually paralyzing the muscles and causing full body seizures."

I grimaced. "Sounds delightful. Where did you learn all of this? I thought my knowledge was good, but I'd never even thought of weaponizing creeping bindweed."

She smiled. "My mother. And you?"

"Corbin," I replied, trying to keep the sadness from my tone. I had sent him so many letters over the past few months, practically begging for his advice. No one had seen or heard from him since he came to visit me after my perilous fall. Not even my mother had had a letter from him, and I couldn't help but worry that something had happened. Especially when I'd ventured into Ocridell to visit his little house, only to find it abandoned.

"You'll find him," Erisa insisted, handing the little bottle and cloth to me, "he'll be fine."

I tried to take comfort from her words, and focused my attention on coating my swords and arrow heads with the oil, taking care not to nick myself on any of the sharp points or edges.

❖ ❖ ❖

The scent of the sea grew stronger as the afternoon wore on, the tall cliff edge exposing itself on our right hand side. Closer to Zingal, the coast was lower, and sheltered enough that the sheer drop didn't pose a threat, but as we traversed through the southern half of Ocridell, the climbing land dropped away into the lapis blue waters of Zagina Bay.

"Theo …" Nook called uneasily from behind me.

I turned in my saddle, my eyes briefly catching on where he held Ezra's hand in his own, before focusing on where he was looking. Aran's men were filtering out of the city, their dark red and gold uniforms unmistakable.

Erisa caught my eye, her look questioning. "We weren't supposed to meet up with Aran until tomorrow morning. They should be waiting in Kusig and meeting us at the juncture to Ocridell at dawn."

My heart seemed to climb up my throat as I noticed them surrounding us, flanking us from every side and pinning us to the cliff's edge.

"None of them are ours," I said quietly, not able to see a single soldier in Zingali green. "Where are they? They should make up at least half of Aran's division."

"Something's not right." Erisa's voice wavered, the sound of her unease repeated in murmurs and whispers throughout the marching men and women around us.

I called them all to halt and approached one of Aran's men who stood at the side of the road, watching me carefully.

"What's going on?" I asked him. "This wasn't the plan."

"Just following orders, my Lord," the man replied, his jaw set firmly. "Lord Seirsun should be arriving shortly."

His words had barely left his mouth when I heard Erisa gasp behind me.

"Theo!" she shouted.

I turned to see her eyes wide, pointing ahead at a large, dark mass cresting the hill above us. Row after row of soldiers began the descent toward us, led by a tall, masked figure astride a horse as black as their armor.

My stomach plummeted to the ground when the rider came close enough to reveal the sharp, angular beak of a crow mask.

The Autarch. And Aran *fucking* Seirsun cantering beside him, golden hair and velvet cape streaming out behind him.

"DEFEND YOURSELVES!" I bellowed, already leaping from Moth's back and reaching for my sword to slice down Aran's soldiers who had come down upon us with vicious brutality. It was as if the arrival of their Lord had shaken them from their peaceful stalling, an unspoken command to spur them into action.

My incomplete army lost any remaining composure, panicking from the unexpected attack and forgetting all of their previous drills and training. No one was prepared, most weren't even carrying weapons, armed only with tent poles and canvas sheets.

Erisa was a blur, darting between the knots of fighting and leaving crumpling bodies in her wake.

Screams filled the air, rivaling the roar of adrenaline sounding in my ears. Men and women were being slaughtered from every angle and that wasn't even the worst of it; the Autarch's army continued to creep closer. I saw a single rider break away from the looming troops and gallop toward us, ignoring the bellowing orders of his commanders.

Slicing down the two men in front of me, I reached behind me for my bow, knocking an arrow and aiming at the approaching rider. Just as I was about to release it, the man jumped down and ran to me, ripping off his helmet to show me his face.

"Verrill? What the fuck is going on?" I demanded, loosing my arrow into a soldier coming up behind him. I saw him scan the area and focus on Erisa's lethal performance.

"I would think that it's obvious," he sneered, drawing his own sword and throwing himself into the fighting, covering my back. "I've been hiding in their ranks. Aran made a deal with the Autarch before you and Erisa even went to Kusig. No one knew about it until this morning."

The string of curses hadn't even left my mouth before a velvet-clad arm came flying toward us, courtesy of Erisa. She was like nothing I'd ever seen before. With fatal precision she sunk dagger after dagger, cutting and slicing into every opponent within a six foot radius. Had I not been fighting for my life, I would have fallen to my knees and worshiped at her feet.

"Verrill," she panted, "please tell me Malah will be here soon."

"I can't," he called back, thrusting his sword into a man's throat, cutting his scream short. "Malah isn't coming."

"What do you mean?" she yelled.

"The rest of our army are locked up in Katmu, the boats aren't coming. Malah betrayed us too. We're on our own."

I barely stopped my knees from buckling beneath me. Confusion and betrayal fogged my mind, tuning out Erisa's shrieks of rage. I hadn't thought it was possible for the situation to get even worse. We had planned for every eventuality, except this one. I had even come up with a contingency for Aran's treachery, but I had never considered Malah's.

That was my first colossal mistake. I felt like an idiot, a naive fool willing to place his trust in anyone for showing the slightest shred of decency. Guilt washed over me like a tidal wave, knowing I'd condemned all of these people from the start.

"Theo," Erisa yelled, halting my descent into despair, "the shield! We can't let them take it."

I knew she wasn't suggesting that we use it, none of us even knew how. But it was supposed to be our greatest weapon. Even if we were completely defeated today, there was no way I could let the Autarch have it.

"Call Silas," I ordered, "we need him now!"

She nodded and positioned herself between Verrill and I to reach into her bodice and extract a small, worn piece of paper.

"*Syrus, Hemushidun!*" she called, reading from the scrap.

Just as I was about to tell her she'd used the wrong name, the air warped and cracked, causing everyone around us to pause momentarily. Silas emerged from thin air with a thunderous expression on his face.

"We don't have time to listen to your whining complaints," Erisa snapped as he opened his mouth to speak. "There's something wrong with the shield, either fix it or take it and keep it safe!"

"The shield is not complete," Silas said, seeming to ignore the din of battle around him. "Lord Seirsun gave you a false relic."

"Then find it and complete the shield! If you knew this, why didn't you say anything? We've been asking for your help for weeks!"

"You don't want to complete it," he snarled. "You have no idea what it will do when you combine them all."

"I know that if you don't cooperate, I'll rescind our bargain," she warned, her eyes wild with fury. "I'll tell everyone about the pretty little thing you're so desperate to hide away. In fact, I think I'll kill her myself."

"Do not test *me*, you callous bitch," he fumed, seeming to grow so much in size that everyone cowered away from him. Except Erisa.

"These are my terms. You owe me, Silas. Keep the shield safe and help us. That is an official exchange."

Without a word, he vanished, splitting the air once more. Erisa glanced at her arm, where the thick band glowed bright for a heartbeat before disappearing completely. She nodded to me, confirming that Silas was bound to fulfill her request, before jumping back into the fight.

The Autarch's army was almost upon us, seconds away from entering the fray. Aran's men still dutifully held the perimeter of the battleground, preventing anyone from fleeing into the city.

We were pinned against the cliff edge.

"Verrill," I demanded, gripping his shoulder and turning him to me, "take her and go."

He didn't need to be told twice. Anyone could see the hopelessness of the situation. Our reserve forces were over a day's ride away and all of our allegiances had failed. This war was over before it had even begun.

We were all going to die today.

Erisa tried to dodge Verrill's grasp, but he was too quick, too versed in her moves, and grabbed her arms.

"Don't you fucking dare, Verrill," she seethed, bucking against him. "I won't forgive you if you do."

He made no move to stop, avoiding each flailing limb she sent toward him.

"I swear to every god that ever existed that I'll make you pay for this, Theodoraxion Lusilim," she shrieked. "Don't you dare make him take me away!"

I allowed myself a brief moment to look at her one last time before she disappeared into the frenzy of grappling bodies and clashing weapons. I trusted her with Verrill, knowing he would protect her with his life.

Ezra and Nook were flanking me and we charged toward the Autarch and Aran, the feel of them beside me so familiar it was almost comforting. We fought like a well-oiled machine, feeling Suenna's absence like a missing part.

Adrenaline powered my fatigued body, not allowing the day's march to slow me down as I cut a path through the fighting toward my goal. I could feel the sweat coating my skin and the trickle of blood from the wounds across my body. None of us had been marching in armor, we were all vulnerable.

There was a brief opening in the carnage and I felt my heart plummet once more as I saw the Autarch and Aran closing in on Erisa and Verrill. He pointed at them and yelled something I couldn't make out over the roar of the battle.

More men ran to them, but they were ferocious; fighting like two halves of a single person, forbidding anyone to even touch them. Bodies were sinking to the ground one by one, unable to control their muscle spasms and seizures from Erisa's poisoned blades. Even from fifty paces away, I could see her fiery eyes were alight and burning with rage.

The Autarch raised his arms, palms facing toward the sky. Reaching for my bow and pulling the nocked arrow back as far as it would go, I took aim. Straight through the eye of his crow mask.

Just as I released my fingers, white hot pain shot through my left leg, causing the arrow to divert. Another lashing of blinding pain seared through my right shoulder and I fell.

Everything happened in slow motion. I hit the ground roughly, but my eyes remained fixed on my arrow, which had pierced through the front of the mask. The Autarch reeled back in shock and fumbled with the clasp, pulling it off and revealing the familiar face hiding beneath the crow's features.

Corbin.

I would have fallen to my knees at the sight, had I not already been on the ground. I felt bile rise up my throat and there was nothing I could do to stop it from heaving itself out of my body.

Time seemed to stand still as my mind raced over the events of the last few months. Corbin, *the Autarch*, had seen me with the stone. He had been the one to suggest I ally myself with the Feline. He had seen my correspondence with Malah organizing the divisions. I sent him letters. Letter after fucking letter, hinting at my plans.

This had all been some big, elaborate scheme of his to manipulate everyone around him, and I'd played into it like an absolute fool.

A sharp scream snapped me back to reality and made my blood run cold. Erisa and Verrill were both bound with thick, writhing ropes encircling their limbs, tugging them toward the ground.

No. Not ropes. Snakes.

I was convinced the blood loss must have been making me delirious, because those were *snakes* holding her down, they were bleeding when Erisa sliced through them.

Hands gripped beneath my arms and my vision went black around the edges as I was hauled up, the wound in my shoulder screaming in protest.

"Get up, Theo!" Ezra was dragging me to my feet and cursed when he looked down to see the arrow speared straight through my thigh.

An unfamiliar horn sounded somewhere to my left, but the resonance was lost in the deafening boom of an explosion. The earth shook, sending me keeling over once more. I looked up to find the Autarch on his feet, his long staff spearing the ground beneath him, feathering out cracks that caused the small rocks beneath me to tremble.

Everything else melted away as another shriek escaped Erisa. She and Verrill were at the edge of the cliff, the crumbling ground beneath them slowly giving out. It was then I realized that I had witnessed this scene before. There was never any fighting in my nightmares, because there was none now. I could see nothing but her, bound and helpless against the pull of gravity calling for her death.

My actions were automatic. I forced myself to my feet, gasping in agony as I took my first step. I mentally grappled the pain away, shoving it into the farthest corner of my mind as I took the second step toward Erisa.

The sickening sense of déjà vu overwhelmed me as my left leg gave out on the third step and buckled beneath me. Dragging the useless limb behind me, I crawled through the dust and dirt, scraping my hands and arms against the rock and debris littering the ground.

I was trampled and kicked, and bile flooded my mouth with every rotation of my right shoulder, but I couldn't stop.

I was going to see her die, as I had countless times before.

# Chapter 28

## Erisa

There was something freeing about the knowledge of my impending doom. I knew I was going to die, but I would take these traitorous bastards down with me.

I ripped away a snake encircling my throat, as Csintalan brought his hand up to summon more from their nests in the cliff face. I had never made the connection before, but his control over animals seemed laughably obvious now. He prowled toward us, Aran at his side. Wind whipped at my face and I could feel the ground crumbling beneath us, the looming drop mere feet away, beckoning us down.

"You motherfucking son of a whore, Aran Seirsun," Verrill raged, his brown eyes fixed on their approach. "I hope she died rotting—"

"Don't you dare finish that sentence, Fox," Aran seethed, tightening his hand around the hilt of his sword. "Don't you dare disrespect my mother!"

"Well it had to have been some kind of festering cunt to have produced *you*," he sneered, "maybe she was already decomposing when she birthed you."

Verrill smiled when his words had the effect he wanted; Aran came charging toward us, sword swinging. Twisting at the last second, Verrill avoided the blade, allowing it to slice cleanly through the serpents binding his wrists to his ankles. The writhing mass caught Aran's feet and he stumbled, allowing me to throw my knee out to trip him. He sprawled out next to me and I sunk my teeth into his calf for good measure before Verrill tackled him, sinking blow after blow into his handsome face.

I turned my attention back to Csintalan, who was now less than ten feet away. Seeing him once again in person made anger cloud my vision, tinting it red. I had scoured the realm for him, desperate for revenge. But he knew how to hide, how to blend into the shadows as though he was born to them.

Someone had shot at him, I could see the arrow piercing the discarded crow mask and a thin trickle of blood dripping from his brow. I was ferociously grateful that they'd missed. I wanted to be the one to end him.

"I'm disappointed in you, Kitten," he said sadly, his voice raised to cover the distance between us. "I took you in, raised you as my own. And this is how you repay me?"

"I know what you did, Csintalan," I snapped. "I know you killed my mother, my family."

A look of horror flashed across his face before he concealed it again, but I saw the way he clenched his staff, his knuckles white from the grip. The ground shuddered again, our fragile piece of cliff slipping a few precarious inches.

Csintalan looked into my eyes. "I have never forgiven myself for what happened that day. But you were supposed to be *mine*, Erisa. You were supposed to be *my* daughter from the very beginning. I cannot regret the events that finally made that happen, I even nam—"

"YOU KILLED HER!" I screamed, trying to tear my limbs free. "She trusted you, and you slaughtered her!"

He closed his eyes and pain twisted across his features, making him appear softer and younger than I'd ever seen him.

A horn sounded behind him, and his eyes snapped open to see the rush of soldiers dressed in pale Atturynnian blue silk and silver armor piling into the battle. I didn't recognize them, and had I not already accepted that we were defeated, this new addition would have been the very last nail in our army's coffin.

Csintalan raised his hands to the sky once more, and animals came scurrying from nowhere toward me. The snakes tightened, rodents nipped at my clothes and birds clawed into my hair. It wasn't until I heard Verrill's curses beside me that I understood what he was doing. He wasn't trying to kill us, he was capturing us.

He said he wanted us alive, and I knew that if we let him, we would never escape again.

I opened my mouth and began to sing, forcing all of my persuasion and coercion into the very fabric of my voice, directing it toward Csintalan in a way I'd never dared to before. His face paled as he froze and dropped his arms. I immediately felt the snakes relax and the creatures begin to scurry away.

I could feel him fighting against me in my mind as I rose shakily to my knees, expelling every ounce of my effort and concentration into holding him. Never before had I attempted to sing with such direct intent; it was like trying to overexert an unused muscle. I lasted for three more heartbeats before he broke free.

Csintalan's blank expression morphed into one of deranged fury and his hand flew to the long, curved knife at his belt. Quicker than I could comprehend, he threw it. I saw only flashes of setting sunlight reflect off the gleaming metal as it twisted through the air toward me.

Then I was slammed back into the ground, with Verrill on top of me. The abrupt shifting of weight caused the earth to slip and shudder beneath us, cracking away from the rest of the cliff edge. I glanced over Verrill's shoulder to see Csintalan retreat back out of danger and we locked eyes for a single heartbeat before he melted back into the swirling mass of blue soldiers.

"Help me hold on, Ver," I huffed, reaching up to try and secure us in the vines winding up the cliff. I looped my arms though the thickest ones and anchored his body against mine. As I did, I felt something sharp graze against my stomach. I looked down at the same time as Verrill, to see the end of Csintalan's blade barely visible, protruding from his torso.

"Verrill," I demanded, forcing his face to mine, "what did you do?"

"It's nothing," he rasped, but I knew he was lying. I could see his face pale and feel his grip tighten around my body, as though desperate to hold on.

"You saved me," I whispered, feeling my voice break and heat burn behind my eyes.

"Always, my music."

Then, for the first time in our lives, he kissed me. His lips were soft and wild against mine, pouring years of unfathomable love into me, showing me every ounce of his unwavering devotion.

He tasted like sage and juniper. Like *home*.

After an entire lifetime had passed, he pulled away, tears flowing freely down his cheeks, and gave me the most heartbreaking smile I had ever seen.

"Verrill, please," I choked out through my closing throat, "please get up so we can get help."

He shook his head, his eyes never leaving mine as he pressed his forehead to my own.

"I have to say it now, before I lose the chance to forever. I love you, Erisa. I have loved you every single day of our lives, and I don't regret not telling you, because you knew. I made sure you knew, without having to fear that you'd lose me too. Words cannot even begin to express what we have. I've shown you my love in every act, every touch, and every breath I've ever taken; they've only ever been for you."

He kissed away the tears from my cheeks before continuing, his voice straining from his waning strength. "Not all soulmates are lovers, but *I do love you* ... With everything I've ever had. It has been my greatest honor to spend my life at your side and ... I wouldn't change a single second of it. You're my ... greatest treasure; the music of my soul. And ... I'll hear your song as it calls me to the gates of heaven, where I'll wait for you to join me."

"We're not making it to heaven, Ver," I lamented quietly, clutching him in desperation.

"Then we'll rule … the deepest pit of hell together," he whispered, closing his eyes, "for eternity."

His grip loosened and I could see his body slacken. My heartbeats sped, as though they were trying to compensate for the slowing of his. Each one counting down sluggishly to the last.

"Verrill!" I wailed, shaking him, clawing my nails into his pale, clammy skin. "Don't leave me, Verrill! You promised you wouldn't leave me! Please!"

"I'm … always with you, my music … always."

His strained words were barely audible and he raised his eyelids to meet my gaze once more. I committed his warm brown eyes to memory before he closed them again, for the final time.

I could feel him leave, prying a part of my soul away to take with him.

I didn't need to look down at my arm to know that the traitorous burn across my skin was the proof I didn't want to see; that the only bargain he had ever made was vanishing, unfulfilled and untraceable.

He was gone. But I couldn't let him go. I wrapped my legs around him, securing his cooling body against me as we balanced over the fatal drop, held up with a few straining vines.

Large hands gripped me beneath my arms, attempting to drag me back over the edge, their touch so warm compared to Verrill's it felt like fire against my skin.

"Let him go, Erisa," Theo grunted, struggling to heave us up, but failing when Verrill's limp leg snagged into the tangle of exposed underground roots.

"I won't," I cried, sobs wracking through my body.

"Please, Erisa," he begged, "I can't hold you both. He's gone, let him go."

"NO! Get off me! I don't want you!"

He used my struggle against me, finding purchase around my waist and roughly prying my fingers from Verrill's clothes. I could feel Theo slipping. We were all so close to falling over, but I didn't care. I wasn't going to abandon him.

"I'm sorry, Sunflower," Theo murmured breathlessly. "You can hate me later, but I'm not going to let you go."

I hadn't even registered his words before he yanked me up and reached down to dig his thumb deep into my right calf, causing it to spasm away from Verrill's side.

As if in slow motion, I watched his body plummet down toward the crashing waters below, his dark blonde waves fanning out around the face I knew better than my own.

Theo pulled me up and onto the flat expanse of dusty, trampled grass, littered with bodies. Blue and silver soldiers swarmed the area, but I couldn't focus on anyone but the man in front of me.

Blood coated Theo's shoulder as he shuffled away, giving me space. There was an arrow protruding from his left leg and his trousers had turned a dark red. The tears in his eyes snapped my final fraying shred of self-control.

"This is your fault!" I screamed, flying at him, wanting to hurt him in every way possible. "You're the reason we failed! You're the reason he's dead!"

I had told him not to trust Aran, I had tried to convince him that something wasn't right, but he'd done it anyway. Had spilled every secret we had into the ear of the enemy.

A dagger was in my hand before I even realized what I was doing and I lunged, blinding fury taking over my every thought. I hadn't even noticed the figure standing next to him until they thrust their arm out in front of his face, just before I sunk my blade into it.

My dagger splintered into wood, shocking me enough to pause and watch Theo's eyes widen as they traveled up the arm and landed on his savior's face.

And he gasped.

"Karasi?"

# Epilogue

Verrill Fedelis was floating. He was no longer cold, but no longer hot. Just … floating. His body was gone. He didn't need it anymore.

There was only her.

His Erisa. The music of his soul.

Verrill watched as she was pulled to safety, despairing as she wept. He wanted to comfort her and brush away her tears. He hated himself for being the cause of her pain.

He tried to reach out, to go back to her and feel her in his arms once more.

But he could not.

He could only watch in silence as her anger built and she exploded into a glorious detonation of fury.

She was a storm, roiling and violent, her tongue a fork of lightning lashing out to singe, and her freckles drowning in the flood of tears.

Verrill mourned for her. For himself. For every song he would never get to play for her on his lyre. For every second he could no longer spend lost in her strange, beautiful eyes. For every other kiss they could have shared.

Verrill could sense himself slipping, unable to deny the pull that wanted to rip him away from his love. He wanted to rebel, but there was a voice. One he'd know in any place, in any lifetime.

Erisa's voice. Her song.

It danced along the fibers of his being, enticing him to journey to whatever lay beyond. He stole one final glance at Erisa's mortal form, feeling nothing but love and joy and the whispers of an ache in the back corners of his cheeks, where a smile used to take the place of her name.

He surrendered to the call, knowing that if he was patient, he would play for her again.

Verrill could almost see it as he was swept away—caressing the strings of his lyre as the sun kissed his closed lids in the waning radiance of day's embrace—the final close to his unending devotion.

# Acknowledgments

First of all, I'd like to say a huge thank you to whoever is reading this and giving The Place of Her Name a chance. This entire series is a true passion project and I'm hoping you'll be joining me along for the ride!

I'd like to thank my amazing editor, Hannah Close, who truly transformed the manuscript into something wonderful, for making so many improvements while keeping the original vision alive.

Thank you so much to Georgia and Clare, and to all my beta readers, every single comment and piece of feedback was taken on board and used to shape the story and bring the characters to life.

Thank you to Marta for the beautiful cover and to Rob for the wonderful maps, you both absolutely smashed it!

Names are important to me, and I wanted as many as possible to give a nod to the Sumerian and Akkadian periods that inspired these books. So, I'd like to give a shoutout to James at Sumerian Language, whose online resources helped influence many of Irkalla's names.

Thank you to Jade for enduring my endless "which is better?" questions, you have the patience of a saint!

I'd also like to thank all my friends and family who have

supported me through this process. Even if it was just a small word of encouragement, it meant a lot!

And finally, Shula, I know without a doubt that this book would not have been completed if not for your constant encouragement (and threats). Thank you for your unwavering support from the very beginning, from when The Place of Her Name was merely an idea. I truly cherish our friendship

Printed in Dunstable, United Kingdom

65255404R00221